The Boy

"[A] tightly plotted whodunnit . . . prepare to gasp."
—*Peop*

"Thoughtful, character-driven . . . Hoag keeps the twists and turns coming all the way to the shocking conclusion."
—*Publishers Weekly*

"You're going to be staying up late at night as the pages turn with this one."
—*New York Journal of Books*

"Hoag puts on quite the juggling act here, dazzling us with multiple theories about the boy's murder, numerous potential suspects, and plot twists that keep us just slightly off-balance. A welcome return for a compelling investigative duo."
—*Booklist*

"With her signature style in building up suspense as the plot develops, Hoag has written a commercial novel which is definitely a joy to read."
—*Mystery Tribune*

"Husband-and-wife detective teams stretch back as far as Dashiell Hammett, but Hoag ensures that her pair have a very individual quality, encapsulated in their razor-sharp dialogue."
—*The Guardian* (UK)

"This is the perfect book for suspense fans to while away a cold afternoon with."
—*All About Romance*

"Every Tami Hoag book is deviously plotted, compulsively page-turning, with dead-on dialogue and twisted characters. You're in the hands of a master with Tami Hoag."
—*New York Times* bestselling author Lisa Scottoline

The Bitter Season

"A masterful tale of two colliding cases that become one tightly coiled plot, *The Bitter Season* is Tami Hoag at her down-and-dirty best. Authentic, dark, and intense, this is a portrait of flawed characters on both sides of the law that will surprise you and make you laugh as you double-lock your doors."
—*New York Times* bestselling author Tess Gerritsen

Cold Cold Heart

The 9th Girl

"Cannily plotted and peppered with some of the sharpest dialogue in t business."

—*Entertainment Weekly (A*

"Thought-provoking."

—*Bookli*s

"A smartly written one-day read."

—*Suspense Magazine*

"A gripping plot."

—*South Florida Sun Sentinel*

Down the Darkest Road

"Eerie, suspenseful, tragic, and thought provoking."

—*USA Today*

"A mesmerizing psychological drama on loss, guilt, frustration and im-placable, explainable evil."

—*Kirkus Reviews*

"The setting and [Hoag's] consummate skill as a plotter add to plenty of old-school thrills that pack a punch and will leave fans breathless."

—*Booklist*

"Hoag . . . rais[es] the tension with every page that turns."

—*The Huffington Post*

"Well written, well executed, and darn near brilliant."

—*All About Romance*

"This taut novel of suspense is a true nail-biter."

—*Library Journal*

"If you have time to read only one book, you really should make it this one. You won't regret it."

—*Suspense Magazine*

"With complex characters and crisp, believable dialogue, [this] is a so-phisticated thriller."

—*Houston Press*

"A masterful tale . . . Ms. Hoag knows how to take her readers on a frightening ride."

—*New York Journal of Books*

for the Other Thrillers of Tami Hoag

"One of the most intense suspense writers around."

—*Chicago Tribu*

"Hard to put down."

—*The Washington Po.*

"A snappy, scary thriller."

—*Entertainment Weekly*

"A chilling thriller with a romantic chaser."

—*New York Daily News*

"Hoag's cliff-hanger scene endings and jump cuts leave the reader panting and turning the pages as fast as possible."

—*The Boston Globe*

"[A] no-holds-barred, page-turning thriller."

—*The Philadelphia Inquirer*

ALSO BY TAMI HOAG

With my most heartfelt thanks to my amazing team at Dutton, most especially Stephanie Kelly—you are the ultimate cheerleader— and Christine Ball, who just calmly adjusted course again and again. And to my agent of lo these many years (how did we get so old?), Andrea Cirillo, who took it all in stride. Some books are more labors of love than others. This one was like giving birth to an elephant.

Thank you all for seeing it through with me.

AUTHOR'S NOTE

In *The Boy* I return to a setting my longtime readers know is a favorite of mine—Louisiana's French Triangle, Cajun country. It is a place like no other—ecologically, sociologically, culturally, and linguistically. I have done my best to try to impart some of the rich flavor of the region to you, in part through language and dialect. Cajun French is a patois as unique to Louisiana as gumbo. Imagine Elizabethan-era French that evolved isolated from its home country, influenced by the spice of Spanish, Creole, Native American, and African languages. Because Cajun French evolved predominantly as a spoken language, spellings and even meanings of words may vary from one area to the next. According to the last census, about one in ten families in south Louisiana still speak French in the home, and many words and phrases find their way into the speech of English speakers. I have included a glossary in the back of the book for words and phrases used throughout the story.

ONE

She ran down the gravel road, struggling, stumbling. Her breath sawed in and out of her lungs, ragged and hot; painful, like serrated knives plunging into and pulling out of her chest. The night air was too thick, too heavy. She thought she might drown in it. Her legs wobbled beneath her like rubber, heavy with fatigue. Sweat streamed from her pores. It felt like her skin was ready to peel away, leaving her red and raw and bloody.

Blood. So much blood. On her hands. In her hair. On her face. She was painted with it. When she found someone—*if* she found someone—they would see the blood, too. They would see the whites of her eyes and the red of the blood that streaked down her cheeks and across her jaw. They would see the blood that stained her hands like red lace gloves. They would be horrified without even knowing the true horror of what had happened.

She replayed it over and over in her mind's eye, the images flashing like a strobe light, like random scenes from a movie. The flash of the knife. The flailing arms. Blood spraying everywhere.

She could taste the blood: bitter and metallic. She could taste the salt of her sweat and her tears. The mix made a nauseating cocktail in her mouth. She choked on it as she tried to swallow. She could smell it. The ench of fear: blood and body odor, urine and feces. The memory was strong and so real she gagged on it.

Then suddenly she was falling, sprawling headlong. The road rushed up to meet her, slammed into her, the gravel biting into the flesh of her hands and bare arms and knees and the side of her face. The impact rattled her brain and knocked the wind from her. She tried to gasp for air, frantic, thinking she might die.

Maybe it was better if she died. Maybe she should just lie down and quit. Everyone in her life would probably be happier, relieved, unburdened.

The night waited, ever-patient, oblivious to her pain, not caring if she lived or died. Things died in the swamp all the time. Death was just a part of life here.

As the roar of her pulse in her ears subsided to a dull throb, the sounds of the bayou came through: crickets and frogs, the groan of an alligator somewhere nearby, the splash of something hitting the water, the distant rumble of thunder as a storm rolled up from the Gulf. Something moved suddenly in the brush at the side of the road. A bird flew up, its wings thumping against the thick, still air.

Startled, gasping, she scraped and scrambled, swimming on the rock, struggling to get her feet under her and to get herself upright.

Headlights appeared around a bend in the road. A driver in the dead of night in the middle of nowhere—would this be help or harm? She knew all about the kind of men who prowled the darkness and preyed on women. A part of her wanted to crouch in the brush and hide. A part of her knew she couldn't.

She stood in the middle of the road and waved her arms above her head.

"Help me! Stop! Help me. Please!" In her mind she was shouting, but she could barely hear the words. They seemed nothing more than a rasp in her throat.

The car drew closer. The headlights blinded her.

The driver had to see her now.

"Help me!"

The vehicle slowed to a crawl.

"Help!" She flung herself at the driver's side of the hood as if s could physically force the car to stop. "Please, help me!"

She slapped the hood with one hand and the windshield with th other, smearing the glass with blood. For just a second her eyes locke on the terrified face of the driver, a woman, and then the engine roared. The tires chewed at the gravel. The car leapt forward, and she fell to the side, trying to grab hold of a door handle. Her head cracked hard against the window. *Bang! Thump! Thud!* She hit the ground and rolled, chok-ing on the dust, spitting out blood and gravel and a tooth.

She could have closed her eyes and willed it all away, slipping into the deep abyss of unconsciousness. She might lie there and die, be run over by a truck, or dragged into the swamp by an animal. But then she was on her hands and knees, crawling, coughing, crying, blood and tears and snot dripping from her face.

The thunder rumbled in the distance, but above her the moon was still white-bright, so bright that the sky around it glowed metallic blue. Down the road she could see the outline of a house, a shabby little box of a house, a yard with an old pickup parked near a sagging porch. A yellow bug light burned beside the front door.

She wobbled to her feet like a newborn deer and staggered on, one foot in front of the other, her focus on the house. Would someone come if she made it to the door? Would they call the police at someone knock-ing in the middle of the night? Or would they just mistake her for an intruder and shoot her?

Exhausted, she tripped on the front steps and fell onto the weathered boards of the old porch. Beyond feeling pain, she dragged herself the last few feet and banged a fist against the screen door. She wanted to cry out, to call for help, but her voice died in her throat. She slapped at the screen door, her strength draining out of her, rushing out of her like water down a hole.

Help me. Help me. Please God, someone help me . . .

"You done forgot your key again?"

The complaining voice seemed to come from a long distance, from a dream.

"I swear! I ought to leave you sleep with the hound dogs! Dat's all hat you deserve, you! I oughta shoot you first, coming home at this our. Stinkin' drunk, no doubt."

The inner door creaked open.

Genevieve looked up at the woman in the doorway—a narrow, lined face, eyes popping, mouth open in shock, teeth missing, a halo of frizzed red hair shot through with gray. The face of an angel.

"Oh, my God in heaven!" the woman exclaimed.

"Help me. Please," Genevieve whispered. "Someone killed me and my boy."

And then the blackness of oblivion swallowed her whole.

TWO

Annie Broussard listened to the thunder rumble in the distance. The sound echoed the restlessness that stirred inside her. She felt anxious, on edge, as if she was waiting for something bad to happen. This had been going on for weeks now, ever since that night in June, when a call had awoken her from a deep, peaceful sleep.

Not that she wasn't used to the phone ringing at all hours with bad news, but it was always someone else's bad news, and she or Nick or both of them were being called on as sheriff's detectives to come out and sort through the latest human catastrophe in Partout Parish. She had never been called to a catastrophe of her own until the night her tante Fanchon had been rushed to the hospital after suffering a stroke.

What had followed that call had been days and nights of breathless anxiety, Annie clinging by her mental fingertips to hope that ebbed and flowed like an erratic tide.

Fanchon Doucet had been her anchor since childhood. And even though Annie's mother had exited her life without warning when she was small, Annie had never imagined Tante Fanchon doing the same. Fanchon and Uncle Sos were as constant as the North Star, as solid as stone—until that night in June.

Now, every time the phone rang in the middle of the night, Annie's heart bolted at the thought that the call would be for her, not as a detective but as next of kin. She hadn't had a decent night's sleep in four months.

Carefully, she slipped out of bed and padded across the cypress-wood floor to the window to peek through the blinds. The moon had yet to be overrun by the clouds, casting the night in a silver glow. Lightning spread across the sky in the distance like spiderweb cracks across dark glass. The thunder rolled after it and right along her nerves.

She liked to think she was too logical and practical to believe in signs and portents, but she couldn't escape the fact that she had been raised by superstitious people in a superstitious place. The French Triangle of south Louisiana may have embraced all the modern amenities technology had to offer, but there were people in bayou country who still half believed in the *loup-garou*—a mythical swamp werewolf. Uncle Sos, as Catholic as any Cajun man in these parts, still wore a dime on a string around his neck to ward off bad *gris-gris*—curses and such. "Just in case," he would say with a grin and a playful gleam in his dark eyes.

Annie wouldn't have gone so far as to drill a hole in a dime, but she secretly wished for some protection against that now-familiar sense of dread that sat like a rock in her stomach.

It didn't help that the unrelenting heat and humidity had everyone on their last nerve. Summer should have been a distant memory by now, but like a big ugly snake, it had sunk its fangs in deep and hung on, pumping its venom into the citizens of south Louisiana. Tempers and patience were running short. Bar fights and domestic calls were up, along with the temperature and the consumption of alcohol.

Everyone in the Sheriff's Office was feeling the effects—on the job and off. And if the rise in calls to come between contentious citizens wasn't enough, ten months into the tenure of their new boss, there were still problems and personality conflicts in the office. Most of the staff had worked their entire careers under the long reign of Gus Noblier, and no matter how any of them had or hadn't gotten along with Gus, he had become a saint in absentia.

The new sheriff was an outsider, a usurper; too stiff, too arrogant, to brash. It didn't matter that Gus himself had brought Kelvin Dutrow o board as chief deputy the year before his retirement. Dutrow wasn't from here. He wasn't one of them. Tensions within the department exacer bated the tensions out on the road. It was a vicious cycle, and every deputy and detective took that tension home to his or her family at the end of their shift. The Broussard-Fourcade household got a double dose.

The chaos and fury of a good old-fashioned thunderstorm would be a welcome break.

As if in answer to her thought, way out over the Atchafalaya Basin, lightning again chased itself across the sky, and the ominous low rumble of thunder followed seconds later.

On the other side of the room, Annie's husband stirred in his sleep, grumbling, sweeping an arm along the empty space beside him.

"'Toinette? Where you at?" he asked, his voice a low, raspy growl.

She didn't answer for a moment, still irritated with him for something he'd said to her earlier in the evening. He sat up, the sheet puddling around his narrow waist. It was too dark to make out his features. He was a broad-shouldered silhouette as he rubbed a hand over his face.

"There's a storm coming," Annie said.

She turned away from him and opened the blinds. The wind was starting to come up, ruffling the treetops and fluttering the ribbons of Spanish moss that draped the limbs of the big oak trees in the yard. That sense of anticipation rose within her again. Behind her, the sheets rustled and the bed creaked as Nick got up.

"Good," he said.

He stepped too close. She slipped to the side.

"You gonna be mad at me forever or what?" he asked.

"Maybe."

He bent his head and sighed, his warm breath stirring the hair at the nape of her neck as he moved close again, corralling her between his arms, trapping her between himself and the window. He whispered something in French and brushed his lips against the curve of her shoulder.

"Don't." Annie shrugged him off and ducked under his arm. "You

...ow that just pisses me off," she whispered. "I'm angry with you, and
...ou think you can just brush it aside like it doesn't even matter, like I'm
...able to just forget about it if only you can get me to have sex with you."

Of course, he wouldn't have been wrong in that assumption—a truth
that made her even more irritated with herself.

He tipped back his head and blew out a sigh. *"Mon Dieu."*

Annie's temper spiked another notch. "Oh, I'm sorry my feelings are
so tedious for you."

"I didn't say that."

"You didn't have to."

"It's the middle of the damn night," he said wearily. "Do we have to
fight now?"

She didn't want to fight at all, but that seemed to be their new normal of late: too many sharp words and tense silences. It seemed the only place they didn't rub each other the wrong way was in bed, where the tension between them seemed only to ratchet up the sexual heat. What transpired between them during sex was explosive and incredible as they both tried to reach beyond their frustration to connect as they always had on this other plane of being that was beyond words. Out of bed they were out of step with each other, like awkward dancers hearing two different beats.

They both blamed their jobs and the heat, the stress of Fanchon's stroke, and Nick's difficulties with a sexual assault case he'd been working all summer and fall to no conclusion. The various pressures had rubbed their nerves raw.

It was an unfamiliar place for them to be, this awkward limbo. To the bemusement of many, they had a rock-solid marriage—six years now. Considering their relationship had essentially begun when Annie had arrested Nick for assaulting a murder suspect, it wasn't surprising that people had doubted they would last. She was a hometown good girl, while Nick had a long reputation as a difficult man with a checkered past.

Plenty of people had believed he was more than a little disturbed and dangerous when he had first come to Bayou Breaux—many thought that still. He had a volatile nature, always teetering on the edge of darkness.

His temper was a thing of legend, and he did not suffer fools. But he w
the way he was, not because he was crazy but because he cared too muc
about what he did and the people he did it for.

"Bobby Theriot called last night," he confessed.

"Oh, Nick." Annie sighed, her annoyance with him instantly gone.
"Why didn't you tell me?"

"What's to tell? The man wants justice for his daughter, and me, I
can't give it to him."

"It's not your fault."

"Whose fault is it, then? It's my case. That buck stops with me, does
it not?"

"You can't give him what you don't have."

"And therein lies my failing."

The Theriot case was a straight-up whodunit. The sexual assault of
Vanessa Theriot, a nonverbal girl with autism, who was unable to com-
municate what had happened to her. If she knew the identity of her molester, that secret was locked inside the labyrinth of her mind. The forensics
had given them nothing to go on. No witness had come forward to point
the investigation in any direction. They had no clear suspects.

"The Theriots want someone to blame," Nick said. "Until we have
the person who hurt their daughter, I'm it."

Annie's protective instincts rose up like hackles. She knew how hard
Nick was working the case. She knew how much sleep he'd lost, the toll
it had taken on him. She wanted to rush to his defense against Bobby
Theriot's verbal abuse, which had steadily escalated over the past month,
but Nick wouldn't have it.

"I'm sorry," she whispered, sliding her arms around his lean, hard
torso, pressing her cheek to the thick muscle of his chest.

"Me, too," he murmured, softly kissing the top of her head. He
wrapped his arms around her tight and whispered, *"Je t'aime, mon coeur,
ma jolie fille."*

He had grown up a swamper's son, speaking French at home as a fair
number of families in these parts did. French was still his preferred
language. He thought in French, spoke French to their son, made love
in French.

"I love you, too," Annie whispered.

"Come back to bed, 'Toinette," he said. "I need to hold you for a while."

She tipped her face up to look at him and met his lips with hers. He kissed her slowly and deeply. As always, the wave of heat was instantaneous, washing over her, through her, pooling deep within her body. When he lifted his mouth from hers, she murmured, "I think you may need to do more than just hold me."

He groaned deep in his throat and took her mouth again, with more urgency, sweeping a hand down the curve of her side and pulling her hips hard against his.

Across the room, his cell phone came to life on the nightstand. They both sighed in frustration. A call this late at night to a sheriff's detective was never anything good or anything quickly resolved.

Outside, lightning cracked like a whip across the night sky. Thunder boomed like distant cannon fire behind it.

"I'm going to go check on Justin," Annie said, as Nick moved to answer the call.

She slipped into her robe and padded barefoot down the hall. She could hear their son stirring in his sleep, whimpering softly as she cracked open his bedroom door. At five, he was still afraid of thunderstorms, most times ending up tucked between her and Nick in their bed. He was a sweet, sensitive little boy—a little too sensitive to the recent tensions between his parents, making him moody and clingy. Bad timing, as he started kindergarten. Another stressor for Annie, another pang of guilt.

The nightlight allowed her to see his face. He was a miniature of Nick with his straight dark eyebrows and full lower lip. He was frowning in his sleep, just as his father did. Her heart swelled to overflowing with love every time she looked at him.

"I gotta go," Nick said, suddenly behind her.

Annie jumped and turned to face him.

His expression was set in the grim lines of a comic book hero's: the high cheekbones and iron jaw, a hawkish nose, brows lowered over dark eyes. He had pulled on a black T-shirt and a pair of camouflage cargo

pants. His badge hung on a ball chain around his neck. This was wh
he wore to death scenes: the badge hanging for easy identification, th
cargo pants for the usefulness of the pockets.

"You're up, too, *cher*," he said. "That thunder's not the only storm
brewing tonight. Our victim is a little boy."

THREE

The house was less than a mile from town, a small, sad rectangle of cheap siding and asphalt shingles squatting on concrete block pilings in a yard of dirt and weeds. It was one of those houses that would inevitably end up miles down the bayou when the next flood came. The nearest neighbor wasn't near enough. The property lines out here were defined by trees and scrub—nature's privacy fencing—all trembling now as the wind picked up and shook the branches.

There were no streetlights on this road, just a yellow porch light on the house and the headlights and red-and-blue roof lights of two Partout Parish sheriff's cruisers parked on the road. What was left of the moon shone intermittently as the clouds scuttled past in advance of the coming storm.

Nick pulled in his Jeep at an angle alongside one of the radio cars and got out, slinging his backpack over one shoulder. A deputy sat sideways out of the driver's seat of the cruiser with his head in his hands, sobbing, the anguished sound punctuated by staccato bursts of noise from the radio. A second deputy was patrolling a line of yellow crime scene tape across the driveway. He shined his flashlight in Nick's face as he approached.

"Detective Fourcade," he said, turning the bright beam to the side. "Hell of a night this is."

"It's about to get worse, Ossie," Nick said. His words were followed by a drumroll of thunder and the rattle of tree branches in the wind.

"I don't see how," Ossie Compton said grimly. He was a veteran on the job, nearer to retirement than not. He had seen a lot of crime scenes in his day. If he thought one was bad, there was no need to doubt him.

"You were first on the scene?"

"No. Young Prejean here." He waved his flashlight toward the deputy sobbing in the car. "His first murder, poor kid."

"What do we know?"

"The call come in from a house down the road. The mother ran there for help. I guess they don't have no phone here, or the lines were cut or something."

"No cell phone?"

Compton shrugged. "Anyway, Prejean got here first. He was coming out the house, hysterical, when I pulled up."

Nick glanced over at the young deputy, his head still bowed beneath the rolling blue-and-red lights of his vehicle. He remembered his first murdered-child call. He remembered all the time, even now, so many years later. A little girl, three years old, scalded to death by her mother's boyfriend for wetting her pants. He saw that baby girl's face in his nightmares still, more than a dozen years later. Hers and too many others. He wanted to go to Deputy Prejean and tell him to get out now, to go get a job selling shoes or working on a shrimp boat or something where death didn't look you in the face on a regular basis and follow you home at night.

"Anyone else in the house?" he asked.

"No. I went in, seen what I seen, and come back out to wait for y'all," Compton said. "Made me sick, too. I'm not ashamed to say it. What kind of evil bastard kills a little child that way?"

"The devil," Nick said as a black Dodge Charger pulled up.

"A junkie kills another junkie for drugs," Compton said. "One man kills another for messing with his woman. A robber shoots a store clerk to get rid of a witness. There's always a reason. But to kill a l'il child . . ."

"There'll be a reason for that, too," Nick said. "Just not a good one."

"Hell of a night this is," Chaz Stokes grumbled as he joined them. A call out on something like this in the middle of my beauty sleep and it has to fucking rain on top of it. I've got to rethink my career choices."

He was in the same clothes he had worn to work the day before—gray slacks and a black button-down, a thin red tie pulled loose at his open collar. There was a good chance he hadn't been home—not to his own home, at any rate.

They had been working together for the better part of a decade. Stokes, the department lothario, quick with a joke and a strategy to benefit himself. Fourcade, the department time bomb, dark and brooding, always on the edge. Somehow, they balanced each other out. Nick tolerated Stokes, and Stokes had sense enough to stay just on the right side of Nick's boundaries most of the time.

"Any sign of a break-in?" Nick asked Compton.

Compton shrugged his thick sloped shoulders. "The back door is locked, but the front door was wide open when we got here. And half the windows are open. The air-conditioning don't seem to be working."

He pulled a handkerchief from his hip pocket and mopped the sweat from his forehead.

"Young Prejean!" Nick called out to the deputy in the car. "Make yourself useful and get the lights out your trunk. We need to light this yard up as best we can and see what we can see before this rain comes down."

"Where's our fearless leader and his toy box?" Stokes asked sourly, ducking under the crime scene tape.

"Lost, if we're lucky," Nick muttered.

They were a small department in a small rural parish—just six full-time detectives to cover everything. Most of their crimes were the small-time variety: break-ins, thefts, petty drug deals. Personal crimes generally involved people known to one another—barroom brawls, domestic violence, disputes between neighbors or rivals.

The detectives had always done their own evidence collection at crime scenes. Nick preferred it that way. They were trained to do it, had the experience of many cases. Having too many people at a scene was a re-ipe for trouble, as far as he was concerned. He wanted people he knew and trusted. He wanted to know exactly who found what, who touched what, who stepped where. When they had a big scene, a complicated scene, they had the option to call in the state police crime scene unit to collect and process the evidence. It was a system that worked well. He saw no need to change it.

The new sheriff, however, had won the office on bold promises to bring the Sheriff's Office into the new millennium. Part of that promise had been a dedicated crime scene unit—something the voting public had decided was essential after Dutrow had told them that it was. People liked to think they knew about such things because they watched CSI on television. But the reality of the shiny new van purchased with grant money was a staff of one Dutrow-recruited seasoned crime scene investigator, a retired deputy, and a handful of trainees who had little experience and a steep learning curve. And they were on their way to Nick's murder scene.

"Y'all walk the outside," Nick ordered as he dug a pair of latex gloves out of a pocket on his cargo pants and pulled them on. "Find a point of entry. Find some footprints."

"How about a bloody knife with fingerprints on it?" Stokes asked sarcastically. "And a driver's license with an address."

"That'd be good, too."

Pelted by the first fat, slow raindrops of the storm, Nick hustled up the steps to the sagging little front porch. A crack of lightning, a boom of thunder, and the porch light went out. He swore under his breath and held up his flashlight to examine the doorjamb. Several bloody smears stained the peeling paint where someone might have grabbed hold on their way out the door. The assailant? The mother?

Was the assailant someone known to her? A spouse, a boyfriend, an angry ex? Or was this the rare monster in the dead of night, intent on harm, preying on a mother home alone with her child? Every woman's worst nightmare.

Nick could still feel the tension in the air as he entered the house.

iolence had an energy that lingered. It made the hair stand up on the ack of his neck.

He took a pair of paper booties out of a pocket on his backpack and pulled them on over his boots. The beam from his flashlight illuminated the room in vignettes: a broken lamp and a chair on its side; streaks of blood on the wall and a picture hanging askew, belongings scattered on the floor. The aftermath of a struggle.

He turned and made his way down a short hall, careful not to step in any of the blood smears on the floor. Tension dug into his shoulders like talons as he made his way toward the first of the bedrooms. Acid burned in his stomach and up the back of his throat in anticipation of what he was about to see. Dread pressed down on him like a giant hand.

Because he was human, a part of him wanted to turn around and leave now, before it was too late. Because he had a duty, he moved forward, knowing that what he was about to see would change him. The dead always did that. What lingered of their souls grabbed hold and tore away a little piece of him, never to be recovered. The last breath of the victim's pain and fear seeped into him like a stain. He had never become immune to it.

He stopped at the open doorway to the first bedroom and shined his flashlight inside. The first thing he saw was a kitten. A little black-and-white kitten, two or three months old, walking back and forth in the small puddle of light, looking up at him expectantly. It meowed at him and arched its back, padding in a figure eight, its white-tipped tail straight up in the air.

Nick stared at it, allowing himself to be mesmerized for a moment. He hadn't expected to see a kitten, something innocent and alive. He let himself be distracted by it, just for a few seconds. Then slowly he realized the cat was rubbing itself along the pajama-clad leg of a small boy lying motionless on the floor.

Spider-Man pajamas. His own son had gone to bed wearing a pair just like them.

"I like Spider-Man 'cause he's a good guy and he helps people and he can climb everywhere on everything. I wanna be Spider-Man when I grow up."

"I thought you wanted to be Karate Kid."

"I can be Karate Kid when I'm not Spider-Man. I can turn into Spider-Man and then turn back into Karate Kid. Right, Papa?"

"You can be anything you set your mind to, but what you need to b right now is asleep."

Nick thought his heart would burst every time he watched Justin fall asleep. Until the birth of his child, he had never imagined it possible to contain that much love within his being. He loved his wife with all his heart, but even that love paled in comparison. It amazed and terrified him every day.

Now he stood over the lifeless body of another father's son, trying not to imagine what he would feel if this boy were Justin.

Lightning split the sky outside, as bright as day in a black-and-white movie, as bright as the explosion of an old-fashioned camera flashbulb. The illuminated image burned itself into the backs of his eyes. It would be there for eternity. He would see it every day for the rest of this life and the next.

The boy lay on the bedroom floor, one arm outflung, one hand curled on his bloody chest; one leg straight, one bent at the knee. A dancer's pose, frozen in death. He might have been six or seven—a little bigger than Justin, but still just a little boy. He should have been a picture of innocence, not a picture of violence. He should have been asleep in his bed, not dead on the floor. He shouldn't have been painted in red by a madman's brush.

Nick didn't know how long he stood there. It could have been a minute. It could have been an hour. He felt detached from his body, as if the essence of him might float free of its shell and go wherever this child's being had gone.

At least the boy was free of the pain that had been inflicted upon him. He had been stabbed again and again. Wounds to the upper chest, to the arms, to the face. It was impossible not to imagine his terror. He had gone to bed in his Spider-Man pajamas, curled up with his kitten, dreaming the sweet, simple dreams of childhood. He had awakened to a nightmare. Now he would never wake again. He would never grow up. He would never drive a car or drink a beer or kiss a girl.

As he stared at the body, the smell of blood coagulated into a thick not in Nick's throat that threatened to gag him. Tears burned hot against the backs of his eyes. He felt like he couldn't breathe. He sank to his knees on the floor beside the boy, reached out, and touched the child's dark hair. The pain that rolled over him was crushing.

"Nick. Hey, Nicky, come on," Stokes said softly, carefully resting a hand on Nick's shoulder. "Let's take a breather, man. I need a cigarette. You need a cigarette? Come on, dude. Let's step outside."

Nick flinched away from the touch as if it hurt. Slowly, he got to his feet.

"When I find the person who did this," he said, his voice low and rough with emotion, "I'm gonna send him to hell, if I have to carry him there myself."

He was trembling. He felt hot and cold and sick and angry. His pulse was roaring in his ears. He wanted to hit someone, smash something, scream.

"You're gonna have plenty of help with that, my friend," Stokes muttered. He groaned and swore as he shined his flashlight down at the dead boy. "Fucking hell. I really do need that cigarette now."

"Did you find anything outside?"

"No," Stokes said. "Dude, it's pouring rain out there."

Beyond the open bedroom window, the rain came in a pounding downpour, erasing any small hope of finding footprints outside the house or tire tracks in the driveway. Nick went to the window that had been propped open with an old paint stirring stick, cursing whatever entity had brought the weather this night of all nights. Carefully, he lowered the window to preserve the crime scene as best he could.

"There's no screen," he noted.

He shined his flashlight on the floor near the window, wet now with rain, looking for footprints, seeing none. The floor was covered in old gray linoleum tile that looked like it hadn't been truly clean in decades.

"There's no screens on half the windows," Stokes said. "This place is a fucking dump."

"Check the other bedrooms."

Had the killer come in through this window because it was the easiest access point? he wondered. Had the child been killed for the sake of silencing him before he could alert anyone else in the house? That made some kind of cold, heartless sense, at least. If the assailant had come in through the window of the mother's room, would the mother be the one dead on the floor? Or had the killer been invited in? Or living here?

What would have been the point of breaking into this house anyway? These people clearly had nothing of real value to steal—unless there might be drugs somewhere. Or unless the motive had been a sexual assault. Had the mother been assaulted? How had she managed to get away? She had somehow made it to a neighbor's house to beg for help.

Who murdered a small child and let an adult escape?

"The window in the other bedroom is painted shut," Stokes said, coming back into the doorway.

"Does it look like anything happened in there?"

"Looks like a bomb went off in a women's boutique, but I didn't see any blood."

Nick shined his light on the unmade bed and the tangle of bloody sheets. The attack had initiated on the bed. The child must have awakened, possibly screamed, certainly struggled, tried to get away, ended up on the floor . . .

Another wave of sick fury washed over him.

"Do you know anything about these people?"

"Me?" Stokes said with surprise. "Why would I?"

"'Cause you're nosy, that's why."

Stokes was always in everybody's business at work and beyond, just on the off chance that knowing something might in some way give him an edge down the road. It wasn't a bad trait for a detective to have, as far as that went.

A frown curved his mouth inside the framework of his neatly trimmed mustache and goatee. "Man, I don't even know where the hell we're at. This ain't my neighborhood."

"The mother ran for help," Nick said. "Where's the father?"

"Who's to say there is one?"

"There's one somewhere."

"Where's the mother now?"

"At the hospital. 'Toinette's there with her."

As much as he hated to disrupt their son's life with the grim reality of their profession, as lead detective he knew whom he wanted interviewing a female victim or witness: Annie. Unlike himself, she was good with people. She had a way of putting them at ease and getting them to talk. And she was nobody's fool. She knew bullshit when she heard it.

She had taken Justin to her cousin Remy, their designated babysitter on the rare occasion they both got called out at night, and had proceeded to Our Lady of Mercy.

"What's the mother's condition?" Stokes asked.

"I don't know."

"Why ain't she dead?"

"I don't know."

"How'd she get away?" Stokes asked. "There's a car sitting in the side yard, but Ossie said she ran to a neighbor's house down the road."

"There's blood in the hallway," Nick said. "The front room looks like there's been a fight."

"Let's see."

Nick looked down at the dead boy. He didn't want to leave the child alone. As if it mattered now.

"Come on," Stokes prodded. "Tick-tock, man. Time's a-wasting. We gotta see what we can see before Dutrow gets here."

They made their way down the short hall, flashlight beams bobbing and crossing each other as they hit on the evidence of a struggle: blood smeared on the wall, on the floor; furniture tipped over and shoved aside. A chair had been overturned near a small dining table toward the back of the main living space. The table itself was loaded down with stacks of mail and magazines, a pile of unfolded laundry, an opened bag of Cheetos, an abandoned can of soda, a half-drunk glass of who-knew-what.

Nick leaned over and sniffed at it. Whiskey and Coke.

An open doorway led into a small, cramped kitchen that smelled of grease and garbage. Dirty dishes filled the sink and were stacked on the counter. A woman's handbag sat on a tall stool near the back door.

Nick fished forceps out of his backpack. Stokes shined his flashlight in the handbag as Nick picked through it with the tool. Kleenex, gum, a handwritten grocery list, two prescription bottles of pills, a wallet, car keys.

He carefully plucked out the wallet with his gloved hand and opened it to see a small amount of cash and several credit cards. A woman's Louisiana driver's license was tucked into a clear plastic window.

She was pretty. Brown hair, brown eyes. Five feet, six inches. One hundred fifteen pounds. Twenty-seven years old.

"Genevieve Gauthier." He pronounced the name the French way: *Jhun*-vee-ev *Go*-tee-ay.

The address was not the house they were standing in or even the parish they were in. The address was a good hour away, a small town down in Terrebonne Parish. He wondered how long she had been living here and why she had come, trading one small town for another. Mostly, people moved from one place to another for a fresh start. Genevieve Gauthier had moved all the way to Bayou Breaux to have her little boy murdered in the night.

Setting the wallet aside, he reached back into the handbag and plucked out one of the pill bottles and held it in the beam of the flashlight. Xanax (benzodiazepine) prescribed to Gauthier, Genevieve. Antianxiety medication. What was she anxious about? Her job? Her life? A bad boyfriend? A threat?

He dropped the bottle back in the bag and picked out the other one. Oxycodone, a narcotic painkiller. An opioid—the prescription drug of choice among abusers these days. This bottle was prescribed to Marcel, Clarice. The address was in town. There were three pills in the bottle.

"Pill freak?" Stokes asked.

"Could be."

"That's a popular combo: Oxy and benzos. The house is a mess. Looks like she don't have a pot to piss in nor a window to pitch it out of."

Common traits for an addict. They were too strung out to bother with housekeeping and spent what money they had on drugs. Oxy wasn't cheap on the street—about a buck per milligram, fifteen to thirty dollars per pill, depending on the dose. That added up as resistance built and the addict needed more and more to achieve the kind of high they wanted.

Nick put the bottle back in the handbag and stared at the dark window in the back door. Lightning brightened the yard beyond, giving him the briefest glimpse of a small car parked in front of a ramshackle little garage.

"Her car keys are in her purse. She left the bag on this stool," he mused. "She must come in and out through this door. But for some reason she didn't try to leave this way tonight."

"Probably she was being chased," Stokes ventured. "But then why he didn't catch her?"

Nick walked past Stokes as if he were invisible, back into the main room, shining his flashlight from the doorway to the hall, across the trail of a struggle. If the killer came in through the boy's window . . . If the commotion brought Genevieve out of her room . . . A struggle down the hall into the living room . . . Escape out the front door . . .

He stepped onto the front porch. The rain was still coming down, though the worst of the storm had already moved north. The lightning flashed, but without the sharp bullwhip *crack!* The thunder rumbled, rolling away into the distance.

"What neighbor did she run to?" he asked as Stokes joined him.

"Up the road this way," Ossie said. "Half a mile or so."

He pointed to the right. Deeper into nowhere. Headed into the swamp. Nick looked to the other direction, to the glow of town in the night sky, less than a mile away with the promise of more houses and more people between here and there. Had she run east for cover of darkness? Had she run to hide in the brush? There was another house less than fifty yards away. Had no one been home to answer her cries for help?

How had a small woman on foot, presumably injured, escaped? Had the killer panicked? Had he chosen to run over risking a second murder? Had something or someone interrupted him, spooked him?

"It doesn't make sense," he muttered.

"Yeah, well," Stokes said, nodding in the direction of headlights and strobe lights coming down the road. Dutrow and the crime scene unit. "If you think it doesn't make sense now, hang on to your hat, partner. Here comes the damn circus."

FOUR

Kelvin Dutrow pulled his Suburban to the side of the road, shoved it into Park, and stared at the house. It seemed to crouch in the darkness just beyond the reach of the portable lights that had been set up along the driveway. The storm that had knocked out the power was trailing away, rolling on toward Lafayette, but the rain continued.

The Suburban's windshield wipers beat against the glass, keeping time with the pounding in Kelvin's head. He was tired and anxious, thinking about the scene he was about to enter. A child murder. Everyone in Partout Parish—everyone in south Louisiana—would be watching, waiting, wanting answers. The burden would fall on his shoulders. He welcomed it. He did. He would show the voters they had chosen well when they had chosen him to be their sheriff.

The house lights came on suddenly, revealing two figures standing on the porch. Stokes and Fourcade. Stokes smoking a cigarette at a crime scene. Fourcade—instantly recognizable by his fighter's build—powerful shoulders, hands jammed at his narrow waist. He was staring out across the yard, straight at Kelvin's vehicle. Kelvin imagined he could feel Fourcade's dark gaze, intense with the detective's dislike for him.

The man had an edge that hinted at potential problems. He had a history—albeit an old history—of crossing lines that shouldn't be crossed during his days with the New Orleans PD and in his early time with the Sheriff's Office here. He had famously once beaten a murder suspect senseless, six or seven years past. The story went that the female deputy who had later become his wife—now Detective Annie Broussard—had arrested him at the scene.

Gus Noblier had told Kelvin that Fourcade was best left to his own devices, that he didn't play well with others but was a first-rate detective, well worth the headache of having to deal with his volatile personality. He had gone so far as to promote Fourcade to Detective Sergeant, giving him a certain amount of power and autonomy within the division. The other detectives answered to Fourcade. Fourcade answered to no one save the sheriff himself.

Noblier's philosophy made Kelvin uncomfortable. He liked to run a tight ship. Nonconformists didn't fit into his picture. A former military man, he wanted order and respect from the people beneath him. But Fourcade was by far his most experienced detective, and the squad functioned well with him as their unlikely leader. Fourcade: the antihero.

And so, he kept Fourcade on.

Against my better judgment, he reminded himself as he opened his car door. He settled his hat on his head as he stepped out, the rain pecking at the plastic cover and running down his slicker. He was immediately sweating inside the jacket. Damn this weather.

The crime scene unit pulled up, stopping with the van's nose on the yellow warning tape that had been stretched across the driveway to the house.

This was not going to go well. Kelvin already knew that. Fourcade had automatically—and defiantly—called the state police to request their assistance processing the scene. That had been their standard operating procedure for years with complex crime scenes. Cops liked to cling to their ways. Kelvin had come to the Partout Parish Sheriff's Office with the determination to modernize and expand the department in creative ways he believed would ultimately benefit the community. He had written the grant proposal for the CSI van while Gus Noblier had still been sheriff.

Kelvin believed having their own crime scene unit would free up the detectives to do their investigating instead of losing valuable time collecting fingerprints and fiber evidence. On a case where they would ordinarily call in the state CSI unit and then have to wait for them to arrive, there would be no wait time. Having their own unit provided jobs and encouraged local young people to pursue schooling as technicians and stay in a parish that steadily lost its population to more metropolitan areas for lack of opportunity. And contracting with nearby rural parishes and municipal police departments to attend their crime scenes would mean revenue for Partout Parish.

Kelvin was a visionary. Nick Fourcade was not, nor was he going to accept this progress without a fight. That was a fight Kelvin was prepared to have.

A heavyset black deputy in a bright yellow rain slicker stood at the driver's-side window of the crime scene van, shaking his head and gesticulating with his hands.

Compton, Kelvin recalled. He prided himself on memorizing the names of as many of his personnel as possible. When he had first come to the Partout Parish SO as Noblier's second-in-command, he had set up a flashcard program on his computer with the ID photos of all his deputies, detectives, and unsworn employees. He went through sections of it every day as a mental exercise. It was good for morale and inspired loyalty for the people beneath him to feel a personal connection to him.

"Is there a problem here, Deputy Compton?" he asked.

"No, sir," Compton answered. "Not as long as the van stays on this side of the tape."

"That's bullshit," Keith Kemp declared.

The senior crime scene investigator, Kemp was a lean, hard stick of a man with a sour expression that spoke of his general outlook on humanity.

"We're supposed to collect evidence and carry it all the way across this yard in the goddamn rain?" Kemp asked.

"Unless you can fly," Compton replied. "Detective Fourcade set the perimeter, and here it is. Storm came before we could get a good look around. He don't want no vehicles in the yard in case we might find some tracks or something once we can see again."

"So we make footprints everywhere instead? That's fucking genius," Kemp said sarcastically.

Compton shrugged, unconcerned with Kemp's opinion.

Kelvin glanced up at the house, at Fourcade, who was still standing on the front porch, staring at them.

"This is ridiculous," Kemp complained. "I didn't move to this fucking backwater to get bossed around by some coonass detective."

"That's enough," Kelvin warned.

"How am I supposed to do my job?" Kemp demanded.

The sheriff turned toward Compton. "Take the tape down, Deputy."

Compton hesitated, frowning. "Detective Fourcade's crime scene—"

"Is now my crime scene," Kelvin said. "Take the tape down. That's an order."

"Yassir," Compton said, then muttered half under his breath as he turned away, "Lord have mercy."

He moved like molasses as he reached for the tape.

Instantly, Fourcade was off the porch, coming toward them at an aggressive pace.

"Is there something about a perimeter you don't understand?" he demanded. He wore no hat or jacket. The rain soaked his dark T-shirt, plastering it to his chest and shoulders.

"No," Kelvin returned. "Is there something about authority you don't understand, Detective?"

"No. My crime scene, my authority."

"That's easily remedied."

Fourcade arched a brow. "Oh? You gonna investigate this case yourself, Sheriff, or what? Maybe you wanna do all our jobs for us."

"I can do without your attitude."

"Likewise."

Kelvin weighed his options. Push the issue into an all-out battle or find some more diplomatic way to work around the detective in front of him. Fourcade wouldn't back down, and he wasn't entirely wrong. The detective in charge took control of a scene and established the perimeter. No one was allowed inside the perimeter without his knowledge and consent. That was procedure for a reason. Nor was it all that unusual for a detective to take a proprietary attitude toward a murder scene. Emotions ran high in the aftermath of a crime like this one.

Still, Kelvin could see Ossie Compton and Keith Kemp and the trainee in the van's passenger seat watching him, waiting.

"Give me your flashlight," he said to Kemp.

The crime scene investigator handed him a heavy black Maglite through the van window. Kelvin ducked under the yellow tape and swept the beam of light back and forth over the dirt and crushed shells and muddy puddles of the driveway, looking for discernable tire tracks, something with a tread pattern, anything they could use.

"There's nothing here," he declared. "We've got a crime scene to process. I want this van as close to the house as possible."

"I don't want these people touching my scene," Fourcade said loudly.

"You got no say in that, Detective."

"I called the LSP—"

"And I canceled them," Kelvin said. "We have our own crime scene unit—"

"That don't know a damn thing about a scene like this!"

"Fuck you, Fourcade!" Kemp shouted out the van window.

Fourcade didn't spare him a glance.

"Kemp has plenty of experience—" Kelvin started.

"Not on my scenes, he doesn't."

"Coonass motherfucker!" Kemp yelled, half hanging out the window of the van. "Come over here and say that!"

Kelvin wheeled on him and shouted, "Shut up!" then turned back to Fourcade. "Kemp's been running crime scenes for years. I can vouch for him myself."

"And the rest of them?" Fourcade asked. He pointed at the kid in the passenger seat. "Is that one old enough to vote? I don't want—"

"It's not up to you, Detective," Kelvin said. "The taxpayers of this parish are paying for a crime scene unit. I won't have them double-billed by the state of Louisiana for no good reason."

Fourcade's eyes widened. A muscle pulsed at the back of his square jaw. "No good reason?" he said, his tone of voice dangerously quiet, somehow more unnerving than rage. He stepped to within a few feet of the sheriff. "There's a dead child in that house. Someone came into his bedroom and stabbed the life outta him. You want to turn his justice over to a pack of amateurs?"

"Every person on this team is a trained professional."

The detective barked a laugh. "Oh, right. For what? Five minutes? Five weeks' training and a fucking Wheaties box top? They're certified? The hell!"

"Stand aside, Detective," Kelvin said. "Don't make me say it again."

Stokes finally joined the party then, reaching out carefully to touch Fourcade on the shoulder. "Hey, Nicky, come on. It ain't like you can't stand right there and watch 'em do the job. Come on. Let's go back inside."

Fourcade shrugged him off violently, cursing in French. He threw his hands up in the air, waving them off, as if they might just go away and leave him, then he turned and stormed off toward the house.

"You need to put a leash on him," Kelvin snapped.

Stokes laughed without humor. "Yeah, right, boss. I'd sooner crawl up an alligator's ass and work my way out through its teeth. He barely tolerates me—and I'm his partner going on seven years."

"He can rein in that temper or he won't make that anniversary."

"It's a kid," Stokes said.

"What?"

"The victim. It's a little boy. Nicky's got a boy about the same age." He tilted his head and gave a shrug. "Just sayin'."

Kelvin swallowed back his anger. The aftertaste was bitter.

"Our people are going to process this scene," he said. "If Fourcade doesn't like that, he can leave. His choice."

"You'd have better luck taking a bone from a pit bull," Stokes said. "Nick won't walk away before he gets justice for this boy."

He motioned toward the road as a hearse drew near. "Great," he said without enthusiasm. "The coroner's here, too. We got us a regular goddamn three-ring spectacle. Let the shit show begin."

* * *

INHALE. FOCUS. CALM. Patience. Exhale. Focus. Calm. Patience. Inhale.

Nick moved around the boy's bedroom, forcing himself to breathe slowly, in through his nose, out through his mouth, counting the seconds—four seconds in, four seconds out—focusing on his watchwords in the attempt to disconnect from his temper.

His heart was still beating too hard, too quickly. His hands were still trembling with rage as he photographed the scene. His thoughts kept racing over the top of his mantra.

The hell if Dutrow's people were coming in this room before he was finished. He wouldn't have it. Dutrow would have to have him physically removed, and there was no one here stupid enough to lay hands on him except maybe for Kemp. What a welcome diversion it would be to beat that cracker asshole to a bloody pulp.

Four seconds in, four seconds out. *Inhale. Focus. Calm. Patience. Exhale. Focus. Calm. Patience. Inhale.*

He looked at the screen on the back of the camera. The truth seemed less real reduced to two inches by three inches. The boy looked like a doll that had been cast aside by some careless child. Even so, Nick could feel the emotions amplifying inside him: anger rising to rage, sadness sinking to despair. He pulled in another long, slow, deep breath. *Inhale. Focus. Calm. Patience. Exhale. Focus. Calm. Patience. Inhale.*

He photographed the body from all angles, moving as quickly as he could. He photographed the floor, the bed, the window, the doorway to the hall. With the electricity back on, he was able to see the details that had been left to the imagination in the dark. Blood spatter on the wall and ceiling. Cast-off spatter from the blade of the weapon as the killer pulled it out of the victim and raised his arm to deliver another blow. Blood smeared on the floor where someone had stepped and slipped. A partial shoe print.

He crouched down, zoomed in, and snapped several pictures. The tread of a sneaker, maybe. Just a few wavy lines. Probably too small to discern much in the way of identification. He would follow the blood trail into the hall and to the front room in hopes of finding a better example.

"Damn."

He looked up to see the sheriff standing in the doorway, sober-faced as he stared at the dead boy.

In his late forties, Dutrow stayed fit in the gym, where people could see him. He had the physique of someone who lifted too much iron, with his black uniform shirts tailored to advertise that truth. Despite the fact that he was really a politician with an office job, he favored the black uniform and boots of a tactical squad leader, as if there was some chance of his needing to be ready to fight danger at a moment's notice. It was a costume, a fraudulent image the public gobbled up with a spoon. Kelvin Dutrow: Man of Action.

He had removed his raincoat and left it somewhere and had put paper booties on over his boots so as not to track anything into the crime scene. *Fastidious* and *vain* were the words that came to Nick's mind when he looked at the sheriff, as if the booties were to protect Dutrow from the gore of the crime scene instead of the other way around.

"You have a son, don't you?" the sheriff asked as Nick went to photograph what might have been a palm print in blood on the wall near the door.

The answer stuck on Nick's tongue for a moment. Somehow, sharing that information seemed too intimate, as if it was knowledge that might be used against him. Dutrow looked at him expectantly. His small dark eyes were hard and bright beneath straight dark brows that were a stark contrast to his close-cropped salt-and-pepper hair.

"*Oui,*" Nick admitted.

"About the same age?"

"He's five."

Dutrow nodded. "My fiancée has a son. He's fourteen. She'd lose her mind if something like this happened to him."

Nick said nothing. He didn't give a shit about Kelvin Dutrow's fiancée. He didn't like Kelvin Dutrow, even though Gus Noblier had recruited the man from Houma PD to be his chief deputy. Nick loved Gus like an uncle and had respected him as sheriff, but he had pegged Dutrow as an opportunist and a showboat from the start, and nothing that had happened since had changed his mind. How Gus hadn't seen that was beyond him.

Dutrow embraced the spotlight and was a creature of social media. Following in the footsteps of several Louisiana law enforcement personalities who had gained national attention doing so, Dutrow had built a following on the Internet as the tough-talking star of his own YouTube videos, calling attention to himself in the name of fighting crime. It was a style that grated on Nick like a rasp.

"If someone did this to my boy," he said, "me, I'd kill 'em with my bare hands, and I'd take my damn time doing it."

Dutrow's brow knit with disapproval. "That's not the wisest thing to tell your boss, Detective."

Nick shrugged a shoulder. "*C'est vrai.* That's for true, but true it is."

He looked at the boy on the floor, took a measured breath, and released it slowly. *Inhale. Focus. Calm. Patience. Exhale. Focus. Calm. Patience. Inhale.*

"If you wouldn't do that for your child, you shouldn't have one," he said.

"You'd condone murder?" Dutrow said. "Vigilantism?"

"It would be my obligation to avenge my family. Let the law call that what it will."

Dutrow scowled. "That attitude has gotten you in trouble before. You—or any man in this parish—would go to prison for taking the law in his own hands. I'd make sure of it."

"A man has to be willing to do the right thing," Nick said, "regardless of the consequences or the moral injustice of the price he might pay. That's the definition of sacrifice, is it not?"

Dutrow's face was growing red. "You're sworn to uphold the law, not advocate for vigilante rule. If you're going to have a problem with that, you shouldn't be working for me."

"I do my job," Nick said calmly. "I do it well. That doesn't mean my societal obligations and my higher beliefs always mesh. Inner conflict is the evolving man's daily struggle, no?"

Dutrow clearly didn't know what to make of him. Nick knew he made the man uncomfortable. He made most people uncomfortable. Sometimes it seemed to be his purpose in life to make people uncomfortable, to make them step back and question. He accepted that role, embraced it, even. What else could he do? He was the way he was.

"Professionally, I am on the side of law enforcement, if not the side of the angels," he said. "The two are not always the same, are they?"

"Both answer to a higher power," Dutrow said. "Remember that."

"'You get justice in the next world. In this one you have the law,'" Nick said, quoting William Gaddis, not that Dutrow would recognize it.

He sighed and went to look more closely at the partial handprint on the wall. The shape was right; the pattern was wrong. Not the random lines and whorls, which demarked human flesh. Not the smooth smearing of a glove. The pattern had almost a stamped quality, like a stencil. Strange . . .

"Detective Broussard is with the mother?" Dutrow asked, surrendering the philosophical discussion for the moment.

"At Our Lady."

"Do we know the extent of her injuries?"

"No. She was able to make it down the road to a neighbor before she collapsed, but she's a mother trying to get help for her child. In my experience, there is no more fierce a creature on the earth. She might have dragged herself there with no legs."

"Why didn't she call nine-one-one?"

"There doesn't appear to be a phone in the house."

"Cell phone?"

"Haven't seen one yet."

"What do we know about this woman?" Dutrow asked.

"Her name. Genevieve Gauthier. Moved here from Terrebonne Parish. Don't know when."

"Where?"

"Dulac. You know it? It's not far from Houma."

The sheriff seemed to ponder the question—or the answer to it. The kitten chose that moment to dash from under the bed and pounce at the dead boy's bloody bare foot.

"Jesus!" Dutrow startled. "What the hell? Get that cat out of here! We can't have animals running around a crime scene!"

Nick scooped up the kitten in one hand and held it close to his chest. It curled against him and immediately began to purr, a sound that might have offered him some comfort if not for the voices coming from the front room of the house.

"The coroner is here," Dutrow announced.

Nick muttered a curse. A small, rural parish, Partout Parish had no medical examiner, only a coroner, an elected official who got the job by default because he had no natural aversion to touching dead bodies. Ulysse Wilson was neither a doctor nor a forensic pathologist, and yet he had the power to determine where a body would go and what would be done to it.

"You're gonna send a murdered boy to the funeral home with that old fool?" Nick asked. "Let him decide whether or not there needs to be an autopsy? I want the body sent to Lafayette."

"The cause of death is not exactly a mystery here," Dutrow said. "We don't need to send this boy out of the parish to know he was stabbed."

"Right," Nick said. "But what was he stabbed with? A knife? A screwdriver? How long was the blade? How wide? Was it smooth? Was it serrated?"

"I take it you haven't found the murder weapon."

"Your powers of deduction are astonishing," he snapped, his voice dripping sarcasm as his blood pressure began to rise again. "It's a damn good thing you're a politician—"

"You can leave the rest of that statement in your mouth, Detective," Dutrow snapped back. "I'll request the body go to the morgue at Our Lady for the time being. And if you have so little faith in my decision making, I can assign you duties elsewhere in the department and this case will cease to be a problem for you. Do you understand me?"

Nick looked down at the kitten sleeping against him. He looked down at the little boy lying broken on the floor. If he had any sense, he would get himself fired and find another line of work. Instead, he would swallow his temper because it was already too late for him to back away.

This boy was his boy now, his responsibility. He had made a promise. He would no more walk away than he would stop breathing.

"I asked you a question," Dutrow said. "You might be my best detective, but you are not my only detective. I won't have you question my authority every time I turn around. I'm damned tired of it already. I know you're used to Gus letting you run your own show, but I am not Gus Noblier. *I* run the show now. Do you understand me, Detective Fourcade?"

Nick said nothing, too stubborn to concede defeat, his attention still locked on the boy.

"Detective?" Dutrow asked with irritation.

"I heard you."

"Good," Dutrow said, with more satisfaction than the answer warranted. "Now you stand back and let these other people do their jobs."

FIVE

I don't know how coherent she'll be," Travis Benton said.

They walked down the ER hallway toward a private examination room, shoulder to shoulder, their voices hushed. He'd been a grade behind Annie in school, the annoying little brother to her first big junior high crush, Big Ben Benton. Big Ben had tragically died of lymphoma at the tender age of nineteen. Travis had gone off to college and come back to Bayou Breaux with a medical degree.

"Has she said anything about what happened?" Annie asked.

"Not that's made much sense."

The hospital was quiet. Weeknights in Bayou Breaux, the sidewalks were rolled up by ten. The population consisted of working people who saved their hell-raising and sport heroics for the weekend. The only lights on in the hallway were down low, giving the polished floor a pearly glow. The conversation going on among staff at the front desk faded behind them.

The hair on the back of Annie's neck rose as she became aware of an eerie, soft keening in the distance.

"That's her," Travis said. "She's been going back and forth between near-catatonia and hysteria since the ambulance brought her in. She wouldn't say anything at first, then all of a sudden she jumped off the gurney and tried to run, screaming like a banshee. It took three of us to hold on to her 'til the drugs kicked in."

"Do you think she was high on something?"

He shrugged as they approached the closed door. He'd been at Our Lady of Mercy long enough to have seen pretty much every kind of chemically induced high that had made it to the bayou country in the past five years.

"Could be. But her pupils were normal. She doesn't smell like she's been smoking anything. Maybe a little whiskey on her breath. I guess we'll see what the tox screen says. But the woman has been through something horrific. That can be worse than any bad drug trip."

"What are her injuries?"

"Knife wounds. She's got cuts on her hands and forearms, consistent with defense wounds. She's got a deep cut on the top of her left shoulder. The knife must have come down like this," he said, pantomiming a downward chop with his right hand to his left shoulder and slicing toward his chest. "Actually nicked the collarbone. Missed her jugular by a few millimeters.

"Other than that, she has a lot of bruises and abrasions, a couple of cracked ribs. Her feet are cut up pretty bad from running barefoot down a gravel road. I want to get a head CT. She might have a fractured orbital. Her left eye is just about swollen shut. Looks like she took a pretty nasty punch.

"I've called the CT tech," he said. "He lives up in Plaquemine, so he won't be here for a while."

"Sexual assault?"

"She wouldn't consent to the exam. Freaked out when I even made a move in that direction. That could mean she was raped, could mean she wasn't. For what it's worth—just as a visual observation—I didn't see any obvious outward signs of a violent sexual attack. No ligature marks, no finger marks on her throat or her thighs. But that certainly doesn't mean she couldn't have been raped.

"I didn't press the issue," he said. "She's upset enough. I thought you might be able to persuade her to say yes to the exam. We have a nurse available to do the rape kit if she consents."

"Did she have clothes on when they brought her in?"

"A T-shirt and panties. Something she might have worn to bed. Covered in blood. They're bagged and ready for you to take."

He cracked the door open, and Annie looked in. Genevieve Gauthier lay on the hospital bed across the room, the head of the bed raised up. She looked young and small and forlorn against the stark white sheets, her face swollen, misshapen, and discolored in splotches. She was as still as death, the keening sound coming from her the only indication she was alive. The sound rose and fell like a distant siren call, strange and otherworldly.

"No one's brought the son in," Travis murmured. "I guess we have to assume the worst."

Annie nodded and whispered, " 'Fraid so. Dead at the scene."

"Damn, Annie. What's the world coming to?" He shook his head, his mouth twisting. "I sound like my old man."

"People been asking that question since Cain," Annie said. "We still don't have an answer. I sure don't."

"You're not shoring up my faith in law enforcement, Detective," he said, joking the way first responders often did in the face of tragedy—wry, sarcastic, a little jolt of absurdity to take the edge off a terrible situation.

"You'll have to appeal to a higher power on that," Annie said. "I'm just part of the cleanup crew, catching the bad guys after the fact."

"I sure hope you get this one," he said. "Ring the buzzer if you need anything."

"Thanks, Travis."

Annie took a deep breath and let it out as she stepped into the room. The woman in the bed seemed not to notice her at all. She stared off at nothing, one eye nearly swollen shut, the other unblinking, and began another long keening note, starting soft, slowly growing louder and then tapering off, fading to nothing.

"Genevieve?" Annie asked softly. She walked to the far side of the bed, stepping into the woman's line of sight. "Genevieve, my name is Annie Broussard. I'm a detective with the Sheriff's Office. I'm here to talk to you about what happened tonight."

No response.

She pulled a rolling stool to the side of the bed and sat down, slipping her phone out of the pocket of her khaki pants. She set it to Record and placed it on the stand beside the bed then looked at Genevieve Gauthier, taking in the bruises and bandages, the IV that snaked into the woman's thin, pale arm. She had a look of birdlike frailty—small bones, slight frame, hollow cheeks. It wouldn't take much for someone larger and stronger to hurt her.

"Can you tell me what happened?"

Silence. Annie waited, giving the woman time to accept the idea of reliving the horror of what had happened to her by retelling the tale. A victim was victimized many times over by the system. There was no avoiding it. The crime was only the beginning.

"Where's my son?" Genevieve asked, her voice barely more than a whisper. "Where's KJ?"

Annie hesitated, wishing she could get the answers she needed before having to answer that question. To tell a mother her child was dead and then interrogating her about how that tragedy had come to pass was nothing short of cruel. But it was her job to get answers from this woman, and the sooner she got those answers, the sooner she could relay them to Nick at the scene. There was a killer on the loose. Time was of the essence.

"He's dead, isn't he?" Genevieve made eye contact for a second and then let her gaze slide away before the answer could come. "My baby's dead."

"I'm so sorry," Annie said. "Yes, your son is dead."

Tears welled up, making the young woman's good eye look huge. A fine trembling shuddered through her, and that eerie keen twisted up out of her soul, escaping her body like a wraith to swirl around the room. The ghost of grief. It would slip under the door and float down the hall to touch anyone in earshot and run a chill through them.

Automatically, Annie reached out and touched her on the shoulder to offer the comfort of human contact. "I'm so sorry. I have a son, too. I can only imagine the pain.

"Is there someone I can call for you?" she asked. "Someone you might want to have come stay with you? A relative? A friend?"

The woman shook her head. "No . . . There's no one . . . Just me and KJ."

"What about your son's father? Would you like me to call him?"

"No."

"Does he live in the area?"

"He's not part of our lives."

"You shouldn't have to go through this alone, Genevieve."

"I'm always alone," she murmured, her empty gaze sliding past Annie again. "That's just how it is."

"You don't have a work friend who might come?" Annie pressed. "Someone from your church, maybe?"

Genevieve didn't answer, clearly tired of having to say she had no one in her life who cared about her at all.

For a second Annie flashed back to her childhood. Her mother had come to Bayou Breaux pregnant and forlorn, no friends, no family. The couple Annie had always known as Tante Fanchon and Uncle Sos had taken in Marie Broussard, had given her a place to live and work.

Annie had been absorbed into the Doucet family from birth even though she was no blood relation to them, as far as she knew. She had no idea what it was to be alone in the world. You couldn't swing a stick in Partout Parish without hitting half a dozen Doucets. But her mother had been intimately acquainted with that kind of emotional isolation. Her mother had always been alone, even in a roomful of people. Marie Broussard had lived her life in a crystal-clear bubble of isolation, never letting anyone truly know her. She had died by her own hand when Annie was nine years old, a mystery even to her own child.

"How old is KJ?" Annie asked.

"Seven . . . Almost eight . . . He'll be eight . . ."

But he would never be eight.

Annie sighed. "Genevieve, I know this is hard and you're in pain, but we need as much information as you can give us tonight so we can find the person who did this to you and your son. I know you ran to get help tonight. I'm it. I'm your help. The other detectives who are at your home right now looking for clues—they're your help. You need to tell us what happened."

Some victims opened the floodgates and spilled information in torrents, talking so fast they barely made sense. Others were so traumatized they could barely speak at all. Genevieve Gauthier seemed like she might drift away into a fog of physical pain and emotional numbness and whatever pharmaceutical haze Travis had injected into her veins. Annie rolled her chair a few inches to the left, back into the woman's line of vision.

"Who did this to you? Did you see? Was it someone you know?"

No answer. Annie snuck a glance at her phone, touching the button to check the time, half expecting to see a text message from Nick, asking for information. There wasn't one.

"We were asleep. I was asleep," Genevieve began at last, her voice a murmur. "I was having a dream, a bad dream, that there was someone in the house, someone who wanted to hurt us . . . And then there was . . ."

"What woke you?"

"The pain."

"What pain?"

"The pain in my chest."

Travis had said nothing about a chest wound. There was no telltale blood on the front of her gown, though the wound on her shoulder had bled through the bandage. Annie could see the dark stain in the gauze through the flimsy cotton garment.

"Do you mean the cut on your shoulder?"

"No . . . I felt it . . . Here," she said, lifting her bandaged right hand toward her sternum. "I sat up. I cried out. I heard KJ cry out."

She was seeing it in her mind. Her eyes had that glassy glaze that reflected vision inward on the memory. Her respiration rate was picking up, quicker, shallower breaths that came with fear and an increased pulse.

"I heard KJ cry out, and I-I jumped out of bed. My foot got caught in the sheets, and I tripped and fell on the floor. He was crying for me, and I couldn't get to him. Like that horrible nightmare . . . you're running and running . . . you can't get there . . ."

The tears came again, streaming down her battered face. The end of her upturned nose turned bright red.

"He was calling for me, and-and I-I ran into the hall. I w-was scr-screaming his name. And-and-and he came out of the bedroom—"

"Who came out of the bedroom? Your son?"

"No. *Him*. He-he h-had a knife."

"Did you see his face? Can you describe him?"

She was quiet for a second, glancing around as if looking for eaves-droppers. Then she looked at Annie and whispered, "He was a demon. A demon straight from hell."

A visible shudder went through her body as she recalled the image. "His face was twisted . . . eyes empty, black holes . . . his mouth was like a black horseshoe. He had horns. Like the devil."

"He was wearing a mask?" Annie asked, trying to discern if the memory was real or imagined.

"I was so afraid . . . It happened so fast . . . He came at me with a knife, slashing and slashing."

She raised her arms as if to fend off the attacker. Annie pictured the assailant's knife cutting Genevieve's hands and arms as she tried to defend herself. One stroke had breached her defenses, slicing deep into the top of her shoulder, just inches from her neck. A blitz attack. She would have been frantic, just trying to survive from one second to the next.

The memory seemed to be nearly as real to her as the event had been. She pressed her lips together, squeezed her eyes closed as if to hold back the coming flood of tears. But the wave of emotion was too strong, overwhelming, and it burst out of her in a terrible, wrenching sob.

"Oh, my God! Oh, my God!" she cried, her small, frail body curling in on itself, shaking with the force of her hysteria. "He killed me! He killed my baby!"

Annie reached out again, placing a hand gently on Genevieve's back, trying to offer some kind of comfort, trying to calm her with words as empty as air. What could she say that could possibly soothe emotions so raw and so justified? Nothing.

She rubbed the woman's back, and said she was sorry, and waited for the worst of the storm to pass so she could poke a stick in the open wounds with more questions to elicit more terrible memories.

Was he tall? Was he short? Was he black? Was he white? Was he thin?

Was he fat? Did he speak? Did he smell? What was he wearing? What color was his hair?

Questions with no reliable answers. Victims of brutal crimes often had very distorted memories of the event. The part of the brain that took over during an attack was the part of the brain where animal instinct lives. Fight and flight, self-preservation. It was not the orderly, logical, problem-solving, list-making part of the mind. There was no time to think and reason, only to react. All energy went to survival, not to making plans and storing memories. Consequently, memories couldn't always be trusted. Assailants described as massive often turned out to be average-size, black turned out to be white, a cannon of a handgun turned out to be a .22, a machete turned out to be a steak knife.

"Genevieve," Annie said. "Did he harm you sexually? Did he rape you?"

The answer was too long coming to be believed.

"No," she whispered.

Annie let it go. Her time for getting information was running out. Genevieve was exhausted from the ordeal, from her injuries, from the emotional roller coaster. She curled on her side in the bed, looking smaller and smaller as her energy ebbed away.

A nurse stuck her head in the door, frowning at Annie. "The technician is here for the CT scan."

"We're about done."

"I should hope so," the nurse said, her eyebrows pinched low and tight with disapproval.

"Just a few more minutes," Annie said, earning herself a curt *tsk* as the nurse disappeared.

"What happened then, Genevieve?" she asked softly, like a child wanting more of a scary bedtime story. "How did you get away from him?"

Genevieve blinked slowly, barely hanging on to consciousness. "I just ran," she said. "I ran and ran . . . I had to get help, but there wasn't anybody . . . There never is . . . I'm always alone . . ."

The door swung open, and Travis Benton stepped in with a strapping orderly dressed in purple scrubs behind him. Annie pushed away from the bed and stood up.

"We're going to take Ms. Gauthier for her head CT now," he said.

"Then she should get some rest. Maybe you can come back later, Detective."

Annie nodded. She bent down and touched Genevieve Gauthier on her uninjured shoulder. "I'll be back, Genevieve. You're in good hands here. And you're not alone anymore. Myself and the other detectives are going to do everything in our power to find the person who did this to you and your son and bring them to justice. That's a promise."

"Take care of my baby," Genevieve whispered. "Please take care of KJ. Tell him I love him. Tell him I'm sorry."

"I will."

ANNIE LEFT THE room and went down the hall, past the nurses' station and the triage desk. She went into the ladies' room and washed her hands and splashed cold water on her face, trying to wash off the imagined grime of dragging a victim through the gruesome details of the crime that had been perpetrated against her.

As she stared at herself in the mirror, she thought she looked every bit as weary as she felt: dark smudges beneath dark eyes, sallow complexion, a worry line digging deep between her eyebrows. Even her dark hair looked tired and limp. She looked and felt like shit. But she hadn't been attacked by a madman, she reminded herself, and she wasn't on her way to a head CT. Her son was safe in bed at her cousin Remy's house. She had a life full of family and friends.

"I'm always alone . . . That's just how it is . . ." Genevieve Gauthier was alone, had no one—not a relative to come to her aid or a friend to sit by her side. The father of her child didn't even warrant a phone call in the wake of this tragedy.

There was a story there. That's what an investigation was: a story put together piece by puzzle piece until it all made sense. It was not just the story of the crime itself but the stories of each individual involved. All those pieces had to come together and fit in exactly the right way at exactly the right moment in order for the crime to happen. If one of the people in this night's story had turned left instead of right at some point in time, their paths might never have crossed, and KJ and Genevieve Gauthier would be home, asleep, safe in their beds.

The storm had come and gone, but the heat and humidity remained, Annie noted as she walked out of the ER into the night. Such strange weather for this late in the fall. Though, technically, hurricane season was not quite over; people had usually quit worrying about it by now and moved on to more pleasant seasonal thoughts like fall football and decorating for Halloween.

The parking lot gleamed wet like a smooth black sea under the security lights. A bright white statue of the Virgin Mary stood in the center of the driveway, its arms opened wide to welcome the sick, the wounded, the people who loved them, and the people who worked to save them.

A large two-story brick *L*, the hospital had been built in the '70s when money ran as thick as Louisiana oil and philanthropy was a status symbol. Even now, years and economic ups and downs later, Our Lady of Mercy was an anchor of the community, always featured on the cover of the annual Junior League calendar. The broad manicured lawn and carefully tended gardens sloped down to the banks of the bayou.

Annie turned away from the parking lot and took the path to the garden. She breathed deep the familiar dark, rich scents of wet vegetation, flowers and earth, and the bayou. The reassuring smell of home, of normalcy. This was the place to come to walk, to pray, to escape the chaos of trauma and the grief of illness and death. The live oak trees were hung with fairy lights and ringed with benches—too wet to sit on now.

Annie stood under one of the trees and pulled out her phone to call Nick just as the phone began to vibrate. His name came up on the screen.

"Where you at, 'Toinette?" His voice was gruff with smoke. Once a pack-a-day smoker, he had curtailed the habit early in their relationship because he knew she didn't like it. He had given it up entirely, cold turkey, the day they found out she was pregnant with Justin. Nearly six years later, he still never smoked at home, but he would take it up again at work if the case was bad enough. He'd been at it heavy of late. It was a point of irritation between them.

"I'm still at Our Lady," she said. "They just took our victim away for a head CT."

"Is she conscious?"

"Yes."

"What kind of shape is she in?"

"Physically: cuts and bruises. A couple of cracked ribs. She's got a bad-looking eye—that's what the scan is for. Emotionally: she's hanging on to the ragged edge with broken fingernails."

"What did she say? Did she see the guy? Did she give you a description?"

"Yeah," Annie said on a sigh. "She said it was a demon from hell."

Nick was silent for a beat then echoed her sigh. She could imagine the smoke drifting through his lips and curling into the night air.

"Hell, 'Toinette," he said wearily, "I coulda told you that."

"It's that bad?"

He said nothing.

"I'm on my way."

SIX

The first thing that struck Annie about the location was that it was so close to town yet seemed so remote. The road ran along a shallow, tree-choked bayou populated with snakes and nutria. It wasn't a place for pleasure boating or sport fishing. No one would come down this road if they didn't have to. Yet not half a mile from here was one of Bayou Breaux's newer subdivisions, Blue Cypress, where the houses were fashioned after Caribbean plantation-style homes and traditional Acadian houses.

No pricey architect had been involved in the design of Genevieve Gauthier's house. It was a cheap cracker box with a sagging front porch. No doubt she lived out here because it was all she could afford. Surely there was no better reason. Even with all the lights on, and an array of law enforcement vehicles parked along the road, the place gave Annie the creeps.

She got out of her SUV and walked toward the driveway with a cardboard carrier of steaming cups of coffee in each hand. Caffeine was like molten gold at a crime scene in the middle of the night. They had been here for hours already. They would probably be here for hours more, examining every inch of the scene. And it would be hours beyond that before they got a chance to sleep. She had swung into the Quik Pik on her way here, the only convenience store in Bayou Breaux that stayed open all night, serving cops and shift workers from the oil refinery and the lamp factory.

"Coffee?" she said by way of greeting as she came up to the two deputies standing guard at the head of the driveway.

"Annie, you an angel of mercy, you are," Ossie Compton said, snagging a cup.

"That's Detective Angel of Mercy to you," she quipped back.

She had known Ossie Compton since her first days in a uniform. He had been one of her lesser tormentors when she had been the only female deputy in a department of hard-ass chauvinists. They had been relentless in their teasing and bullying, some of it good-natured, most of it not. She had learned to give as good as she got. Seven years had somehow gone by since her promotion to detective, but she would always be Annie or just Broussard to the old guard—out of either affection or disrespect. With some, she minded. With Compton, she did not. He had a good heart and a good sense of humor. She considered him a friend.

"You coming late to the party," he said.

"I was at Our Lady with the mother."

"She all right?"

"I wouldn't say that, exactly. She's alive. Her wounds will heal—at least the physical ones."

She held out the carrier toward the younger deputy, who had yet to speak. Everyone called him Young Prejean because he was a nephew to the Prejean with whom Annie had once worked. He looked too young to have a job and had grown a scraggly goatee, as if that might fool someone into thinking he was a grown man.

"I hear it's bad in there," she said, nodding toward the house.

"Terrible," Compton said. "Somebody punched their own ticket straight to hell tonight. And the sooner they get there, the better."

Young Prejean shook his head. "I don't ever want to see anything like that again."

"None of us do," Annie admitted. "But all of us will if we're at this long enough."

"You remember your first homicide, Annie?" Compton asked.

"I sure do. Pam Bichon."

"That was a bad one."

"I'll have that in my head 'til the day I die."

"What happened?" Prejean asked, sipping at his coffee like it was too hot for his delicate young tongue.

"A real estate agent lured to an abandoned house out on Pony Bayou," Annie said, wishing she could keep the mental picture at bay, knowing she wouldn't be able to. "She was nailed to the floor, tortured, eviscerated. It was horrific."

On patrol, she had been the one to find the body days after Pam Bichon had been reported missing. She could still hear the buzz of the flies. The sickly sweet rotten smell of decaying human flesh came back to her and lodged in the back of her throat like a fist.

"Damn," Young Prejean whispered, his eyes wide.

The sound of raised voices came from the house. Annie looked at the crime scene van and knew Keith Kemp would be here. No good would come of that. Having opposed the idea of the crime scene unit, Nick had taken an instant hatred to Kemp. And Dutrow was here. His big black Suburban was parked on the road.

The sheriff's job was primarily as an administrator, not an investigator. Gus Noblier had rarely ventured to crime scenes, preferring, like most men in his position, to let his people do their jobs. But Dutrow liked to be visible. He would be posting on Instagram from the scene come morning, ever the politician. And the crime scene unit was his baby. He would be here to hover like a helicopter parent on his child's first day at kindergarten.

Kemp, Dutrow, and Nick. That was a three-man recipe for disaster, right there.

Compton hummed a note of concern. "Detective Fourcade, he's none too happy."

Annie blew out a weary sigh and started toward the house. "Pray for me, Ossie."

Chaz Stokes came out onto the front porch as Annie climbed the steps. He was a good-looking man with photogenic, symmetrical features—a square jaw centered with a perfect white smile, a slim nose, and piercing light turquoise eyes beneath thick black brows. His skin was a shade more brown than white, hinting at his mixed racial background.

Unsuspecting women routinely fell under the spell of his looks and his dubious charm. Annie had never been one of them, and that had made them adversaries back when. The years and shared experiences had softened both their edges. Their relationship had gradually morphed from disgruntled would-be lover and sexually harassed target to something more like annoying big brother and smart-mouthed little sister. They had reached a truce of sorts because they had Nick in common.

"Slipping out of the line of fire, as usual," Annie said.

"Damn straight," he confessed, snagging a cup of coffee from one of her trays. "I done risked my life several times tonight already trying to keep your husband from tearing somebody's throat out."

"Let me guess. Kemp."

He made a face. "Hell, I'd buy a ticket to watch that redneck piece of shit get his clock cleaned. Not that it would even be sporting. That'd be like watching a panther tear apart a muskrat. I'm talking about the sheriff."

"Great," Annie said on a sigh.

"You, on the other hand, have perfect timing. You have my blessing to go in and save the day."

"And here I forgot my whip and chair."

"TMI, Broussard. I don't need a vision of y'all's sex life in my head."

"Ha-ha."

"You know, as a detective, you make a fine errand girl," he said as she set the cup carriers off to the side on the porch railing and wiped her hands on a napkin.

"Isn't that funny?" Annie returned. "Was the sheriff just sending you out for sandwiches, Chaz? There's a bag of them in the back of my car."

"Said the woman just showing up at long last."

"Yeah, I've been slacking the night away interviewing the brutally beaten mother of a murdered boy. It's so much fun to torment victims by making them relive the horror of the worst moments of their lives," she said with heavy sarcasm.

"She's conscious, then. Did she give you anything? A name and address for the assailant would be great."

"No such luck."

"A suspect at least?"

"Oh, yeah," Annie said. "A demon from hell, she told me. So, naturally, I thought right away of you. Where were you tonight?"

"Very funny."

From inside the house came an angry raised voice: "Get the fuck away from me, you coonass cocksucker!"

"Oh, shit!" Annie snapped, bolting for the door.

In the front room Kemp and Nick were standing much too close together, Kemp leaning into Nick's personal space, trying to assert dominance even though he was the smaller of the two. Nick stood with his hands out to his sides like a gunslinger, his feet slightly apart, his expression impassive, disinterested, even. Deceptively emotionless.

Annie held her breath.

"My God, the two of you! Stop it!" the sheriff snapped, exasperated. From where he stood near the dining table he could see Kemp, but he couldn't see Nick's hooded eyes and wouldn't have known how to read the dangerous tension in his stillness.

Nick shrugged in that very French way that somehow managed to embody condescension. He never took his eyes off Kemp. "Me, I'm just making sure he's getting everything I want preserved, Sheriff. Working in a spirit of cooperation. That's what you wanted, no?"

Kemp's hard, chiseled face was nearly purple with rage. "I know my job! I don't need this asshole looking over my shoulder, questioning every goddamn piece of lint on the ground!"

"If that piece of lint came off my killer and you don't pick it up and a murderer goes free because of your laziness," Nick said, "that's not gonna end well for you, *mon ami*."

"Let the man do his job, Fourcade," Dutrow growled. "He's not gonna follow you around, looking over your shoulder while you conduct your investigation. You can do him the same courtesy."

"Maybe he should," Nick said. "He might learn something."

"Nick—" Annie began, trying to break his focus.

"Oh, fuck you," Kemp sneered. "You arrogant, overrated son of a—"

He stepped forward and went to shove, planting his hands on Nick's chest.

Quick as a snake, Nick had one hand cupped behind Kemp's head and a forearm shoved up against his windpipe, choking him ever so slightly.

"Insults are the last resort of an insecure man with a crumbling argument," he said quietly, his face just inches from Kemp's.

"Fourcade!" Dutrow shouted, rushing forward. "Let him go!"

Kemp was free before the words were out of the sheriff's mouth. He coughed, red-faced, grabbing at his throat, and croaked, "You're out of your fucking head!"

"Don't you ever put your hands on me again," Nick said calmly, wagging a finger at him like he was a recalcitrant boy. He took a step back, rested his hands at his waist, and cocked a leg. Relaxed. Bored, even. The moment was over.

Annie let out her breath. "There's coffee outside," she announced.

Sweating, trembling with residual emotion, Kemp let his gaze dart around to the other people in the room. With a final pathetic show of bravado, he said stupidly, "There's your wife coming to save you."

The smile that curled Nick's mouth was predatory. His eyes narrowed. He reached out and patted Kemp's cheek like he was a poor, dimwitted child and chuckled low in his throat.

"*Mais non, couillon.* She's here to save you." He laughed out loud—a rich, low sound that undoubtedly ran like iced daggers through most of the people in the room.

Kemp slapped his hand away and backed out of reach.

Nick bent down and pinched up a tangled collection of colored threads between a gloved thumb and forefinger and held it out to Kemp.

"You missed something."

"Kemp, bag it," Dutrow snapped. He turned on Annie. "Broussard, get your husband out of here. I've had enough of this bullshit for one night."

"Yes, sir."

Annie started to say something to Nick just as the coroner's assistant wheeled the stretcher into the room from the side. Annie's breath caught at the sight of the small black body bag. The memory of his mother's wail of mourning went through her, an echo of grief, and chills chased over her from head to toe.

Frowning darkly, Nick grabbed one end of the stretcher and backed toward the door. Annie hustled ahead of them, pushing the screen door all the way open and holding it for them to pass through. Stokes moved aside, sober-faced as Nick and the coroner's assistant maneuvered the stretcher down the steps and around the crime scene van.

Annie followed as they made their way down the drive. Compton and Young Prejean hustled to the coroner's hearse parked on the road and opened the back. No one said a word as the body was loaded into the vehicle. Ulysse Wilson, the coroner, a small, thin gray man so old he looked like he should have been riding in the back, watched until the door was closed and then climbed in on the passenger's side. His assistant got behind the wheel.

Young Prejean crossed himself as the hearse pulled out and headed toward town, then turned and walked back toward the house, followed by Compton. Nick stood on the road, watching the hearse's taillights grow smaller and smaller.

Annie walked up beside him, her arms crossed in front of her. They stood there, side by side, listening as the sound of tires on gravel faded away to nothing, swallowed up by the sounds of night on the bayou: insects, frogs, small things splashing in the water, an owl calling from the thick canopy of trees.

"He was stabbed," Nick said at last. "Eight times, ten times, maybe more. In a frenzy. In a fury. Stabbed once in the eye. Right in the eye!" he said, incredulous that anyone could do such a thing. "A little boy! *C'est fou!*"

Annie listened to the emotions in his smoke-hoarse voice. The shock. The horror. After all the things he'd seen in his career—much of which had been spent in New Orleans, where death and depravity had come in near-daily doses—he still had the capacity to be morally outraged at the deepest level of his soul, as if it were the first time.

She stepped closer and rubbed a hand against the taut muscles in the

small of his back. His T-shirt was damp with sweat. He smelled of cigarettes and frustration. He turned and pulled her to him and held her
tight, resting his cheek on top of her head.

"We need to find justice for that child," he said.

The boy was his now. His responsibility. He had already taken that
truth to heart. He wouldn't rest until he had answers. Already stressed
with the Theriot case, Annie wished he could have stepped away from
this one, but he wouldn't—not voluntarily, at any rate.

"You'd better watch yourself," she cautioned, taking a step back. She
wagged a warning finger at him. "You piss Dutrow off bad enough, he
won't care how good you are at what you do. You'll be wearing a uniform and mopping out the drunk tank for the rest of your career."

Nick scowled. "He's a fool."

"He's our boss. And Kemp is his man. Like it or not."

"I say not."

"That was made abundantly clear while you were choking the man."

"He put his hands on me. Me, I had to defend myself."

"I was afraid you were going to snap his neck like a chicken bone,"
Annie confessed. "I'd just as soon you don't get sent to prison, thank
you."

"How is the mother?" he asked, bluntly dismissing her concerns for
his job security.

"Broken," Annie said simply.

"Did she say any more about the demon who did this terrible thing?"

"No."

"Then we'd best get back to work, 'Toinette," he said, turning back
toward the house. "Justice seldom delivers itself."

SEVEN

Oh, you're just in time for breakfast! What a nice surprise! Look, Cameron! Kelvin is joining us for breakfast!"

"I'm only having coffee," Kelvin said as he walked into the kitchen. He went to the stove where his fiancée was stirring scrambled eggs and bent to peck a kiss on her cheek. The flowery notes of her perfume cut through the heavy scent of bacon cooking. "I have to shower and get changed. I have a press conference this morning."

She gave him a slightly scolding look. "You can't just have coffee, Kelvin. I'm sure you have a full day ahead of you. Sit down and let me bring you a plate. The bacon is just getting done. I make mine in the oven, you know, so the grease doesn't go everywhere. I don't know why everyone doesn't do it this way."

She was an attractive woman in a 1950s kind of way: curvy, always nicely dressed, her auburn hair always done just so and sprayed in place. At seven in the morning she already had her makeup on.

Sharon reveled in both her femininity and her domesticity. She was an old-fashioned kind of woman who actually enjoyed cooking and cleaning and being a mother. Even though she and her son had only just moved to Bayou Breaux in the summer, she was already chairing a committee in her church group and volunteering for the hospital ladies' auxiliary. She felt it was important for the sheriff's soon-to-be wife to set a good example for the community.

Kelvin sighed and took a seat at the round table that was tucked into a bay window alcove with a view of the back patio and the scenery beyond. He had bought the house on the edge of the Blue Cypress development shortly after coming to Bayou Breaux. It was a nice Caribbean plantation-style home, a single-story house with a roof that overhung the building by several feet to create a shaded gallery all around. The quarter-acre property featured an oversize detached second garage that housed his RV and workshop, and a little dock for his bass boat and the small rowboat he had bought for Sharon's son. The backyard was an entertainer's dream with a small pool and a barbecue area.

Beyond his backyard lay woods and wetlands. He routinely saw herons and egrets. Deer were common. This time of year squadrons of ducks raised a racket coming and going to and from the wilder reaches of the Atchafalaya Basin on their way south for the winter.

He usually found it restful to watch the birds. Now he watched a group of mallards fly to the east, knowing they would quickly pass over the murder scene he had just left. Sharon would be upset to know a murder had been committed so nearby while she and Cameron slept in this house, half a mile but a world away. He would emphasize that when he told her. This was a nice, safe neighborhood, and he made sure deputies cruised through the streets here enough to deter any would-be prowlers. It was a far cry from where Genevieve Gauthier and her boy lived.

Sharon and her son had moved to Bayou Breaux as soon as the school year had ended in Houma. After three years of dating, Kelvin had finally popped the question on Valentine's Day. Sharon had immediately set to work planning like a general preparing an invasion. They would be married in Bayou Breaux. It only made sense for her to move here and get established as soon as possible.

Unable to fault her logic, Kelvin had moved himself into a small apartment near the Sheriff's Office to avoid the appearance of impropriety until their wedding, which would take place in February, a year to the day since his proposal. He came to the house for meals most nights and spent time there on the weekends, easing into the idea of having a family, something that still felt awkward to him.

Sharon brought him a cup of coffee—strong and black, the way he liked it—and turned back to fetch him a plate.

"Morning, Cameron," he said to the boy sitting across the table from him.

Sharon's son from her first marriage, Cameron favored his mother with his fair skin and his slightly almond-shaped eyes and wide mouth, though his hair was a brighter shade of red. At fourteen, he was in that awkward stage of growth when a boy's arms and legs seemed too long and spindly for his body. His feet had outgrown three shoe sizes practically overnight. His body was morphing into a young man's, though he still had the face of a boy with his freckles and teeth that seemed a little too big for his mouth.

The boy glanced up at him without lifting his head and mumbled, "Morning, sir."

"Sit up straight," Kelvin admonished, irritated. "You need to look a man in his face when you speak to him."

"Yes, sir." Cameron pulled himself up in his chair, seeming to grow by six inches. "I'm sorry, sir."

"That's better. You're a young man now, Cameron."

"Yes, sir."

"Ninth grade already."

"Yes, sir."

The boy didn't seem to know what to do next. He looked down at his plate, not sure if he should eat or not.

"Go on with your breakfast," Kelvin ordered impatiently.

He had never seen himself as a father. He had always dedicated himself to his work. He was a natural leader, but this more intimate role had yet to settle on him. He didn't understand children. Never had. When he was Cameron's age, he was in his first year of military school. No one had ever coddled him. He had been expected to toe a certain line and be a little man. That wasn't the way of parenting nowadays, much to the detriment of society, in his opinion.

He had suggested to Sharon that Cameron might benefit from going away to school at this point in time, as he and Sharon began the new chapter in their own relationship as man and wife, but she wouldn't hear of it. Cameron had been through too much in the past few years—the unexpected death of his father from a sudden brief illness, his mother's new relationship a year later, the upheaval of moving from Houma to Bayou Breaux, where he knew no one. It wasn't easy to be the new boy in a small town, and Cameron was shy and awkward.

In Kelvin's opinion, the boy was timid, and his mother enabled him. He had told Cameron to step up and join some clubs at school and to go out for the junior varsity football team to toughen him up. Weeks into the school year, he still didn't seem to have any friends, and he came home from football practice dejected, sometimes crying, according to Sharon, looking like he'd been used for a tackling dummy. Sharon wanted to let him quit. Kelvin insisted he stick it out. The topic was an ongoing sore point between them.

"You look a mess, Kelvin!" Sharon said, setting his plate in front of him. "Did you not shave this morning?"

"I haven't had the chance," he said, self-consciously rubbing a hand across the stubble on his jaw. "I've been at a crime scene half the night. There was a murder not far from here."

Across the table, Cameron's eyes went wide. His freckles stood out like copper pennies in a bowl of cream.

"A murder?!" Sharon said, wringing her hands in her apron. "What is this world coming to?"

"I don't want to frighten you," Kelvin said, "but it's better you know the truth than don't. We don't know all the circumstances of the people involved, but a small boy is dead and his mother is hospitalized."

He dug into his scrambled eggs, suddenly realizing his hunger.

"What do you mean when you say 'not far from here'?" Sharon asked.

"Half a mile or so as the crow flies. Out in the country on a little bayou road."

"Is it anyone we know?" she asked, sinking down onto the chair between him and her son.

"I shouldn't think so."

"What's the name?"

"Gauthier," he said, watching for her reaction. "The woman is in her late twenties. The boy was about seven or eight."

"Oh, my word!" Sharon exclaimed, pressing a hand to her heart. "Who would do such a thing? Kill a little boy!"

"We don't know. The investigation is just beginning."

Kelvin glanced at Cameron, who was staring down at his plate. He had lost some color and looked younger than he had a minute before. He had a purple bruise on the crest of his cheekbone, one of many souvenirs from football practice. It stood out against his pale skin like a grape stain.

"People do terrible things, Cameron," Kelvin said. "It's my job to find out why and to bring those responsible to justice. We'll find who did this. I'll make sure of it."

"Was it a robbery?" Sharon asked. "Did someone break in? Should we be worried?"

"We don't know the motive at this point. I don't want people to be frightened, but everyone should be vigilant. Keep the house locked, be mindful of strangers, and so on."

"Is the mom gonna die, too?" Cameron asked with tears in his eyes, clearly frightened.

"No. She's in the hospital, but she'll be all right," Kelvin said. "She was hurt, but she managed to run for help."

"Does she know who did it?" Sharon asked.

"She seemed not to last night. The detectives will speak to her again today. Needless to say, she was badly shaken."

"The poor thing!" Sharon exclaimed. "She'll wish it had been herself that died. No mother should have to bury a child. What of her husband? Was he not home?"

"Not married," Kelvin said, snapping a piece of bacon in two. It was the perfect degree of crispness.

"Does she have family here?"

"I swear, I should hire you for the detective division," he muttered.

"I don't have answers at this point. I haven't spoken to the woman. This only just happened last night. I shouldn't even be talking about it except that I want y'all to be safe. I'm sure we'll learn more today."

"Find out if she belongs to a church."

"That is the least of my concerns."

"She'll need the support of friends and community," Sharon said. "She'll have to make arrangements for a funeral. I can't even begin to imagine how terrible it would be to face that alone."

Kelvin said nothing, his mind on a more immediate issue: where to stage the press conference—in the briefing room or in front of the building.

Sharon made a little huffing sound. "Never mind. I'll find out for myself. I volunteer at the hospital today anyway."

Focused on his career, Kelvin had never been tempted to marry earlier in life. Girlfriends had come and gone over the years, filling his needs, all of them gradually giving up on the idea of becoming Mrs. Dutrow. He was older now, established. As an officer working his way up the ranks, a wife and family would have been a distraction, a burden, even. As sheriff, it made more sense for him to be married than not. If he wanted to have as long a career as his predecessor, he needed to have roots in the community, to be invested in life here.

Sharon had come to his attention at just the right time. She had been working as a secretary in the Houma PD when she first caught his eye. He had recently made captain, overseeing the anti-crime community relations unit. She had set her cap for him, to be sure, but he had admired her purposefulness. When Gus Noblier had lured him to Bayou Breaux, he had decided he would marry her rather than start over in a new town. She suited him well enough.

The boy was a drawback, but it wouldn't be that long before he was grown and gone to college. In the meantime, Kelvin would negotiate his way through parenthood as best he could.

"Cameron, finish your breakfast," he admonished. "You're going to be late for school."

"I don't feel good," the boy whined, pushing his plate away.

Sharon heaved a sigh. "Oh, Cameron . . ."

Kelvin checked his watch, impatient to escape the oncoming exchange between mother and son. Cameron had a nervous stomach. The least upset and he wanted to stay home. *Weak* was the word that came to Kelvin's mind. It irritated him to no end. And the more irritated he became, the more anxious Cameron was and the more Kelvin wanted away from the whole situation.

"I have to go," Kelvin said, shoving his chair back. He took a last drink of his coffee. "Don't count on me for supper. We've got crime to fight."

"We've got crime to fight" was his closing line from his YouTube videos. Strong. Positive. Inclusive. His was the voice of authority that instilled a sense of confidence in the public. That he included them in the idea of fighting crime fostered a stronger sense of community. A murder in a small town would shake people to the core. The people of Partout Parish would look to him for answers and leadership.

He left the house, pulling in a big deep breath of humid air, rich with the scents of earth and wet grass, not wanting to think this might be what it felt like to walk out of jail a free man. Thinking it just the same.

EIGHT

Nick stood on the road at the end of the Gauthier driveway watching Annie drive off toward town. She would pick Justin up from her cousin Remy and take him to school, where she would speak with the principal and with the Gauthier boy's teacher. He envied her the first part of that. After the hours spent on this crime scene, focused on a murdered child, the thing he wanted most to do was hold his son and feel the life pumping through his little body. Death needed to be countered with life.

The day had dawned with a clear, electric-blue sky. Early as it was, the air was already as heavy and warm as summer, magnifying the fecund smell of the sluggish bayou across the road. A desultory breeze stirred the treetops. A flock of ducks cut across the blue above them. Down the way, an armadillo poked its nose out of the weeds and waddled across the road toward the water.

The world didn't look any different than it had the previous day. This patch of countryside was unchanged by the violence that had been committed in the shabby yellow house the night before. The fabric of the lives of the people involved had been torn asunder, never to be the same again, but the rest of the world went on about its business.

Nick found that at once disturbing and comforting. He looked at one side of the coin, and then the other by turns. A life had been stolen and snuffed out. Whatever this child might have contributed to the world was gone, his potential forever unrealized. But the world would keep turning, nevertheless, largely oblivious to the tragedy, no more impacted by the death of this boy than by the death of an armadillo that had crossed the road to get a drink only to become breakfast for an alligator.

"Whatcha thinking, boss?" Stokes asked, walking toward him from the yard. He had retrieved one of his many straw fedoras from his car on the excuse of cutting the sun. Nick suspected it was as much that as his hairline had begun to recede in the past year or so.

" 'Nature is neither cruel nor kind, but utterly indifferent to all suffering,' " he said, quoting the Darwinist Richard Dawkins.

Stokes blinked. "Huh?"

"But nature and human nature are not one and the same," he went on, not giving a shit one way or the other if Stokes understood him. "There's a practical reason for everything in nature. There is no intension of cruelty, only survival. Evil for evil's sake is an invention of man."

"Dude, seriously?" Stokes said wearily. "It's too damn early in the morning for philosophy. Where'd your wife go?"

"To take Justin to school. She'll tell the principal what happened here and speak with the dead boy's teacher. Hopefully get some background on the family."

He looked past Stokes to the Gauthier yard, where deputies and the younger crime scene investigator were doing a grid search for anything that might remotely resemble evidence. Kemp had finished in the house and left with the van as soon as Dutrow had gone. Nick couldn't decide whether he should be relieved or pissed off that the incompetent ass had skipped out, leaving a green boy to finish his job for him.

"You find anything?"

Stokes made a face. "Yeah, a whole lotta nothing. The trash can in the backyard blew over in the storm. There's garbage all over the damn place."

"Anything under the boy's window?"

"Nope, and I'm going cross-eyed staring at the ground. Let's go knock on some doors. I'm craving human interaction here."

Nick stared at the house with its sagging front porch. He could see Genevieve Gauthier's car sitting in front of the ramshackle garage at the back of the property. Her keys had been in her pocketbook in the kitchen.

"What makes the most sense from the scene is that she struggled with the killer in the front room of the house and came out the front door and ran. Ran for cover or ran for the neighbor's house. Whichever—she turned south toward the swamp instead of north toward town."

"If this killer was chasing her, she had to run where she could," Stokes said. He pointed toward the next property, half-obscured from the road by scrub and trees. "Young Prejean said he knocked on this door last night and wasn't nobody home."

"So she had to keep going," Nick said. "But if the killer was chasing her, why he didn't catch her? She's hurt, bleeding, getting weak. Say she goes to this house and there's nobody home. Why didn't the killer catch her there?"

"Maybe he wasn't chasing her. Maybe he split."

"Why would he leave her alive? That don't make sense. But for the sake of argument, say he wasn't chasing her. Why would she run deeper into the countryside? If he wasn't chasing her, why run at all? Why not take her car and go for help?"

Without waiting for Stokes to answer, Nick started walking, his gaze automatically sweeping back and forth along the ground in front of him. Genevieve had been wounded, cut, bleeding. Unfortunately, the rain had washed away any blood trail she might have left—or any evidence of anyone chasing her.

"If she has a head injury, she might have been confused," Stokes said. "It sounded to me like she wasn't in her right mind when Annie was talking to her. She said she was attacked by a demon from hell. That ain't exactly rational."

"That doesn't make it untrue."

"Oh, really? When was the last time you arrested a demon?"

"Somebody stabs a child in the eye and kills them, what else do you call them?" Nick asked. "You wake up in the middle of the night with someone trying to kill you, someone's attacking your family, how rational are you gonna be?"

"She could have been high, too," Stokes pointed out as they turned in the driveway. "You get fucked up enough, you don't know frigging up from sideways."

Nick arched a brow. "Is that the voice of experience talking?"

"As a man of the world, I plead the Fifth. Life is short, my friend. You gotta grab it by the balls every once in a while, you know what I'm saying?"

He knew Stokes lived in his own zone where rules were as easily bent as willow switches. Stokes felt that drawing a paycheck for wearing a badge somehow gave him a free pass to step over certain lines, as long as he stepped back quick enough. Not that Nick hadn't crossed a line or two in his time, but his excuses had been founded in his own fundamental truth. Stokes's capacity for rationalization was capricious. Nick considered that a weakness. Stokes considered it a talent. They could not have been more different philosophically and remained in the same species.

"What all did you find in the medicine cabinet?" Nick asked.

"Children's Benadryl. Cold medicine. Cough syrup. A second bottle of Xanax, half a dozen Vicodin—"

"Her 'script or someone else's?"

"No bottle, in a shot glass on the top shelf. There wasn't enough of any one thing to scream 'addict,' but that don't mean she ain't one."

"It makes no matter right now," Nick said as they went up the steps to the front porch of Genevieve Gauthier's neighbor. "We'll find out soon enough from the ER if she was on anything last night."

Other than having been painted a now-faded dark blue sometime in the past decade, this house looked no better or different than the Gauthier home. The porch floor was sagging with rot. The yard was full of weeds.

He went to knock on the front door and hesitated as he saw a smear of blood on the peeling white paint of the doorframe. Another smudge striped the door.

Stokes arched his thick brows. "I guess that answers that question. She came here knocking."

"Who's to say that's her blood?" Nick said, his voice low.

He slid his weapon out of its holster. It could have been the killer's blood. It could have been the child's blood, smeared there by the hand that had wielded the knife. There could be a shotgun waiting for them on the other side of this door.

"Shit, man," Stokes muttered, drawing his weapon. He took a position up against the wall on the far side of the door.

Nick stepped to the other side of the door and knocked hard. The cop knock. *Bam, bam, bam!* "Sheriff's Office! Come to the door!"

He waited for an answer, barely breathing, listening for any sound of movement inside the house. Nothing. He banged on the door again. "Sheriff's Office!"

Nothing.

He tipped his head at Stokes and murmured, "Go around. See what you can see."

Stokes ducked past the window and slipped over the porch railing, disappearing around the side of the building. He came back half a minute later and peered up at Nick through the railing.

"Somebody's back in the kitchen cooking breakfast."

"What?"

Stokes shrugged. "If I'm lying, I'm dying. There's a dude in the kitchen cooking breakfast."

Nick banged on the door a third time, irritated. "Sheriff's Office! Open the damn door!"

Stokes jogged back down the side of the house and came back, shaking his head. "He ain't coming."

"What the hell?"

Temper snapping, Nick jogged down off the porch and made his way to the back of the house, Stokes on his heels. A matte black jacked-up four-by-four truck sat parked in front of a shed that looked about to fall over. The back porch was crowded with junk and garbage cans. A rat leapt off into the weeds, squealing as Nick pounded up the steps and banged on the back door.

"Sheriff's Office! Come to the goddamn door!"

He caught a glimpse of the guy through the window. He looked on the hard side of middle age with the start of a potbelly stretching a dingy wife-beater. A cigarette dangled from his lips.

Nick grabbed his badge on the ball chain that hung around his neck and held it up in his fist, tapping it hard on the window. "Come to the door! I need a word with you, sir!"

The man startled then backed away, out of sight.

Nick glanced at his partner. "What the fuck is with this guy?"

Stokes shrugged, taking his position at the far side of the door, banging into a rusty barbecue grill.

Nick flexed his hand and repositioned it on his Glock, ready for whatever might come through the door.

They waited. Just when he was about to tell Stokes to go cover the front door, the back door finally opened.

"Put your hands where I can see them and come out the house!" Nick ordered.

"I ain't done nothing! Why the hell you after me?" the man said loudly as he pushed open the screen door with his hip and stepped out with his hands in the air.

Nick put him in his late fifties, early sixties. He had a head of thick but receding silver hair that grew sparse on the right side of his skull where he had been severely burned. The ear had been melted down to a crescent-shaped nub of cartilage. The flesh around it and down the side of his neck was red and shiny, roped with keloid scars. The tightness in the skin pulled down at the corner of his right eye and at the corner of his mouth—something he tried to hide with a mustache and goatee.

"Roddie Perez?" Stokes said uncertainly, lowering his weapon.

Perez scowled at him, emphasizing the length of his lined, weathered face. His eyes were a bright, crystalline blue. He looked down his considerable nose at Stokes. "What? You worked your way through ever'body in the parish and come back to trump up some more charges on me?"

"Nope," Stokes said. "Just your dumb luck, Roddie—me knocking on your door."

"You know him?" Nick asked, stepping forward.

"Yep. I helped Roddie here take a vacation on the state back in the day when I was a dope cop," Stokes said. "What was it? I get my scumbag drug dealers mixed up. You were cooking up crack cocaine—or was it meth?"

"It wasn't nothing," Perez said belligerently. "I was in the wrong place at the wrong time."

"Says ninety-nine percent of dirtbag felons," Stokes pointed out.

"Why you didn't come to the door?" Nick asked irritably. He lowered his weapon but didn't put it away. "We been knocking for five minutes. What took you so long coming out? You cooking drugs in there now? You had to go flush something?"

Perez turned toward him. "Cooking my breakfast," he growled, his voice low and rough with the corrosion of five decades of cigarettes. "I didn't hear no knocking. I'm deaf in one ear and can't hear out the other." He turned so Nick could see his left ear and his hearing aid. "I had to put my ear trumpet in. See?"

"What happened to you?"

"Explosion at work, cleaning chemical tanks at Tri-Star refinery."

"Freebasing cocaine, more like," Stokes said.

"I don't need to listen to you running your mouth like a bad case of diarrhea," Perez said. "And I sure as hell got nothing to say to you."

He gave Nick the stink eye. "Nor you, either, whoever you are. I'm gonna have my breakfast. Y'all can just go piss up a rope."

"Entertaining as that might be, I need to ask you some questions about your neighbor," Nick said. "You can eat your breakfast and talk, or we can take a ride to the law enforcement center and you can talk to us there. Your choice. Wait long enough, and I'll choose for you."

Perez looked from one to the other and back, his mouth turning down in a hard horseshoe of a frown.

"Is there some reason you don't want us in your house?" Nick asked. "Something in there you don't want us to see? You might as well know I'm coming back out here with a warrant either way."

"You got no probable cause to come in my house," Perez challenged.

Nick arched a brow. "Really? Are you a lawyer now? Did you take up the law at the University of Angola Penitentiary?" he asked sarcastically. "I don't know many ex-con lawyers who spend their free time cleaning out chemical tanks at the oil refinery."

Perez narrowed his eyes and then sucked a wad of mucus out of his sinuses with a rude noise and spat on the rotting porch deck in the general direction of Nick's boots.

"There was a crime committed at your neighbor's house last night, and there's blood all over your front door," Nick said. "Me, I don't even have to ask you nice. I could put you in cuffs right now. I got half a mind to."

"You better think twice, Roddie," Stokes cautioned. "Nicky, he's cranky in the morning without his coffee."

"Then I might as well have my egg scramble then, hadn't I?" Perez grumbled.

They went into the kitchen that smelled of sour garbage and boudin sausage. Perez picked up his smoldering cigarette in one hand and a spatula in the other. He stirred his egg scramble in a cast-iron skillet—eggs and sausage and green peppers and onions, all of it flecked with the black crud from a pan that hadn't been properly cleaned.

Nick's upper lip curled in distaste as he took in the state of the place. He couldn't tolerate a dirty kitchen. He saw it as a reflection of a man's inner life. Chaos and filth were the interior of Roddie Perez.

"You haven't asked what happened, Roddie," he said, prowling the room like a restless panther, taking in every grungy detail—the film of grease on the cabinets, the dirty linoleum floor. The counters were piled with dirty dishes and canned foods, half a loaf of Evangeline Maid bread left open. A wicked-looking butcher's knife lay on a cutting board along with the remains of a green pepper and the fatty aftermath of cutting up the sausage.

"You haven't said, 'Oh, my God, there's blood on my front door? How'd that get there?' Is that because you already know? Or are you just a strangely uncurious man?"

Perez dumped his breakfast onto a plate and ditched his cigarette butt in the skillet. "I'm sure you'll tell me all about it," he said, turning around to face them. "Maybe after you introduce yourself."

"Me?" Nick stepped close enough that Perez had to lift his plate and pull it tight up against his chest. "I'm your worst fucking nightmare if you don't start to answer some questions. That's who I am."

Perez glanced at Stokes as he fell into a chair at a tiny kitchen table layers deep in clutter, making himself at home. He set his hat toward the back of his head at a jaunty angle.

"How well do you know your neighbor—Genevieve Gauthier?" Stokes asked, flipping open the cover of a *Penthouse* magazine.

"Don't know her. Never heard of her."

Nick took a step back to lessen the pressure and crossed his arms, settling in. "You got a beautiful young woman living next door to you, and you would have us believe you have never seen her?"

Perez shrugged and forked up some eggs.

"What about the little boy?" Nick asked.

"What boy?"

"You're keeping your nose clean, Roddie," Stokes said. He tossed the magazine aside and helped himself to an open bag of Manda's Hot & Spicy Pork Cracklins. "You got no desire to see the inside of a prison again."

"I done chopped enough sugarcane for the state of Lou'siana to last me a lifetime," Perez said. "I ain't going back to the Farm."

"Where were you last night between, say, ten and two this morning?" Nick asked. He scowled at Stokes as he offered the bag of cracklins.

"Right here at home in my own bed," Perez said.

"You didn't see anything going on next door?"

"I wadn't looking. Can't see that house from this one, anyway."

"You didn't hear anything?" Nick said, glancing out the window to confirm Perez's words. Through the curtain of trees and scrub, he could see a bit of yellow siding, a glimpse of a window toward the back of the house.

"What would I hear? I take my hearing aid out to sleep."

"So you didn't hear anyone banging on your door in the middle of the night?"

"I didn't hear you banging on my door just now, and I'm wide awake."

"And you didn't hear Sheriff's Office cars rolling in there with sirens screaming?" Nick asked, moving again.

Eyes narrowed, Perez watched him as he chewed his breakfast and swallowed. "I'm beginning to think you're the deaf one here, Detective Whoever You Are. No. I didn't hear no sirens. I was A-SLEEP!"

Nick looked down into the open trash can beside the stove, his gaze zooming in on a wad of paper towels half hidden by the slimy plastic wrap from the sausage—Comeaux's Cajun Wild Pork Boudin.

"You have an accident, Roddie?" he asked.

"What?"

"There's bloody towels in this trash you seem never to remove from the place where you prepare your food," he said with disgust. "Where'd this blood come from?"

"I don't know what you're talking about."

Nick took a step toward him. "Let me see your hands."

"Why?"

"Let me see your hands."

"I don't have to show you nothing," Perez said belligerently. "I know my rights."

His rights. The image of the dead boy flashed through Nick's brain. This piece of shit had rights, but a seven-year-old innocent child was dead. His temper snapped like a dry twig. He snatched the plate out of Perez's hands and flung it aside like a Frisbee. It smashed as it hit the wall and fell to the floor.

"Show me your goddamn hands!" he shouted, lunging at the man.

Perez leaned back, trapped against the counter, holding his hands up in front of him, yelling, "What the fuck is wrong with you?"

"I'm half past sick of your shit, that's what! I been up all night looking at a dead child, and you're gonna stand here giving me a fucking attitude? The hell!"

Perez looked to Stokes, his eyes wide. "Do something!"

Stokes dug another cracklin out of the bag and munched on it, unconcerned. "I ain't your friend, Roddie. What do I care if Nicky here beats the ever-loving shit out of you? No doubt you have it coming for one reason or another."

He got up lazily and tossed the bag on the table, making a face. "These cracklins are stale, man."

He sounded far away, like a voice from another room. Nick's attention was focused on Perez's hands—weathered and battered and cut—a couple of old cuts, a couple of fresher cuts on both hands.

It was common for the hand to slip on the knife during a stabbing, common for assailants to cut themselves—often badly. Were any of these cuts fresh enough? Deep enough?

"How'd you get those cuts?" he asked, looking the con hard in his crystal-blue eyes.

"Working with sheet metal!" Perez said indignantly. "I didn't kill no child!"

It might have been a plausible excuse. Or not. If he had attacked the Gauthier boy and cut himself in the process, his blood would be at the scene—provided Kemp hadn't fucked up the collection of it. His blood would be mingled in the blood on the front door as well.

Without a word, Nick stepped back and turned, leaving the room.

"Where's he goin'?" Perez asked.

Stokes shrugged as Nick stalked past.

"Where you goin'?" Perez called after him. "You can get your goddamn warrant before you look through my house!"

Nick paid no attention. The house was laid out the same as the Gauthier floor plan. From the kitchen he went past a dining table heaped with unfolded laundry and unopened mail. A laptop computer sat open on one end of the table. Beyond the dining area was a ratty-looking brown plaid couch and a fancy black leather reclining massage chair. A huge new flat-screen television took up most of one wall.

These things Nick noted in passing as he looked for any sign of blood inside the house. If Perez had come into the house bleeding, he might have touched the inside frame of the door. He might have touched the light switch or dripped blood on the floor.

He pulled the bottom of his T-shirt out of his pants and used it to protect the doorknob as he turned it and pulled the door open to scrutinize both sides and the edge. He saw nothing other than the blood smears on the outside of the door. No bloody hand had gripped the edge of the door to open it or grabbed hold of the interior door trim. The light switch and the switch plate cover on the wall inside the door were grimy with dirty fingerprints, but there was no visible blood.

All he had for his warrant was blood on the outside of the door. The victim had made no mention of Roddie Perez, either explicitly or implicitly at this point. It looked like she had come here in search of help and, finding none, had continued on down the road. Nick didn't like the idea of Roddie Perez, a known felon with a history as a drug dealer, living next door to a murder scene, but there was no line on the search warrant affidavit for "I don't like this guy." He needed facts, not assumptions. Other than some paper towels in the garbage that may or may not have had blood on them, he had seen nothing inside the house to support his request for a warrant.

He had outfoxed himself pressing to come inside—a calculated risk that would now weigh against him. Swallowing back his frustration, he turned and faced the room. Perez had seated himself at the table and closed the laptop. Nick made a mental note of it but said nothing. He would now go to the office, write the affidavit, spend hours trying to get a judge to sign it—and possibly fail. The idea didn't sit well.

Perez laughed out loud and slapped a big hand on the table. "You got nothing, Detective X!" He looked from Nick to Stokes and back. "Fuck y'all. And get out my house before I sic my lawyer on you!"

Nick walked over to the table, spun a chair around on one leg, and straddled it, resting his forearms on the back. He stared hard into the eyes of Roddie Perez.

"Are you listening to me, Roddie?" he asked. "Can you hear me all right? You with your bad ear and all? Do you hear me right now?"

Perez sobered, his eyes narrowing in suspicion. "I hear you fine," he said, his voice a low growl.

"Good," Nick said, nodding. "The name is Fourcade," he said. "You remember that, Roddie. Because if I find so much as a nose hair linking you to this murder—if I find so much as a flake of your dead skin at this murder scene—I will personally drive you right up to the gates of hell and deliver you to the devil, myself. Are we clear on that? Roddie?"

"Like crystal," Perez said.

"Très bien," Nick murmured on a sigh, rising. "Now, me, I'm gonna collect the evidence off your front door, then I'm gonna go visit Ms. Gauthier in the hospital, and see what she has to say about you, Roddie. Better hope for your sake you been a good neighbor."

Perez said nothing.

"Don't buy any green bananas, Roddie," Stokes said as they started for the door. "If we find out you put a step wrong here, you'll be a guest of the parish before you can eat them."

Perez flipped them off with both hands as they walked out the door.

NINE

"Where's Papa?"

Annie glanced at her son in the back seat via the rear-view mirror. Strapped into his booster seat, he was dressed for school in shorts and a purple polo shirt with a dancing alligator embroidered on it. He was a little carbon copy of his father, right down to the haircut—close-cropped on the sides, slightly longer on top with a razor-sharp part on the left. Going to the barbershop had become a monthly father-son ritual that was followed by lunch at Madame Collette's diner.

"Papa's working," Annie said.

"Is he helping people?" Justin asked, walking his Captain America action figure along the car door.

"Yep."

"We didn't get to do our tai chi."

"Not this morning."

It was Nick's habit to rise before the sun to meditate and work through his tai chi ritual to center himself. On days when Justin got up early enough, Nick included him in a few final easy steps at the end of the routine, patiently teaching his son the discipline of the martial art, which always ended with the two of them bowing to each other with great ceremony.

The sight of them on the front lawn as the sun came up, the mists rising off the bayou in the background, touched Annie's heart in an especially tender place. She had never known her father. She had no idea who he was. Marie Broussard had taken that secret with her to her grave. Annie had never danced on top of her father's shoes or squealed with delight as he tossed her up into the air. Uncle Sos had filled that void in her life, but as much as she loved him, it wasn't quite the same thing as she had imagined having a real father would be. To watch her own child forge that bond with his father filled her with an overwhelming rush of love underscored by a faint ghostlike longing.

"You should ask Uncle Remy if he might do tai chi with you some time when you stay over," she suggested. "You could teach him how, like Papa teaches you."

"Uncle Remy says he doesn't bend that way."

Annie smiled at that. Remy had gone to LSU on a football scholarship back when. At forty-two, he was still built like the corner mailbox: square and stout.

"He said Tante Danielle tried to make him do yoga once and he got stuck and couldn't get up from the floor. Do you think that's true?"

"I don't know, but it's a pretty funny story, isn't it?"

"He said she had to call the fire department to get him up. I don't think that's true," he said, shaking his head.

"You think Uncle Remy was pulling your leg?"

"Uh-huh."

Annie hit her turn signal and pulled into the parking lot of the elementary school. It was early. The teachers and administrators had arrived, but the buses were still on their routes, picking up students. Only a few kids were on the playground, getting in an early round on the swings and monkey bars.

Justin looked up, peered out the side window, and then turned to Annie, looking betrayed.

"I don't wanna go to school! I wanna go home!"

Annie sighed. The last thing she wanted was a fight. She had gone directly from the crime scene to pick him up rather than taking Remy up on his offer to drop Justin off when he dropped off his daughter, Gracie, who was in fourth grade. Justin had been clingy and needy of late, and she didn't want to give him a reason to feel insecure. Despite the sometimes odd hours and demands of her job and Nick's, they both insisted on keeping their son's life as normal as possible.

"Justin, you're a big boy now. You go to kindergarten."

Tears welled up in his big dark eyes. His full lower lip began to quiver. "I don't want to! I want to go fishing with Papa!"

"Papa can't go fishing today. He's working. And you're going to school."

"You're mean!"

The tears came in earnest then, an honest-to-goodness sobbing tantrum. He banged his Captain America toy on the door and then threw it at her, hitting her in a glancing blow off the chin.

Annie gasped. "Justin Fourcade!"

She turned off the car, got out, and stormed around the hood to the back passenger side. She threw open the door and grabbed hold of her son with both hands on his little shoulders. "You stop this right now! This minute!"

Justin wailed and twisted, kicking out with both feet.

Annie let go of him and stepped back, at a loss. She couldn't keep him home if she wanted to. She had a job to do. And she had no intention of letting a five-year-old set a precedent for not going to school because he simply didn't want to.

Red-faced, he wailed and kicked and pounded his fists. She watched him with a rising sense of frustration. Tears rushing up inside her like a sudden tsunami. She pressed her hands to her face as if to push them back inside. She closed her eyes so tight colors burst like fireworks behind her eyelids. Then came the memory of the small body on the stretcher being wheeled through Genevieve Gauthier's living room and the memory of the photographs Nick had taken of the scene—KJ Gauthier lying dead on the floor of his bedroom in a pool of his own blood; a small, broken body in Spider-Man pajamas just like Justin's.

Genevieve Gauthier would never have another argument with her son about going to school. She would never again get to feel the frustration of being a parent. Someone had stabbed her son to death. His body was lying in the morgue at Our Lady, down the hall from where she lay in bed, cut and battered from trying to save him.

The emotions that came with those thoughts tore out of Annie on a sob. She tried to catch it with a hand over her mouth.

"Maman? Maman! D-d-don't c-c-cry!"

Justin's small, shaky voice seemed to come from far away. She opened her eyes and swiped away the tears with her fingers, focusing on her son. He had given up on his tantrum. The expression he wore now was one of fear and uncertainty.

"Maman!" He reached out for her, trapped in his booster seat.

She went to him, sniffing back the last of her own tears, her hands fumbling to unbuckle his seatbelt. He scrambled free and into her arms, clinging to her like a monkey.

"I'm sorry, baby," she said, holding him tight, rubbing his back. "It's all right. Don't cry. Maman is just tired, that's all. Everything is all right."

It took her another ten minutes of reassurance and a promise of extra television time to talk him around to thinking he could go to school and have fun with his friends while Maman and Papa did their jobs. The buses had begun to arrive in front of the school. The minivans and station wagons of carpool kids were pulling up to the side entrance.

Annie walked him to his classroom and was instantly forgotten when he saw his friend Sawyer playing with a giant stuffed dinosaur on the far side of the room. After a few words with his teacher, she made her way down the hall to the girls' bathroom, ducked into a stall, and threw up. She was tired, and her head was pounding from too much coffee, too little sleep, and too much stress. She would have given anything for a few hours to close her eyes and regroup, but time was a luxury she didn't have. She had to just pull herself together and march on.

The bathroom sinks were so low she felt like a giant trying to wash her hands and splash some water on her face and rinse out her mouth. The place hadn't changed at all since she had attended school here when she was a child—the same sexist pink subway tile on the walls, the same pink sinks and toilets. The color should have given her reflection a healthy glow, she thought as she looked at herself in the mirror. It didn't.

She wet a paper towel with cold water and pressed it to her face for a moment, composing herself. She needed to pull it together and figuratively change hats, set aside her emotions and concerns as a mother, and—*presto-change-o!*—become a detective again.

Wading through a sea of noisy children, she made her way to the school office and asked to see the principal. The receptionist's drawn-on eyebrows scaled her forehead when Annie showed her badge and said she was on official business. The young woman disappeared down the hallway and came back a moment later.

"She'll see you now," she murmured, as if they were in a library.

"Thank you." Annie mouthed the words, moving past her.

Pamela Samuels Young greeted her at her office door, effortlessly elegant in a figure-skimming mustard skirt and a crisp white cotton blouse. Pamela was one of those women who was always put together— perfectly accessorized, perfectly made up, her kinky, curly black hair piled artfully on her head. It would have been nauseating if she hadn't been a friend.

"Sheriff's business?" she said, a bright smile lighting her face as she invited Annie in with a sweep of her arm. "I hope that's not as ominous as it sounds."

"I'm afraid it is," Annie confessed.

The principal's smile faded into a look of concern. "You're serious," she said. Her gaze swept over Annie from head to toe like a spotlight. "Girl, you look like hell."

"Thanks. This is what the glamorous life of the sheriff's detective gets me," Annie said, sinking down into one of the two visitor's chairs in front of the desk. She covered a massive yawn and ran her hands back through her hair. "I've been up all night working a murder."

"A murder?" Pamela repeated. She went behind her desk and sat down, pressing her hands down on her spotless blotter as if to balance herself. "Oh, my God," she murmured. "Please tell me it's not one of my teachers."

"Not a teacher. A student."

"No. A child? No, that can't be." She shook her head, trying to dismiss the notion.

"KJ Gauthier."

Pamela's brow furrowed slightly. "That name doesn't ring a bell."

"His mother is Genevieve Gauthier. They're fairly new to the area. The boy was seven, nearly eight. That should make him a second-grader, right?"

The principal turned to her computer and brought it to life with a wiggle of the mouse. "You said Gauthier? G-a-u-t-h-i-e-r?"

"Yes. KJ. I don't know what the initials stand for."

The principal stared at the screen as she clicked purposefully through commands. She wanted to look and not find a student by that name, Annie knew. She wanted this to be some kind of misunderstanding. No one would want this news to be true.

Annie glanced around the office, taking in the neatness and normalcy and order—the small bouquet of fresh flowers on the credenza, the framed photographs in the bookcase: Pamela's nieces and nephews, and a picture of her parents when they were young and beaming with happiness. She had no children herself. Her marriage was in the past tense. But she had dedicated her life to children, to shaping their futures through education. She was a motivator, a goal achiever. Stenciled on the wall behind her desk was her motto: *Dreams Don't Work Unless You Do.*

She sat up a little straighter in her chair, as if something on the computer screen had startled her.

"Oh. Here he is," she said with a mix of reluctance and dread. "Second grade. Jaime Blynn's class. He transferred here from Grand Caillou Elementary, Terrebonne Parish school district."

She turned back to Annie. "I'm embarrassed to say I haven't met his mother. She should have been at the orientation for new families, but she must have been a no-show. She should have gotten a letter and an email asking her to call and schedule an appointment for a one-on-one, but it hasn't happened. And now you're telling me this boy is dead?" she said. "Murdered? How can that be? What about the mother? Is she—?" Her eyes widened. "She didn't—"

"She's in the hospital," Annie said. "She managed to run for help. I can't go into a lot of detail at this point, but it sounds like some kind of home invasion situation."

"Oh, my God. Here? In our community?"

As if violence here was inconceivable. Decent people were always shocked to learn bad things could happen within the boundaries of their quiet lives. Violence was something that happened to other people, rougher people, people who lived on the other side of town, people who tempted fate. Violence was a petty drug deal gone bad, a thug beating up his girlfriend, a brawl at Mouton's, the bar down on Bayou Noir south of Luck, where troublemakers went to practice their avocations.

"They live just outside of town," Annie added. Like knowing this had happened outside the city limits might somehow be a comfort.

"We'll have to tell the children—all the children, but his classmates first," Pamela said, her organized mind doing what came naturally in a time of crisis. "They're so young. They shouldn't have to know what it is to lose a friend to death. We should bring in a counselor."

"The victim assistance coordinator at the district attorney's office can help you with that," Annie said. "Actually, Jaime has done some work with their office in the past. You know she volunteers with the court-appointed special advocates group."

"Yes. We have resources within the state school system as well."

"I'll need to speak with Jaime now," Annie said. "The sooner we can start filling in details on this family, the better."

"Of course."

The bell rang loudly as they walked out of the office and down the hall. Locker doors banged up and down the corridor. The cacophony of children's voices rose in a final crescendo as they hurried to their classrooms. In an instant the hall was empty, the noise shut behind the classroom doors.

Jaime Blynn's second-grade room was designated by a large, glittery purple-and-gold 2B held up by a cutout of the school mascot, a grinning, dancing cartoon alligator, taped to the door. With big bright eyes and a toothy smile, Gilbert the Gator beckoned children to come into the classroom and have fun learning.

Fun would not be on the curriculum today.

Pamela stuck her head inside the classroom and motioned for the teacher to join them in the hall.

"Good morning!" Jaime Blynn greeted them in an animated whisper, her face bright with good cheer as she slipped out the door, not quite shutting it behind her. "Annie, hi! What are you doing here?"

"I'm afraid I have bad news," Annie said softly. "Your student KJ Gauthier passed away last night."

The teacher looked from Annie to the principal, back and forth, her expression crumbling. "What? What did you say?"

"It seems there was a break-in at their home last night. KJ was killed."

"Killed?" she repeated, as if the word was foreign to her even as her brown eyes flooded with tears. She pressed a hand across her mouth to keep from crying out.

Pamela placed a comforting hand on her shoulder. "I'm going to step in and sit with your class. You go with Annie. She has some questions for you.

"Use my office if you like," she offered Annie.

"I-I need some air," the teacher said breathlessly.

Annie hustled to keep up with her as she rushed for the nearest exit. She pushed open a door and flung herself out into a small courtyard off the administration offices, gasping in a lungful of the thick damp air, and then another, and another.

"Jaime, sit down," Annie said, taking hold of her arm and steering her toward an iron-scrollwork bench. "You're hyperventilating."

"I feel sick."

She sank down onto the bench, curling into a seated variation of the fetal position for a moment. Annie sat beside her, resting a hand on her back, feeling the tremors of emotion going through her.

"I'm sorry, Jaime. I know it's a shock. There's just no good way to deliver this kind of news."

"I saw him just yesterday," the teacher said, sitting up a little, her forearms resting on her thighs. "You're telling me someone killed him last night?"

"Yes. I'm afraid so."

"But he's just a little boy! Why? Oh, what am I saying?" she murmured, shaking her head. "People do terrible things to children every day. We both know that."

She had seen it firsthand for herself, volunteering as a special advocate for children in the court system, working with children who had been abused and neglected. Somehow she had managed not to become hardened to it or burned out by it. Children were her life—the children she advocated for, the children she taught, and her own two little boys, Sawyer and Jax.

"You don't usually know the victims personally," Annie said. "At least not until after the fact."

"That's true." Jaime sighed. Her hands were trembling as she swept back her straight blond hair, tucking it behind her ears. She pressed them on her lap, smoothing the fabric of her long, flowy cotton skirt that was sprigged with tiny yellow flowers. "Oh, KJ . . . I'm so, so sorry . . ."

They sat in silence for a moment. The courtyard was a small oasis of garden and grass with a sweet olive tree in the center. It was a quiet spot for teachers and staff to get away on their break time. Annie focused on a statue of a winged fairy reading a book beneath the tree. Birdsong filled the silence.

Jaime wiped the tears from her cheeks and worked to compose herself. She was a tiny thing—five-three and petite, but fit and strong. Annie knew her to be a competitive runner. They ran together with a group of women that met Thursday nights after work. Jaime was always with the serious runners at the front. Annie hung around mid-pack, hating every step. Jaime ran because she loved it. Annie ran because she might have to chase a criminal or run to save her own life. As far as Annie was concerned, the best part of the evening was when they arrived at Frenchman's Landing for a glass of wine and a light dinner on the patio.

"What happened?" Jaime asked at last.

"We're trying to put the story together now."

"What about his mother—Genevieve?"

"She's at Our Lady. She was wounded but managed to run for help. Do you know her?"

"I've met her. *Genevieve.* Such a pretty name, the way she pronounces it. I don't *know* her. I sat down with her the first week of school to talk about KJ."

"What was he like?"

"Oh, he's a sweet little boy, but he struggles—struggled—with ADHD. That can be so trying, especially with the young ones. They don't understand why they feel the way they do, and they don't understand how to control their feelings."

"Was he on medication?"

"No. Genevieve didn't have insurance when she came here, and she had only just started a job that would provide insurance. It hadn't kicked in yet."

"Where does she work?"

"Evangeline Oaks—the assisted-living facility. I believe she said she has an aunt living there."

"What was your impression of her?"

She gave a little shrug. "Harried. A little bit at the end of her rope. Typical poor single mom, I would say—not enough resources, no help, run ragged. Plus she was dealing with a hyperactive child. That's tough."

"Did you get the impression there was a daddy involved at all?"

"No. She didn't have anything to say about KJ's father other than that he isn't in the picture. Maybe she doesn't know who he is."

"You mean maybe that's a multiple-choice question?"

"Maybe. Or maybe KJ is a product of rape. Who's to say?"

"How was she toward the boy? Loving? Close? Distant?"

"I only saw her a couple of times. She seemed exasperated, bless her heart, but I don't want to judge," she said, clearly wanting to do just that. "We all have our moments."

"Tell me about it," Annie said. "Justin pitched a fit this morning. He didn't want to go to school. I had a meltdown in the parking lot. I'm tired, out of sorts. We were at the crime scene all night. I love my son, but that wasn't my finest moment as a mother."

"You should send Justin over for a playdate," Jaime offered. "He and Sawyer always have a good time together."

"Oh, I don't know that you'd want him right now. He's going through a clingy phase."

"Nonsense. He'll be fine. Reg will take the boys out on the boat. They always love that."

"Maybe."

"Maybe, nothing. You and Nick will have your hands full working this case. A few child-free hours will not go to waste, will they? If only to give you a chance for a nap."

"A nap would be worth more than gold. Thank you."

"That's what friends are for."

"And here I am, supposed to be comforting you," Annie said. "I know how attached you get to your students—even if you haven't had all that much time to get to know KJ."

"Oh, he already stole my heart," Jaime admitted. "You know I have a special soft spot for the ones with tough home situations. I talked his mother into putting him in my after-school story time twice a week."

"You paid the fee, you mean," Annie said, giving her a sideways look.

Jaime shrugged off the suggestion. "Whatever. KJ loved to be read to. He could almost manage to be still through a whole story. He tried so hard. He stayed yesterday for *Leonardo, the Terrible Monster*."

"Did his mother pick him up after?"

"No. The babysitter did."

"Who's that?"

Jaime rolled her eyes. "A sixth-grader. Can you imagine? Would you send Justin home with a twelve-year-old?"

"God, no. I think thirty is a good age for a babysitter. Nick is even worse than me. He practically requires a government security clearance. Thank God I have a lot of relatives who pass muster."

"Well, I was none too pleased about this situation," Jaime said, "but what can I do? His mother arranged it. She saw absolutely nothing wrong with it. She said she used to babysit when she was that age, and it was only for a few hours after school. The girl took KJ to her house and kept him occupied until Genevieve got off work."

"How did they get there? The bus?"

"They walked. It's not far, I guess. Still . . . It's easy for me to criticize," she said. "I can afford better options."

"What's the girl's name?"

"Nora Florette. She's in Dan Blakely's class. I asked him, and he rolled his eyes, too. It would be one thing if she was mature and responsible for her age, but she isn't. She's a silly, immature girl, and her home situation is chaotic, to say the very least. I don't think that mother knows where her children are half the time. Nor does she care. They grow up wild as weeds."

"I'm sure it's small comfort," Annie said, "but KJ's not dead because of the babysitter. He was home in his bed. Everybody's worst nightmare: being attacked in their sleep in their own home."

"That's too horrific to even contemplate," Jaime said. "And here I am criticizing Genevieve. I feel terrible. Is she allowed to have visitors? I should go see her."

"I'll know more later this morning. I'll text you."

"Please do. I can't even begin to imagine what she must be going through. I feel absolutely sick about it."

"Do you know if she has family in the area?" Annie asked.

"I got the impression she's on her own, other than I believe she said she has an aunt in the assisted-living place. She and KJ just moved here over the summer. I gave her the information to join the PTA, so she could meet some of the other moms, but she hasn't come to a meeting yet."

"Neither have I," Annie confessed.

"Kindergarten moms get a pass. We're too shell-shocked from separation anxiety to be expected to do PTA."

"Good, because I think I'd rather break up a drunken brawl at Mardi Gras."

Jaime managed a chuckle. "It's not that bad."

"I'm not the bake-sale type," Annie said. "And how many PTA moms carry a weapon?"

"Probably more than we'd care to know about."

"That's true."

They shared a chuckle that died quickly.

"I feel like I shouldn't be allowed to laugh," Jaime confessed. "How can I think anything is funny or normal, even? I have to go tell my students one of their friends is dead."

"I don't envy you that. What do you even say to kids this young?"

"I don't know. What can I tell them that they'll understand? I don't want to frighten them, but *I'm* frightened. *I* don't understand. Why would someone kill a child?"

"He was probably just in the way," Annie offered, as if that somehow made sense of a senseless act. "We think his room was maybe the easiest way into the house, and he was killed to silence him."

"Do you think this maniac was after Genevieve? Was it a rapist?" Jaime asked with a fresh touch of horror. "Was that what he was after?"

"We don't know the motive yet." Annie sighed and glanced at her watch. "I need to go," she said, rising reluctantly from the bench. "I'll call you later."

"Will you see Genevieve?"

"Yes."

"Please tell her I am so, so sorry," Jaime said sincerely.

"I will." Annie nodded. "We all are."

TEN

An old groundskeeper was wiping down the white statue of the Virgin Mary as Nick drove toward the entrance of Our Lady. He wheeled the Jeep past a parking space reserved for law enforcement, scanning the hospital entrance for any sign of reporters.

The good fortune of having Dutrow as the media magnet for sheriff was that he happily drew all the attention to himself with his staged events, buying the detectives a little breathing room. But the cleverer of the press scavengers would fall for that only so many times before they broke from the pack to hunt on their own. With the furor kicked up over the summer and fall with the Theriot sexual assault case, Nick suspected that time would likely be quickly at hand, with himself as the prime target.

Unlike his boss, he had little use for the press. In his experience, they caused more harm than good to most investigations, reaching for the most sensational headlines, leaking details that should have been held back, reporting rumors and half-truths. The media had helped to nearly end his career in New Orleans, playing right into the hands of corrupt men in positions of power whose goal had been to divert attention onto an overzealous, allegedly mentally unhinged detective and away from the brutal murder of a young prostitute. They had come after him again during the Bichon case, his first big investigation here, though the fault had been his own, getting drunk and going after the suspect he had been so afraid was getting away with murder on a technicality.

His name had quickly become a dog whistle to the media in these parts. As the lead detective on high-profile crimes, he was as attractive to them as metal filings to a magnet. They would be all over this case, a brutal child-killing in sleepy bayou country. And as soon as his name came up, they would dig into their Pandora's box and bring up the Theriot case, and the Bichon murder, and all the way back to New Orleans. It was like being flayed alive over and over, and the truth was, there was no escape.

The Vanessa Theriot sexual assault had drawn them out like cockroaches—a pack of lascivious voyeurs, their usual appetite for details on a sexual assault intensified by the fact that the victim was autistic. Nick's disgust at their behavior was palpable and sour. He knew what it was for a victim's family to live under a spotlight. He knew what that scrutiny did to the people involved. And for what? For the public to be entertained and distracted from their mundane existence as they worked up outrage in order to feel alive.

A crime as shocking as the murder of the Gauthier boy would make headlines anywhere, but it was all the more sensational in a place like Bayou Breaux, a small town where people supposedly still had values. Reporters would come all the way from New Orleans and Baton Rouge for this. But GPS notwithstanding, they wouldn't easily find their way out to the Gauthier house, and their first stop would be the law enforcement center for the Kelvin Dutrow Show.

He swung back around the statue a second time and parked in the red zone of the ER entrance for a potential quick getaway. The parking valet looked up from his phone, raising a hand in acknowledgment as Nick held up his badge on his way to the doors.

Annie had chosen a corner table on the far side of the cafeteria, away from the few other diners. She sat staring at a plate of scrambled eggs as if the unappealing mass might transform into something better if only she could wait it out.

"You trying to wish that into a plate of chicken or something?" he asked.

She looked up, startled, taking in his change of clothes. "You went home."

"I figured I should make an effort to look civilized. Town's gonna be crawling with reporters soon. They have enough to say about me as it is." He bent and pressed a kiss to her lips. "Better that I don't look a vagrant and smell like a wild animal."

"And you brushed your teeth," she murmured. "Mmm . . . minty fresh."

He hadn't taken the time to shave, and she brushed her fingertips along the stubble on his jaw but made no comment. Enough that he had showered and put on a pair of slacks and a shirt and tie.

"Did the mother say anything about her next-door neighbor?" he asked, pulling out a chair and sitting down. It was the first time he had been still in hours. The fatigue hung on him like dead weight. He shoved his sunglasses on top of his head and rubbed a hand hard across his eyes.

"No. Why?"

"'Cause he's a piece of shit low-life drug-dealing ex-con."

"Wow. Every single woman's dream neighbor," Annie declared. "Is he a pedophile, too?"

She made a face at the eggs and shoved the plate toward him and then picked up a piece of toast and nibbled at a corner.

"Not that I know of—yet."

He doused the eggs with Tabasco sauce and forked up a bite. The eggs didn't taste any better than they looked, but he needed the protein. "There's some blood on his front door like maybe she came knocking, but he says he never heard anything."

"Can we get a search warrant?"

"Depends on what judge we get to look at the affidavit," he said. "Stokes is on it. Me, I'm not hopeful. If the victim isn't pointing the finger at him, and we don't have anything more than a little blood smear on the outside of the door . . . I'd sooner bet on a horse race.

"I pressed my luck as far as I dared while we were in the house talking to him. I didn't see much to make a case on, but I'm sure as hell not ruling him out. He's a two-time loser on drug charges. If he goes back to Angola, he will never see the free world again. That's a dangerous animal to put in a corner. If this woman knew something or saw something she shouldn't have—or if the boy did . . . Murder is a viable option to a man like that."

"But he didn't kill Genevieve," Annie said. "What would be the purpose of him killing her child and letting her live? To scare her? To shut her up? For what? What's the point in keeping her alive so she can testify against him?"

"I don't know."

"Any reason to think he's dealing drugs now?"

Nick arched a brow as he took a sip of her coffee. "Any reason not to think it? Past behavior being the best predictor of future behavior . . . And it's easy money. Beats the hell out of cleaning chemical tanks at the oil refinery."

"He's not exactly living high off the hog down on that road," Annie pointed out, setting her toast aside.

"The house isn't much. *C'est vrai*," he conceded. "But he has a nice big TV and a fancy chair to sit in and enjoy it. Maybe he's just not into appearances."

"He should rethink that. That's a creepy place to live, out on that nasty backwater in those ramshackle houses."

"Not a lot of prying eyes around. Fewer today than yesterday."

"Eat your toast, 'Toinette," he admonished. "You gotta fuel the fire, *cher*."

"I'm not hungry," she said, pushing her plate toward him.

"You need to eat," he insisted.

"I don't want it."

"Eat something else, then," he said. "You gonna tell me you don't have a Snickers bar in your purse calling your name?"

Instantly, she narrowed her eyes at him, readily taking offense. This was the way of things between them lately. He was too quick to lose patience. Her feelings were too easily hurt. They stepped on each other's raw nerves on a daily basis.

He heaved a sigh and attempted to scrape together some diplomacy. "I didn't mean for that to sound that way."

"Well, it did."

"I said I'm sorry."

"No," she corrected him, "actually, you didn't."

"*Mon Dieu!* I'm sorry," he said with more impatience than sincerity, holding up his hands in surrender. "There."

Annie rolled her eyes. "And you're so gracious about it!"

"Can we just back this up to the part where I was expressing my concern that you eat something to keep up your strength?" he asked.

She considered her options. He could see she might go either way. Her face was pale with purple smudges beneath her bloodshot eyes. She had worked the same hours he had, had been sleeping as poorly as he had been these past months.

She was a brave little thing, his Antoinette, fierce in the courage of her convictions even when it scared the hell out of her. She had never hesitated to stand up to him and set him straight when no man would. That was what had won his admiration and respect from the start—her heart, her courage. That she was pretty was a bonus.

She had been still a girl, really, when they met. Twenty-something, wide-eyed and idealistic. His opposite in almost every way. From the start of their relationship, he had pushed her to push herself, to challenge herself, to seek the truth, to grow. She had met that challenge every time—right up to and including marrying him.

He sometimes felt guilty she had accepted that challenge. He was not an easy man. She could have married a deputy DA. A nice guy in a suit and tie. Mr. Nine-to-Five. A man who had loved her but didn't fulfill her. She would have settled into that life eventually and compromised on stability over satisfaction. The idea pained him, but that was what he would have done if he had been a better man: seen to it she had that life.

Lucky for him he was a selfish son of a bitch.

"*Allons,*" he murmured, reaching out to touch her shoulder. She twitched away, her eyes narrowed, brows lowered.

"Come on, *cher,*" he cajoled, leaning closer. "*S'il vous plâit.* Truce, eh? We're both tired. I'm sorry. I am."

She sighed and looked down at the cold toast, frowning, her arms crossed over her chest. This time when he reached out to touch her, she allowed it.

"I'm sorry," she confessed softly. "I'm so tired, I can't see straight. And I keep thinking about that poor little boy. I keep hearing the mother crying. The sound of her grief . . ."

A shudder went through her at the memory. She hugged herself, as if to ward off a chill. Nick stroked a hand over her hair to comfort her, wishing they were alone instead of on duty.

"It's hard not to put yourself in her place," he admitted. "To think if something like that happened to Justin . . ."

She shook her head. "I don't think I could take it. I'd be a puddle on the floor.

"The Gauthier boy was in Jaime Blynn's second-grade class," she said. "Jaime took it hard."

"Did she have anything to say about the mother?" Nick asked.

"That she's a typical single mom: overworked and not enough money. Jaime doesn't think she has much of a support network here. She said the boy was a bit of a handful—ADHD."

"On medication?"

"Not that she knew of."

Nick sat back, thinking about the Children's Benadryl, the cold medication, and the cough syrup Stokes had mentioned finding in the family medicine cabinet. Genevieve Gauthier wouldn't have been the first mother to use those drugs to calm a hyperactive child.

"Jaime said Genevieve recently started working at Evangeline Oaks, the assisted-living place," Annie said. "She may have a relative there."

"She had a prescription bottle for Oxy in her purse with the name Clarice Marcel on the label," Nick said.

"She could have taken the bottle to go get it refilled for her aunt or whoever."

"Or she could be a pill freak stealing from old people and living next door to a drug dealer."

"Is that what this guy deals? Oxy?"

"Opioids are where the money's at these days. Opioids with a side order of benzos is a popular combo, and she has a 'script for Xanax, as well."

Annie shrugged. "I'd have a 'script for Xanax, too, if I was a stressed-out single mom trying to raise my ADHD child next door to a convict out in *Twilight Zone*–ville. Why are you trying to make her look bad?"

"I'm not. I'm just stating the facts and the possibilities. And there's some things about her story that don't make sense to me: If she was being chased, why didn't the killer catch her? She had to go half a mile to get someone to open a door for her. Where'd this killer go? Why he didn't run her down? Why would he let her go? Who kills a child and leaves an adult to tell the tale?"

"I don't know. Maybe he got interrupted. Maybe a car came along and scared him off."

"But this mystery car didn't stop to help the woman?"

"Not everyone is a good Samaritan. Imagine driving down that creepy road in the dead of night and a bloody, screaming woman comes up in my headlights. If I'm a woman alone, would I dare stop? Or would I get the hell out of there?"

"You'd stop and get yourself ass-deep in alligators," Nick said. "Or you'd call nine-one-one at the least. But not everyone is you. Not everyone would do either of those things."

"I'm trained to know how to react in a crisis."

"You'd do the right thing, trained or no. That's who you are."

"We all like to think we know what we would do in a crisis," Annie said. "We're all superheroes in our own minds. But in the reality of chaos? I think about this girl, Genevieve. Imagine waking up in the middle of the night and there's some monster in the house. Her child's being attacked. *She's* being attacked . . . It's a nightmare come true. Regular people aren't going to know what to do. She was in a fight for her life with a knife-wielding maniac. She reacted. There was no thought to that, no plan, just instinct. No time to form clear memories, even."

"True enough," he said.

Memory making was delegated to a meticulous part of the brain that took time to paint those pictures and absorb the emotions that went with them. The part of the brain where instinct lived had to function quickly as a matter of life or death. There was no luxury of time to process information. That was why eyewitnesses to traumatic events often got key details wrong.

Nick glanced at his watch. Dutrow would be about to start his dog and pony show for the media. He rubbed the back of his neck and blew out a sigh.

"Let's go see what she has to say. Fill in some of these blanks, maybe."

He went around the table to pull his wife's chair out for her, leaned down, kissed the side of her neck, and whispered in her ear, "I'll take you for pancakes after."

A weary smile turned her lips. "Sweet talker. I guess I'll leave that Snickers bar in my purse, then."

"Save it for later," he murmured. "Come on, partner. Let's go to work."

GENEVIEVE GAUTHIER LAY in her bed, staring into space at some imagined scene, paying no attention to them as they entered the room. He would never have recognized her from her driver's license photo. She had taken a beating. Her left eye was nearly swollen shut. The deep purple bruising had come to the surface overnight, painting a grim picture on what Nick knew was a pretty face in normal circumstances. Her left shoulder was heavily bandaged, her arm in a sling. An IV line ran to the back of her right hand.

"Genevieve?" Annie asked quietly as they came alongside the bed. "I'm Detective Broussard. Do you remember me from last night?"

She looked at Annie without recognition, saying nothing, giving no indication whether she remembered her or not. She gave Nick the same blank look.

"This is Detective Fourcade," Annie said. "He's in charge of your case."

"I'm sorry for what happened, Ms. Gauthier," Nick murmured. "I'm sorry for your loss."

"Where is he?" Genevieve asked, her voice little more than a rough whisper. "Where is my son? I don't want him left alone," she said. "He's just a little boy."

Annie flicked a glance at Nick. He kept his attention on Genevieve, checking her pupils, the vaguely glassy quality to her eyes. She was on something for pain, but the doctor had said nothing strong enough to alter her reality. The shock of what had happened to her may well have been enough to do that. Her mind was no doubt swimming in a whirlpool of shock, disbelief, denial, and residual terror. She wanted to believe her son was still alive. No one could fault her for that.

"Genevieve," Annie said gently, "do you remember what happened last night? You told me someone came into your house and hurt you and hurt your son?"

The young woman glanced away, her respiration quickening. "Yes."

Nick could feel the tension in his wife, the reluctance to be the one to deliver the bad news—for a second time, no less—though she would do it anyway. He touched his hand to the small of her back as a gesture of support.

"KJ didn't make it, Genevieve," she said sadly. "I'm so, so sorry."

Tears magnified Genevieve Gauthier's good eye. Her delicate, bruised chin quivered. "No. I don't want to believe that. Where is he? I want to see him."

"He's in a safe place," Nick said. "You don't need to worry. No one can hurt him anymore."

"I want to see him."

"We can arrange that," he said. "But right now, it's very important that you tell me everything that happened last night. I need to get as much information from you as possible so we can catch the person who did this and put that person behind bars. We want to catch him before he can hurt anyone else."

She nodded and sniffled. Two slow, fat tears rolled down her cheeks. Annie pulled a tissue from the box on the bedside tray and handed it to her.

"Do you have any idea who did this to you?" Nick asked. "Did you recognize anything about this person?"

"No."

"He didn't look familiar at all?"

"It looked like the devil," she whispered. "It was mostly dark. There was light coming from my room and KJ's nightlight. Everything happened so fast . . . It didn't seem real. I thought it was a nightmare. That red face. Black eyes . . ."

Nick thought of Roddie Perez, half of his head burned, the flesh red and gnarled; his long, deeply lined face. In a rage he might well look like the devil. But Genevieve Gauthier had said nothing about her neighbor.

"Ms. Gauthier, I want you to tell me everything what happened last night, starting from when you got home from work," Nick said. "Was there anything unusual about the evening?"

"No," she said, staring off into the middle distance, as if she was seeing a replay on some invisible screen. "We got home and had dinner. KJ had his bath. We went to bed."

"Nothing unusual happened? No strange phone calls? No visitors?"
"No."

"You didn't notice a strange car go by? Nothing like that?"
"No."

"When you turned in for the night, did you check your locks?"
"I always lock my doors."

"But you had windows open."

"It's been so hot," she said. "The air conditioners don't work. I complained to the landlord, but . . ."

She let the sentence trail off. She seemed to struggle against the emotion that came with the idea that she may have lost her child for want of a working air conditioner in his bedroom window. A few hundred dollars that she didn't have to spend and a skinflint landlord too cheap to do the right thing might have cost her her son.

"You went to bed," Nick said, prompting her toward the worst of the story. "What woke you?"

"KJ," she said. "I heard him cry out, and I felt a terrible pain in my chest, like I was being stabbed," she said, pressing a hand against her sternum as if feeling for the knife.

"I tried to run to him," she whispered, tears sliding down her cheeks. "I tripped and fell and hit my head so hard . . . And then I was in the hall, and I saw that creature standing there with the knife, but I didn't . . .

It didn't make sense. I had to get to KJ, and I ran into his room, and he was there on the floor, and there was blood everywhere . . ."

In contrast to the image she painted with her words, she was as white as chalk.

"And I-I grabbed him and p-pulled him a-against me, and I-I screamed. And-and then he came at me with the knife."

"Who came at you?" Nick asked.

"The devil! He came after me with the knife."

"He came back into your son's room from the hall?" Annie asked.

"I-I just— I had to fight him."

"You fought with him," Nick said. "Did he try to force himself on you, sexually?"

"No," she said, glancing away. "No. I had to get out. I had to get help! I thought he was going to kill me! I made it out the front door, and I j-just ran! Oh, my God! I was s-so a-afraid!"

"Where did you run to, Genevieve?" she asked.

"T-to the n-neighbor's h-house."

"The blue house next door?" Nick asked.

"No one answered," she said. "I knocked and knocked. N-no one c-came. There was a light on, b-but no one came. It was like a terrible dream. And then I-I j-just kept r-running."

"The man who attacked you. Did he follow you to the neighbor's house? Did he chase you?"

"I-I just k-kept running," she whispered.

Nick plugged Genevieve's version of events into his memory of walking through the crime scene, matching her story to the evidence. The crime had begun in the boy's room. A struggle had taken place in the hall and in the front room of the house. He believed Genevieve had been on Roddie Perez's front porch, that her blood was on his front door.

But why was she still alive? Had the attacker panicked at the idea that she might alert her neighbor, and the neighbor would call 911? Had that spooked him into bolting? If Perez was their bad guy, if she ran to his house, why hadn't he finished the job?

"Did you see or hear a car?" Annie asked.

She shook her head no. "I don't understand why this happened," she murmured, almost to herself. "Why would somebody do this to us?"

"It's our job to find those answers, Ms. Gauthier," Nick said. "Can you tell us if there's anyone in your life you're not getting along with? A boyfriend, ex-boyfriend?"

"No."

"Are you in a relationship?"

"No."

"What about your boy's father?"

"He's not part of our lives."

"We'll need to speak to him, just the same."

"That's not possible," she said, looking away.

Meaning he was dead or gone or unknown to her; a one-night stand or a rapist or a love lost. Perhaps this man she wouldn't name was the reason she had left Dulac and moved to Bayou Breaux for a fresh start in a strange place where no one knew her and she had no memories. She had memories now.

"How well do you know your neighbor in the blue house?" he asked.

"I don't know him at all."

"Have you seen him? Do you know what he looks like?"

"I've seen him drive by. I've seen him in his yard. That's all."

"You haven't had any interactions with him?"

She said nothing for a few seconds, as if she was scouring her memory, then, "No. Well— Once, he yelled at KJ for climbing a tree near his property. KJ came crying. I was angry. He's just a little boy. What harm was he doing, climbing a tree?"

"Did you say anything to this guy?" Annie asked.

"No. I just thought it best not to. I mind my own business. I don't want any trouble. I told KJ to stay away from his yard—"

Her good eye widened as the possibility struck her. "You don't think he—? Who would kill a little boy for climbing a tree? Oh, my God."

"When did that happen?" Annie asked.

"A couple of weeks ago."

"And your son didn't say anything more about the man after that?"

"He was afraid the man would yell at him again or chase him, but it was just him being afraid. Nothing happened. He had some bad dreams, but it was just dreams. Do you think—? I don't even know this man's name!" she said, sounding incredulous at the idea a man she didn't know might shatter her life for no reason. "Do you think he did it?"

"We're just asking questions at this point," Nick said. "We need to get a clear picture of everything going on in your life, who you might know, people you might have crossed paths with. Anyone who might have been angry with you for any reason."

"I can't believe someone I know could do such a thing."

"Who do you rent the house from?" he asked.

"Mr. Carville. Roy Carville."

"How long have you lived there?"

"We moved here in June."

"From Dulac, yeah?"

"Yes."

"What brought you to Bayou Breaux?"

She gave a little shrug with her good shoulder, looking away. "I needed a job. There was an opening where my aunt Clarice lives—Evangeline Oaks."

"Clarice Marcel?"

"Yes," she answered, giving him a quizzical look. "Do you know her?"

"What do you do there?" he asked, leaving her question hanging.

"I'm an aide. And I help out some in the office. Mr. Avery, the administrator, says I might work into being a receptionist soon. He thinks I have good people skills. When can I see KJ?"

"You get along with your co-workers?"

"Yes," she said, glancing away, looking toward the door. Her respiration had picked up. She was growing anxious, tired of the tedious questions. "When can I see my son? You said I could see him."

Nick glanced at Annie and stepped back from the bed. She moved with him, turning her back to their victim.

"What do you think?" he asked softly. "The boy is right down the hall. Is it better for her to see him or not? That's gonna be a bad shock all over again."

"If it was me and I knew my child was down the hall, wild horses wouldn't keep me from him," Annie murmured. "Shock or no. Alive or not. And if it was you," she added, "you would've already torn the doors off the morgue."

"True enough," he conceded as Genevieve Gauthier began to cry behind them, a soft, eerie keening sound that slowly rose in pitch and volume, making the short hairs stand up on the back of his neck.

"Please," she sobbed. "I just want to see my baby! Please let me see my baby!"

Annie turned back to her, to offer what comfort she could. "We'll take you to see him now, Genevieve," she said on a sad, weary sigh. "We'll take you to see your baby."

ELEVEN

Do you have any idea who did this to you?" the detective asked.

Me, she thought. *It was my fault. It's always my fault, one way or another.*

She didn't say it.

"Did you recognize anything about this person?"

Evil. She recognized evil in all its forms.

"It didn't seem real," she said. "I thought it was a nightmare . . ."

"Was there anything unusual about the evening?"

"No."

She replayed the day in her mind: Jeff's callous coolness to her in the office. She'd spent most of the day on the brink of tears. Picking up KJ at the Florettes'. KJ crying, wound up like a top, no sign of Nora anywhere. Jojean's snippy, dismissive remark when Genevieve had called her to complain. This was her life—just another day full of hard work and disappointment.

She'd had a sick headache by the time they got home. Pills for her dinner: one for the pain, one for her nerves, neither making a difference. Her patience was frayed down to the nub. KJ had refused to eat anything but Cheetos, whining and fighting with her at every turn. She had been at the end of her rope. She had lost her temper with him.

Was there anything unusual about the evening?

No, not at all.

". . . KJ had his bath. We went to bed . . ."

. . . in the stifling heat of a house with no working air-conditioning and not a breath of wind coming in through the windows.

". . . you had windows open."

". . . I complained to the landlord, but . . ."

Roy Carville. She could see him in her mind's eye as plain as day: bald as a billiard ball, skin stretched as tight over his bony little skull as a condom on a bulging penis. He had a laugh like a hyena's, and when he laughed, his eyes disappeared into slits in his face.

"Air conditioners don't grow on trees, Miss Gauthier," he said in his squeaky, scratchy voice. *"But maybe, if you're a good girl . . ."*

He'd laughed at what he left unsaid.

Her stomach turned at the thought. Why did men always have to be that way? Everything in their world had a sexual price. No need for a woman to have money as long as she had a vagina she didn't mind sharing or a mouth she didn't mind using like one.

"Can you tell us if there's anyone in your life you're not getting along with?" the detective asked. ". . . A boyfriend, ex-boyfriend? . . . What about your boy's father? . . . How well do you know your neighbor in the blue house? . . . What brought you to Bayou Breaux?"

The questions swarmed around her head like bees, loud, annoying, dizzying, dangerous bees. She didn't have the answers he wanted. Her head was pounding. The pain in her shoulder throbbed and burned. She wanted yesterday back. She wanted her boy back. Could she just turn back time—a day, a week, a year, eight years?

"When can I see my son?" she asked, tears rising. "You said I could see him . . . I just want to see my baby! Please let me see my baby!"

THEY TOOK HER by wheelchair, the woman detective pushing her, the male detective going on ahead of them and disappearing into a room at the far end of the long hallway.

Strange, Genevieve thought, how it made her feel special to have the attention of these people, even though the circumstances were terrible.

In the normal course of things, she lived her life unnoticed. In her experience, she was safer that way, off to the side, at the edge of the shadows, quietly putting one foot in front of the other, keeping her head down. But she was the star of the story today. The starring actress in a real-life horror movie.

"This is going to be hard," the female detective warned her. "Your son sustained some terrible injuries. You may have blocked that out of your mind. No one would blame you if you had. But I want you to be prepared, Genevieve."

Genevieve said nothing. In her brain, the images flashed, one and then another and another: the knife, the blood, wide eyes, and mouths torn open in screams of rage and terror. She remembered the heat, the smell of sweat and fear, the taste of tears and blood and bile and guilt.

Her heart was beating too fast. She felt a little faint. A sign on the wall pointed to the morgue.

The male detective appeared again, holding the door open as they neared the end of the hall. He was handsome in the way of a dangerous animal, like a panther: fit, sleek, overtly male, all muscle and sharp angles. His dark eyes were hard and keenly watchful. She felt the heat of his gaze as she rolled past him. Not in a sexual way, but like a predator looking at prey, like she was something to pounce on the second she made a mistake.

The room was white and sterile. Harsh fluorescent lights and cold tile. A stainless steel wall of small doors, like she'd seen on TV. Doors hiding drawers of dead bodies.

Her heart beat faster still as the female detective pushed her toward a gurney in the middle of the room. The small draped figure on the cart would be KJ. Panic formed like a ball in the pit of her stomach and rose up into her chest, into her throat, threatening to choke her. She screamed to let it out as the detective drew back the sheet. She tried to catch the sound with her hand and shove it back inside her mouth.

"I'm so sorry, Genevieve," the detective murmured, touching her shoulder.

Genevieve struggled to pull herself to her feet, grabbing hold of the gurney. KJ lay there on the steel table, small and pale and lifeless. Her mind wanted to reject the image. He didn't look real. This was a dummy, some kind of Hollywood prop made to look like her son. And yet, of course she knew it wasn't that at all.

She reached out and touched his arm, wanting to feel his warmth, wanting to feel life pulsing through him, but he was as cold and unresponsive as a doll. Tears fell from her eyes and splashed against his flesh like raindrops as she bent over him, a storm of emotions swirling through her: love and heartbreak, rage and terror, guilt and blame.

She had made the decision to bring him into the world—against advice, defying threat. She had regretted her choice on many occasions. The weight of that guilt was like an anchor. She had been pelted with shame hurled at her by the judgmental: how selfish, how shameful, what a slut she was. And she had drunk in the accolades given by others: how brave, how selfless, to have a baby on her own and keep him and raise him as best she could, accepting the sacrifices that choice entailed. She had been a bad mother and a good mother, depending on the point of view. Now she was a mother without a child.

Her fault. She should have been stronger, tried harder. She should have controlled herself. She should have protected him. What if she hadn't taken the pills . . .

"I'm so sorry, Genevieve," the female detective said.

I'm so sorry, Genevieve echoed in her mind.

"I'm so sorry," she whispered to KJ, bending down over him, touching her cheek to his body. "I'm so sorry, baby."

She saw him as an infant, red-faced and screaming, enraged at the ordeal of being born. She saw him at two years old, his face and hands a mess from a half-eaten chocolate Easter bunny. She saw him crying over his first lost tooth, and his last skinned knee. His life passed before her eyes, over too soon, gone like smoke through her grasping fingers. It didn't matter how sorry she was. All the apologies in the world could never bring him back.

The sobs began as a low siren, a moan from the depths of her soul, a wave that grew to a crescendo and broke on the jagged pieces of her shattered heart.

I'm so sorry. I'm so sorry, baby. I'm so sorry I killed you . . .

TWELVE

My message to the scum who perpetrated this heinous crime is this: You can run, but you *CANNOT* hide!" Kelvin Dutrow shouted at the camera, his face set in an exaggerated scowl, like a tough guy in a cheesy action movie. "I, Sheriff Kelvin Dutrow, am going to make it my personal mission to see to it that your next hiding place will be BEHIND BARS! I will see to it that every investigative tool at my disposal will be brought to bear in the effort to bring you to JUSTICE!"

He leaned toward the camera, thrusting an accusing finger at the lens. He was dressed in his black tactical uniform, complete with boots and black felt trooper hat. In the background, a row of six trim young deputies in uniform stood pointlessly at attention, the entrance of the law enforcement center behind them.

The TV coverage cut back to the news anchor in the studio, a woman with bright red lipstick and a spray-starched helmet of black hair.

"Partout Parish sheriff, Kelvin Dutrow, added during the press conference that a tip hotline will be set up by noon today. Anyone having any information regarding the crime is encouraged to call—"

Scowling darkly, Nick muttered a string of nasty French only half under his breath. A tip hotline for a murder that happened in the middle of nowhere in the dead of night. What would that get them? A hundred phone calls from the lunatic fringe, people who sat at home listening to police scanners for excitement, people who watched too many fictional crime dramas that bore no resemblance whatsoever to real police work. He would now have to dedicate manpower to chasing down phantom leads that would evaporate into nothing.

"I just *love* that Sheriff Dutrow!" the waitress exclaimed as she led them to their table. A petite, sinewy woman, her red hair was striped with gray and gathered in a loose pile on top of her head, damp tendrils clinging to the fine sheen of sweat on her forehead. She'd been working in this place for twenty years or more.

"He's a man of action, him!" she declared, pointing at the television that was mounted on the wall in one corner of the room. A freeze-frame shot of Dutrow filled the screen as news of the homicide crawled below.

Annie elbowed Nick gently. A preemptive reprimand for whatever unpleasant thing he might have wanted to say.

They had come in the back way to Madame Collette's diner, into the small private dining room where they could talk and strategize away from the eyes and opinions of the restaurant regulars. They were able to park off the alley and slip in unseen. Had they tried to return to the SO, they would have run smack into the media. The longer that could be avoided, the better.

An institution in Bayou Breaux, Madame Collette's had changed little since the Great Depression. The slow-turning ceiling fans had cooled the brows of generations. The cypress-wood floors were worn in the traffic patterns of legions of waitresses before Miss Crystal.

"I'm your man of action right here, Miss Crystal with a *C*," Stokes said, flashing his square, white smile. "You know it's so. Don't try to deny it!"

The waitress rolled her eyes and swatted at him halfheartedly. "I know you're full of something, Chaz Stokes!"

"My love for you," he teased, taking his seat.

"You gonna settle for grits," she shot back, filling his coffee cup.

"You wound me, Miss Crystal. Here I been up all night fighting crime. I just need a little sweetness from my favorite waitress."

"I'll bring you extra sugar for your coffee. That's what you'll get," the waitress quipped. "You want something more than that, you go up front and flirt with Krystal with a *K*."

"Krystal with a *K* has a boyfriend, I hear tell."

She arched a finely drawn eyebrow at him. "Since when did that ever stop you, *cher*?"

"Since he's the size of a mountain gorilla."

"And here I accuse you of having no common sense," Annie remarked.

"Self-preservation is a base animal instinct," Nick said. "I'll have the number two platter, Miss Crystal, *s'il vous plâit*."

"You're gonna catch the scum what did this terrible thing? Killin' that little Gauthier boy?" the waitress asked, nodding toward the television. It was more of a directive than a question.

"Yes, ma'am."

"You send him straight to hell if you can."

The look on her face said she would do the honors herself if possible. She wouldn't be the only one with that sentiment. An attack on a child in a small town was an attack on family, whether anyone knew Genevieve Gauthier personally or not.

"Are we getting our search warrant?" Nick asked as the waitress disappeared into the hall.

"No, sir, I am sad to say," Stokes reported. "I begged, I pleaded, I worked up tears. Hell, I did everything but go down on the man. Judge Monahan was unimpressed with our probable cause—or lack thereof. He axed me straight-up did the victim have anything to say against Perez? I told him she was delirious, in and out of a coma. How could we even ask her? He didn't wanna hear about it. Come back when she points the finger, he tells me."

"Yeah. Let's give the man plenty of time to destroy any relevant evidence," Nick grumbled.

"Did you talk to her?" Stokes asked. "Did she say anything about him?"

"She ran to his house looking for help," Annie said. "If she thought for a second he was the assailant, she wouldn't have done that."

"That doesn't mean it couldn't be him," Nick pointed out. "She said that he yelled at the boy a couple of weeks ago for getting too close to his property. What's he got going on over there he didn't want a child to see?"

"I don't know," Stokes said. "I'm gonna talk to the guys on the drug task force, see if they have Roddie on their radar for any reason. But if he was the assailant, why didn't he just kill her?"

"That's the magic question. That's the magic question no matter who did this. Why is she still alive?"

"Does this guy, Perez, have any history of violence against women?" Annie asked.

"Ol' Roddie, he's got a rap sheet long as an elephant's dick," Stokes said. "There's a little bit of everything on it—drugs, assault, B-and-E. He's a regular cornucopia of crime. I just spoke to his parole officer. He said Roddie moved back here about eight months ago. He had been living up in Breaux Bridge for a couple of years. According to the PO, he's been keeping that long nose of his clean since he got out of the can—as hard as that is to imagine."

"Why'd he come back?" Nick asked. "He doesn't seem the nostalgic type."

Stokes shrugged.

"Is he really working at the refinery?"

"Was. He wasn't lying about that accident. He's been milking the disability and trying to sue for a year and a half. The company's gonna try to starve him out on that. They say he lit a cigarette and caused the explosion himself. He'll never see a dime."

That nice truck, the TV . . . "So he could have an alternate source of income?"

"Absolutely. And, why not fall back on what he knows best?"

"Drugs," Annie said.

"Beats chopping sugarcane in the hot sun."

"Any word about that on the street?" Nick asked. "Him dealing?"

"My CIs are all under their rocks at this time of day," Stokes said. "I've made a couple of calls. I'll hear back or go digging for them. Did y'all get anything new out of the victim?"

"Kind of a sketchy story at this point. Full of gaps and holes," Nick said.

"She has a head trauma," Annie reminded them. "We're lucky she remembers as much as she does."

"Somebody breaks into my house and tries to kill me, and kills my kid, I'm gonna remember every second of that," Stokes declared.

"Good for you," Annie bit back. "Can I volunteer to be the one to hit you in the head for that experiment?"

"Ha-ha," Stokes said flatly. "Did you ask her about the drugs?"

"No," Nick said. "I'll wait for the tox screen to come back. I want to know the answer before I ask that question."

"Boyfriends, ex-husbands, lovers?"

"She says no."

"So this kid of hers was the immaculate conception?" Stokes asked. "There's gotta be a dick involved in there somewhere."

"I'll look up the birth record," Annie volunteered. "But that's no guaranteed answer."

"No," Nick said. "Give that to Dixon. Call her ASAP. She can do the background on this girl. I need you elsewhere, 'Toinette. Have her check for any record of a marriage or a divorce, too, and any kind of criminal record or criminal complaint made by her. Could be she moved here to get away from the boy's father. Could be a history of abuse, for all we know. There's a reason she doesn't want to talk about him."

"If the baby daddy did it, why wouldn't he kill her, then?" Stokes questioned.

"It would be worse punishment to kill my child and leave me alive with the knowledge that it was somehow my fault," Annie offered.

Nick nodded. "That's a thread worth pulling. Eliminate a child support payment and have the added bonus of continuing to terrorize the ex."

"But if I thought my ex did it," Annie said, "I wouldn't hesitate to give him up for it. She won't even say his name."

They fell silent as the food arrived. As he ate, Nick's attention flicked back to the television, where Dutrow's press conference was being replayed for the first of what would be many times in the coming days. Everyone in the parish would be made to feel as if KJ Gauthier had lived next door, the boy who might have grown up to cut their grass or deliver their newspaper.

Dutrow at his podium pointed to a reporter in the crowd, and a faceless voice asked, "Who will be heading up this investigation, Sheriff?"

"Detective Nick Fourcade will be the lead investigator on this case."

"He's heading the investigation on the Theriot sexual assault case as well," the reporter stated. "Is there any reason to believe the two cases might be related?"

Dutrow frowned. "One is a sexual assault on a girl; the other is the murder of a small boy. There's no correlation between the two."

"Two cases perpetrated against children. Two instances of an assailant gaining entry to a home—"

"There is no connection between the two that we know of at this time," Dutrow said curtly.

Another voice came from the other side of the podium. "Has there been any progress in the Theriot case?"

"I'm not here to comment on that case," Dutrow said. "The investigation is ongoing. We're here this morning to focus on a murder perpetrated last night. It's vital that anyone having any information relating to this case contact us immediately."

"Will Detective Fourcade be available for comment?"

"No, he will not. His attention is focused on investigating the crime. Direct your questions and comments to me."

"Will you be directly involved in the investigation, Sheriff? You have a reputation for being very hands-on."

Dutrow pulled one of his authoritarian faces and looked straight at the camera. "Rest assured, I will have my finger on the pulse of this investigation every step of the way!"

Somewhere in the background, applause broke out. Probably Dutrow's office staff, Nick thought cynically. It wouldn't have been the first time his secretary and chief deputy had been pressed into service as acolytes.

Stokes made a rude noise. "He can put some K-Y on that finger and stick it right up his ass."

"Let's be grateful he and the media can keep each other enthralled,"

Annie said. "Maybe we can solve a crime while they're busy gazing into each other's eyes."

"That sounds like a plan," Nick said, pushing back from the table. He could all but hear a stopwatch ticking off the seconds in his head. "Let's get on it."

THIRTEEN

I saw it on the news!" the office manager said with equal parts excitement and dismay. "I was in a resident's living room—Alphonse LeComte—and he had the news on. The volume was just blaring loud—Alphonse is deaf as a post, bless his heart—and I was just about to hit the Mute button, and the sheriff came on and said her name, plain as anything: *Genevieve Gauthier*. He practically shouted it right in my face!"

Her name tag read MAVIS PARSONS in large block letters. She stood behind the counter in the administrative offices of the Evangeline Oaks Center for Assisted Living. With coiffed blond hair and retro cat-eye glasses, she might have come from a bygone era, though Annie put her in her mid-to-late thirties at most.

"I couldn't believe it!" the woman went on. "I mean, how many times do you hear the name of someone you know on television?" she asked, without pausing to hear an answer. "It just didn't seem real. It didn't seem real at all! Poor Genevieve! Is she going to be all right?"

"She's injured," Annie said, "but she'll recover."

"Thank goodness!" Mavis exclaimed, glancing up at the heavens, literally clutching the pearls at her throat. "But her poor little boy!"

Beside her, Annie could feel Nick's impatience humming like an electrical field around him. He had no patience for nervous talkers. He wanted answers to his specific questions. For Nick, an interview was a psychological chess match, and he was always three moves ahead of his opponent, manipulating them into corners, tricking them into giving up information. Annie, on the other hand, was willing to let people ramble, willing to sift through a lot of nonsense while mining for a few gold nuggets of truth they might not otherwise have gotten. The contrast made them an excellent team.

"I need to speak with your administrator," Nick said flatly.

"Oh, yes, of course!" Mavis said. "I told him you were on your way. Just let me ring him."

"No need, Mavis. I'm right here."

Jefferson Avery emerged from his private office looking tired and harried. His thinning sandy hair had been subjected to a hasty finger combing. In his early forties, he might have been Mr. Popularity in high school, Annie thought. He was still good-looking, but he had gone a bit soft around the middle and along his jawline, worn down by the inevitability of male pattern baldness and the disappointing mediocrity of his life.

He offered a hand to Nick. "Jeff Avery."

"Detective Fourcade," Nick said. "This is Detective Broussard. We need to speak with you and some of your staff regarding an employee—Genevieve Gauthier."

"We've all seen the news already, Detective," Avery said on a sigh. "It's terrible. I don't know what else to say."

"I have some questions for you, if we can speak privately."

"Of course."

"Detective Broussard has questions for any of your staff who might know Ms. Gauthier."

"Whatever you need," he said, gesturing Nick toward his office.

Annie watched them go. As soon as the door closed, the office manager started in again.

"He's such a good man—Mr. Avery," she said. "Very civic-minded, even though he hasn't lived here all that long. He belongs to I don't know how many groups—the Chamber of Commerce, the Rotary Club, and

I don't know what all. I don't know where he finds the time. He's working here all hours."

"And Genevieve . . . ?" Annie prompted.

"Just tragic. I felt so guilty right away when I saw the news," Mavis confessed in a half whisper, leaning over the counter, woman-to-woman. "I was angry with her this morning for being late. I said something very unkind. Donna Goldberg, our head nurse, heard me—and she agreed with me, frankly. I mean, in all fairness to me, Genevieve *is* often late and suffers no repercussions whatsoever."

"Why is that?"

"Well, I wouldn't know, as I'm *married* to the father of my children, but I'm sure it's difficult being a single mother—"

"No," Annie interrupted. "Why no repercussions?"

"Oh, I don't want to speak out of school—"

"Of course not."

"—but it's no secret she plays the Poor, Poor, Pitiful Me card with Mr. Avery, and he is *far* too kind."

"Is there a reason for that?"

"I'm sure I don't know what you mean," she said, pulling back in offense.

"She's a pretty girl. He's a man."

"Mr. Avery is *very* dedicated to his wife and children."

"That never stopped any man I ever knew from looking," Annie said. "Or giving preferential treatment, for that matter."

"Well, Mr. Avery is *not* that way," Mavis insisted. "He has a kind heart, is all. In fact, he and his wife put together a box of clothes and shoes their son had outgrown to give to Genevieve for her boy. That's the kind of people they are: charitable, God-fearing Christian people."

"Do you know Genevieve very well?" Annie asked, refraining from telling Mavis how many "God-fearing Christian people" she had put in prison for all manner of hideous behaviors. Showing up in church on Sunday didn't automatically make anyone good, as far as Annie was concerned.

"No, not really. She's not what I call a woman's woman, if you know what I mean."

"I don't. What do you mean?"

"She doesn't have much to say to other women. Now, whenever a man is nearby, that's a whole other story. She just lights right up," she said with a sharp hint of acid. "But who am I to judge? I have a husband."

"So Genevieve wouldn't have confided to you if something had been bothering her," Annie said.

"If her moods are anything to go by, something is *always* bothering her. But I know she struggles to make ends meet. And her little boy is—was—a handful. She has a hard life, bless her heart."

"Do you know if she's friends with any of the other staff here?"

"I don't think so."

"Has she ever said anything to you about a boyfriend, ex-boyfriend, anything like that?"

"No."

"Has she ever said anything about her boy's father?"

"No." Mavis's eyes narrowed in suspicion. "Why are you asking all these questions about Genevieve? She's the victim. Shouldn't you be out looking for whoever did this?"

"We don't know who did it," Annie said. "Genevieve doesn't know who did it. We're hoping people who know her might be able to help fill in a few blanks. We don't always see the bad in people close to us. Sometimes folks who pretend to care about us turn out to be jealous and spiteful."

Mavis didn't blink, apparently lacking the self-awareness for shame.

"Well, this wasn't somebody she knew," she said with certainty. "Surely not. This was some maniac. We'll be locking our doors tonight, hoping y'all can catch this murderer faster than you've done anything about the pervert who molested that Theriot girl."

She nodded in the direction of Jeff Avery's office. "He's the detective for that investigation, too, isn't he? I saw him on the news when that happened. Maybe Sheriff Dutrow should put someone more capable in charge."

Annie clenched her jaw and reminded herself that the general public only had what information the press and the gossipmongers gave them. This woman had no idea what had gone into the Theriot investigation.

She knew nothing about Nick's sleepless nights or how many hours he had spent going over and over the meager details of a case with a silent victim. She knew nothing about police work or the frustration of having a case with no leads and no viable suspects. She only knew someone had been hurt and no one had been made to pay.

"I can assure you, Detective Fourcade is very good at his job, ma'am," Annie said.

Mavis sniffed. "Well, I hope so. Here we are living with maniacs running around loose in the dead of night."

Annie tuned out the diatribe and looked through the glass office doors to the facility's large, sunny common area, where residents gathered to socialize. It was a homey place full of chintz and overstuffed couches and round oak tables topped with adult coloring books and half-done jigsaw puzzles.

"Genevieve has a relative here, doesn't she?" she asked. "An aunt?"

"Clarice Marcel. Genevieve calls her Aunt Clarice, though I don't know what kind of niece she is," Mavis said. "Clarice and her husband lived here two years before he passed, God rest his soul, and we never saw hide nor hair of Genevieve. Better late than never, I suppose."

"Can I meet Mrs. Marcel?" Annie asked. "Maybe she'll have some insights to share."

"Probably not from this decade," Mavis quipped, coming out from behind the counter. "But you're welcome to try."

"HAVE A SEAT, Detective," Jeff Avery offered as he seated himself behind his desk. The knot of his navy blue tie had been pulled slightly loose at his throat, jerked off-center, the collar button beneath it hastily undone. He was already rattled, and they had yet to begin the interview.

Good, Nick thought. His specialty was making people uncomfortable, putting them off balance. People lied to the police all the time. Bad people wanted to look good. Good people wanted to look better. No one wanted to be a rat if they could find a creative, venial way out of it. But lies were twice as hard to keep straight as the truth, and harder still when the liar was nervous.

"I'll stand, thank you," Nick said politely, knowing this would immediately make Avery slightly uncomfortable, both physically and psychologically. Avery would have to look up at him and follow him as he moved restlessly around the small, messy office. He would wonder why this detective wouldn't bring his energy level down to have a simple, quiet conversation about an employee.

It was a drab room with putty-colored, utilitarian furnishings and a window that looked out on the parking lot. Papers and periodicals were piled on a credenza. Pictures of the family hung on one wall at the end of a row of framed certificates, diplomas, and such. The larger photo was of the entire Avery family dressed in khakis and untucked white shirts, posing on a sand dune somewhere.

Jeff Avery had a pretty, gently plump, dark-haired wife and three nice-looking stair-step children—two girls and a boy. The All-American middle-class family. They had probably met in college—or just out of—him and the missus. They had probably followed the expected track: courtship and a big Southern wedding with too many bridesmaids. A career for him, children for her. Fifteen or so years on, that track might have worn into a rut. Life might have become stale, predictable, monotonous. Enter the troubled twenty-something single girl with the pretty smile and sad story . . . A tale as old as time.

"How old are your children?"

"The girls are fourteen and twelve," Avery said. "My son just turned ten. Makes me sick to think of anyone harming them. I hate to imagine what Genevieve is going through, losing KJ. It's just terrible. Incomprehensible.

"Is she hurt badly?" he asked. "All they said on the news was that she was hospitalized."

"Her condition is stable."

"Is she conscious?"

"Yes."

"Does she know who did this?"

"How long have you known Ms. Gauthier?" Nick asked, blatantly ignoring Avery's question. He moved away from the family photos, pausing to look over a framed diploma for a bachelor of science degree in General Family and Consumer Sciences from Nicholls State University down in Thibodaux.

"She started here part-time as an aide mid-June. We didn't have a full-time position available for her until a few weeks later.

"I can't imagine how she's going to pay these hospital bills," Avery said. "Her health insurance isn't due to kick in for another two weeks. I checked this morning. We have a waiting period from start of employment. There's a high rate of turnover in this business at the lower levels. People take these aide jobs and quit within a week or two. It's more prudent for business to wait and see if the employee is committed."

"She may be able to get some assistance through Victim Services," Nick offered, moving again. "Do you know what brought her to Bayou Breaux?"

"She wanted to be closer to her aunt Clarice—a resident in our facility," Avery said. "She doesn't have any other family—Genevieve, that is. Clarice has family in Mobile—a niece and a nephew of her late husband. They never visit. They just pay the bills.

"Some people think assisted living is just a storage facility," he said with disgust. "A place to stick their old people until they die or go into full-time nursing care. And then you have people like Genevieve."

"You're fond of her," Nick said, watching him carefully.

"She's a young woman with a difficult life, trying to do the right thing," Avery said. "She works hard, does the best she can with her son, spends time with an old woman the rest of her family has forgotten. That's admirable. She deserves a break. Now this happens . . ."

"She told us you let her do some office work in addition to her work as an aide."

"She's had clerical jobs before. She was a receptionist for a dentist in Dulac. She worked as a file clerk at City Hall in Houma for a time. Our front-desk receptionist will be going on maternity leave in a few months. Genevieve could take her place. She's personable, polite—"

"Attractive."

"—presents herself well," Avery continued, refusing the bait. "In the meantime, I've had her helping Mavis some so she could earn a little extra on top of her aide's pay. I know she's struggling financially. Her regular shift ends at three; then she does a couple extra hours in the office."

"You're a good man," Nick said, pacing slowly back and forth in front of the desk. "You see a young woman struggling, you try to help her out. Chivalrous. That's what that is. Me, I don't get to see much of that behavior, you know? My line of work, I see the worst of people. I'm more apt to run across the man who has a little power in a certain circumstance—a boss, for instance—who decides to leverage that into something for himself."

"I'm not that man," Avery said, pushing to his feet, color rising in his cheeks. "I don't appreciate the insinuation."

Nick said nothing. He stared at Jeff Avery, letting the silence hang until Avery was uncomfortable enough that he felt a need to move. It didn't take long. He went to the wall of pictures and unnecessarily adjusted the one of his family.

"I'm a happily married man," he added, almost as an afterthought.

"Hmmm. Were you aware of anything troublesome going on in Ms. Gauthier's life?" Nick asked. "Did she ever mention being bothered by anyone? A boyfriend? Ex-boyfriend? Would-be boyfriend?"

"She never mentioned anything like that to me," Avery said, moving back to his desk to straighten a pile of papers. "It wouldn't have been appropriate for me to have that kind of conversation with an employee."

Nick shrugged. "People, I find, are often inappropriate in times of need. Self-preservation takes precedence over decorum—rightly so. This girl looks up to you, appreciates your kindness, sees you as a benefactor, a mentor of sorts, perhaps. Not hard to imagine she might turn to you with a confidence or for advice. Nothing wrong with that."

Avery held his silence—which was neither an admission nor a denial but was almost surely more the former than the latter, Nick thought.

"Ms. Gauthier was here at work yesterday?"

"Yes."

"Did anything seem out of the ordinary? Her demeanor, the quality of her work . . . ?"

"I couldn't really say. I was very busy yesterday," Avery said stiffly. "We're getting ready for an inspection. My mind was on a million details I need to see to before that happens. I've only been here a year, myself, and my predecessor left something of an administrative mess for me to sort out.

"What are you implying with this line of questioning, anyway?" he asked. "That Genevieve somehow might have seen this attack coming? That's absurd."

"Do you know where Ms. Gauthier lives?"

Avery's reply seemed to stick in his mouth.

"That's a yes-or-no answer," Nick said calmly.

The man rubbed a hand across his jaw as if to unlock it. "Yes," he said on a short sigh. "I once drove her home when her car wouldn't start, but I don't want you getting the wrong idea from that—"

"Does that seem to you to be the kind of neighborhood anyone would find by accident?"

Avery was silent for a beat, no doubt picturing the desolate road he had driven down while taking his lovely employee home.

"No," he admitted. "Are you saying you think she knows the person who did this?"

"Statistically, most perpetrators are known to their victims," Nick said. "Do you drug test your employees, Mr. Avery?"

Avery all but grabbed his neck for the whiplash from the change of subject. "Why would you ask such a thing?"

The question was hardly out of his mouth when he raised a hand in surrender, acknowledging that he didn't expect an answer.

"Yes," he said. "We drug test at the start of employment."

"Can I assume Ms. Gauthier had a clean test or you wouldn't have hired her?"

"Of course."

"And you've had no cause to suspect she might be abusing substances since she's been working here?"

"No, of course not. She's been a model employee. Why would you—"

"Would it be up to Ms. Gauthier to refill prescriptions for her aunt? Or is that a service provided by the facility?"

"It depends on the resident. Some have auto-refill and delivery from local pharmacies. Others prefer to get out and pick up their own. We're not a prison, you know. People are free to come and go. We help them as much or as little as they need."

"And Mrs. Marcel?"

"You'd have to ask our head nurse, Mrs. Goldberg." Avery set his hands at his waist and huffed a sigh as if he'd been running. "I find your whole line of questioning very strange, Detective. Genevieve is the victim here. Is there some reason to believe drugs were involved—?"

"You said, 'She does the best she can with her son,'" Nick said. "What did you mean by that?"

"Nothing! It's just a figure of speech!" Avery said, exasperated. "She's a young mother trying to raise a child on her own. That's not easy. She does the best she can, that's all. I didn't mean anything by it! You can't think Genevieve did that to her son!"

"I'm just trying to get a complete picture of their home life," Nick said calmly.

"You are *way* off base thinking something like that," Avery said adamantly. "Genevieve would never be capable—"

"People are capable of all manner of things when under sufficient pressure."

"No. Not Genevieve." Avery shook his head, agitated. "And she's in the hospital, for God's sake! She didn't put herself in the hospital—"

"No need to work yourself up, Mr. Avery," Nick said softly. "These are just routine questions."

"None of this sounds routine to me!"

Nick let the man's statement hang in the air—a little too loud, a little too emotional. Avery worked to rein himself in, to compose himself. Color mottled his face in red splotches.

"You have a very antagonistic way about you, Detective," he said.

"You seem to have very strong feelings about a minor employee you've only known for a few months," Nick pointed out. "Why is that, Mr. Avery?"

Avery came out from behind his desk and strode for the door. "I've had about enough of you, Detective Fourcade. It's my duty to cooperate, but I am a happily married man, and I won't have you insinuate otherwise."

"I didn't," Nick said with the same infuriating calm he'd used the whole interview. He leaned back against the edge of Avery's desk and crossed his arms over his chest, settling in even as Avery put his hand on the doorknob.

"My wife has been equally involved in helping Genevieve and KJ," Avery went on. "She got her ladies' group at church to add Genevieve to their outreach program for families in need—"

"When did you last see Ms. Gauthier?" Nick asked, uninterested for the moment in the Christian charity of Jeff Avery's wife.

"I'm not sure," Avery said impatiently. "Late in the day yesterday, I guess. I told you, I was very busy all day. I don't have time to oversee every employee."

"Mr. Avery, where were you last night between eleven and one in the morning?"

Avery gasped. "Oh, that's it!" he exploded. "I've had it with this bullshit! You need to leave. *Now*."

Nick didn't so much as twitch a muscle. "I don't get paid to be a diplomat, Mr. Avery."

"My tax dollars pay your salary," Avery said, indignant. "So you do, in fact, work for me. I will feel free to lodge a complaint—"

"You do that. Me, I don't worry do you like me or not. I'm not shopping for friends."

"Good thing. I can't imagine you have any."

"I'm still waiting for an answer," Nick said, unperturbed. "Where were you last night between eleven and one A.M.?"

Avery looked out through the glass in his door, like a trapped animal longing to escape. His pulse was visible in the side of his neck where his carotid artery stood out like a length of cord.

"I was here," he said with resignation. "Working. I have paperwork to catch up on before the inspection. I suppose you'll try to twist that into something."

"The truth will twist itself into the light," Nick said, lazily pushing away from the desk. "It always does. I am but a facilitator, a gatherer of facts. Thank you for your time, Mr. Avery."

FOURTEEN

T his is so exciting! Me, I don't get many visitors. Do I know you, *cher*?"

"No, ma'am," Annie said, smiling gently at Clarice Marcel.

She was a petite woman with dark eyes and a soft cloud of nicely done blue-gray hair. Eighty-five, the nurse had told Annie. She was a bit stooped and leaned on a cane but was still relatively healthy, save for the Alzheimer's that had begun to erode her memory several years past.

"This is Detective Broussard from the Sheriff's Office, Clarice," Donna Goldberg, the facility's head nurse, said loudly for the second time. "She needs to ask you some questions."

Clarice chuckled. "Well, good luck with that, my dear!" she said, reaching out to pat Annie's arm. "I don't always remember things anymore. That's what happens when you get old. The parts start wearing out, starting right up here," she said, tapping her temple with a finger gnarled by arthritis. "Come sit down, you!"

She shuffled her way to a brown velvet recliner that sat with its mate tucked into the alcove of a bay window that looked out on a broad lawn studded with live oak trees heavily draped in moss. Annie chose to sit on a wheeled ottoman so she could get closer to the woman and hopefully avoid the need to shout. The nurse excused herself to see to her duties, closing the door on her way out.

"I don't care for that one," Clarice said, making a face. "She's bossy. Thinks she knows everything. She give me a tin of stale cookies on my birthday, like I wouldn't know the difference. Hard as rocks! Bought them at the drugstore, if you can imagine that! Giving people stale cookies from the Walgreens! Talk about! You wouldn't do that, would you, dear?"

"No, ma'am."

"You was raised good right here, yes?"

"Yes, ma'am. Right here in Bayou Breaux."

"That one, I think she's not from here. Maybe she don't know no better. Maybe she's from up north."

"Maybe. You have a lovely home, Mrs. Marcel," Annie said, glancing around. The entire place could be seen from right where she sat—a tiny kitchenette on one end of a living area furnished with generic oak pieces and a flat-screen TV tuned to a home improvement show, a single bedroom, and a bathroom wafting out the cloying scent of some flowery air freshener through the partially opened door.

Annie swallowed against the urge to gag.

"Oh, it's not my home," Clarice corrected her. "I have a lovely home, but I don't recall how to get to it. I lived there with my husband. He passed, God rest him. No one here will take me back to my house. I asked Genevieve, but she don't know how to get there either. She's not from here.

"Where is she?" she asked. "Do you know? She didn't come dress me this morning. That fat Hebert girl, she dress me today. Look at this!" she said with disgust, gesturing to her mauve velour tracksuit.

"You look very nice," Annie said.

"Bah! These aren't my clothes! Where is my Genevieve? She get my right clothes. She's a good girl. She's my sister, you know."

"Your niece, you mean?"

"My niece?"

"Genevieve Gauthier. Your niece," Annie said, though she assumed the term was not technically accurate. The age difference made it implausible. Clarice Marcel was eighty-five. Genevieve Gauthier was twenty-seven. She was more likely a great-niece. Still, Annie asked, "Is she your sister's daughter? Or brother's?"

Clarice Marcel blinked at her. "What you talking 'bout, *cher*? I don't have a brother."

Annie took a deep breath and started over. "Mrs. Marcel, Genevieve isn't here today because she was injured last night. She's in the hospital. She'll be all right, but she won't be to work for a few days. Maybe a week or more."

"Oh, no!" the old woman said with genuine distress. "What happened to her? Was she in a car accident?"

"No, ma'am. I'm afraid not. Someone hurt her."

Tears rose in Clarice Marcel's eyes. She pressed a wrinkled hand to her cheek. "Who would hurt my Genevieve? She's a good girl! Who would do such a thing?"

"We don't know yet," Annie said. "But we're looking into it. That's my job. I'm a detective with the Sheriff's Office."

"You're a detective? *Mais non!*" she exclaimed with a mix of amusement and disbelief. "A purty girl like you, *cher*? *Non!* That's a man's job, that!"

"I am. I swear," Annie assured her, showing the woman her badge. "I'm trying to find out who might have wanted to hurt Genevieve. Did she ever tell you if anyone was bothering her?"

"*Mais non.* She never said such a thing. I told her, you find you a good man, Genevieve, and you hang on to him 'cause most of them ain't worth a damn. She already knew that."

"Did she tell you about any bad man in particular?"

She made a face and shook her head. "She's a quiet girl, that one. But she had her heart broke, for sure. I can see that, even with my old eyes."

She reached over to the end table that squatted between the two recliners, picked up a small, framed photo, and held it out to Annie. "Here we are. Once a week she dress me up nice and we go out for lunch."

Annie looked at the photo. Clarice Marcel in a lavender sweater set and a long gauzy summer skirt, and Genevieve Gauthier, in capri pants and a simple black top, her slender arm wrapped carefully around the older woman's frail shoulders. It was hard to reconcile that image with the image of the battered woman Annie had left at Our Lady just a few hours earlier. The young woman in the picture was pretty, with soulful brown eyes and a shy smile. The two women stood in a gravel parking lot in front of a long two-story wood-frame building with a wide front porch. A placard in the window behind them read ICI ON PARLE FRAN-CAIS. Annie's eyebrows rose as recognition dawned.

"You go out to the Corners for lunch?" she asked.

"Sometimes. They got good fish, them. All the time fresh, their fish. And a good gumbo."

"I know," Annie said. "I grew up there. Sos and Fanchon Doucet raised me."

"Oh!" Clarice looked delighted. She wagged a finger at Annie. "That Sos, he's a rascal, him!"

Annie laughed. "Yes, he is."

She could easily imagine Uncle Sos laying on the Cajun charm with Mrs. Marcel and her young companion. He loved to play the host to ladies, young and old—not in a predatory way but because he genuinely loved women of all shapes, sizes, ages, and races. He was a champion flirt and considered it his duty and his calling. Tante Fanchon had always just smiled and shook her head. *"That's just Sos,* chérie," she would say, waving a hand as if to shoo away any concerns. *"He wants every woman to feel beautiful, but me most of all."*

And that was true. Annie had never known two people more in love, more devoted, than the two of them.

"Are they well?" Clarice asked. "I don't remember when I saw them last."

"Fanchon had a stroke this summer."

"I'm sorry to hear that."

"Thank you. It was a hard few months," Annie said. "But she's doing better now."

"Getting old isn't for wimps, *cher*," Clarice said. "Me, I used to be all the time on the go. Then I fell and hurt my hip. Now I sit in here like a bird in a cage. Genevieve, she flies around for me."

"She runs errands for you?"

"*Oui.* Me, I pay her a little extra on the side. She don't want no money for it, but I give her some, just the same. She's a good girl, her."

"Does she pick up your medications for you?"

"Sometimes. And she goes to the grocery. She picks up my maple leaf cookies that I like. Would you like one?"

"No, thank you, ma'am."

"Well, I think I'm out of them, anyway. Genevieve, she gonna bring them. Maybe today," she said hopefully. "Maybe later."

"Genevieve won't be coming today," Annie reminded her. "She's in the hospital. Someone hurt her last night."

She hoped to God the woman didn't ask about Genevieve's son. It was hard enough to explain the one tragedy.

Clarice let out a soft sigh as she took the photograph back from Annie.

"Oh, no, that's too bad," she said, touching Genevieve's face in the picture. "Bad things happen to my poor Genevieve. She's too pretty to be all the time so sad, *pauvre 'tite bête.*"

PAUVRE 'TITE BÊTE . . . Poor little thing . . .

Something in the quality of Clarice Marcel's voice—the sadness, the pity, the patina of age—took Annie instantly back in time to the day she had learned of her mother's death. She was a little girl, nine years old, just back from her first-ever vacation trip with Uncle Sos and Tante Fanchon. The doting surrogate grandparents, they had taken her to Disney World, and it had been the most wonderful, magical, happiest time of her young life. And then they had come home to the Corners, where Annie and her mother lived in the apartment above the store and café, to be greeted by the parish priest with the news that Marie Broussard had taken her own life. Out of sight and out of mind, Annie's mother had quietly slipped the bonds of a burden she had never shared with anyone.

How many times had Annie heard those whispered words of pity in the days that had followed? A hundred or more as family and friends had come calling on the Doucets. Fanchon and Sos had taken Marie in when she was pregnant and destitute, a stray cat from who-knew-where, and loved her like the daughter they never had. Now Marie had gone and left them behind with her fatherless child. *Pauvre 'tite bête . . .*

Poor little thing . . . Annie could still see them in her mind's eye from the perspective of a child, looking up at the sad faces, the sorrowful eyes. She was the poor little dear, the child abandoned by the woman who had sheltered her from whatever truth she had herself been unable to bear. Even as a child Annie had seen the irony, even if she hadn't known what to call it.

Those same adults had doubtless used those same words to describe Marie Broussard, herself, when she had been alive. *Poor Marie. Poor little thing, all the time so sad.* Poor Marie, locked inside herself with her secrets.

The picture of Annie's mother easily morphed into the picture of Genevieve Gauthier, another young woman with a secret sadness in her eyes and a past that cast a shadow over her present. Had that past come calling in the night? Had it taken her boy instead of her life?

". . . hey, Earth to 'Toinette!"

Annie startled back to the moment. She sat behind the wheel of her SUV in the Evangeline Oaks parking lot, swamped by the memories and the heat. She hadn't bothered to turn on the car. Hadn't thought of it, she'd been so lost in her own head.

Nick reached in through the open window and touched her cheek with the back of his hand. "Are you okay?"

"I'm fine. I was just . . . lost . . . thinking," she corrected herself.

"*Bébé*, start the car," he chided gently. "It's hot. Your face is flushed."

Annie turned the key in the ignition and breathed a sigh of relief at the cool air that rushed out the vents. She took a deep breath, glad to bring her attention back to the moment at hand, to the sounds of birds and traffic, to the sight of her husband and the view of Veterans Park across the street.

"What did you find out?" Nick asked, leaning his forearms on the window frame.

"The head nurse says they dispense all of Clarice Marcel's meds because of her Alzheimer's, but she had a fall a couple of months ago while she was out of the facility with Genevieve. Genevieve went with her to the ER. That's probably where the 'script for the Oxy came from."

"She didn't turn the pills over to the nurse?"

"Clarice refuses strong drugs. She doesn't want anything more than Tylenol. So the ER doc might have written her the 'script, but the nurse here wouldn't have been looking for those pills."

"So Genevieve wound up with that prescription. Serendipitous for her," Nick said. "Find out from the pharmacy if she ever had it refilled. Or she might have duped it at another pharmacy. Call around."

"But you only found the one bottle?" Annie asked.

"Far as I know. I haven't looked at the inventory from the house."

"If she's pharmacy hopping, there should be multiple bottles."

"Not if she's selling those pills—or using heavily herself. Stokes said he also found some random loose Vicodin in the medicine cabinet. Did the nurse say anything about drugs going missing in general?"

"She said no, but she was slow to answer," Annie said. "I'm sure that's not a rumor they want floating around town. Won't look good on the sales brochure: *Retire to Evangeline Oaks, where our staff will rip off your meds.*"

"That'd be some bad publicity," Nick agreed. "Avery said they're getting ready for some big state inspection. He needs everything here to look shipshape."

"As an aide, Genevieve is in and out of a lot of different apartments," Annie said. "Residents who are more independent than Mrs. Marcel take care of their own medications. It would be a simple thing to pick up a pill or two here and there. But I should think the administration would have been quick to fire her if they thought there was a problem like that."

Nick hummed a note. "Maybe, maybe not."

"Something going on with the boss?" Annie asked, and sighed. "Oh, I do hate a cliché."

"That story line is a cliché for a reason," he pointed out. "He does seem to have more than a passing interest in her. Mr. Happily Married Man, he didn't like me poking around that subject."

Annie arched an eyebrow. "And if someone suggested to you that you were fooling around on me, what would your reaction be?"

"They'd be picking their teeth up off the ground," he said with a wry smile. "But that's not what I got from him. I got a lot of puffed-up outrage on the heels of some lame excuses. There's plenty more to that story."

"For what it's worth, the office manager champions him as the perfect pillar of the community and a God-fearing Christian man."

"That only makes me want to double down on the idea, given his level of discomfort with me. Adulterous guilt shouldn't sit well on the shoulders of a religious man."

"Well, Miss Mavis believes he walks on water and multiplies loaves and fishes on the weekends," Annie said. "She does *not* like Genevieve. At all. While Mrs. Marcel thinks Genevieve is an angel."

"Avery had all good things to say about her. Called her a model employee."

"And Miss Mavis claims Genevieve is perpetually late to work and suffers no repercussions for it. Genevieve's supervisor, Nurse Goldberg, falls somewhere in the middle. She gives Genevieve a B-plus for her work and extra credit for the time she spends with Mrs. Marcel."

"But no one has any idea who might have wanted to hurt this girl," Nick said, frowning.

"Not a clue. Not a word about an ex or current boyfriend. According to her supervisor, she doesn't seem to be close with any of the other aides here. She does her work and goes home. No one here seems to know anything about her social life, if she has one."

"She had one once," Nick pointed out. "Maybe it came up from Dulac for a visit last night."

"Let's go to the office and regroup," he said. "We should have some background on her and the boy by now."

As he started to step back from the car door, a news van pulled into the parking lot, halting not more than ten feet in front of Annie's SUV, blocking her way out. Her heart sank, knowing exactly what was about to go down.

"That didn't take long," she muttered, looking to Nick for his reaction. She could feel his tension instantly as he straightened away from the car door, his shoulders squaring and flexing, as if he was preparing for a physical fight.

"Detective Fourcade! Detective Fourcade, can we have a word?" The reporter was shouting at him before her feet even hit the pavement as she all but tumbled out the passenger door of the van.

Kimberly Karstares was instantly recognizable by her bottle-blond, spray-starched mane and the predatory gleam in her eyes. From the waist up she was dressed for the camera in a red blouse and too much makeup. From the waist down, white shorts revealed a mile of tan legs. She wore neon green running shoes, advertising her willingness to literally chase down a story if she had to. An ambitious rising star at one of the Lafayette stations, she had been a thorn in Nick's side for months with regard to the Theriot case.

"Detective Fourcade, can we get a comment from you on last night's murder of the Gauthier boy?"

"No, you may not." He stood like a statue, feet apart, jaw set, his sunglasses hiding a glare that might have made Kimberly Karstares think twice if she had had the sense to do so.

"Don't you want to make some kind of appeal to the public for information?" she asked, microphone in hand as she stepped too close.

"Sheriff Dutrow has already done so."

"But you're the lead detective on this case. Don't you—"

"You should stay out of my way while I see to it then, yes?" he said, his voice a low growl.

"How are you supposed to investigate this murder while you still have no resolution in the Theriot sexual assault case?"

"Crimes don't wait their turns to be committed, Ms. Karstares," Nick said. "Nor do they wait their turns to be solved."

The reporter glanced over her shoulder for her videographer, a young man with a bad complexion and a camera perched on his shoulder. He hustled toward them from the back of the van, hiking at the waist of his baggy jeans with one hand.

"Clovis, get up here!" Karstares snapped. "Are you rolling?"

"I am!"

She turned back to Nick, thrusting the microphone at him like a fool poking a stick at a tiger. "Detective, would you please repeat what you just said so we can get that on camera?"

"No."

"Have you spoken with the Theriot family about this? Are they aware you'll be abandoning their daughter's case as you take charge of this investigation?"

Annie wanted to jump out of the car and snatch Kimberly Karstares by her hair extensions. Instead, she said loudly, "Detective Fourcade, we need to go! We have a briefing to get to."

Nick remained still save for a muscle pulsing in his jaw.

"Let's go!" Annie prodded. "Sheriff's waiting!"

"Duty calls, Ms. Karstares," he said quietly. "Report that. Detectives couldn't be bothered to comment as they were busy trying to solve the crime."

He stalked past her and around the hood of the SUV. As the reporter started to give chase, Annie revved the engine and leaned hard on the horn, sending the woman bolting sideways.

"Y'all have to move that van!" Annie shouted out the window. "Preventing us from leaving is interfering with the business of the Sheriff's Office."

Karstares's eyes narrowed, and she hustled back around toward Annie on the driver's side of the vehicle, the hapless Clovis the cameraman stumbling to keep up with her.

"And you are?" she asked curtly, as if she had a right to know.

Annie held up her badge. "Broussard. Direct your questions to Sheriff Dutrow's office. They'll be all too happy to entertain you."

"I'm not looking to be entertained. I'm looking for the truth."

"Well, isn't that funny? That's our job, too," Annie said as Nick got in on the passenger's side and slammed the door. "We'll let you know soon as we find it."

"Broussard . . . ?" Karstares said, realization dawning alongside derision. "Oooh. You're the *wife*."

"It's *Detective* Broussard," Annie said. "And you're out of line, Blondie. Now move that van before I call to have it impounded. And don't think I won't."

"The people have a right to know what's going on when their Sheriff's Office can't keep them safe in their own homes," Karstares snapped in a parting shot, even as she backed toward the news van.

Behind the shield of the dashboard, Annie flipped her off with both hands. Karstares said something through the window to her driver and the van rolled forward just enough to let Annie squeak by.

"Drink that bleach next time instead of putting it on your hair, you nasty piece of business," Annie grumbled, glaring at the reporter in the rearview mirror.

Nick looked over at her as they turned onto the street, his expression unreadable.

"Are you mad at me?" Annie asked, watching him out the corner of her eye.

"Because you thought I needed saving? Again. No." He shook his head. "That's hardly the first time that's happened. Won't be the last. How can I fault you? Your brave heart is the first thing I fell in love with, you know.

"I remember the night you came up to me at Laveau's back when," he said. "I'd had too much whiskey and too much bullshit, and you were scared to death of me, but you stepped right up and had your say, just the same."

Annie smiled at the memory. She had been terrified—of him, of what she wanted to ask of him, of where that might lead. She had wanted in on his murder investigation when she was just a deputy and so low on the totem pole she should have carried an umbrella to deflect all the piss rained down on her from above.

"But this is liable to get ugly, you know," he said. "I can take it. I don't want them going after you because you're my wife. If we can't solve this murder in a hurry, Dutrow will figure it reflects badly on him, and that will be my fault. He'll be all too happy to take it out on me any way he can, including turning the media on me like a pack of starving dogs. He don't want them near me now, as long as there is still the potential for him to look the hero, but that's not gonna stop them coming at me."

"You don't deserve it," Annie said, knowing it wouldn't matter. The mix of anger and helplessness made her want to hit something.

"Well, in terms of karma, we don't know what I might deserve—"

"Stop it," she snapped. "I don't want to hear about how you were some kind of badass ninja in a past life, therefore . . . I know who you are in this life, in *my* life, in our son's life. I know what *we* deserve. And I'll be damned if I sit quietly by and let Aqua Net Barbie try to use you for a stepping-stone out of East Ass-Crack, Lou'siana, on her way to some imaginary stardom."

A sudden smile split Nick's face, as surprising and dazzling as the sun bursting forth in the middle of a storm.

Annie scowled at him as she slowed the SUV for the turn into the law enforcement center. "Don't you dare be amused at me, Nick Fourcade."

"You're something else, 'Toinette," he murmured. "My tigress."

She hit the blinker and glanced over at him as she waited for oncoming traffic to pass. "Don't you forget it, mister."

FIFTEEN

The Partout Parish Law Enforcement Center had been built in the late 1960s. The SO had long since outgrown the main building, purchasing the property adjacent from a road construction outfit in the '90s, turning the heavy equipment yard into an impound lot and giving the construction office over to the detective division for their exclusive use.

Known to all as the Pizza Hut—in homage to the many pies delivered there over the years—it was a low, snot-green concrete block building, still sporting the original bars on the windows and doors, as if anyone might choose to break in on a pack of gun-wielding cops. Inside, one large, open front office housed a bullpen of detectives at half a dozen beat-up steel desks, only two of them occupied as Nick opened the door.

Stefon Quinlan glanced up from his computer screen in acknowledgment, a telephone receiver pressed between his meaty shoulder and his ear as his thick fingers tapped his keyboard. A fine sheen of sweat gleamed on his dark bald head, giving lie to the noisy efforts of the two window air-conditioners in the back wall.

Nick looked past him to Wynn Dixon, their resident techie. Tall, rawboned, and red-haired, she had been dubbed with the obvious nick-name Winn-Dixie (after the supermarket chain) by Stokes when she had first come on board with the team a year past. As the newbie, she had been too diplomatic to object. Now it was too late. The name had stuck with every man in the SO whose sense of humor hadn't advanced past the ninth grade—which was most of them.

Nick had no tolerance for such foolishness. He had assessed Dixon's abilities as a detective, pinpointed her specialties, and used her accordingly on his cases. She knew her way in and around every conceivable database available to them and could track a paper trail like a blood-hound on a scent.

"Dixon, what you got?" he asked, taking a stance at the end of her desk, his arms crossed over his chest. Annie snagged a chair from the next desk over, rolling it close enough to look at Dixon's computer screen.

"Genevieve Gauthier: no wants, no warrants," Dixon said. "She does have a record. Mostly petty stuff. A couple convictions on shoplifting, one for check kiting, one disturbing the peace. She does have two convictions for driving under the influence—"

"When was that?" Nick asked. "The DUI."

"One eight years ago. One a year ago."

"Any drug charges?"

"Misdemeanor possession of a controlled substance. Looks like that went together with the first DUI. The charge was dismissed."

"Dig into that. Find the arrest record. I want to know what the substance was and how much she had on her. See if she was actually charged with the misdemeanor."

Annie arched an eyebrow at him. "From eight years ago?"

"If she had enough of whatever it was on her that she could have been charged, then got to plead down for some reason, A: she might have flipped on somebody to get that deal, and B: she for sure had known associates who provided that substance to her, yes? Who's to say she might not still have the attention of one of those people? Maybe last night was payback."

"That seems a long stretch."

Nick shrugged. "*C'est vrai*, but what's to lose? We're just digging in the dirt at this point. Let's see what we scratch up. Maybe nothing, maybe something. All it costs us is a little of Detective Dixon's time. You don't mind, do you, Detective?"

"No, sir," Dixon said. "Anything you need—for this case, especially. I have three nephews. This hits too close to home."

"Did you find the birth certificate on the Gauthier boy?" Annie asked.

"Yes. He was born at Terrebonne General Medical Center in Houma to Genevieve Gauthier. No father listed."

"No marriage licenses, divorce decrees, anything like that with her name on them?" Nick asked.

"No."

"I want to know if she's ever been a victim of a crime," he said. "Specifically, domestic violence or sexual assault. Has she ever taken out a restraining order on anyone, that kind of thing."

"I'm on it, boss."

"I want hard copies on everything. And call me immediately when the results come in on her tox screen."

He turned and went down the hall to what had at one time probably been the construction foreman's office in the building's past life. Nick had commandeered the room for himself upon his promotion, not because he fancied himself an executive but because he needed a retreat from the noise and personalities of the bullpen. He needed to be able to step away and just be still, to gather his thoughts and his focus.

He thought of Jeff Avery's office as he walked in—messy, crowded with clutter and obvious reminders of who the man was and how he had gotten there. Nick had no wall of fame displaying his diplomas and citations. He kept nothing personal in the room at all. No mementos, no photos of his family. His private life was not for public display. His desk was immaculate, orderly, with nothing extraneous on the surface. A pair of simple straight chairs served anyone needing to speak privately with him—utilitarian, but not inviting a visitor to linger.

The only visitor invited to stay in this office was the kitten from the Gauthier house, curled up sleeping in a towel-lined box under the desk. The kitten had moved in lock, stock, and litter box.

Along one wall filing cabinets squatted beneath a long countertop where the paperwork related to his pertinent cases was all perfectly organized. The wall opposite his desk was taken up by a large whiteboard, on it his meticulously handwritten notes on his most prominent case of the moment—before today—the Vanessa Theriot case.

He had taped a photo of the girl in the middle of the board and stood in front of it now, staring at the thirteen-year-old, a dark current of emotion pulling at him. It was a school photo, though Vanessa did not attend a traditional school. Her parents worked three jobs between them so they could afford to send their daughter to a special facility for severely autistic children in Lafayette.

Even in a photograph Vanessa couldn't make eye contact. Her gaze went not to the camera, nor to the photographer, but up and to the left. Her expression was that of a child mesmerized by something she couldn't understand. Nick always had the feeling she was seeing something no one else could see, something wondrous in another dimension.

Vanessa was just reaching puberty and her features had begun to morph from the soft roundness of childhood to hint at the angles and lines of the young woman she would become. Her thick, dark hair had been pulled back on one side with a barrette to show off the small pearl pierced earrings she had gotten for her birthday that year—a momentous event, her mother had said.

As detached as she was from the world around her much of the time, Vanessa still sometimes showed an interest in the things her older sister liked—pretty things like jewelry and hair ribbons. She liked to make art and dance to pop music and giggle like any teenage girl. At least, she had done. Before.

Nick hadn't been allowed to see Vanessa Theriot in weeks. Her parents wouldn't have it. There was no point in it from an investigative standpoint. The girl couldn't or wouldn't speak to him—or to anyone else, for that matter. She hadn't told him what had happened to her or given him any idea who might have molested her. Her communication with her parents, primarily with her mother, consisted of little more than guttural sounds of emotion: need, comfort, discomfort, excitement, fear.

Her existence was largely internal. No one had a key to that world. Vanessa lived there alone.

Nick understood that, as well or better than most. He had always fiercely guarded his internal life, even as boy. That was just who he was. When he was small, his mother had referred to him as *petit homme de mystère*—her little man of mystery. Very few people had ever been invited past even the first of his fortress walls.

Someone had trespassed on Vanessa Theriot's barriers and violated her—not in an attack a detective or a doctor would categorize as brutal or violent, as wrong as that sounded. Her physical injuries had been minor, thank God, nothing but a few bruises on her thighs and some minor vaginal bruising. The assailant had penetrated her with the handle of a hairbrush—an act she had later pantomimed to her mother—but not viciously, seemingly not with the intent to punish or damage.

That as a detective he had to make those distinctions objectively offended Nick deeply, personally, beyond the law and order aspect of the case. He believed any breach of personal boundaries was inherently violent, existentially speaking. The lasting damage was to the fabric of one's being, to the veil of trust, to the shell of self-image, to the pillar of confidence. Those things could not be altered by force and ever return to their original shape. It wasn't possible. The damage was done. And how much worse that had to be for Vanessa, who had no real means to express what she felt or to grasp the tools conventional psychotherapy could offer to help her heal herself.

The frustration that he had been unable to do anything to at least avenge her was like a hard lump in Nick's throat that he could neither swallow nor dislodge. He wanted nothing more than to bring to justice the person who had hurt Vanessa Theriot, but the case had gone nowhere. They had no witnesses, no DNA. A couple of random unknown fingerprints in the girl's bedroom had not found a match in any database.

That frustration was no stranger to him. He understood the anger of Vanessa's parents better than they would ever know. He knew what it was to lose a loved one. He knew what it did to the family to have their questions go unanswered, to have justice hang in the limbo of not knowing. He knew the helplessness and the misplaced guilt. He knew the whys and the what-ifs and the if-onlys. He knew there was no escape from any of that and that the only thing that even marginally relieved the pressure was to vent it onto someone else—namely the detective in charge of the case.

His sister, Justine, had been a sophomore at LSU in Baton Rouge, studying to become a teacher for children with special needs. Had she lived, she would have been helping kids like Vanessa. A beautiful girl, sweet, funny, the apple of their father's eye, Justine had gone out for a run one fall evening and never returned to her dorm. Her body had been found two days later in the underbrush off a jogging path in a park just off campus. She had been raped and murdered and dumped like a sack of trash. The crime had gone unsolved for years.

Just seventeen at the time, Nick had watched the stress and strain and heartache of not knowing, of never being able to see their daughter's killer punished, destroy his parents. Racked by grief and anger, his father had died of a heart attack two years after Justine's murder. His mother had been heartbroken, and her health had failed. She passed less than a year later. Their family had disintegrated, all of them victims of the faceless predator who had taken Justine Fourcade's life.

Nick knew what the Theriots were going through just as well as he knew that, until something shook loose in the case, there wasn't a goddamn thing he could do about it.

"You're not abandoning her," Annie said softly.

She stood in the doorway, not five feet away. Too far. He could have stood to put his arms around her for a while, to feel her arms around him, but that wasn't an option, not here.

"I know," he said on a sigh. "That doesn't make it easier to have to set her aside for the time being. And it certainly won't make it easier to explain it to Bobby Theriot."

"You can only do what you can do when you can do it. Focus on the task at hand, Fourcade. Murder trumps everything."

He gave her a look from under his eyebrows. "How'd you get to be so smart?"

A little smile turned the corners of her mouth. "I have an excellent mentor. He's a hard-ass, to be sure, but he knows his stuff."

"You learn well."

"I'm a work in progress."

"So are we all, *cher*," he murmured. "That journey has no end."

"Well, my journey is taking me out of here," she said. "I'm going to try to track down Genevieve's babysitter, see if she noticed anything out of the ordinary yesterday."

"Good."

"Don't expect too much insight," she warned. "She's twelve."

"*Years old? Mon Dieu.* She left her child with a child?"

"Just for a couple of hours after school," Annie explained. "Jaime said the girl collected KJ when school let out and entertained him until Genevieve got off work. It's not much of a thread, but I'll give it a tug."

"Tug away. Are you picking Justin up?"

"No, Remy is. He's taking the kids out to the Corners for supper with Fanchon and Sos. I had a feeling we could be in for a late night. If not, we can always go get him."

"Tell Remy I'll stop by later one way or the other," Nick said, going to his desk. His next job would be downloading the crime scene photos of KJ Gauthier's murder from his camera to his computer. Already his memory was calling the pictures up in his mind: the boy lying dead on the floor in his Spider-Man pajamas, his kitten rubbing against his lifeless little foot. "I'm not going this day without hugging my son."

HE LOOKED AT the photographs on his monitor one by one as he orga-nized them into a folder for the case, duplicating, cropping, enlarging, zooming in on individual wounds, making notations, and jotting down questions as he went.

In photographs, the dead never looked real. Crime scenes always looked like scenes from a movie. Absent the smell of death, absent the lingering air of fear and violence and evil, Nick could more easily sepa-rate himself from the emotions that saturated a death scene. And still it was all he could do to keep the rage at bay looking at the photos of KJ Gauthier.

He worked hard to focus on what the sequence of events must have been. The assumption was that the killer had come in through the open bedroom window—the point of least resistance in a house where half the windows were painted shut. That was the assumption. Because of the rain, they didn't have any physical evidence from outside that window to confirm the assumption. If the universe was feeling benevolent, they might get a hit on fingerprints from the window frame. Nick wasn't going to hold his breath for that.

Had the assailant known the child would be there in that room? If the answer was yes, then he was probably known to the family or had at the very least cased the place on a prior occasion and was familiar with the layout of the house and the habits of its occupants.

Judging by the blood spatter, the attack had initiated on the bed, meaning the assailant had come armed. Thinking of the wounds he had observed on the dead boy's body at the morgue—small with clean, smooth edges—his educated guess was that the weapon was a sharp knife with a narrow blade. Something like a boning knife as opposed to a hunting knife.

The child must have awakened, possibly made a sound. Otherwise, why not just creep through the room and go on to Genevieve? The killer had struck the boy in a frenzy, in a panic. The child had struggled, had made it out of the bed. The blood told the story.

An inexperienced killer, Nick thought. It didn't take ten or more strikes to kill a small child if the killer was calm and focused. The wounds were all over—the face, the neck, the chest. One or two stabs to the chest would have done the job. One slice across the throat would have ended life in an instant.

An inexperienced killer—or an emotional one.

Overkill was always an indicator of emotion—anger, hatred, fear, sexual excitement (stabbing was commonly considered a sexually motivated method of killing, depending on the victim). This murder didn't appear in any other way to be sexual in nature, though nothing was outside the realm of possibility. Nick had seen firsthand that there was no bottom to the depths of depravity in mankind. He had seen children used and abused in the most horrific ways imaginable—beyond the imagining of most right-minded people. But he didn't feel that was the case here. KJ Gauthier lay on the floor of his room, his pajamas undisturbed, his body unmolested save for the stab wounds.

Genevieve said she had awakened to her son's cries. She fell and struck her head getting out of bed. Did that fall account for her black eye and concussion?

She proceeded to go into the hall, going toward her son's bedroom, and saw a figure standing in the hall, brandishing a knife, but the assailant allowed her to continue into her son's room.

She saw KJ on the floor. There was blood everywhere, she said. How did she see the blood? Had KJ's nightlight and the moonlight coming through the window been sufficient?

She fell to the floor and pulled him to her—which explained the blood that soaked the T-shirt she had been wearing when she had arrived at the hospital.

The shirt was now hanging on a clothesline in Evidence, drying. Because Dutrow had nixed the call to the LSP to process the scene, the shirt would now go with the other testable evidence gathered to the regional Acadiana Criminalistics Lab in New Iberia—a facility besieged by budget cuts and staff reductions, which meant backlogs and longer wait times for results. But he couldn't allow that frustration to distract him just now. He had to remain focused on putting together a probable scenario for what had happened to Genevieve Gauthier and her son.

Genevieve said she had gone to her child and the assailant then entered the bedroom and came at her with the knife.

Here the story became very sketchy, far less detailed—which could have easily been attributed to panic. Nick had to try to envision the scene and imagine the details that would fill in the blanks. Was Genevieve kneeling on the floor with her son in her arms when the assailant came into the room? With the position of his body on the floor beside the bed, she would have had her back to the door.

Nick visualized the assailant's point of view, coming through that door. Two steps and he would have been plunging the knife into her back or grabbing her hair, yanking her head back and slitting her throat. If his intent had been sexual assault, he would have easily gained control of her there. How had she gotten away? How had she even gained her feet?

She said she pulled her son against her and screamed. If she was screaming, she wouldn't have heard footsteps coming. Could her angle have been such that she could have caught a blur of movement out the corner of her eye?

She had somehow gotten to her feet. There had been a struggle. A struggle between a concussed, unarmed woman who weighed 115 pounds, according to her driver's license, and an armed assailant of undetermined size, presumed to be male, yet she had managed to fend him off. How? With what?

At some point during that struggle, someone had touched the wall near the door, leaving what might have been a partial handprint. Nick clicked on the enlarged photo and stared at it. He guessed the shape was maybe the lower third of a hand, but there were no whorls or ridges indicative of flesh. Nor was there the smooth smearing that might have suggested a glove.

The struggle had continued through the door and down the hall, into the front room. Genevieve had managed to make it to the front door, unlock it, and get out. She had fled down the gravel road, barefoot, to Roddie Perez's house.

Why hadn't the killer run her down? Had she somehow managed to injure him in the struggle? Had he weighed the possibility of the neighbor intervening or calling 911 and decided it wasn't worth the risk?

Or was *he* the neighbor?

But if Roddie Perez had perpetrated the attack, why then wouldn't he have finished the job?

Releasing a big sigh, Nick stood up, stretched, and rubbed his hands over his face. He needed coffee and wanted a cigarette. He would settle for the first.

Quinlan had gone from the bullpen, leaving Dixon alone, still clacking away on her computer.

"Got anything for me yet?" Nick asked, pouring himself a cup of coffee from the pot on the counter. God only knew how long it had been sitting there. It was black and bitter, and the caffeine hit him in the head like a hammer.

"I'm not sure," she said, her attention on her monitor. "I'm looking into that possession charge. It shows up in one place but not in another. I mean in one universe, that was part of the arrest, and the charge was dismissed, and in another universe, it never happened at all."

"Clerical error?"

"Could be. Must be."

"Keep at it. See if you can get hold of the original arrest report."

"I can't find it in the database."

"Then call the arresting agency and see if someone might dig it up for you. Gotta be in the archives somewhere."

"I'll try harder," Dixon said. "I also found she has a juvenile record. Do you want me to look into that, too?"

"The other is the priority—"

The office door swung open and Stokes made his usual entrance, looking left and right for an audience.

"Winn-Dixie! Where y'at? What's the special of the day? You got something sweet for me?"

Dixon didn't bat an eye. "The big fat knuckle sandwich with a side of whoop-ass."

Stokes grabbed an apple out of the basket on the counter and polished it on his chest. "Damn, girl, you crush my heart on a daily basis."

"Then why ain't you dead yet?"

"Enough with the sexual harassment," Nick growled at Stokes. "If Dixon makes me write you up, I'm gonna kick your ass. I got no time for bullshit now."

"It's not sexual harassment," Stokes argued. "Winn-Dixie and I have an understanding. Just a little teasing among friends. Am I right, or am I right?"

"Right," Dixon said, a smile tugging at one side of her mouth. "I understand you're an aging dinosaur who doesn't know any better."

"*Aging?!*" Stokes winced. "Ouch!"

"Truth hurts, *mon ami*," Nick remarked. "Now, did you just come in here to act a fool, or have you got something to say that isn't legally actionable?"

Stokes took a big bite out of the apple, nodding. "I came to take you away from all of this, my friend. I tracked down Miz Gauthier's landlord, Mr. Roy Carville. Turns out he keeps some interesting company."

"Such as?"

"Everybody's favorite drug dealer, Roddie Perez."

SIXTEEN

Club Cayenne squatted on the industrial edge of Bayou Breaux, convenient to a liquor store that offered check cashing, and half a dozen businesses with predominantly male employees—welders, pipe fitters, heavy-equipment mechanics, and the like. The building was long and low, made of concrete block, and painted purple, with a roof of rusted corrugated tin. Neon signs in the dark windows advertised Bud Light and topless dancers.

Stokes pulled the Charger into a handicapped parking spot near the door, killed the engine, and flipped down the visor with the sticker for the Sheriff's Office on it.

"Trust you to know what lowlifes are hanging out at the topless bars," Nick remarked.

"Excuse me!" Stokes exclaimed with a show of offense, pressing a hand to his chest like an old woman with the vapors. "I'll have you know I am a patron of the arts. I have a fine appreciation for modern dance."

"Uh-huh."

"I take it upon myself to encourage these young ladies in this formative stage of their careers."

"That's mighty big of you."

"Just trying to contribute to humanity, you know what I'm saying? Giving back to the community."

"You're a regular philanthropist, I'm sure."

Nick shook his head and climbed out of the car. He had spotted Roddie Perez's matte black four-by-four truck at the far end of the crushed-shell parking lot as they had approached the bar. He walked down to it now and circled it. It was a nice truck, newer and nicer than an ex-con on disability should have been able to afford. A drug dealer, on the other hand . . . A small red light blinked on the rearview mirror, indicating the alarm was on.

He went over to the dumpster at the end of the building, pulled a bottle crate out of the pile beside it, took it back, and used it for a step so he could peer inside without touching the truck.

The interior of the cab was as much of a mess as Perez's kitchen— junk mail and fast food bags, an ashtray full of butts, a couple of empty crushed beer cans on the floor of the passenger's side.

"The man is a pig," Nick announced. "And that's an insult to pigs."

"He got anything good in there we can bust him for?" Stokes asked. "Guns? Drugs? A kidnapped woman?"

"No such luck. He's a slob, but he's not stupid. What's him being here seeing the sights got to do with Roy Carville?"

"Carville brothers own this place. T-Rex and Roy. 'Course there's about eighty-two Carvilles 'round these parts, three or four of them named Roy. It took a couple of phone calls to get pointed to this one. As I was driving up, I see Roddie heading inside. I figured you might want to tag along."

"You never saw Perez here before?"

"Contrary to your low opinion of me, I don't spend all that much time here."

"Only because you prefer strippers to topless dancers."

"A better value for my hard-earned dollar."

"You're a practical man," Nick remarked. He hopped down off the crate and took it back to where he'd gotten it.

Cold beer and naked dancing girls being a siren song on a stifling hot day, the parking lot was filling up with men whose work shift had ended at three. The smell of sweat, beer, and cigarettes filled the entrance to the club like a thick, acrid perfume.

Nick followed Stokes in, shoving his sunglasses on top of his head and scanning the scene. The music was loud and lively swamp pop—Waylon Thibodeaux's apropos "My Baby Don't Wear No Drawers." The air temperature was frigid to encourage stiff nipples and enthusiastic dancing by the two girls on duty on the pair of catwalks that jutted out from the far end of the room.

As they walked into the bar, a waitress with blond pigtails and a cutoff, see-through Club Cayenne T-shirt made a beeline for Nick, leading with her breasts.

"What can I get for you, handsome?" she asked with her best sexy smile, eyelashes batting.

"You're wasting your time on him, Doreen," Stokes said, trying to draw her attention to himself.

"Why is that? Is he gay?"

"Worse than that, sugar. Nicky, he's a moral man."

"They always turn out to be the kinkiest kind," she said, her eyes still on Nick. "All those repressed desires. You can unleash them with me, Moral Man. I get off at nine. Bring your handcuffs. In the meantime, we got a two-drink minimum, gentlemen."

Nick held up his badge. "We gotta pass on that, ma'am. We're looking for Mr. Roy Carville."

"What's that weasel done now?"

"What'd he do before?"

"He's always got some kind of hustle going on," she said. "But you didn't hear that from me, honey. I need this job. He's on the far side of the bar, the bald-headed little squinty-eyed, rat-faced bastard."

He spotted Carville off the description—a small bald man with a pinched face, gesticulating with a cigarette in his hand as he spoke to none other than Roddie Perez.

Nick glanced at Stokes. "Tip the lady."

"That's the other thing," Stokes grumbled, fishing a five-dollar bill out of his pants pocket. "He's cheap."

"You're the one only giving me five bucks, Chaz," the waitress pointed out.

Nick was already moving through the crowd toward the far side of the bar. He came up behind Perez and placed a hand firmly at the base of his neck.

"Fancy finding you here, Roddie," he said loudly into Perez's hearing aid.

Perez jumped and twisted around on his bar stool. "Well, if it ain't Detective X," he said loudly. "Me, I'm just here complaining to my landlord about the vermin what got into my house this morning."

"You can't be referring to my partner and me," Nick said, helping himself to a cigarette out of the pack on the bar next to Perez's drink. "We were invited in, as I recall," he said, on a long stream of smoke.

"You have a poor memory. And you never came back with no warrant, neither. Now here you are, harassing me, a law-abiding citizen."

"I believe number four on the list of supervisory conditions for parole by the Louisiana Department of Corrections includes the phrase 'I will avoid bars and casinos. I will refrain from the consumption of alcohol,' does it not?" Nick asked. "You, being the felon, should know these things, Roddie. Ignorance of the law is not an accepted affirmative defense. It'd be a shame for you to end up getting your ass violated over your reckless desire to hang out in a tittie bar."

"Oh, now, hold on there, Mr. Po-lice Man," Roy Carville piped up, flashing a smile of oversize yellow teeth. "Don't be such a hard case! Mr. Perez here is just enjoying an icy Co-Cola on a hot day."

"Is that so? And you're his landlord?"

"I am."

"You own both those shit holes out on that little bayou road?"

"I own several . . . *properties* on that road, yes," Carville said, struggling to keep the smile.

"I need to have a conversation with you, Mr. Carville." Nick looked around, his lip curling ever so slightly with distaste for the surroundings. "Elsewhere. Do you have an office we might retire to?"

Carville threw up his hands like he was at a tent revival. "Absolutely! Not a problem! Follow me, Officer!"

"Detective," Nick corrected him. "Detective Sergeant Fourcade."

"Detective Sergeant. Yassir! Come right this way!"

Carville hopped off his bar stool and started toward a hallway. Nick glanced at Roddie Perez as Stokes walked up.

"Don't be in a hurry to leave, Roddie," Nick said as Perez began to shift his weight off his stool. "Your old friend Detective Stokes here will keep you company while I chat with your friend."

Nick followed Carville down the short hall to a small cluttered office painted the color of tomato soup. The place smelled of mold, mice, and cigarettes. Carville sat back against an old wooden desk heaped with papers, grinning like they were old friends there to shoot the breeze.

"What can I do you for, Detective Sergeant Fourcade?" he asked cheerfully.

"How do you know Roddie Perez?"

"As I believe you've already surmised, he rents a house from me."

"And how did that come to pass? Are the two of you old friends? You used to run together back when, before Roddie was a guest of the state?"

"No, sir, not at all! I'm an honest businessman. I don't truck with criminals. I do not," Carville said, shaking his head, still smiling.

"Well, apparently you do," Nick said. "Because there he sits, right out there."

"Mr. Perez has done his time. He's a free man now. Free to start his life over and become a productive member of society," Carville said. "I believe in giving all men a second chance, don't you, Detective Sergeant?"

"No," Nick said flatly, more to be contrary than anything else. There were people who deserved second chances in this life, but he guessed Roddie Perez probably wasn't one of them.

He took a deep drag on his cigarette and exhaled through his nostrils to burn out the smell of the room.

"Mr. Carville, you may or may not be aware a crime was committed last night at the house you rent to Miz Genevieve Gauthier."

"I did hear that, yes," Carville said, the smile finally sliding away. "That's a tragedy, that is. My condolences to Miz Gauthier."

Nick nodded, letting his anger build for a moment as he looked at Roy Carville, sleazy weasel purveyor of lurid delights for voyeurs. *Smug* was the word that came to mind. Like he thought whatever might happen to other people was nothing but amusement because it didn't really touch him.

It wasn't hard to imagine him making life difficult for a woman like Genevieve Gauthier—poor, alone, without much real control over her circumstances. The idea infuriated Nick. He had been raised to treat women with deference and respect, and to treat any person or creature weaker than himself with kindness. He couldn't abide men who sought any opportunity to exert their power to manipulate and control over the powerless.

"Why you didn't fix the air conditioners?" he asked.

Carville almost startled at the question. "What?"

"I said, why you didn't fix those air conditioners?" Nick asked again, his temper rising one degree hotter, and then another, and another . . . "That house was a hundred fucking degrees last night. They had to leave the windows open."

"W-well, I didn't know—"

"Don't insult me with lies," Nick snapped, stepping forward, one step, two steps, compressing the space between them. Carville leaned back.

"She complained to you the air conditioners were broke, and you didn't do shit about it."

"Well, I fail to see how—"

He took another step, closing the small distance between them to almost nothing, leaning into Roy Carville's space.

"*Fils de pute.*" He all but spat the curse words in Carville's face, his anger at a boil now. "They had to leave the windows open. The killer came in through a window. Came in through the window and stabbed that little boy to death. If you fail to see how you are complicit in that, I sincerely hope Miz Gauthier hires herself a lawyer who can explain it to you."

"Now look here," Carville said, slipping to the side and away from the pressure and the implied threat of Nick's body language. "I couldn't foresee something like that happening! Maybe she did ask me about them air conditioners, but you got to understand she's already two months behind in her rent!"

"So you sought to force her out into the street by making the home uninhabitable? Clearly, I need to bone up on my real estate law. I gotta think that's not legal."

"Uninhabitable?" Carville scoffed. "Hell, didn't nobody have air conditioners when I was growing up here. We all managed to survive.

"And don't let her tell you I never did nothing for her," he argued. "I offered her a job here to help make ends meet."

"Oh, I'll bet you did," Nick said, his temper spiking another notch. In his mind's eye he pictured Carville leering at Genevieve Gauthier through his squinty eyes, grinning like the Cheshire cat with his big yellow teeth as he invited the single mother to come earn her keep in this place.

"So because she didn't want to dance naked in front of a bunch of drunks every night, she should lose her child?"

"I was being generous!" Carville insisted. "These girls make good money!"

"And Genevieve, she's a pretty girl," Nick said, nodding, stalking Carville around the cramped space as he tried to move away. "A fresh face, a perky new set of breasts—that's a boost for your business, isn't it, Roy?"

"I won't argue it would have been mutually advantageous, but she said no."

"Maybe you didn't take that well, huh, Mr. Carville?" Nick asked. "Maybe you thought she should have been more appreciative. Maybe you thought to send someone to give her a little scare. Someone like your friend Mr. Perez, who lives conveniently next door."

Carville's eyes went as wide as they could at the accusation. "That's ridiculous!"

"But you can't control Mr. Perez, who you claim not to know very well. Maybe you don't know that he's been convicted of assault in the past. Or maybe you do."

"I did not—"

"So, it wouldn't really be your fault if he lost control and killed that child."

"You're out of your mind, Fourcade!"

Nick took a step back then, killing the physical pressure entirely, like flipping off the power switch. He cocked a leg and smoked his cigarette and watched Roy Carville, like a mouse trapped in a cat's keen view trying to figure out what the hell might happen next.

"Well, people, they do say that about me," Nick conceded softly, nodding, the perfectly reasonable man. "Me, I don't suppose I could be a fair judge of the subject."

Carville just stared at him, afraid to show an emotion that might trigger a wrong reaction.

"Has Mr. Perez ever said anything to you about Miz Gauthier?" Nick asked. "That he noticed her, spoke to her, had designs on her?"

Carville shook his head. "No, sir."

Nick arched a brow. "Really? I find that hard to believe, the two of you being such aficionados of beautiful women. And you having offered Miz Gauthier a job and all. Seems like that might have come up in conversation."

"It didn't."

"Curious. Well," he said with a shrug, "we'll see. The crime scene unit processed the scene today. We're all done there. If I get a call that Mr. Perez's fingerprints turned up in that house, he gonna have some 'splaining to do."

"That's got nothing to do with me," Carville said, sitting back against the desk again, relaxing ever so slightly.

"You're just the landlord."

"That's right."

"*Très bien,*" Nick murmured, glancing away. He let silence fall between them for a moment.

Carville looked relieved. "Will she be going back to the house—Miz Gauthier?" he asked.

"I shouldn't think so. Would you? She's in the hospital, at any rate. Why?"

"Well, I'm just wondering. I mean, we're near the end of the month here . . ."

Nick stared at him for a moment. Amazed anew that he could be surprised by a human being's callousness.

"You want to be able to rent out the scene of a murder?" He shook his head. "You're a piece of work, you are."

"I'm a businessman. I will understand if she don't wanna live there no more. Hell, I'll even waive the last month's rent."

Nick counted to himself: *Inhale. Focus. Calm. Patience. Exhale. Focus. Calm. Patience . . .* He wanted to beat this man to a bloody pulp and dump his body in the swamp. The world would be a better place for it. He took another measured breath and let it out slowly.

"I'll let you know when you can have the house back. Shouldn't be more than a few days," he lied. "I think we're done with it, but I might have an afterthought to look through it again in a day or two—just in case we might have missed something. I can't think about it right now. My focus has to be elsewhere tonight."

He checked his watch and sighed, surreptitiously watching Carville through his eyelashes. The man was twitching, uncertain as to whether he was off the hook or not, wanting to let his guard down but not sure he should.

Très bien, Nick thought. Très bien. *You twitch, you motherfucker. You keep twitching,* fils de pute . . .

Clipped to his belt, his cell phone vibrated, announcing a text message. He glanced down at the screen. Dixon: *Tox screen in.*

He moved forward suddenly to stub out the last of his cigarette in a dirty ashtray on the desk. Carville flinched sideways.

"Merci beaucoup," Nick murmured, staring into the man's little rat eyes. "Thank you for your time, Mr. Carville. You have a wonderful evening, sir."

He turned and walked out of the room and back down the hall, emerging into the bustle and noise of a crowd on their third round of drinks, and Ryan Foret belting out "Tee Nah Nah" over the sound system.

Both Stokes and Perez looked at Nick expectantly. He spared not a glance for Roddie Perez but cut a look at Stokes and said, "We gotta go. Our victim has something to tell us."

SEVENTEEN

You *will never see your son alive again . . .*
You will never see your son alive again . . .
You will never see your son alive again . . .

"I will never see my son alive again," Genevieve murmured. "I will never see my son alive again . . ."

She rolled the words around in her mouth like marbles, hard and cold. Her throat closed at the idea of trying to swallow them. She imagined them chipping her teeth as she forced them out.

"I will never see my son alive again . . ."

And yet, when she heard the words, she felt weirdly numb, as if they didn't touch her. As if they meant nothing. In her mind's eye she imagined the words like razor blades, cutting her flesh a thousand times. She watched her blood running everywhere, soaking her hospital gown, soaking the sheets, dripping on the smooth polished floor. But she felt nothing. No pain, no sorrow, no fear, no nothing.

It was the drugs, she supposed. Whatever they were giving her for the pain was leaving her numb physically, emotionally, psychologically. Numb was good. She tried to achieve a certain amount of numbness every night of her life to dull the pain of her existence. She would stay numb for as long as possible.

She looked around the generic hospital room they had moved her to on the second floor of the hospital. A private room—like she was somebody special. The walls were a pale cool green. A picture of the Virgin Mary hung above a nondescript gray metal cabinet of drawers opposite the bed.

A picture of what people wanted to imagine the Virgin had looked like, she corrected herself. No one could possibly know for sure. In fact, it was easier to safely say she had looked nothing like the woman in the picture, with her flawless ivory skin and small, slender nose. For two thousand years people had been reimagining Mary to suit their own needs. But that was what people always did—remold history into a shape that pleased them.

Mary was always depicted as peaceful, an idea that gave people comfort. Resigned to her fate, Genevieve had long thought, powerless to change the course of her life. As a teenager, Genevieve had wondered what it must have been like for that young girl all those centuries ago, facing her parents, pregnant with no plausible explanation. Everyone glossed over that part of the story.

She knew what it had been like for herself to be pregnant without support. No one had ever forgiven her anything. She had never felt acceptance or peace. But she had never truly resigned herself to her fate, either—though she would have been better off if she had. She had never let go of wanting something more, something better, something special just for her.

KJ had been just for her, she reminded herself.

You will never see your son alive again . . .

What would her life be like without him?

Quiet.

Life with KJ had been a constant, exhausting cacophony. Without him, she imagined silence. No more boy noise—yelling and roaring and crashing and clattering and belching and farting. No more racket of rowdy play. No more temper tantrums. No more crying from frustration or disappointment or fatigue or hurt feelings or pain. No more of the noise that had come from both of them, each directed at the other.

What would her life be like without him?

Silent.

Not the kind of silence that wrapped itself around them after he had fallen asleep in her arms but the kind of silence that pressed in on you and filled your ears until you had to scream to relieve the pressure. The kind of silence that eventually became a piercing white noise.

A sense of dread seeped beneath the drug-induced numbness. She didn't want to let it in. She didn't want to be alone with it. She didn't want to be alone.

She looked at the phone on the bedside stand for a long moment, wondering if she should, wondering if he would answer. If he answered, would he be angry with her for calling? Probably.

Even as she thought it, she reached for the phone anyway.

The phone on the receiving end rang once, twice, three times—

Please, please, please, please—

—and straight to voicemail.

She hung up without leaving a message and blinked back tears. She had no one else to call, no one who would come and see her. Clarice Marcel was the kindest person she knew, but no one would bring Clarice to visit, and Genevieve could only imagine how confused the old woman would be talking on the telephone. She didn't have any friends, not really. Jojean Florette was an acquaintance, not a friend, and the last time they'd spoken—just last night, though it seemed a hundred years ago—hadn't been pleasant. Jojean was hardly the type to come with comfort and cheer, anyway.

She didn't have any choice but to be alone, shut up in this room like a prisoner.

A deputy stood watch outside the door to her room. She could see the slope of his broad shoulders through the frosted glass. She had caught a glimpse of him when the nurse had come in to check on her. He was tall, trim, young, white.

Was he there to protect her or to contain her?

He shifted positions, turning sideways. Voices rose and fell outside the door. Genevieve caught a few words at a time.

". . . orders . . . no visitors . . ."

". . . be ridiculous . . . Sheriff Dutrow . . . representing . . . auxiliary . . ."

The door swung open, and a woman walked in carrying a small bouquet of white flowers in a clear glass vase. *Neat* and *tidy* were the words that came to Genevieve's mind. She was one of those neat and tidy women who always had her hair done and fresh lipstick on, like Mavis Parsons at work. Stepford Wives, Genevieve called them in her less charitable moments. Women who had it all together and seemed never to put a stylish pump wrong. They raised families, tended to their husbands, lunched with the Junior League, and volunteered at church as if they somehow had more hours in the day than women like Genevieve.

This one came directly to her, her head tipped slightly to one side, hazel eyes full of superiority and pity, not a single auburn hair out of place. She had a prim little mouth that quirked up on one side, as if she found the situation somehow ironic.

"Ms. Gauthier," she said softly, her voice like butter on warm biscuits. "My name is Sharon Spicer. On behalf of the Our Lady of Mercy hospital auxiliary, I want to express our sincere condolences on the loss of your son."

She set the vase on the bedside stand and clasped her manicured hands together. Genevieve's eyes went to the tasteful diamond engagement ring she wore.

"I don't know if you have family in the area," the woman went on, "but if you need assistance with anything, anything at all, please feel free to contact me. I'll leave you my number. Between the auxiliary and my church group, you will have all the support you need during this trying time.

"Do you belong to a church here?" she asked. "If you need someone to call your pastor, I'll be happy to do that. Or to call family. Do you have family here? Who are your people?"

It took Genevieve too long to process the questions. Numbed by chemicals, her brain was much slower than Sharon Spicer's mouth. By the time she formed an answer, the woman was asking something new.

"I have a son, myself," she said. "Cameron. He's fourteen. A young man now, I know, but he's still my little boy. My heart just stops at the idea of something happening to him. I understand your son was younger. Just an innocent little child—"

"How do you know me?" Genevieve asked. "How do you know about my son?"

Sharon Spicer hesitated for a split second, as if she was surprised to have someone interrupt her, then regrouped with a knowing look. "You're all over the news, my dear."

She gestured toward the television that hung high up on the wall across from the bed. *Murder in Bayou Breaux* crawled across the screen beneath the image of a newscaster reading soundlessly. Genevieve hadn't even noticed the TV. She had no idea how to turn the sound on, didn't know if she wanted to.

"As it happens," the woman went on, "I am engaged to be married to Sheriff Dutrow. So, I suppose I heard the news before anyone. Has he spoken to you?"

"No," Genevieve murmured, staring at the television.

On the screen, Sheriff's Office personnel were going in and out of her house. Deputies in uniform. Crime scene people. Detective Four-cade stood off to the side at the bottom of the porch stairs, talking to another man. Yellow crime scene tape fluttered in the foreground.

The house looked even worse on television than it did in real life. People would watch this and think she lived in a dump—because she did. They would have no way of knowing it was only temporary, that as soon as Jeff was able to give her an office job and she had managed to scrape together enough for a deposit and first month's rent, she planned to move someplace better.

That was the story of her life: there was never enough money. There had not been enough money when she was a child in a single-parent household, nor as a single parent herself. People liked to say money couldn't buy happiness, but that was a lie. Money could buy comfort in the form of a nice home and clothes and a car that worked. Money could buy security and status. All those things added up to happiness in Genevieve's eyes.

Everything cost money. Rent cost money, and food cost money, and her beater car cost money because it was always breaking down. It cost money to raise a child. Children needed things—food, clothing, toys, health care.

She needed a second job just to make ends meet, but she couldn't get a second job because a babysitter cost money, and it made no sense to pay a babysitter when she could make no more than a few dollars an hour. She couldn't get a job that paid better because she couldn't afford college. And she couldn't go to college anyway because she had a child.

You will never see your child alive again . . .

What would life be like without him?

Less expensive.

Less complicated.

"I'm sure the sheriff will be by to see you," Sharon Spicer was droning on. "Kelvin is taking a personal interest in your case. The idea of a young mother and her child being attacked this way . . ." She shook her head, her perfect auburn bob swaying just so. "Family is very important to him."

Genevieve said nothing.

"Do you know him?" Sharon Spicer asked.

"Why would I know him?"

"Well, he's practically a celebrity," she said with a small chuckle. "It seems like everyone around here knows Kelvin."

"I'm not from around here."

"That makes this all the more sad, then," the woman said. "You came here to make a fresh start, no doubt, and this happened. I'm sure you wish now you had stayed where you were."

"Could you leave now?" Genevieve asked abruptly. "Please. I'm very tired."

"Of course," Sharon Spicer said, seeming to take no offense. "You need your rest. I'm sorry to prattle on."

She picked up a hospital notepad from the bedside table and wrote down her name and phone number in perfect, beautiful cursive.

"Please do call me if you need anything at all," she said. "I can't stand the idea of you going through this alone. If I can help in any way, I will."

Genevieve couldn't muster the strength or the grace to thank her.

She watched Sharon Spicer leave knowing she would go on about her day of being Miss Everything to Everyone, then go back to her comfortable home to fix dinner for her almost-famous fiancé, the sheriff, and her precious son.

You will never see your son alive again . . .

What would life be like without him?

She thought of going home to that sad, run-down house on the bayou road. No one to greet her. No one to cook for. No one to fight with. No one to love.

What would life be like without him?

Empty.

Peaceful.

EIGHTEEN

School was letting out as Annie swung into the parking lot and parked in the space reserved for law enforcement near the main set of doors. Children spilled out of the building onto the sidewalk, swarming like a colorful army of ants, scrambling onto buses and hurrying toward the line of vehicles waiting in the carpool lane. The buses would load up the elementary school kids and then pull around the broad curved drive, past the park, to the junior high school to load the next batch of students.

The junior high kids had only begun to trickle out of their building, some of them walking toward downtown, a few meandering in the opposite direction to the park. Just like any normal day, Annie thought, except that it wasn't.

She spotted Remy's Range Rover at the head of the carpool line and waved him over rather than risking the gauntlet of carpool parents whose focus was already on their children's next scheduled activity. Woe to anyone holding up the carpool lane—even a cop.

"You're not here to steal my godson, are you?" Remy asked as he ran his window down. "'Cause we're going fishing. Catch us some sac-a-lait for supper."

He flashed his wide, easygoing smile dressed up with a thick mus-

tache. Annie had always teased him he should have been a cop with that
'stache. Instead, he had parlayed his geology and biology background
into a boutique environmental consulting business. He worked out of
offices on his property just outside of town, allowing himself a flexible
schedule to spend time with his daughter and his cadre of nieces and
nephews. Remy was every Doucet kid's favorite uncle.

In the back seat, Gracie Doucet made a face and shuddered. "Fish
are slimy and gross!"

Remy rolled his eyes. "Said the girl who wanted a seaweed body wrap
for her birthday."

Gracie smiled like the pixie she was, meeting her father's eyes in the
rearview mirror. "That was different. That was part of my spa experience."

"Yeah, well, that stuff smelled like a mud bog in the hot sun."

"You have no appreciation for the finer things, Daddy."

Remy shook his head in good-natured dismay. "Fourth grade and
my daughter is a spa maven."

Annie chuckled. "You're in for a long haul, cousin."

Gracie had always been the epitome of a princess, the girliest of girls,
all pink glitter and fancy hair bows. She was something of a mystery to
her parents. Her mother was, even as they spoke, in the Middle East
photographing a refugee crisis for *National Geographic*, not a spa or a
glitter manicure to be had for miles. But Danielle and Remy both delighted in their only child's sparkling individuality. Rough-and-tumble
athlete Remy, who had hands like catcher's mitts, bragged he had mastered no fewer than five different hair-braiding techniques by studying
YouTube videos.

"Maman?" Justin piped up from his car seat behind his uncle. "Are
you coming with us? Come fishing! We're gonna have fish for supper
and I'm gonna catch them!"

Annie leaned in his window and kissed his cheek. "Nope, not tonight, little man. Papa and I have to be detectives tonight, but we'll try
to stop by later and tuck you in, all right?"

She held her breath, waiting for his mood to turn, ready to flip on
her maternal guilt switch, but the prospect of going fishing and spending time with other people he loved won out.

"Okay," he said. "But you're gonna miss out on all the fun."

"I know. I'm sad."

"Let's go, Uncle Remy!" he called, dismissing her. "We're burnin' daylight!"

"So much for missing me," Annie said with a wry smile, going back to Remy's window. "Thank you for taking him."

"You know we love having him," he said. "Justin's my buddy. And Gracie loves to play big sister."

"I know. I want you to know we don't take it for granted. A case like this one makes me appreciate my family all the more."

"Well, we *are* exceptional," he said with a little wink.

Annie mustered a tired smile for him, this cousin who was no blood relative at all. She couldn't imagine her life without him, without the entire Doucet clan. They were her support and safety net. She didn't want to imagine trying to raise a child on her own without the sense of security her family gave her. She would never go through any trial in her life alone. She would never lie in a hospital bed with no one to comfort her and no one to call, no one caring if she lived or died. The sense of loneliness and hollowness that idea brought was painful and frightening.

But that degree of isolation wasn't quite the truth of Genevieve Gauthier, she reminded herself. Someone had cared enough to try to kill her. She may not have had people to love her, but she definitely had one in the other category. And as Annie knew well, the line between *I love you* and *I want you dead* could be very thin indeed.

"WE NOTIFIED MOST of the parents by text and email," Pamela Samuels Young said as they walked into the school office. She went around behind the counter to a computer monitor and woke it up with a wiggle of the mouse. "I've got my secretary calling the few who still live by landline."

"What did you say in the statement?" Annie asked.

"Just that we lost one of our students to a violent crime last night and that we're here for our Bayou Breaux Elementary family, et cetera." She glanced away from the computer screen to give Annie a look of weary hope. "I don't suppose you're here to tell us the crime is solved."

" 'Fraid not," Annie said on a sigh as she leaned against the counter. She looked to Jaime Blynn, who mirrored her pose a few feet away. She looked exhausted, like a wilted daisy, her usual effervescence gone flat over the course of a long, hard day. "How did it go with your class?"

"It was hard. I told them as gently as I could, but how do you tell children news like that and not upset them, not frighten them?" the teacher asked. "Some cried. Some asked for their parents. Others seemed shell-shocked. They're too young to get their little minds around something that horrible. I imagine there'll be some bad dreams tonight—mine, for starters."

She rubbed her hands over her face, her makeup long gone, and pushed her blond hair back behind her ears. "I want a big glass of wine and to hug my boys all night long."

"There'll be a lot of that going around tonight," Pamela said. "Here it is, Annie. Nora Florette. Her parents are Duane and Jojean Florette."

She turned the monitor so Annie could see.

"The father works on an oil rig in the Gulf," Jaime said. "He's gone a lot. Jojean always has at least two jobs. The kids are left to their own devices most of the time. Nora is the youngest."

"You had her in your class?"

"Yes, which is why I was concerned when I found out she was babysitting KJ. There's no adult supervision going on there. The older kids are off doing their own thing after school—none of it good, I'm sure. The older girl was always very mouthy. Takes after her mother, I hate to say. The brother, Dean, must be fourteen now. He likes to hang around the park after school and make trouble. I've run him off more than once myself."

"Charming family," Annie murmured as she entered the Florettes' address and phone numbers into her phone. "What kind of trouble?"

"Teasing girls, picking on boys weaker than he is, smoking cigarettes. He's your basic annoying little punk. But what can we expect if no one is trying to mold him into something better?"

"So you said Nora usually picked KJ up after school and walked him to her house," Annie said. "Did they cut through the park to get there?"

"Yes. The Florettes' neighborhood is just on the other side."

"That's what I thought. You haven't had any creepers hanging around the park lately, have you?"

"There was a raggedy guy camping down in the woods way at the far southeast edge of the park a couple of months ago," Pamela said. "Right before school started. We came across him on a run. Remember that, Jaime?"

"Oh, my Lord, he scared the bejesus out of me," Jaime said.

"How'd I miss this?" Annie asked.

"You were in the middle of everything with your tante Fanchon," the teacher reminded her.

"It wasn't a big thing," Pamela said. "We called the police and they rousted him out of there. He never caused a problem."

"Have you seen him since?" Annie asked.

"I haven't," the principal answered. She looked to Jaime Blynn. "Have you?"

"No. I was out there yesterday," Jaime said. "I didn't see anybody out of the ordinary."

"Did you see Nora and KJ?"

"Nora was hanging out with some friends by the gazebo. KJ was playing on the swings. Too far away from her for my liking, but everything seemed fine. I came inside to get a bottle of water—it was so beastly hot!—and when I went back out, they'd gone."

"Will you walk out there with me now?" Annie asked.

"Sure."

"Is that what you think happened?" Jaime asked as they headed down the cool dark hall toward the main doors. "Some child molester picked KJ out in the park and followed him home?"

"I don't know," Annie said. "It's possible. I don't think it's likely, but it's possible."

"Sick, is what it is."

"That applies no matter who did it. There's no good reason a child gets murdered in his own home."

"Have you seen Genevieve? How is she doing?"

"In shock one minute, in tears the next."

The memory of Genevieve Gauthier sobbing over the body of her child in the morgue at Our Lady lit up in Annie's mind with painful clarity. The worst part of her job was having to be a voyeur to the pain of victims and loved ones left behind. Moments that should have been intensely private but by necessity and circumstance were often not.

"How long will she be in the hospital?"

"A day or two, I should think. Her injuries aren't life-threatening."

"And then what?" Jaime asked. "Is she just supposed to go home? How can she go back to that house after what happened? I couldn't do it. I couldn't ever go back there again."

"She won't be allowed to go back until we release the scene," Annie said. "That could be a while. Nick likes to keep his scenes sealed until he's absolutely certain it's no longer necessary. She'll have to stay elsewhere."

They each pushed open one of the big doors and stepped out into the heat and humidity. Both of them groaned automatically.

"When is this heat going to break?"

"It's hurricane weather, if you ask me," Annie said. "I can do without that, too."

The elementary school playground was empty. It was an almost eerie sight, Annie thought, a place that should have been alive with noisy children, now devoid of all life, the swings hanging still in the thick air. Beyond the playground, around the curve of the drive, the park stretched out, green and studded with sprawling live oak trees. A paved path cut through the center of it for cyclists and pedestrians.

Annie pictured a girl and a little boy walking down that path hand in hand. Nora Florette leading KJ Gauthier on their way to the neighborhood she lived in on the south side of town. Less than a mile beyond that neighborhood sat the house where KJ had died.

Was there a connection? Could some child predator have seen the boy in the park, fixated on him, followed him? The perpetrator would have had to follow the kids to the Florette home, lie in wait for two to three hours—until Genevieve arrived to pick up her son—then follow them home from there just to find out where the targeted child lived. He would then have had to either find a hiding place to wait or leave and return hours later to kill the boy.

A far-fetched theory, to say the least, she thought. The kind of child predators that trolled playgrounds and parks tended to be opportunists. They took the path of least resistance to get the thrill they wanted. They singled out a vulnerable child and acted when and where the chance presented itself. They weren't usually stalkers with long-term elaborate plans.

Still, the notion of the raggedy man in the woods was unsettling. Annie made a mental note to call the patrol sergeant at the Bayou Breaux Police Department and talk to him about it.

She was more interested in speaking to the babysitter to get some idea if there had been anything out of the ordinary in the days leading up to the crime. Had she heard anything, seen anything? Had Genevieve been acting strangely? Had KJ been upset? Might he have innocently mentioned anything that could have been a clue something terrible was headed their way?

"Lola!" Jaime called, waving, her attention on a couple of kids milling around the park's ornate gazebo—a slender girl with a long dark ponytail, bouncing a soccer ball on one knee, then the other, and a russet-haired boy sitting on the gazebo steps. A second boy rode a dirt bike back and forth in little half circles behind the girl, as if corralling her in place. "Lola!"

The girl with the soccer ball looked their way and flashed a wave and a big sunny smile. "Hey, Mrs. Blynn!"

"Lola and Nora are best friends," Jaime explained as they approached the gazebo. "Lola Troiano. Her mom's an attorney—Jessica Troiano. Maybe you know her? Anyway, Lola was out here yesterday. Maybe she saw something."

"And the boys?" Annie asked.

"That's Dean Florette on the bike. I don't know the other boy. He must be new."

"Hey, Lola, this is Detective Broussard from the Sheriff's Office," Jaime said as they walked up on the group. "She has a few questions for you."

Lola's brown eyes widened. She clutched her soccer ball close. "For me?"

"Ha-ha, Lola!" crowed the boy on the dirt bike, his greasy black hair falling in his eyes. "You're under arrest for being an ugly butt-face!"

Lola rolled her eyes. "She's probably here to arrest you, Dean. It should be against the law to be as dumb as you are."

"You're Dean Florette?" Annie asked in the voice of authority. "I'll have some questions for you as well, young man."

The smirk fell off Dean Florette's round face, his small eyes narrowing. Lola Troiano stuck out her tongue at him and turned back around, her ponytail swinging.

"Lola, Mrs. Blynn tells me you're friends with Nora Florette," Annie began. "You heard about what happened last night, right? To KJ Gauthier?"

Tears sprang instantly to Lola Troiano's eyes. "Mr. Blakely told us. It's so terrible! Why would anybody do such a thing?"

"It's my job to find out," Annie said. "Have you spoken to Nora today?"

"No, ma'am. She was absent today." The girl's eyes widened suddenly in horror. "You don't think Nora did it, do you? She wouldn't!"

Annie held up her hands to stem the tide of preteen hysteria. "No, no, I don't think Nora did it. I'm on my way to ask her the same questions I'm going to ask you. I'm just wondering if she might have said anything to you that could point us in a direction. You haven't talked to her on the phone or texted since you saw her yesterday?"

"No, ma'am. Nora doesn't have a cell phone. She was saving up for one, but *someone* stole her money," she said, shooting another nasty look at Dean.

The boy sent the look right back at her, rising up off his bike seat and farting loudly for emphasis.

"Dean Florette!" Jaime snapped in teacher mode. "Have some respect!"

He looked right at her, bug-eyed, and belched.

Choosing to ignore his nonsense, Annie pressed on. "So, you guys were hanging out here yesterday after school. Did you notice any strangers hanging around?"

"Yeah," Dean answered, snickering, pointing at the boy on the gazebo steps. "Spicer. He's strange. He's the strangest thing for miles!"

As Dean Florette laughed loudly at his own joke, the Spicer boy's face went as red as his hair.

"Did you see anyone?" Annie asked him directly.

"No, ma'am," the boy mumbled, his head ducked down like a whipped dog. He squirmed under the sudden attention. All skinny arms and legs, he tried to fold himself up and make himself smaller as he sat there on the steps.

"What's your name?" Annie asked.

"Cameron Spicer," he mumbled, avoiding eye contact as if it might hurt.

The name meant nothing to her. She knew no Spicers, not that it mattered. She dug her cardholder out of her hip pocket, pulled a business card, and held it out to him. "Here, take this."

He accepted the card reluctantly, like he thought it might be some kind of trick or that he might suffer for having accepted it. Probably the latter, Annie thought. He had the demeanor of a natural target for his crueler peers, that no matter what he did, he would be ridiculed for it. There was no right answer for kids like Cameron.

As if on cue, Dean Florette spoke up. "Now you can be a snitch, Spice Girl! Houma Homo."

Annie wheeled in his direction. "That's enough out of you, mister."

Still young enough to be momentarily intimidated by authority, the boy's expression sobered as Annie walked up to him with her hands jammed on her hips. He was about the same size as her, she thought, and he was still more little boy than young man. Soon he would be bigger and stronger, and full of hormones and idiotic machismo, and she wouldn't be able to easily intimidate him with a look or a curt word.

"I'm about to go and speak with your mother," she said. "Do you think she wants to hear about your bad behavior from a sheriff's detective? Hmmm?"

He dropped his head in surrender. "No."

"No, what?"

"No, ma'am."

"Good answer," Annie said. "And I do not want to hear one word from anyone about you mouthing off and being a bully. Do you understand me?"

His breath hitched a little as he inhaled. "Yes, ma'am."

"Now here," she said in a gentler voice, holding a business card out to him. "You take this card, because one of these days that mouth of yours is gonna get your butt in a world of hurt, and you're gonna need someone on your side. You call me when that happens. I guarantee you'll like me a lot better as your friend than as your enemy."

He gave her a suspicious look from the corner of his eye, peering at her through ragged strands of hair that needed to be cut. Finally, he reached out, took the card, and shoved it into the front pocket of his jeans.

"If any of you think of anything from yesterday that stands out at all as troubling or just out of the ordinary, I want you to call me," Annie said as she handed a card to Lola. "If you saw anyone that seemed out of place, or if you remember hearing anyone say something that struck you as odd, just call me and say, 'Hey, Detective Broussard, I just remembered something.'

"That's not being a snitch," she assured them. "You're not gonna get anyone in trouble. Part of my job is just to make a clear picture of everything that happened yesterday, and one small piece of information— even if it seems like it couldn't possibly matter—might help make that picture complete. That's how crimes get solved."

NINETEEN

Cameron watched the sheriff's detective and the teacher walk back toward the elementary school, feeling weirdly detached, as if he was watching a scene from a movie.

If only that was true, he thought as the sheriff's detective got in an SUV and drove away. If only he was a character in a movie and this wasn't his real life.

His heart was pounding from having to talk to the detective. What if she recognized his name? What if she told the sheriff she'd spoken to him? He wasn't supposed to be here. He was supposed to be at football practice, only he had quit football.

His mother had taken pity on him and let him quit more than a week ago, but she had yet to tell Kelvin. He wasn't going to be happy about it. They had already had a million arguments about Cameron just *wanting* to quit the team. Kelvin raging about pride and character building and "sticking it out." His mother arguing that it was dangerous and took Cameron away from his studies, and shouldn't it be enough that he was an excellent student? Kelvin had won every argument so far by declaring that he was right and that was the end of it.

Cameron was stuck in between them, not wanting to let either of them down. What if he disappointed Kelvin so badly he decided not to marry Cameron's mom? She had suggested that could happen. She said most men didn't want some other man's kid. They were so lucky to have Kelvin.

But he was going to find out sooner or later that Cameron had left the football team, and then the explosion was going to come. They would probably get thrown out of their house, and his mom would have to get a job, and it would be all Cameron's fault. Every time he made a mistake these were the thoughts that went through his head, and no matter how hard he tried not to, he kept making mistakes. Kelvin seemed to constantly find fault with everything he did. Cameron knew for a fact that Kelvin would have been happy to send him away to some horrible military school. His mother had yet to give in.

Cameron held himself tense all day every day, waiting for the reckoning. It was only a matter of time. The anxiety made him feel ill. It churned his stomach and gave him headaches—signs of weakness, to Kelvin's way of thinking. Why couldn't he buck up and "be a man"?

Maybe he wasn't a man. Maybe he would never be a man by Kelvin's way of thinking. Every time Cameron thought that, he felt smaller and smaller, and weaker and weaker.

Sometimes—more and more—he felt like his true self was a tiny shrunken thing living inside the giant empty shell of his body, standing on a cheekbone and peering out through a giant eye socket at a world that seemed both hyper-real and surreal. He couldn't believe that no one seemed to notice there was something really, horribly wrong with him, that he wasn't a whole, normal person, that he was some kind of freak.

"Someone we know got murdered!" Lola said, breaking the silence. She propped her soccer ball on her hip and shook her head. "I can't even! What if we saw something and we don't even know it?"

"That's stupid," Dean declared. "How could you see something and not know that you saw it?"

"*You're* stupid," Lola said. "Cameron knows what I mean. Right, Cameron?"

Cameron shrugged, not sure what would be worse for him: pretending he knew what she was talking about or admitting he didn't. Dean Florette was going to come down on him either way.

He wished he could just close his eyes and wake up at home, or—better yet—on a desert island somewhere. He didn't want to be here—not here at school, not at home, not anywhere in Bayou Breaux. He hated this place, and this place hated him. No matter how hard he tried, no one here liked him. His ears were too big; his hair was too red. The kids who grew up here didn't like him because he was new. The athletes didn't like him because he was awkward. The average kids didn't like him because he was too smart. The smart kids didn't like him because they thought he was weird.

He wanted people to like him. They just didn't. The closest he came to having friends were a couple of sixth-grade girls. The only guy who had anything to do with him was a loser who only wanted to beat the shit out of him.

Nobody liked Dean Florette, either, or he would have had something better to do with his life than hang out in the park after school, harassing kids lower on the totem pole than he was. Maybe that was what made him so mean.

"Hey, Spicer," Dean said, rolling his bike toward the gazebo. "If the sheriff is practically your old man, how come that detective didn't know who you are?"

Cameron got to his feet and leaned against the nearest gazebo pillar, ready to duck behind it if Dean rushed him. "I never saw her before. Why would she know me?"

"I bet the sheriff never talks about you because he doesn't even know who you are."

"He does so."

"You're a liar."

"Am not!"

"Prove it."

Lola rolled her eyes. "How's he supposed to prove it, Dean? Is he gonna bring the sheriff to show-and-tell? You're not in kindergarten anymore—although you act like it."

"Who asked you, *girl*?" Dean said, reaching out with one dirty sneaker to kick at her.

Lola hopped back out of the way. "Who asked you to be alive?" she said, wrinkling her nose. "Why don't you just go crawl in a hole and rot? That's what you smell like anyway."

"Fuck you, Lola. Your pussy smells like roadkill."

"You're disgusting!" Lola snapped. "I hope that detective goes and tells your mother you're a juvenile delinquent and you have to be sent to reform school!"

"Well, I hope you get raped and killed on your way home."

Lola gasped aloud. "That's horrible! You're just hateful! Who says something like that?"

"Me! I say whatever I want, twat puddle," Dean said with a menacing smirk. He climbed off his bike and dropped it without a care. He swaggered toward Lola, rubbing his grubby fist into the open palm of his other hand, like he was polishing it.

"I say whatever I want, and I do whatever I want," he said. "Who's gonna stop me? You? Spice Girl over there? You think your faggot boyfriend is gonna stop me?"

"He's not my boyfriend," Lola said, backing up.

"Because he's a gay, cock-sucking butt monkey," Dean said, chuckling at what he clearly thought were his clever name-calling abilities.

"Cameron, why don't you stand up to him?" Lola asked.

Cameron wished he could. He wanted to say that he wasn't gay. He wanted to be brave enough to stand up to Dean Florette, but he wasn't. Even if he stood up to him today, what about tomorrow and the next day? Dean was never going to quit being stupid and mean unless he died.

"You're such a loser, Spicer," Dean jeered as he stalked Lola. "You should just go kill yourself and be done with it."

"Get away from me, Dean," Lola ordered, backing toward the gazebo. "You're *so* not funny."

"What's the matter, Lola?" Dean taunted, google-eyed, stretching out his hands, fingers wide. "Afraid I'm gonna touch your titties? Bwahahahaha!"

He laughed like a maniac in a cheesy movie. Dean was always groping girls. He thought it was hilarious. The girls never thought so, but that only seemed to egg him on. The less the girl liked it, the funnier Dean thought it was.

Cameron couldn't see Lola's face as she backed up. He couldn't tell if she was scared or just angry. He stood frozen, not knowing what to do. If he intervened, Dean would kick his ass. If he didn't, Lola would hate him. He was sweating and trembling, his stomach churning and cramping. He needed to go to the bathroom, even though he'd already gone, like, ten times today, the diarrhea shooting out of him like water from a fire hose.

"Don't you come one step closer to me, Dean Florette!" Lola warned.

"Ooooh, I'm scared!" Dean mocked, creeping closer and closer. "Whatcha gonna do to me, Lola Ebola Stick It in Your Hole-a?"

"This!"

Clutching her soccer ball between both hands, she slammed it as hard as she could into Dean's ugly face. Howling, he staggered backward, pressing his hands to his mouth and nose, trying to stem the flow of blood gushing from his face. Tears poured from his eyes.

Lola followed up by kicking him in the shin like she was kicking the winning goal in the most important championship game of her life.

"That's what you get!" she yelled, furious.

Dean hopped on one foot and then fell to the ground. "I'm gonna kill you, you fucking bitch!" he shouted, the threat spoiled by the fact that he was crying like a big baby.

Lola stood over him, shouting down at him, "I'm going straight to the principal's office! And that detective can lock you up for a sex predator!"

Snatching up her ball, she turned and ran for the elementary school.

Dean struggled to sit up, half crying, sputtering swear words as snot and blood ran into his open mouth. He glared at Cameron. "What are you looking at, faggot?"

Cameron didn't bother to answer. Now was his chance. He turned and dashed across the gazebo and flung himself over the far side, falling into a bush that tore at his clothing and skin with a thousand tiny thorns as he scrambled to get up.

Stumbling, tripping, heart racing, he ran for the paved path that cut from one side of the park to the other. If he could get enough of a head start, maybe Dean wouldn't bother to chase him.

His sneakers pounded hard on the path—*SLAP! SLAP! SLAP!* His pulse was pounding in his ears—*BOOM! BOOM! BOOM!* His breath sawed in and out of his lungs. He sounded like Darth Vader, only he wasn't the bad guy in this movie. The humidity made the air like thick, hot steam, choking him, smothering him, drowning him. As he fixed his gaze ahead on the path, the heat rose up in ripples off the pavement, making his vision dreamlike. *Bad* dream–like.

His neighborhood was just two blocks beyond the end of the path— but so was Dean's. He went by the Florette house every day on his way to and from school. Nora and Dean had been two of the first kids he'd met after moving here. Dean had taken an instant hatred of him, tormenting him on a daily basis. That wasn't going to get better. Not ever. It was only going to get worse.

Cameron's stomach rolled and cramped. He worried he wouldn't make it home in time. He had to run faster, but his legs felt huge and heavy and slow, like he was running through deep sand.

And then it was too late.

The sound didn't penetrate the noise in his head until the threat was almost on him. A war cry, loud and blood-curdling: *"FAGGOT!!!!!!"*

He glanced over his shoulder just as Dean Florette rode up on him. The blood smeared all over his face made him look like he was wearing a samurai mask. His split lip and bashed nose were misshapen from swelling; his eyes squinted down to straight lines.

Cameron took in the sight in a split second, and then Dean hit him hard in the back, and he went flying. The ground rushed up at him in a blur. He landed—*BAM! SLAM!*—like a plane with no wheels, bouncing on the pavement, scraping his hands, his arms, his chin. His brain sloshed and banged around inside his head like Jell-O. He saw double and tasted blood.

His bowels let loose as he bounced to a stop in a heap on the walkway, the smell overwhelming him, making him gag and retch. That was all he needed—to throw up all over himself. That would just be the cherry on top of the shit sundae.

He could hear Dean laughing like a maniac, the sound growing louder and louder as he came closer and closer. He didn't look up to see where Dean was. It didn't matter now. He couldn't get up and run again. He couldn't fight Dean Florette and win. All he could do was give up and take his beating and hope it was over quickly—or that he died.

At this point, all things in his life considered, death didn't seem like the worst alternative.

TWENTY

The Florette home was a big two-story clapboard house in an older middle-class neighborhood. The wide front porch sagged in the middle from decades of heavy foot traffic in and out of the house. Warped by time and weather, the old dark-green wood-framed screen door didn't quite close.

Upkeep was clearly not the owners' forte. The roots of a huge oak tree had heaved up the sidewalk. The grass in the front yard was struggling, scrubbed down to the dirt near the front porch where bicycles and tricycles of various sizes had been abandoned, some standing, some tipped over.

Two minivans filled up the driveway to the detached garage.

A pair of teenaged girls in short shorts and skimpy tank tops burst out the front door, giggling as Annie climbed the steps.

"I'm looking for Nora Florette," she said.

The girls looked at her like she had asked for something disgusting and smelly—a sack of garbage, a roadkill possum. Or maybe that was their impression of her. She held up her badge and arched an eyebrow.

"Is she home?"

"Why would I care?" one said caustically. She was clearly the Florette of the two—black of hair, round of face, like the younger brother, with narrow eyes and too much mascara.

Tired, hot, running on the half-melted Snickers bar she had finally dug out of her purse on the way from the school, Annie had no patience left for teen-girl attitude. She moved to block the Florette girl's path down the steps and gave her a hard stare.

"I don't care if you care, sweetheart," she said. "And I have heard all the Florette smart mouth I can stand for one day. What's your name?"

"Nicole," the girl said grudgingly, as if she was giving up a state secret.

"Nicole, I'm Detective Broussard from the Sheriff's Office. Is your sister, Nora, home? I need to speak with her, please."

"What'd she do now?" the other girl asked—blond hair in pigtails, bra strap falling off one shoulder, shorts barely clearing her hoo-ha. Annie shuddered to think of the trouble the pair of them were headed for, just old enough to think they were grown up, still young enough to be jailbait.

"What'd she do before?" Annie asked.

Nicole shot her friend a dirty look, turned, and went back to stick her head inside the screen door. "*No-ra!* Nora, get down here right this minute!"

Out in the street, a jacked-up electric blue pickup pulled to the curb in front of Annie's vehicle. A shirtless young man, maybe eighteen or nineteen, with a goatee and bleached, spiked hair stuck his head out the passenger window.

"Load up, bitches!" he yelled, then fell into gales of laughter along with the driver of the vehicle.

"Do we have to stay?" Nicole asked, coming back to Annie, one eye on the truck, ready to bolt. "I don't know anything about anything Nora does. She's just an irritating brat child."

Apparently, that ran in the family.

"No," Annie said. "You can go."

Giggling, the girls clattered down the porch steps to the sidewalk and made their way toward the pickup on precariously tall wedge-soled sandals, the blonde snatching the edge of her shorts out of her butt crack as she went. The word *bitch* floated back at Annie.

"Have fun," Annie muttered as she watched them climb into the truck. "Try not to get pregnant."

No one had come to the door of the house. She peered in through the screen to a messy living room with a television blaring and a toddler standing on the couch punching a doll in the face. Somewhere deeper in the house, a baby was crying. The smell of onions frying wafted out from the kitchen, wherever that was.

She knocked and waited and checked her watch. She could hear faint voices rise and fall, and the sound of a utensil banging on a pot. She knocked again and called, "Sheriff's Office! Anybody home?"

The toddler came running on stubby legs and peered up at her through the same narrowed eyes as Nicole and Dean Florette.

"Hi, sweetheart," Annie said. "Where's your mama?"

Who's your mama? She wondered as the child scampered off into the depths of the house, dragging the doll by the hair.

Annie banged on the door and called again. "Hello? Sheriff's Office!"

A petite twenty-something young woman with a crying baby on her hip and a cigarette dangling from her lips picked her way through the minefield of abandoned toys in the living room, the toddler dogging her heels.

"I'm looking for Mrs. Florette," Annie said. "Detective Broussard, Sheriff's Office."

Plucking the cigarette from her mouth and holding it out to the side, scattering ash on the floor, Twenty-Something turned and yelled toward the back of the house, "Aunt Jojean! It's the po-lice!"

An equally strident voice shouted back, "I can't leave my meat! Come on back here!"

Annie followed the mother-and-child procession back through the living room to a messy, cluttered kitchen where Jojean Florette stood at the stove stirring a huge cast-iron skillet full of raw, sizzling ground beef. She was a short, round woman with a belligerent face that easily marked her as the mother of her children. The steam rising from the meat glazed her ruddy skin and frizzed the short dark hair along her forehead. She gave Annie a scathing once-over.

"Miz Florette, I'm Detective Broussard with the Sheriff's Office," Annie began. "I need to speak with your daughter Nora."

Jojean heaved a sigh and jammed one dimpled hand on her hip, continuing to stir absently with the other. "Oh, what now? Is that bitch pressing charges? I don't know who she thinks she is! Comes to town and starts lording it over everybody like her shit don't stink. Nora swears she didn't steal that trinket box, and who's to say she did? Not Miss High-and-Mighty! And here she is sending in the goddamn cavalry—"

"I don't know what you're talking about," Annie confessed bluntly, too tired and impatient to pretend interest in anything not related to the case. In the past hour she had already experienced enough of the Florette offspring to not be surprised one of them had been accused of stealing.

Jojean's eyes narrowed to slits. "Then why are you here?"

"I have some questions for her about yesterday, that's all."

"What about yesterday?"

"She was babysitting KJ Gauthier."

"You don't think she hurt that boy, do you?" Jojean said. "Did Genevieve say Nora did something to him? After all we've done for her—"

"No one is accusing Nora of anything," Annie said. "I just want to ask her if everything was normal yesterday, if maybe they ran into a stranger in the park or if KJ might have said something—"

Jojean cut a look at her niece in the doorway. "Tiffany, go call Nora downstairs."

"It's terrible what happened," she said belatedly as the niece left the room. "People aren't safe in their own beds at night."

"How do you know Genevieve?" Annie asked.

"Work. I'm a cook at Evangeline Oaks."

"That's how Nora came to be her babysitter?"

"*NO-RA!!!* Your mother wants you!" the niece screamed in the front of the house.

Lord, what a family of hog callers.

"She needed someone to watch KJ after school," Jojean went on. "Time for Nora to get some responsibility. Earn her own money."

"Did Nora say anything to you last night? That anything was out of the ordinary?"

She stirred her meat, frowning. "I didn't see her last night. I was working."

"At Evangeline Oaks?"

"No. I work some evenings at the liquor store. Lambert Liquor—that's my cousin Joe Lambert. I didn't get home 'til late."

"And Nora didn't say anything this morning?"

"I didn't see her this morning. I have to be at the Oaks by five to start the breakfast."

"You didn't talk to her on the phone?"

"For what? She's old enough to get herself up for school."

"But she wasn't at school today," Annie said.

"What?"

"She was absent. Didn't you get the text from the school office?"

Jojean made a face like she'd tasted something bad. "I don't pay no mind to those. They're all the time sending texts about this and that and the next thing. And Nora skipping school is not a news flash. I'm not gonna drop everything and go find her. She can just pay the piper and sit in detention when she goes back. She has to learn responsibility."

It was the second time in three minutes she had mentioned her daughter learning responsibility—this mother who hadn't spoken to her youngest child since who knew when, ignored messages from school, and believed her daughter's delinquency was her own business to deal with. Annie wondered if Jojean Florette had any idea or care that her son was a bully or that her older daughter had just gone off dressed like a backwater hooker in a truck with boys too old for her.

The back door slammed, and Dean Florette came thundering into the house, dodging piles of clothes on the floor in what must have been the laundry room just beyond the kitchen. His eyes went wide at the sight of Annie, and he came to an almost-comic skidding stop in the middle of the room. His face was smeared with blood. The front of his shirt was soaked with it.

"What happened to you?" Annie asked.

He dodged her gaze and then his mother's. "I crashed my bike."

"And broke the fall with your face?"

His nose looked squashed and swollen, and he had a fat lip, like someone who had been on the wrong side of a fistfight. His knuckles were skinned as well in a way that suggested he had punched someone.

Annie wondered if the red-haired boy in the park had gotten the better of him. That was hard to imagine, as timid as the other boy had seemed. But then, Dean Florette no doubt had a whole list of kids who might want to punch him in the face. Anything might have happened on his way home.

He shrugged and turned away from her toward a sink full of dirty dishes.

Jojean just rolled her eyes, completely unconcerned with his injuries. "Go wash your face in the bathroom. And don't get blood on my fancy towels!"

"His nose might be broken," Annie suggested.

"Boys get into scrapes," Jojean said. "Especially that one. If he's not crying about it, neither am I."

The niece came back into the kitchen then from the other direction, the baby on her hip red-faced and wailing like a siren. "Nora's not here."

"She's probably asleep," Jojean said.

"I went up to her room. She's not there."

Jojean angrily cracked her spatula handle on the edge of the skillet. "Oh, that girl!"

Annie caught Dean by the shoulders as he tried to escape past her. He was drenched with sweat and smelled like a wild animal. "Dean, did you see your sister this morning?"

He wrenched away from her, scowling. "Which one?"

"Nora."

"No."

"No, what?"

"No, ma'am."

"Did you see her after school yesterday?"

"Yeah—uh, yes, ma'am."

"In the park with KJ?"

"Yeah."

"And later? Was she home?"

"Yes, ma'am," he said, fidgeting impatiently. "Hogging the bathroom and talking on the phone, like always."

"Do you know where she might be now?" Annie asked.

"How would I know?"

"She's probably running around with her friends," Jojean said. "Probably with that Troiano girl."

"She's supposed to be grounded," Dean grumbled.

"No," Annie said to Jojean. "I saw Lola Troiano half an hour ago. She hasn't spoken to Nora all day."

"She probably ran away," Dean said. "I hope so." He looked hopefully at his mother. "Can I have her room if it turns out she's dead?"

"Dean Allan!" Jojean shouted. "Go wash your goddamn face before I slap you!" She turned on her niece. "Give that baby something to chew on before I lose my mind!"

"It's not my fault she's teething!" Tiffany shouted back, tears springing up in her eyes. The toddler flung himself down at her bare feet and began to sob.

Annie thought her head might explode. If this was the usual chaos of the Florette home, she wouldn't have blamed anyone for running away from it.

"Tiffany," she said calmly, "could you please take your children into the front room while I speak with your aunt? There's a little too much going on here."

"Well, whose fault is that?" the girl snapped, shooting a glare at her aunt.

"Oh, really? Seriously?" Jojean snapped back, still stirring her ground beef. "Well, you don't have to come over here, crying about your rotten marriage ever again, little missy. How about that?"

Tiffany gasped. "Well, I won't, then! You're so hateful to me!"

She turned and hurried away through the dining room, abandoning the little boy on the floor before shouting in afterthought, "Cody Matthew, come here this minute! We're going home!"

Blubbering and rubbing his eyes, the toddler got up and trotted after her.

"Oh, boo-freaking-hoo!" Jojean called after her. She sniffed indignantly and muttered, "She'll be right back here tomorrow, crying in her beer."

"Is there any reason to think Nora might have run away from home?" Annie asked, steering the conversation back on track.

"That girl is too lazy to run anywhere," Jojean said. "She's just off with her friends."

"She's supposed to be grounded? What for?"

The mother put a misfit lid over the pan of meat, turned down the burner flame, and picked up a dish towel to mop the sweat from her brow and wipe her hands. She didn't want to answer. Her mouth bent into a stubborn little horseshoe frown.

"Don't make me play twenty questions, ma'am," Annie warned. "I've had enough of this day, and it's far from over. I've got a dead boy laying in the morgue at Our Lady and—"

"Nora wouldn't be involved in such a thing—"

"I'm not saying she would be, but if your daughter might be able to shed *any* kind of light on what happened yesterday between the time she left school with KJ Gauthier and the time Genevieve picked him up, I need to hear it from her. I need to know everything I can know. I need to know everything I can know about every person in this picture. So why was Nora grounded? Did she get in trouble at school? Out of school? What?"

Jojean heaved a sigh. "She got caught shoplifting at the Quik Pik. My friend Arlene was the manager on duty. She called me to come get her."

"When was this?"

"Monday. I grounded her for a month."

A month was a long time to a kid, Annie thought. Long enough that Nora Florette might have thought running away from home was a viable alternative? It sounded like she and her mother butted heads on a regular basis. Had that grounding been the last straw?

And she had chosen to run away the day after the boy she babysat was murdered. Was that a coincidence? A damned strange one, if so. Did Nora know about what had happened to KJ? Did she know he was dead? Did she think she might get blamed? Why would she? Genevieve had picked up her son, as usual, and gone home, as usual, for an unremarkable evening.

"Aside from Lola Troiano, does Nora have other friends she might have gone to?"

"Maybe her cousin Tina or Janey Avery."

"I need you to call anyone you can think of and try to find her," Annie said. "And I'd like to go take a look around in her bedroom, if that's all right with you."

"Fine," Jojean said impatiently. "Do whatever. But I'm telling you right now, she won't stay gone. She'll probably be home in time for supper."

It wasn't hard to pick Nora's room from the others'. Dean's room had a hazmat sign on the door and NO GIRLS! printed in Magic Marker right on the white paint. Nicole's name ran down the center of her door in pink glitter letters. That left a door with NO BOYS ALLOWED! and a dozen stickers of unicorns and rainbows on it. Someone had used a marker to draw giant penises on the unicorns and poop falling from their butts.

Evidence of the living hell of having a brother like Dean.

The bedroom looked like it had been ransacked by thieves. Annie supposed it was probably normal, though it was going to make it hard to determine if anything was missing. The bed was unmade, a wild tangle of sheets and pillows and stuffed animals. Clothes were strewn everywhere—on the bed, on the chair, left in rumpled piles on the floor. The walls were papered in posters of baby animals and pop music heartthrobs.

The dresser was cluttered with figurines and Beanie Babies and a pile of underwear. A small table near the window was covered in craft supplies for making jewelry—beads and baubles for necklaces and earrings.

The current work in progress was a friendship bracelet like all Annie's young cousins were wearing and making for one another. She remembered going through that phase herself when she was that same age. Friendship bracelets and getting her ears pierced. Hanging posters of the singers and actors she had crushes on. She had kept a diary full of her deepest, innermost thoughts and desires, chronicling the dramas of school life.

Hoping Nora might do the same, she poked around for anything resembling a diary, looking in logical hiding spots but finding nothing. She looked around for the other things she wasn't seeing—a purse, a backpack. Something a kid would take with them if they were running away. Kids these days seemed to carry their lives in their backpacks. Remy's daughter, Gracie, a fourth-grader, already carried a backpack half as big as she was.

There was no backpack in Nora Florette's room. No schoolbooks, either. If she had been planning to run away, she might have left them in her locker at school. Or maybe she was just holed up with a friend, thinking to punish her mother by disappearing for a day or two. Too bad her mother hadn't bothered to notice.

Annie plucked a small school photo from the frame of the dresser mirror and took it with her downstairs to the kitchen. Jojean had poured herself a whiskey and was sipping it as she stirred her ground beef in a giant pot of spaghetti sauce.

"Is this a recent picture of Nora?"

"That's last year's school picture. They haven't taken new ones yet."

"Do you have anything more current? In your phone, maybe?"

Jojean sniffed, frowning. "When do I have time to take their pictures? My husband's gone three weeks at a time, working a rig in the Gulf. He's on twenty-one and off fourteen. And those fourteen days when he's home, he ain't home. He's driving long hauls for his brother's trucking company to Florida and back. He is a goddamn ghost to this family.

"I am *it* in this house," she said, turning away from the stove, walking up on Annie, her temper rising. "I am *the* parent. I work my ass off for these kids, and when I'm not working, I'm cooking and cleaning and doing their laundry. I'm a fucking slave to this family. So if you're thinking I'm not a good mother because I'm not making them scrapbooks and recording every waking moment of their precious lives, you can just shove that idea right up your tight little ass, Detective."

Annie said nothing, not caring in the least that Jojean Florette was feeling judged. Her feelings didn't weigh more than a twelve-year-old child.

She put the photo of Nora down flat on the kitchen table and took a picture of the picture with her phone.

"Did you make those phone calls?" she asked. "To the cousin? To the other friend?"

"She's not at her cousin's house," Jojean said, calmer. "And the Averys didn't answer."

Annie checked her watch. It was getting on to suppertime, and the sun wasn't much more than a faint glow out the window.

"I'll put this picture out for all our deputies to see, with a be-on-the-lookout notice," she said. "If you haven't heard from Nora in the next couple of hours, I want you to call me," she said, placing a business card on the table next to the photograph. "You don't want to take this seriously, but I am taking it seriously, Miz Florette. No one has seen or heard from your daughter since last night—"

"She's just being stubborn—"

"You don't know what she's being," Annie snapped. "KJ Gauthier was murdered last night. We don't know why. Could be he was just in the way. Could be he could have identified this person because he'd seen him before. If my daughter had been taking care of that child and now I couldn't find her, I'd be a damned sight more upset about that than you seem to be."

Fed up, Annie started for the doorway but then stopped and looked back at Nora Florette's mother. "When was the last time you actually saw and spoke with your daughter?"

Jojean didn't answer right away. She either didn't want to or had to think about it. At least she finally had the grace to look guilty.

"Monday night," she said at last. "She said she was never gonna speak to me again."

Monday night.

Two days had passed.

TWENTY-ONE

Merde," Nick swore as they rode up the drive to the entrance of Our Lady. Three news vans were parked along a red zone, antennas up. Their crews had staked out areas on the lawn near the entrance to broadcast their six o'clock news segments. *Live from Bayou Breaux . . .*

"They're like mosquitoes," Stokes said. "Swarming right where you don't want them to be, ever-ready to suck your blood. You want to duck in a side entrance?"

"No," Nick said on a sigh. "Might as well run the gauntlet and disappoint them all at once. They're not gonna be happy until they get us on camera being dicks to them. Let's get it over with."

"Like I always say when I'm making love to an ugly woman . . ."

He pulled the Charger into a spot reserved for law enforcement, immediately drawing the attention of the news crews.

"I-i-i-i-it's showtime!" he said, settling his fedora at a jaunty angle over one eye as he got out of the car.

Nick climbed out of the vehicle and slid his sunglasses in place, even though daylight wasn't much more than a glow in the west. He walked with purpose toward the hospital entrance, his expression set in stone.

Stokes ran interference on one side. Kimberly Karstares came at him from the opposite side, shouting his name, shoving a microphone at him.

"Detective Fourcade! Detective Fourcade!"

"Do you—"

"Have you—"

"Will you—"

Their voices were a discordant racket as unpleasant as a flock of crows cackling around his head.

"No comment."

"Detective Fourcade, have you spoken to the Theriot family?" Karstares asked.

No, he had not. He had a murderer running loose in his parish. Solving that crime had to take precedence over a courtesy call to the Theriots.

"No comment."

Bobby Theriot would call him. He had no doubt about that. Bobby Theriot would call him in a couple of hours, after he'd had a chance to steep himself in Jack Daniel's and frustration, and Nick would take whatever abuse he chose to dish out.

"Do you have no consideration for the family that—"

"Do you have no consideration for the victims of *this* crime, Miz Karstares?" he snapped, pausing just outside the hospital doors and turning to face her.

The doors *whoosh*ed open. Behind him, he heard Stokes groan, "Oh, Lord Jesus, take the wheel!"

"You are aware there's a murdered child lying in the morgue here, are you not?" he asked the woman. "And a mother, brutalized in her attempt to save him, lying in a hospital bed, knowing she's never gonna see her little boy again. Maybe you could muster up some sympathy for this family."

He shouldn't have said it. Kimberly Karstares wasn't smart, but she was certainly clever. She knew she had to take a different angle than the others to get attention, and she didn't mind stooping low. She had baited him, and he'd jumped to it like a bass to a fly.

He didn't wait for a reaction or a response from her. He proceeded into the building, knowing the vultures weren't allowed to follow them inside.

"You just had to, didn't you?" Stokes grumbled as they headed for the elevators. "Dutrow's gonna shit a brick when he sees that on the news."

"Fuck him," Nick snapped. "I'm tired and I'm hungry, and I'm disgusted by the base selfishness of society in general, and of that woman in particular."

"She's just doing her job, man."

Nick all but pinned him to the wall with a look. "Are you sleeping with her?"

Eyes wide, Stokes held up his hands in surrender. "No!"

"By God, you'd better not be."

"I swear!"

"Don't let me find out different," Nick warned, shaking a finger at him. "That will *not* work out for you."

Stokes punched the button for the elevator and crossed his arms over his chest. "Not that she ain't worth a fantasy or two," he admitted. "Man, you seen the legs on that girl? Whooo-eee!"

"Don't toy with me," Nick growled. "I'm in no mood. She wants to make her name putting my dick through a wringer. I won't have it. And I sure as hell won't have you help her."

"You wound me, Nicky. Truly, you do," Stokes said as they got on the elevator. "Here I am, practically your only friend, and you think I'd betray you for a piece of ass?"

"I think your logic system too often resides south of your belt buckle."

"Well, that is sometimes true," Stokes conceded. "But you have to know I'd rather be alive and miserable than die happy and satisfied. There's always another pretty girl. There's only one of me."

He flashed the square white smile and thumped his own chest.

Nick rolled his eyes. *"Merci Dieu."*

The deputy who had drawn guard duty on Genevieve Gauthier's room for the evening shift stood leaning back against the wall beside her door, playing on his cell phone.

"Young Prejean!"

Prejean shot to attention, fumbling his phone in the air like a manic juggler, his eyes wide with horror that he'd been caught slacking on the job.

"How long you been here?" Nick asked.

"Since four, sir."

"You have anything to report?"

"No. Well, Sheriff Dutrow's fiancée came by with flowers."

"What?"

"Sheriff Dutrow's fiancée came by with flowers."

"How'd you know it was Dutrow's fiancée?" Stokes asked.

Confusion puckered Prejean's brow. "'Cause she said so."

"C'est sa couillon!" Nick snapped. "What the hell is wrong with you?"

"What?" Prejean whined, looking like a kicked puppy. "What'd I do?"

"Are you dumber than a sack of hammers?" Stokes asked. "You are here to guard the victim of a crime who was attacked by an *unknown* assailant, and you let someone you didn't know go in the room?"

"But she was a lady!"

"And you don't think a woman can be violent?" Stokes asked. "Are you a virgin or something?"

"Umm, no—"

"Jesus Christ," Nick muttered. "Get your head out your ass, Prejean. Do not let unauthorized people in this room. How hard is that to understand? She could have been a reporter, for all you know."

"Oh, man." Prejean winced. "I never thought of that!"

"Well, don't hurt yourself trying to use your brain, Einstein," Stokes said. "Who else just happened to come by that you held the door open for? Jack the Ripper?"

"Miz Gauthier's boss and his wife are in there now, paying their respects," Prejean confessed. "Miz Gauthier said to let them in."

Stokes shook his head and clamped a hand on the kid's shoulder. "Son, you are gonna love that Walmart greeter job! They give you a cute little blue vest to wear!"

Already dismissing the deputy, Nick knocked on the door once and walked into Genevieve Gauthier's room without waiting for permission.

Jeff Avery swung around, frowning at the sight of him. He stood at the foot of the bed, conspicuously far away from the bed's occupant, looking uncomfortable for being anywhere near Genevieve Gauthier. His wife looked first at his face then at Nick, a little worry line tracking up between her eyebrows. She stood beside the bed in a pretty summer dress with a small bouquet of daisies clutched in her hands like an out-of-place matron of honor.

"Mr. Avery," Nick said.

"Detective." Avery nodded, shifting his weight from one foot to the other. "My wife wanted to come by to pay our respects to Miss Gauthier."

"I see that."

"Janine, this is Detective Fourcade and—"

"Detective Stokes," Stokes said, doffing his hat as he came into the room.

"—from the Sheriff's Office."

"I hope you're about to say you've caught the animal that did this," Janine Avery said.

"Do you have news, Detective?" Genevieve asked. Her bruises were in full colorful bloom now, and the swelling around her left eye and cheekbone stretched the skin to the point that it looked shiny and tight.

"I'm afraid not," Nick said. "Detective Stokes and I need to ask Miss Gauthier some more questions."

"We should be going, then," Avery said, pouncing on the excuse, already moving to herd his wife toward the door.

"Genevieve, you call us if you need anything," Janine Avery said, setting the flowers on the bedside stand.

"I may need to have a few more words with you tomorrow, Mr. Avery," Nick said just to watch Avery's reaction—a brief hot flash of panic, quickly covered.

"Whatever you need," he said, but his hand was trembling as he went to press it to the small of his wife's back. "You know where to find me."

Janine Avery shot a look of concern over her shoulder as her husband all but shoved her out the door.

Stokes leaned close and murmured, "I hope he makes it to the shitter in time."

Nick refrained from comment, though he was thinking much the same thing. Jeff Avery was going to have an uncomfortable ride home with his wife asking questions. He could easily excuse one visit from a sheriff's detective. He was Genevieve's boss, after all. But what might warrant a second round of questions? Avery would stew on that himself tonight with the mother of his children lying next to him.

"What questions?" Genevieve asked softly. Her good eye was wide and dark, the pupil almost swallowing the iris entirely, making Nick wonder what drugs the doctor had her on.

"Why would you have questions for Mr. Avery?" she asked.

"Just routine background stuff," Stokes said. "Nothing for you to worry about, ma'am. My condolences on your loss."

"Thank you," she murmured, staring at him, her expression almost wary. "Do I know you?"

"No, ma'am. Detective Stokes. I'm one of Detective Fourcade's partners."

She looked to Nick again as he pulled up a stool beside the bed and sat down to be closer to eye level with her.

"It was very kind of him to come. Mr. Avery," she said. "They're very kind people, the Averys."

"I understand they've tried to help you out," Nick said, keeping his voice low and quiet so she had to pay close attention. "They've helped you get on your feet here."

"Yes, they have."

"Mrs. Avery—is she a friend of yours?"

"No, not really. I don't really know her," she said. "We aren't in the same . . . social circles. But she's been very kind to me and KJ. We're her charity project," she said with just the slightest hint of resentment.

It had to be difficult for her, Nick thought, to see everything the Averys had—a comfortable life, social standing, stability—and to know she and her boy were a project for them, a name to add to the list of their church's outreach program, someone to give their hand-me-downs to.

"And Mr. Avery, he's a good boss?" he asked.

"He's been a godsend."

"He's taken something of a special interest in you, trying to work you into an office job?"

"He thinks I have potential. He sees more in me than most people do."

"It's nice to have someone believe in you," Nick said kindly, with the barest hint of a smile. "Sometimes that's all a person needs—for someone to believe in them, yeah?"

"Yes."

"Mr. Avery told me you've had office jobs before, but you moved up here and took a job as an aide at Evangeline Oaks. That's a noble profession, for true, caring for people, but it probably doesn't pay all that well, I'm guessing. Why would you do that?"

"I needed a job. It's what was available," she said. "Why?"

"Me, I'm just trying to get a clear picture of who you are, Miz Gauthier," he said softly, holding her gaze with his. "Genevieve. May I call you Genevieve?"

"It sounds so pretty when you say it," she said with a shy smile.

"It's a beautiful name," he said, again giving her the slightest of smiles in return.

"Thank you."

"So, Genevieve, the more I know about you, about your life, the better I might be able to see why someone chose you to be their victim. If I can understand that, I can better discern who that person might be."

"It's like we're putting together a ten-thousand-piece puzzle," Stokes added. "But we don't get to see what the final picture should look like until it's almost done. That's why we need all these little pieces that might not look like anything to anyone else—not even to you. For instance, I'm gonna ask did you notice people coming and going from your neighbor's property? The blue house next door—Mr. Perez."

"Last night?" she asked. "No."

"Any night."

"No. Why?"

"Your neighbor, Mr. Perez, has a criminal record as a drug dealer, among other things," Stokes said. "You didn't know that?"

"No!" she said, clearly upset by the idea. "How would I know that? I would never have moved in there if I had known that!"

"Your landlord, Mr. Carville, he didn't mention it to you?"

"Did he know?"

"He owns that property as well. He's well-acquainted with Mr. Perez."

"Oh, my God," Genevieve murmured, shifting in the bed, breathing harder and faster as her anxiety level rose. "That horrible little man! He rented that house to me and my son, knowing there was a criminal next door?"

"But you told me this morning you've never had any real interaction with Mr. Perez," Nick said. "He didn't bother you in any way."

"He yelled at KJ that time."

"But other than that one time . . . ?"

"No. Well . . ." She hesitated, glancing away, uncomfortable with whatever she was holding back.

"Well, what?" Nick prompted. "Don't be shy, Genevieve. Whatever thought you have, please share it. It'll be up to us to decide do we need to pursue it or not."

"Well, he would . . . look at me. If I was out in the yard with KJ and he came by, he would . . . look at me . . . the way men do."

"It made you uncomfortable?"

She nodded, uncomfortable now for talking about it.

"But you didn't hesitate to run to that house for help last night."

"It was the nearest house. I needed help," she said. "You think he did it, don't you?"

"No," Nick said. "I think if Mr. Perez wanted you dead then you'd be dead, but here you are. So, no, I don't think he did it."

"Then why are you asking me about him?"

"Bad men have bad friends," Stokes said. "Maybe one took notice of you."

She looked away toward the window and the last glow of the waning sunset, searching her memory. "I don't remember anyone."

"Genevieve," Nick said, drawing her attention back to him. "You told me this morning there was nothing out of the ordinary about last night. It was just a usual night at home for you and your son."

"Yes."

"Do you normally drink heavily in the evening?"

Her whole body jolted, as if the question had been delivered by cattle prod. "What? Why would you ask such a thing?"

"The attending physician in the ER last night remarked that he detected the smell of alcohol on your breath," Nick said, keeping his voice at the same low, calm pitch.

"No. He was mistaken!"

He shook his head, grimacing a bit. "The thing is, he wasn't mistaken, Genevieve. Your tox screen came back with a point-oh-six blood alcohol content. That's considerable."

"That's not possible."

"Blood tests don't lie."

Her pulse was racing. He could see it beat in the carotid artery along the delicate line of her neck.

"I'm not saying it's a lie," she said. "I just— I had a Jack and Diet Coke after supper," she confessed. "Just to relax a little. It was a hard day at work. But I never drank that much! I swear!"

"It's all right, Genevieve," Nick assured her, keeping his gaze steady on hers. "It's not against the law to have a couple of drinks in your own home."

"You could still drive a vehicle on point-oh-six," Stokes pointed out. "And believe me, no one understands needing a drink after work better than cops, right, Nicky?"

Nick hummed a note of agreement. "Did anything in particular happen at work that stressed you?"

"No," she answered, a little too quickly. She looked down at the sheet that covered her to the waist and picked at the wrinkles with her good hand. "It was just a busy day is all, and KJ was wound up, and . . ."

Tears rose in her eyes, one spilling from each to roll like clear pearls down her cheeks.

"I understand your son had some challenges," Nick said gently. "Hard to deal with all that by yourself—having a job, being his mother, no support . . ."

"He wouldn't settle down," she said so softly, Nick had to lean closer. "He wouldn't mind. I just didn't have the energy to deal with it. I had such a headache . . ."

"Just one of those days," Stokes said, shrugging it off. "The best thing you can do with a bad day is put an end to it. Have a drink and go to bed. We get that."

"The problem is, Genevieve, you didn't just have a drink, did you?" Nick asked. "You had a drink and a couple of pills, too, yeah?"

She wanted to deny it and knew she couldn't.

"You had a pill bottle of Clarice Marcel's for Oxycodone," he prompted.

"I was just going to get that refilled for her—"

Nick raised a finger and shook his head. "Don't lie to me, Genevieve," he said softly. "We're not the drug police. Nobody's gonna bust you for having three Oxy tablets in your handbag. I am not your enemy. But if I'm to find the person who killed your son and injured you, I need the truth. I need the truth to find the truth. Do you understand me?"

She stared at him, frantically weighing her options.

"You take a deep breath and calm yourself," he instructed. "Breathe in slowly. Breathe out slowly."

She inhaled too quickly, her breath hitching in her throat.

"You're all right," Nick said. "Just slow down."

She tried again and did a little better, her gaze hard on his, afraid to look away.

"Tell me why'd you take that pill last night?" he asked in a near whisper, drawing her closer, into his confidence, as if her answer would be just a small secret between them.

"I g-get migraine headaches," she said, wiping a tear from her bruised cheek. "I d-don't have insurance. Sh-she— Aunt Clarice, she gave those t-to me. Sh-she wouldn't t-take them anyway."

"How often do you take it? Every night?"

"No!"

"Once a day?" he asked. "More than once a day?"

"No!"

"How many times have you had that 'script refilled?" Stokes asked.

"Just once."

"You know we'll check the drugstores, yeah?" he said.

Genevieve looked from Stokes to Nick and back, frantic. "I'm not lying!"

"Do you ever get pills from anyone else?" Nick asked.

"No!"

"You in and out of a lot of rooms at Evangeline Oaks. You don't maybe pick up an Oxy here, a Vicodin there?"

"I'm not a thief!" she insisted, but she didn't quite meet his eyes.

"Do you know anyone there who does that?"

"No!"

"And you've never bought pills off anyone here in town?"

"No!"

"How about when you lived down Dulac?" Stokes asked.

"Oh, my God, I can't believe you're asking me these things!" she said, looking like someone trapped in a nightmare, unable to wake. "You're acting like *I'm* the criminal!"

Nick sat back a little, releasing the pressure on her. He looked at Stokes and then away. Genevieve watched him the whole time, swiping at one tear and then another with a trembling hand.

The news was playing silently on the television. He caught a glimpse of Jaime Blynn, Annie's friend, the second-grade teacher, and the principal of the elementary school, Ms. Samuels Young, the two of them standing on the edge of the playground, answering questions, their expressions earnest and sad. Then there he was, himself, looking angry as he snapped at Kimberly Karstares on his way into the hospital.

He took a deep breath and sighed.

"Genevieve, we're not picking these questions out of the sky," he said, turning back to her. "You had drugs and alcohol in your system last night. That's a fact. That suggests to us you might be living a risky lifestyle."

"I'm not!" she insisted. "I had a headache. I was tired. I just had a drink—"

"And you have a possession charge on your record from a few years ago," Nick said. "What are we to make of that?"

"No!" she said on a little gasp of shock, tears welling up anew. "That's a mistake! That's not right! Why are you doing this to me? I haven't done anything wrong! Someone killed my son!"

"That's exactly right," Nick said. "Someone came into your home last night and murdered your child and attacked you. This wasn't an accident, Genevieve. It wasn't random. This killer didn't just wander in off the street. He came to your house for a purpose.

"Maybe he's someone who saw you from afar at the supermarket and spun up a fantasy about you. But maybe he's someone who knows you, has some connection to you. And when I see these possible connections to the drug culture, I have to go there and dig in that hole. It can't matter to me if that offends you or upsets you. And it shouldn't matter to you, either.

"You want me to find who killed your boy, yes?" he asked.

"Yes," she whispered.

"Then we want the same thing," he said softly. "I have a little boy, too. If something happened to him, me, I'd move mountains with my bare hands to find out who hurt him and why. I'll do the same for your boy.

"I'm sorry if that's hard on you, Genevieve. I'm sorry I have to ask you hard questions. But nothing is harder than losing your child, right?"

"Nothing."

"So you need to trust me," he said, leaning closer, holding her gaze. "And I need to be able to trust you to tell me the truth, no matter what that truth might be. For KJ," he whispered. "For your boy."

She nodded, closing her eyes against a fresh wave of tears and grief. She looked exhausted, wrung out by the emotional roller-coaster ride he had just taken her on.

"C'est assez," Nick murmured. "That's enough. You get some rest."

As he rose, he reached out and gently touched her uninjured shoulder in a gesture of sympathy and reassurance. She seemed as slight as a bird. It was hard to imagine her fighting off an armed assailant, but people often found physical strength beyond imagining when faced with the choice of life or death.

He started to turn toward Stokes when she reached out and touched his hand, catching hold of his fingers.

"Where is KJ's kitten?" she asked. "I got him a kitten for an early birthday present. He hadn't even named him yet."

"We have him at the office," Nick said. "He can stay until you get settled somewhere."

"Thank you. You're a kind man. I know you're going to help me, Detective Fourcade," she said, looking up at him with hope and something else, something like admiration, something that at once fascinated him and made him feel vaguely uncomfortable.

"I don't have anyone else," she said. "You'll have to be my hero."

TWENTY-TWO

"I stood right there and watched that go down, and I still don't know how you did it," Stokes said, looking at Nick sideways as they headed down the hall toward the elevators. "I don't get it. You all but called her a crack whore, and that girl is in love with you now."

He batted his eyelashes and clutched at his heart and said in a breathless falsetto, "You're my hero, Detective Fourcade!"

Nick saw no need for a reply. He was already replaying the interview in his mind, picking apart and analyzing Genevieve Gauthier's every response and reaction.

Stokes hit the button to call the elevator. "I personally don't find you all that charming."

"Perhaps she thinks it's to her benefit to fall in love with me," Nick said. "Just as it may be to her benefit to fall in love with her boss—and to try to get him to fall in love with her."

Stokes bobbed his thick eyebrows as he took the point. "This is exactly why I don't do single moms," he said. "That's a spiderweb, man. I don't care how juicy the bait is. I ain't getting wrapped up in that."

"Well, God forbid any woman would want you to be a father to her children," Nick said. "That's reason to call Child and Family Services, right there."

"Hey, I know my limitations."

"Why does she think she knows you?" Nick asked as the bell dinged and they got on the elevator.

"The hell if I know."

He watched Stokes's face carefully, never quite trusting him to tell the whole truth where it involved a woman. "You didn't maybe run across her while trolling ladies' night at the Voodoo Lounge?"

"No, sir. My hand to God."

"God should have withered that hand off your arm by now," Nick said. "You a walking advertisement for atheism, you are."

"Pagans have more fun," Stokes said with a grin. "If I'm lyin', I'm dyin'."

"I want the records on her cell phone," Nick said. "And tomorrow I want to go down Terrebonne Parish and talk to her former employers. Something doesn't add up to me. She told me this morning she moved here to take a job. Now she says she moved up here and *needed* a job, then she takes a grunt job when she's qualified by past experience to make more money working in an office. That doesn't make sense to me."

"You think she came here for some reason other than this auntie in the old folks' home?"

"According to the office manager, she was never a regular visitor to Clarice Marcel before she moved here. Why the sudden devotion?"

"And now the woman is giving her an unlimited supply of Oxycodone," Stokes said. "Every pill head should have such a fairy godmother."

They got off on the ground floor and headed for the main exit, Nick already bracing himself mentally for what would probably greet them as they walked outside. He didn't hold out any hope that the news crews had given up and gone back to where they had come from, not when they knew they would have a second chance to poke a stick at him and get him to respond.

"Try not to get into a fistfight on the way to the car," Stokes said. "I'm fucking starving, man. I got a shrimp po'boy in my sights. I'm making a beeline for Po' Richard's, with or without you."

The doors *whoosh*ed open, and they stepped out into the electric sun of artificial lights, and a cloud of noise that seemed louder than before. Nick squinted hard against the glare and walked forward, not allowing himself to sort out individual voices. He had no intention of answering any of them.

"Detective Fourcade!"

"Detective Fourcade!"

"Detective!"

"Detective!"

"Fourcade!"

Bobby Theriot's voice cut through the others like a thunderbolt—loud, deep, raw with emotion, cigarettes, and whiskey. He came directly at Nick, emerging from the center of the light like an avenging angel.

He was big—well over six feet—with the thick, practical muscle of a man who used his body for a living and the gut of man who self-medicated with too much beer and fried food.

"You bastard!"

He came at Nick like a charging bull, roaring, and stopped just short of making contact, looming over Nick, leaning down into his face, his breath sour, his eyes half-wild, half-glazed.

"You just forget about my little girl," he said. "You don't even have the balls to call me and tell me you're moving on?"

"Bobby, this is not the time or the place," Nick said, trying to keep his voice low so as not to be picked up by a microphone.

"You don't want to admit it on television?" Theriot said, bumping him with his belly, trying to make him step back. "You're not man enough to say it to my face?"

"Bobby, man, step back," Stokes said, moving in like a referee, even as the cameras crowded closer.

Theriot swung toward him, shoving him back with a pair of rough hands the size of war hammers. "Fuck off, Stokes, you useless piece of crap. This is between me and Fourcade—if he has anything to say for himself."

"If you want to sit down and talk, Bobby, let's go do that," Nick said calmly. "We're not gonna do it here."

Theriot spat on the ground and wiped his mouth with the back of his hand, grimacing at the taste. He had a rawboned face, lined and chapped from working in the elements. A grizzled mustache and goatee bracketed his mouth. "You're a fucking coward, Fourcade."

"You're drunk," Nick said, moving a couple of feet to his right.

Theriot stepped awkwardly to match him. "What are you gonna do? Arrest me?"

"Let's not make it come to that," Nick said, moving back the other way. Just a few steps. Just to make Bobby Theriot track him with blood-shot eyes that didn't quite want to focus.

"You'd do it, too," Theriot said, turning, slightly unsteady, his speech just this side of beginning to slur. "You'd arrest me and let the man who molested my daughter walk scot-free."

"We're doing everything we can to find the person—"

"You're doing jack shit!" he shouted. "But here you are, in the big spot-light," he said, flapping his arms at his sides. "The big man. The big detective. Moving on to the big murder investigation. My daughter doesn't mean shit to you. Fuck you!"

Theriot hauled his arm back, winding up for a haymaker of a punch. Nick caught the big man's fist as it came at him and stepped deftly aside, letting Bobby's momentum take him forward. Off balance and overcom-mitted to the punch, clumsy in cowboy boots, he went down face-first on the pavement. Nick rode him down to the ground, twisting Theriot's arm up behind his back to hold him in place.

"Oh, man, this is gonna look great on the ten o'clock news," Stokes muttered, leaning down close, offering Nick a pair of handcuffs.

Hospital staff poured out the doors to see the commotion. The TV cameras rushed in on both sides. The shouts of the reporters came like the loud, rapid fire of a machine gun.

"Are you arresting him?"

"Is he under arrest?"

"Detective!"

"Detective!"

Nick glanced over to see Kimberly Karstares standing off to the side, speaking directly into the camera from her station, composed in the way of someone who might have been expecting exactly what had happened.

Beneath him, Bobby Theriot was sobbing out his frustration and rage in a barely intelligible litany of grievances and profanity.

"You fuckers don't care! . . . My baby girl! . . . Ain't no justice! . . . Fuck all y'all, you fucking fucks!"

"Bobby, you have the right to remain silent." Nick began the Miranda warning quietly, wishing to God Theriot would take the advice. Around them, the news people were still chattering.

"Detective, will he be charged?"

"What will he be charged with?"

"Detective Fourcade!"

In his peripheral vision he caught a glimpse of two deputies running toward them from the ambulance bay. He glanced up at Stokes.

"Help me get him up."

Together they struggled to get Bobby Theriot to his feet. Twice he let his knees buckle and tried to drop back down to the ground, crying, tears and snot and blood running down his face. He had busted his lip in the fall and had scraped his face on the concrete, leaving bright red abrasions, bleeding in spots.

"Take him to the ER," Nick ordered the deputies as they arrived. "Get him checked out."

"Then what?"

"Take him in and book him for public intoxication. He can sleep it off in the drunk tank. I'm not sending him home like this."

Stokes had begun herding the reporters backward, telling them there was nothing more to see, that they needed to pack it up and move it along. Only Kimberly Karstares evaded him, staying off to Nick's left, away from the others.

"Detective Fourcade, can we have a moment?"

"No," Nick snapped, shooting her a hard look then turning it on the videographer. "Get that fucking camera out of my face."

The young man jumped backward like a skittish horse, dropping the camera.

"Turn it off."

The red light blinked off.

"Detective Fourcade," Karstares pressed. "This is your opportunity to say something for yourself—"

"No," he said. "But I have a question for you, Miss Karstares."

"Of course." She had the nerve to smile a tight little professional smile, as if they were strangers and she hadn't already fucked him over half a dozen times on the Theriot story.

"Do you have no human decency whatsoever?" he asked.

"I'm not the one manhandling the father of a victim," she shot back.

"Nor was I, but you'll be all too happy to show that clip at ten and let people think what they will, won't you?"

"You're good television, Detective."

"You want good television?" Nick asked. "Then let's talk about how Bobby Theriot came to be here. What would possess him to come to Our Lady tonight? Did he just happen to turn on your channel for the six o'clock news to see you badgering me on my way inside? Or did you give him a little heads-up on that, Miss Karstares?"

"What are you implying?"

"I am inferring from past experiences that you, Miss Karstares, are a shit stirrer," he said. "And if I find out from Mr. Theriot that you called him and told him maybe he might want to come over here and confront me tonight, I'm gonna make damn sure you have to lick that spoon."

"Are you threatening me?" she asked, pretending affront.

"No. I'm telling you that your actions and your words have consequences," Nick said. "Not just for you personally, although you can't seem to see beyond that pretty little nose on your face. You're messing with people's lives. Bobby Theriot is going in the ER now, to get his busted lip stitched up because he came here tonight to try to punch me in the face. What if he'd brought a gun? Hmmm? What then? Did you think of that?"

His question was met with a carefully blank look. She reached up with a nervous hand and pushed a stray lock of her hair behind her ear.

"You think he doesn't have a gun?" Nick asked. "You think he doesn't have ten guns? You think if somebody pokes at his raw nerves enough he might not just up and decide to kill somebody? Is that what you want? Is that 'good television'? You gonna crawl up out of obscurity on my dead body, on Bobby Theriot's dead body, and get yourself a big job in New Orleans?"

"Hey, Nicky," Stokes said, coming alongside him. "Let's go. I don't want to get chewed out on an empty stomach. Come on."

Nick's gaze didn't waver from Kimberly Karstares.

"You go look up Hunter Davidson," he said. "He's gonna die in prison because he took a gun and killed an innocent man he thought was guilty."

She didn't blink. "And whose fault was that?"

The barb found its mark, though he refused to show it. She had already done her homework. Of course she had. Of course she knew he had been obsessed with the idea that an architect named Marcus Renard had murdered local real estate agent Pamela Davidson Bichon. He had nearly killed Renard himself at one point. Pam's father, despondent with grief and frustration at a justice system he thought had failed him, had shot and killed Renard on the very night the real killer had revealed herself. The weight of that tragedy still hung on him all these years later.

"Mine," he admitted. "And I won't have it happen again."

Stokes tugged at his shirtsleeve. "Nicky, let's go."

"You have a lovely evening, Miss Karstares," Nick said, backing away. "Maybe you go looking for your soul before the ten o'clock news."

TWENTY-THREE

"What did I tell you?" Dutrow asked, his voice crackling with temper. "What did I tell you about talking to the press?"

"Don't," Nick said dispassionately.

He stood in Dutrow's office, formerly Gus Noblier's office, unrecognizable now that it had been stripped of Gus's accumulation of twenty-some years of crap and dust: the ancient case files and stacks of old *Field & Stream* magazines, giant ceremonial ribbon-cutting scissors and lacquered alligator heads, Mardi Gras beads and a jarful of tiny plastic baby dolls discovered in King Cakes over the decades.

Gus's office had been a museum of weird relics. Dutrow was a man who appreciated order. It was practically the only thing he and Nick had in common.

The sheriff sat behind his desk, still wearing his black tactical costume, projecting an image of square-jawed authority, something that made no real impression on Nick, since he only acknowledged Dutrow's authority in the most basic way. He stood with his hands on his hips, his feet slightly spread apart. He had not been invited to sit. This was Dutrow calling him on the carpet, literally, in a vain attempt to shame and embarrass him.

"Don't talk to the press. Is some part of that sentence incomprehensible to you, Detective?"

"No."

"And yet you had to shoot your mouth off."

"I wouldn't call it that."

Dutrow's face turned a darker shade of red. "I don't care what you might call it. I care how it looked and how it sounded."

There was a sarcastic remark to be made about style and substance, but Nick kept it in his mouth. He was tired and irritated, and the last place he wanted to be at the moment was standing here listening to Kelvin Dutrow.

"I asked for compassion for the mother of a murder victim," he said. "Or did you miss that part?"

Of course, that was only his six o'clock sound bite. If Kimberly Karstares ran true to form, his ten o'clock sound bite would be "*Get that fucking camera out of my face,*" followed by an edited shot of him sitting on Bobby Theriot as he handcuffed the sobbing father of a molested autistic girl.

"Do. Not. Talk. To. The. Press," Dutrow said, enunciating each word. He pressed his hands on his blotter, his fingers splayed wide as if he was trying to hold down the desk.

"I'm willing to bet money that Karstares woman made sure Bobby Theriot showed up tonight," Nick said, moving on.

Dutrow arched a brow. "Am I done reprimanding you?"

"I sincerely hope so, as it's a waste of your time and mine," Nick said impatiently, shifting his weight to one side and then the other, wanting to walk away. "And speaking for myself, I don't have time to lose over this nonsense or anything else. I have a murder investigation ongoing."

Dutrow shook his head. "You have got a set of brass ones on you, Fourcade."

"You don't want me talking to the press," Nick said. "Me, I don't wanna talk to the press. That suits me fine. If you can arrange for them to be elsewhere, that'd be great. Maybe they can follow you around all day, filming whatever you do, recording everything you say. You're better suited to it than me. If not, I'll do the best I can. I can't promise more than that. My focus is on catching a murderer. I don't give two shits about TV ratings or the public's opinion of me. Can we now move on to issues pertinent to the case? Sir."

He added the title as a discordant afterthought. Dutrow looked at him for a long moment, mentally sorting the slights and insults, trying to decide which to disregard and which to take exception to. In the end, he gave up.

"What did you do with Theriot?"

"Charged him with public intoxication. Stokes is booking him."

"He attempted to assault a law enforcement officer. On camera, I assume," Dutrow said. "It's probably all over the Internet already."

"I'm none the worse for wear," Nick said. "And charging him for it would be highly unpopular in the court of public opinion, which I'm sure is where your primary concern lies here. Let it go. Make a public statement about compassion, if you feel the need. Bobby Theriot wasn't the most malicious person there tonight. At least his motivation was pure, which is more than I can say for Kimberly Karstares."

"Would you be so charitable if he had landed that punch?" Dutrow asked.

"Bobby Theriot is not my enemy, nor am I his," Nick said.

Giving in to the need to move, he went to Dutrow's wall of fame and let his gaze scan the photographs—Kelvin Dutrow with every politician to draw breath in Acadiana for the past decade or so, giving awards, accepting awards, posing with prominent citizens and civic groups and other cops. In a suit, in a uniform, younger, less gray—the pose and the smile were always exactly the same.

Nick's eye landed on one framed newspaper article in particular. The date was nine years past, stamped beneath the newspaper headline from the Houma *Times*:

HOUMA OFFICERS DEDICATED TO COMMUNITY SAFETY
R.A.D.—RAPE AGGRESSION DEFENSE SYSTEM:
TEACHING SELF-DEFENSE TACTICS TO AREA WOMEN

The photo showed Dutrow instructing a woman to target an assailant's eyes in her attempt to escape an attack. The officer playing the role of the assailant was Keith Kemp. There was no mistaking the crew cut and the sharply chiseled features. It was Kemp in uniform, leaning back and turning his face toward the camera as the woman reached out to gouge at his eyes.

"He's a father hurting for his child," Nick said, turning back around to face Dutrow. "He couldn't be there when she needed him most. He thinks he let her down. That's why he lashes out. He wants someone else to blame, but there isn't anyone—just a ghost, for now. He's alone with all that hate inside. He directs it at me. I'm the surrogate until the case gets solved.

"That day was like any other," he said. "He went to work like he has every day of his adult life. There was no reason for him not to. He couldn't know. No one could—except maybe the person who committed the crime, and maybe not even them. His wife went on about her day like she did every day. She only left the girl alone for an hour or so . . . Now he hates her for it.

"I wish I could give him the thing he needs," he said. "But now my focus has to be on the Gauthier murder."

"And where are you at with that?"

"Nowhere, yet. Given where Ms. Gauthier lives, I don't believe this was a random act. The killer may not have gone there to murder a child, but he almost certainly went there on purpose."

"Suspects?"

"She claims to have no enemies here."

"You don't believe her?"

"Unless she did this thing herself, she has one enemy, for true. Who that might be is a mystery. We're working a possible drug angle. She seems to have a liking for Oxy. And she has an ex-con drug dealer living next door."

"Do you like him for it?"

"Not really. If he wanted her dead, why ain't she? If he went there to rape her, why didn't he? Why kill a child and get nothing for it? It makes no sense, and yet, I feel like there might be something there. I just don't know what."

"What about boyfriends, exes, the boy's father?"

"She says no on all counts."

"Have you spoken to the father?"

"She refuses to give us his name. It's not on the birth certificate. She says he's not in the picture at all."

"And you believe her?"

"Me, I think Miss Gauthier has a lot of secrets. The question is, does she want to keep those secrets more than she wants justice for her child?" Nick frowned and gave an almost imperceptible shrug. "We'll see."

"You said 'unless she did this thing herself,' " Dutrow said. "Do you think that's possible?"

"Anything is possible. She's a single mom, struggling to make ends meet. Maybe has a drug problem. The boy was a handful. Maybe she just had enough.

"Am I getting my autopsy?" he asked.

Dutrow heaved a big sigh. "The coroner isn't inclined. He says he doesn't need to desecrate the child's body to determine either the cause or manner of death."

"And you agree with him?"

"It's his call. He's the coroner."

"And you're the sheriff," Nick said, his temper rising. "And I'm the detective. I want a tox screen at least."

"You think the boy was popping pills, too? A seven-year-old child?"

"I want to know did his mother drug him," he said impatiently. "I want his body examined and X-rayed for old injuries that might suggest a pattern of abuse.

"Do you have some sort of objection to being thorough?" he asked, his tone dripping sarcasm. "Is that how they do things in Houma? Half-assed?"

"Of course not!"

"Then why are we having this conversation?" Nick asked, his patience worn to threads. "A boy was murdered. There needs to be an autopsy. End of fucking story!"

Dutrow pushed to his feet. "Keep a civil tongue in your head when you're talking to me! You forget I'm not the subordinate here, Detective. You work for me, not the other way around."

"I work for the victim," Nick corrected him.

"And I'm just here to supervise, is that it?" Dutrow asked, his face growing red. "I'm just here to sign off on the paperwork?"

"*Mais* yeah!" Nick snapped back, ready to explode with frustration. "That *is* what you do! You can put on a uniform and march around like a goddamn general and have all the power of a dictator, but you *are* in fact a supervisor!"

Dutrow stiffened. "You are perilously close to losing your job, Detective Fourcade," he said softly.

"I am trying to *do* my job," Nick said, matching the sheriff's tone. "I am trying to go through the proper channels to get what I need to solve a murder. I don't think I should have to jump through hoops every time I need something that should be a given in a murder investigation. But if that's what you want—"

"This isn't about me."

Nick pressed a hand across his mouth to stop himself from cursing at the absurdity of the statement. The fucking gaslighting narcissist. This conversation wasn't about anything other than him. His needs, his demands, his own overblown opinion of his importance in the world.

Inhale. Control. Focus. Exhale. Control. Focus.

Nick could barely articulate the mantra in his conscious mind. He couldn't seem to slow his pulse or his respiration.

"I wonder," Dutrow murmured. "Will your wife choose to continue working for the SO if I fire you?"

Nick wanted to hurl himself across the desk and wrap his hands around the man's throat. He was literally trembling from the effort to remain still. The *fils de pute*, bringing Annie into this. What kind of man did that? No man of honor. Whatever abstract scrap of respect he'd ever had for Dutrow turned to ash in that second.

"Is that how you operate?" he asked quietly. "You threaten a man's livelihood, threaten a man's family? That's who you are?"

"I'm just telling you how it is, Detective," Dutrow said. "That's how the food chain works. I am the apex predator here. And if I decide I don't want to put up with your attitude, you will be nothing but a bad memory to me. What impact that has on you and your family is not my problem."

He wouldn't quit. No matter how much he disliked Dutrow, he wouldn't quit. No matter how much Dutrow disliked him, he wouldn't quit. As a matter of principle and pure damn Cajun stubbornness, he would ride this fight into the bowels of hell and outlast the devil himself.

He spread his hands wide in a gesture of false surrender and cocked his head to one side. "Me, I'm just trying to do my job to the best of my ability," he said. "I confess to being guilty of overzealousness in the pursuit of justice for my victims."

"Is that supposed to be an apology?"

"If need be."

Dutrow looked at him, weighing his options. "You're an arrogant son of a bitch," he announced.

"Yes," Nick admitted. "But not without cause. I *will* solve this case. I need that autopsy."

The sheriff gave an exasperated half laugh, shaking his head. "I'll speak with the coroner."

"Thank you."

"Where is Detective Broussard this evening?" Dutrow asked, seating himself again, content for the moment with his thinly veiled threats and emotional manipulation.

"She went to talk to people at the boy's school and to talk to the boy's babysitter," Nick said, matching Dutrow's calm tone. If that was the game he wanted to play . . . "To see if there was any indication of something amiss yesterday or leading up to yesterday."

"And your next move?"

"Provided I still have a job, Stokes and I will go tomorrow to Dulac and Houma and talk to Genevieve's former employers and fill in the blanks on her background. You might be able to help with that, actually."

Dutrow sat back a bit, one eyebrow sketching upward. "Really? How so?"

"She has a DUI charge on her record from some years ago and a misdemeanor possession charge that was dropped. I want to know more about that. Dixon's trying to get a copy of the original arrest report but hasn't been able to. I want to know what this girl had on her when she was arrested. Was that charge dropped because she flipped on a dealer? If someone went away on her say-so, they might just be out by now. That would give us a revenge motive."

"Where did this happen?"

"Not sure if it was Houma PD or Terrebonne Sheriff's Office, but you must have contacts both places. Maybe you could reach out for us."

"And how long ago was this?"

"Eight or nine years ago."

Dutrow scoffed. "That's a long time. How can that be relevant?"

"It's been long enough for some petty dealer to go do a stretch in Angola and get back out."

"She couldn't have had much in her possession if the charge got dropped entirely," Dutrow argued.

"Or she gave the DA somebody they really wanted," Nick countered.

"More likely, it was nothing," Dutrow said.

"When I brought it up to her tonight, she got pretty agitated. She said, 'Oh, no, that's a mistake.' What does that mean?" Nick asked. "What kind of mistake?"

"Could be a clerical error for all you know."

"Then there should be no record of charges being dismissed because the charges never existed."

"You're barking up an old obscure tree here," Dutrow said, getting up from his chair.

Nick shrugged. "It's a thread. I find them, and I pull them all. One unravels the cover cloth and we see the truth. Will you make a couple of phone calls and get the original arrest report or not?"

"All right, fine," Dutrow said, flipping a hand dismissively. "I'll make some calls tomorrow if you think it's necessary."

"I think it's necessary."

"Fine."

"Thank you," Nick said, trying to stifle the sigh of frustration. He glanced at his watch.

"Am I keeping you from something more pressing, Detective?" Dutrow asked sarcastically.

"Yes. As a matter of fact, you are. Are we finished?"

The sheriff gestured toward the door. "By all means . . ."

Nick started to leave, turning back around just as he settled his hand on the doorknob. "Young Prejean said your fiancée brought flowers to Genevieve Gauthier today. Could that be true?"

For a second Dutrow looked surprised, taken aback. The look was gone in a heartbeat. "Oh, well, probably so," he said, shuffling a stack of papers on his desk. "Sharon volunteers for the hospital auxiliary."

"She wouldn't know Genevieve from Houma, would she?"

"I thought this girl was from Dulac."

"She worked for a time as a clerk in Houma City Hall. Their paths might have crossed."

Dutrow shook his head, making a face. "I shouldn't think so, no. She didn't mention it to me."

Nick dismissed the thought as he left the building and walked across the yard to the Pizza Hut. The night was still too warm. It felt like a storm could blow up, though the sky was clear. He looked for Annie's car in the lot. It seemed strange he hadn't heard from her. How much could KJ Gauthier's twelve-year-old babysitter have had to say?

Even as he thought it, his phone pinged the arrival of a text. He unclipped it from his belt and looked at it as he buzzed himself into the building. The aroma of pepperoni and tomato sauce hit him in the face, immediately making his stomach growl.

The text was from Annie: *We have a problem. The babysitter is missing.*
Missing?

Nick walked into the bullpen, his attention on his phone screen, his brow furrowed. He turned and went down the hall to his office, wanting privacy to call Annie, his mind tumbling over possibilities. Why would the babysitter go missing? Did she know something? Had she seen something? Heard something? Done something? Had someone taken her? Had she run away?

KJ Gauthier's kitten had gotten up on his desk and curled up on the papers in his in-box. He reached out and stroked the animal's head with his fingertips.

"Boss?"

Wynn Dixon stood in his doorway as he settled himself in his chair. "Did you find that arrest report?" he asked.

"No, not yet," she said, though it was clear by her expression she had something to say, something she didn't necessarily want to say.

"What then?"

"Remember I mentioned this afternoon she had a juvie record?"

"What of it?"

"It's for murder," Dixon said soberly. "Genevieve Gauthier killed a baby."

TWENTY-FOUR

Lola Troiano and her mother lived in a lovely Caribbean colonial–style house in the Quail Run development on the western edge of town. The neighborhood was little more than a decade old, but due to the traditional style of the homes and the many mature trees the development had been designed around, it had the feeling of having been there forever. It was the kind of place professional people raised their beautiful families and entertained their witty and successful friends at gracious dinner parties where everyone spoke intelligently about politics and world affairs. The driveways were studded with Volvos and BMWs.

Annie recognized the house right away—17 Cheval Court had been filed away in her memory years before. The house had been owned by a real estate agent named Lindsay Faulkner, partner to a murder victim who had become a victim herself. Annie wondered if Jessica Troiano knew that story. Some people would run backward from a murder house. Others would use the sad fact of a violent death to drive a hard bargain and never think of it again. Jessica Troiano was a litigator, a professional negotiator. In Annie's experience, lawyers were given to neither superstition nor sentimentality.

She went to the front door and rang the doorbell, peeking into the foyer through a sidelight. The last time she'd looked in through this glass there had been a beaten, bloody comatose woman lying half naked on the floor with a ginger cat curled up beside her. The huge potted fern in the corner may well have been the same plant as had been there years before.

The house was open and airy. From the front door, Annie could see straight through to part of the kitchen, to the French doors that led out to a brick patio.

Lola came trotting from the kitchen, dressed in black leggings splashed with graffiti in neon colors, and a T-shirt with a big anchor on the front, her long hair down and loose. Her smile faded as she opened the door.

"Hey, Lola," Annie said. "Is your mom home?"

"Lola?" a voice called from deeper in the house. "Who is it? Supper's almost ready!"

Jessica Troiano didn't wait for an answer. She emerged from the kitchen, wiping her hands on a towel, striding purposefully toward the foyer. She was her daughter's older carbon copy—tall, slender, her brown hair swept up in a messy knot on her head. She had the sinewy leanness of a longtime yoga practitioner, a lifestyle given away by the smiling stick figure in downward dog pose on her T-shirt.

"Can I help you?" she asked, peering over her daughter's head as she came to the door.

"Mrs. Troiano, I'm Detective Broussard from the Sheriff's Office," Annie began.

Immediately, Jessica Troiano stiffened, her expression going sober. "Are you kidding me?"

"No. Uh—"

"She's pressing charges? Are you freaking kidding me?"

"Uh—"

"Lola, go in the kitchen," she instructed, sweeping her daughter away from the door.

"But, Mom—"

"Go! I'll take care of this."

Lola backed out of the foyer but hovered just beyond, looking worried.

"Mrs. Troiano, I'm not sure why you think I'm here," Annie started again. "Who do you think is pressing charges? And why?"

Jessica Troiano clamped down on the emotion that had tipped her hand the second before. "Why are you here?" she asked coolly.

"I need to ask Lola some questions."

"About what?"

"About a friend of hers. May I come in?"

"What friend?"

"Nora Florette."

"Oh, my God," Jessica muttered, rolling her eyes. "That family!"

"Dean started it!" Lola blurted out.

Her mother gave her a look of exasperation.

"May I come in?" Annie asked again. Whatever this was about, she wanted to be sitting down to hear it. It seemed that every story involving the Florettes turned out to be long and headache-inducing, and she was tired and hungry.

Annie stepped inside before the woman could change her mind.

"I'm sorry I'm interrupting your supper," she said, her stomach grumbling as she breathed in the aroma of something delicious wafting out from the kitchen.

"Hopefully this isn't going to take long," Jessica said, showing the way to a comfortable, stylish living room straight out of a Restoration Hardware showroom.

Lola hopped onto the sofa and tucked herself into the corner, her feet drawn up, her arms banded around her knees. She couldn't have made herself any smaller.

"I like your nail polish," Annie said to break the ice as she took a seat on the huge, tufted leather ottoman directly in front of the girl. "Blue is my favorite, too."

"Thanks," Lola murmured.

"So, did Dean get into a fight with that other boy after I left the park today?"

"With Cameron?" Lola said, surprised. "I don't think so. Cameron is terrified of Dean."

"I saw Dean later," Annie said. "He sure looked like he'd been in a fight. And you just said Dean started it. That sounds like a fight to me."

Lola cut a glance up at her mother, who perched herself on the thick arm of the sofa, literally hovering over her child. The mother hen with a law degree. Jessica gave an almost imperceptible nod.

"That was me," Lola confessed. "Dean was trying to grab me. He's such a perv! He's always trying to touch girls' breasts! I bashed him in the face with my soccer ball, and I went straight to the principal's office and told Ms. Samuels Young. But by the time we went back outside, he was already gone."

"You said you saw him later," Jessica said to Annie. "Did the Florettes call the Sheriff's Office?"

"No," Annie said. "I stopped at their house looking for Nora. Dean came home with blood all over him. He said he crashed his bike. I guess he wasn't keen to tell me a girl cleaned his clock for him."

Lola bit her lip to keep from smiling. "Am I in trouble?"

"No, you're not in trouble. You have a right to defend yourself. And nobody has the right to touch you without your permission. Dean is the one in trouble."

"So, what exactly is this about, Detective?" Jessica Troiano asked. "If Lola's not in any trouble—"

"I need to speak to Nora, and I can't seem to find her," Annie said. "She may have information that could be helpful in another investigation. I'm hoping Lola can help me with that. I know you saw her yesterday after school."

"Nora." Jessica gave her daughter a stern look. "How many times have I told you I don't want you hanging around with that girl?"

Lola raised her chin in defiance. "You also tell me I should be independent and use my own judgment to make up my mind about people," the girl returned. "Nora is my friend."

"Your friend who is always in detention, who is always in trouble, who is now embroiled in some kind of police investigation. Your judgment needs some fine-tuning."

The mother glanced at Annie. "What kind of investigation? Is she stealing again? I swear. Those Florette children get no adult supervision whatsoever."

"Nora babysits after school for Genevieve Gauthier—"

"Oh, my God." The words were uttered on a sigh that was half distress and half aggravation. The color drained from Jessica Troiano's face. "The little boy that was killed."

"Yes."

"And now Nora is missing?"

"She's not at home," Annie said. "And her family doesn't seem to know where she is."

"Do you know where she is, Lola?" The mother gave her daughter a look more suited to the courtroom than the living room. "No messing around here, young lady."

"I don't know!" Lola insisted, wide-eyed. "She wasn't at school today."

"Yesterday," Annie said. "You saw her in the park after school. Did you speak to her after that?"

"No."

"She didn't call you last night?"

"No, ma'am."

"Would she normally call you in the evening?" Annie asked. Dean had said Nora was hogging the phone. Who would she call but her friends? Lola Troiano seemed to be one of the few.

Lola shot a guilty glance at her mother and murmured, "Yes."

"Lola, has Nora said anything to you about wanting to run away from home?" Annie asked.

The girl glanced away, nervously twisting the stack of friendship bracelets on her wrist.

"Lola . . ."

"She threatens to all the time," Lola admitted. "Her mother grounded her again—for a whole month! And besides, who wouldn't want to run away if they had to live in the same house as Dean?"

"Did she seem like she might go through with it this time? Did she have a backpack with her?"

"Just the same purple-and-pink one she brings to school every day."

"Did it seem more full than usual?"

Lola shrugged.

"What do you know about her getting caught shoplifting at the Quik Pik on Monday?" Annie asked.

"Again?" Jessica exclaimed.

"Were you with her?" Annie asked.

Lola didn't need to answer. Her expression perfectly blended guilt and panic.

Jessica Troiano gasped, moving off the arm of the sofa to stand beside Annie. "Lola Troiano! Why didn't you tell me about this?"

"Because this is how you react!" Lola exclaimed, pointing at her. "Why would I tell you? So you can yell at me?"

"Yes! That's exactly why! And you wonder why I tell you not to hang out with that girl! *THIS* is why!" She turned her outrage toward Annie. "Why wasn't I notified? My daughter is *twelve*! I should have been called *immediately*!"

"There was no law enforcement involved," Annie said. "The clerk on duty is a friend of Jojean Florette. She called Jojean."

"And then what happened?" she demanded, turning back to her daughter.

"Mrs. Florette came and got her," Lola said. "She was really angry. I saw her grab Nora by the hair on their way to the car. She's mean like that."

"And what did you do with yourself?" her mother asked.

"I walked to the library."

"Which is where you were supposed to have been the whole time. And when I picked you up at the library, you had not one word to say about all of this?"

"I didn't do anything wrong!" Lola protested. "I wasn't the one stealing!"

"No, you were just an accomplice."

"I wasn't even in the same aisle!"

"Did you know she was going to steal something?"

"I'm not her keeper! I can't control what she does!"

"No," Jessica said, "you control what *you* do. That is my point. You need to make better choices—"

"What did she steal?" Annie asked, not really caring, more interested in simply derailing the mother-daughter squabble for the time being so as to get back to her own line of questioning.

She didn't expect the answer to be surprising or even interesting. What did girls shoplift in a convenience store? ChapStick, candy, gum, cigarette lighters. It didn't matter. Still, Lola Troiano hesitated to answer.

"The detective asked you a question, Lola," her mother said. "What did Nora take?"

Lola slid down in her seat, miserable, trying to disappear into the sofa cushions. She looked down and fussed with her friendship bracelets, no doubt wanting to be rid of the one Nora Florette had given her.

"A magazine," she said in a small voice.

"A magazine?" Jessica repeated. "What magazine?"

The girl squirmed, color rising in her cheeks. "What difference does it make? She didn't take it, after all."

"Lola, what magazine?"

Lola took a deep breath, sighed, and cringed, bracing herself, as if the truth had a terrible taste to it. Finally, she spit it out. "*Penthouse.*"

Jessica Troiano gasped like she'd been doused with ice water. "Lola Mackenzie Troiano! You are grounded for a month!"

"That's not fair!" Lola said, popping up to her feet. "I didn't steal it! It wasn't for me!"

"No, you're just an accessory to the crime!" her mother argued. "Accomplices go to jail, too, young lady!"

"What did Nora want with a *Penthouse* magazine?" Annie asked.

"I don't know!"

"She didn't say?" Jessica asked. "Nora Florette, who never had a thought that didn't tumble through her empty head and out her mouth, didn't tell you, her accomplice, why she was going to steal a dirty magazine?"

Tears welled up in Lola's eyes. "It was probably for Dean! He looks at dirty magazines all the time! And he steals her underwear, and he spies on her in the bathroom!"

"It is not Dean's fault Nora stole something," Jessica said. "Don't deflect."

Annie stood up between them, holding her hands up like a referee. "Okay, that's enough. It's not important now. I need to find Nora and speak to her. Lola, did you talk to her last night?" she asked again.

"No!"

"Dean told me she was hogging the bathroom and talking on the phone all evening. She didn't call you?"

"No! I'm not a liar!"

"You said she threatened to run away. Did she tell you where she would go?"

She rolled her eyes in tween-girl fashion. "She always says she'll go to Hollywood or she'll go to New York and become an actress or a model. Like that would ever happen."

"You don't think she means it?"

"She would never really do it," Lola scoffed. "She doesn't have any money. How could she go anywhere?"

Annie's mind was rolling over the possibilities, imagining the sixth-grader hitchhiking, getting in a vehicle with a sexual predator, being snapped up into a sex-trafficking situation. Her stomach turned sour at the idea.

"Besides," Lola said, "Nora's a big chicken. She's probably hiding somewhere just to make her mom mad. She's done that before."

"Where would she go to hide?" Annie asked.

Jessica's eyes popped wide. "She's not here, is she?"

"No!"

"Lola, so help me, if she's in your closet—"

"She's not here!" Lola shouted. "Why won't you believe me? You're treating me like a criminal!"

"You are not winning any gold stars for trustworthiness tonight, young lady."

"Who else might she go to?" Annie asked. "Who are her other girl-friends?"

"She doesn't have many—"

"There's a shock," Jessica muttered.

"—so I go out of my way to be nice to her," Lola said pointedly, "because my *mother* always tells me to be kind to kids who don't have friends."

"Not the ones with criminal records!"

"Who else?" Annie prompted.

"Her cousin Tina," Lola said. "But she lives out in the country someplace. And she used to be friends with Janey Avery, but Janey's not supposed to hang out with her anymore, either."

"Avery?" Annie said. "Any relation to Jeff Avery, the administrator at Evangeline Oaks?"

Lola shrugged.

Jessica nodded. "Yes. I know Janey's mom, Janine. They're a lovely family. It's no surprise she wouldn't want her daughter hanging around with Nora Florette, either."

"You're a bully," Lola declared angrily. "You're like the mean girls in the cafeteria. You're the Mean Moms of Bayou Breaux!"

"Yeah," Jessica returned, "we're a bunch of mean ol' moms trying to keep our children out of reform school. Call child services!"

"Does Nora have a boyfriend?" Annie asked.

Jessica looked horrified. "She's *twelve*!"

"I don't even want to tell you what that doesn't mean anymore," Annie said. She looked again to Lola. "Does she?"

Lola shook her head. "No. She has crushes on practically every boy in school, but they don't pay any attention to her 'cause she doesn't have boobs yet."

"Oh, my God," Jessica said with a groan, pressing a hand to her forehead.

"Lola, how was Nora with KJ Gauthier?" Annie asked.

"What do you mean?"

"Did she enjoy babysitting him?"

The girl shrugged, frowning just a little. "No. Her mom made her do it. He was like hyperactive or something."

"And there are a lot more fun things to do after school than hang around with a second-grader, right?" Annie suggested.

"Well . . . sure . . ."

"Did she ever lose her temper with him?"

"Sometimes," Lola murmured. "She yelled at him a lot."

"Did she ever do more than yell at him?"

". . . . No . . ." The syllable was barely audible. She dodged Annie's gaze.

"Oh, my God," Jessica Troiano murmured again, hugging herself, tears rising in her eyes. "You don't think she hurt that child, do you?"

"I'm just gathering information," Annie said. "We need as complete a picture as we can get of everything leading up to what happened last night—who might have seen something, heard something, knows something."

To Lola, she said, "Did you hang out with her when she was babysitting KJ?"

"Not really. I mean, when we'd hang out in the park, but I don't like going to her house."

"Because of Dean?"

"Because of everything," Lola confessed softly, hastily swiping away a tear. "They're always yelling and fighting, and their house is dirty, and . . . yeah . . . Dean."

Annie's phone chimed the arrival of a text message. She glanced at the screen. Nick.

Meet me at Remy's.

She typed *Yes* and hit Send.

"Okay," she said on a sigh. "I have to go."

She reached out and touched Lola on the arm. "Thank you, Lola. I know this isn't fun, but it's important. You've got my card. If you hear from Nora, you call me. I don't care if she makes you swear on a stack of Bibles not to tell. You call me right away. Got it?"

"Yes, ma'am."

She pulled another card out of her pocket and handed it to Jessica Troiano. "Thank you. I'm sorry I had to disrupt your evening."

"Is there anything else we can do?" Jessica asked as they moved toward the front door.

"Call anyone you think might have seen Nora," Annie said. "If she shows up here, keep her here."

They had arrived at the foyer when the question occurred. Annie had already started to reach for the doorknob. She turned back to Lola.

"What time were you at the Quik Pik on Monday?"

"About four thirty."

"So KJ was with you?"

The girl shook her head and looked down at her feet, her long hair falling like a curtain around her face.

"Where was he?" Annie asked.

"She left him," Lola admitted reluctantly. "She just left him at her house, watching TV."

"Did she do that a lot? Leave him at the house and go do whatever she wanted?"

"Sometimes. When her mom wasn't home."

"And that was okay with you, was it?" her mother asked, eliciting the smallest of shrugs.

"And who else was at the house that day?" Annie asked.

"Dean."

TWENTY-FIVE

Mean Dean the Killing Machine. Cameron drew him with a head as round as a pumpkin, with slashes for eyes and pointy, triangular teeth in a mouth shaped like a football.

He wasn't very good at drawing. He got the proportions all wrong. The heads were too big and the limbs were too skinny. The bodies were too small, and the legs and feet always came out looking like hockey sticks. It didn't matter. Drawing was something he did just for him. He didn't have to be good at it.

He didn't ever show his drawings to anyone. His mother would have just picked his pictures apart. She was a firm believer in what she called "constructive criticism," though Cameron seldom saw anything constructive about it. She would have hated the terrible cartoonishness of his drawings. She would have found them grotesque and disturbing, because he tended to draw when he was angry, and he drew pictures of fights and car crashes and volcanoes going off and bombs exploding. If his mom looked at his drawings, the next thing anyone knew, she would be signing him up for proper art instruction and making him talk to the youth pastor, who would tell him to pray his anger away.

The youth pastor wasn't going to ever do anything about Dean Florette beating him up or calling him a faggot. He'd tell Cameron to turn the other cheek and then lecture him on the evils of homosexuality, like he probably secretly agreed with Dean that Cameron was gay. And Cameron would come away just feeling even worse about himself and his life.

"You should just go kill yourself and be done with it," Dean's voice murmured in the back of his mind. *"Faggot!!!"*

"I AM NOT A FAGGOT!!!!" he wrote in a word bubble above the image of himself, red-faced with anger, burying an axe in Dean's round pumpkin head. He touched his electronic pencil to the color bar on the side of the iPad screen and then drew bright red blood spurting out of Dean's brain like a geyser.

He drew on his iPad so he could quickly hide his pictures if his mom came in his room. She always wanted to see what he was looking at on the Internet, but she never demanded to see anything stored in his hard drive or on the cloud. Cyberspace was the only place he had any real privacy. She routinely searched his room, turning over the mattress and going through his drawers, looking for marijuana and cigarettes and whatever else grown-ups did but forbade kids to do.

When they lived in Houma, shortly after his dad had died, he had found a *Playboy* magazine in the recycling bin when he was taking the trash out to the curb. His mom had been on a tear, clearing out the closets and dumping everything out of his dad's desk and dresser drawers, bent on getting rid of every trace of him.

Cameron had been shocked to find the magazine. Shocked, and curious, and excited in a way he didn't quite understand at twelve years old. He had snuck it back into the house and hid it between the mattress and box spring of his bed. Late at night he looked at it with a flashlight under the covers, mesmerized and horrified by the naked girls and the feelings they stirred in him.

His mother had found the magazine the following week when she changed his sheets and had gone completely ballistic. She had screamed at him for an hour about male perversion, and women being sluts and whores, and hellfire and damnation. She had then dragged him to the youth pastor at their church, and she had totally lied about where Cameron had gotten the dirty magazine. The youth pastor had lectured him on all the same things his mother had already done, telling him only perverts looked at pornography, and only whores posed for pictures with their clothes off, touching themselves and trying to tempt men into sin.

Cameron had wanted to blurt out that the magazine had belonged to his father, so his father, who had been on the church council, must have been a sick pervert. But he had known that would only have made more trouble for himself, so he kept quiet. People had respected his father. Telling the truth about him would have only made everyone angry. In Cameron's experience, adults wanted to believe only what they wanted to believe—whether that was the truth or not.

The truth was his father had not been a nice man, constantly finding fault with everyone, ruling the house with an iron fist and a raging temper. Cameron had always been torn between wanting his father's approval and wishing he was an orphan. He and his mother had walked on eggshells around his dad, neither of them wanting to be the one to set him off.

Cameron had both hated his father and loved him in a tangled, toxic mix of emotion he could never understand. He had always tried so hard to make his father proud by being the best student, by being a good Boy Scout, by keeping his room clean and helping around the house and mowing the lawn and taking out the trash. Of course, he was never quite good enough no matter how hard he tried. There was always something he could have done better.

When his father died, the emotions that swamped Cameron were even more confusing and shameful. A part of him had been relieved. Another part of him had felt ashamed and guilty and desperate, wanting him back, hurting so hard he cried himself to sleep at night.

Now he had Kelvin to contend with, which was pretty much the same, only worse. Kelvin wanted him to be an athlete and learn how to shoot animals and gut fish, and all kinds of things for which Cameron had no desire and no talent. He was not a talented kid. That was just the truth of it. He was book smart, and he worked hard, but he had no real talent for anything. He couldn't escape the idea that no matter how hard he tried, he was going to be a source of constant disappointment for his new dad, just as he had been for his original one.

His hands began to tremble and his stomach churned and rolled as he thought of the lady detective asking him questions that afternoon. He could imagine her telling the sheriff how she'd seen him and questioned him in the park when he should have been at football practice. Kelvin hadn't come to the house yet for supper, but he would be here soon. It was only a matter of time before the shit hit the fan.

Cameron closed his iPad and got up to pace his bedroom on shaky legs. He liked his room. He liked this house. It was newer than their house in Houma. The furniture was new. His room was larger than his old room—big enough that he could have a desk, and a big easy chair in one corner. And he had his own bathroom. He didn't have to share the space with his mother and all her makeup and beauty creams and whatnot. His room was at the end of the hall, right next to a door that went out to the pool area—a real swimming pool.

What if Kelvin got mad enough that he didn't want them around anymore? What would they do? Where would they go? His mother would hate him for ruining everything. She deserved to be happy. She told him so all the time. She deserved to be married to a man like Kelvin Dutrow.

Anxiety went through Cameron like a current of electricity. Yet again, he felt his sense of himself shrinking and shrinking, disconnecting from the shell of his body and becoming a tiny little duplicate, a teeny tiny little version of his big self that stood in his eye socket and stared out at the world, terrified, his heart pounding.

He'd been a nervous wreck since he'd gotten home, terrified his mother would come home before he could clean up and do something about his clothes. He'd torn his pants and scraped his knee, his hands, his arms, and his chin when Dean knocked him down on the bike path. His shirt and pants had been smeared and stained with blood. And then there was the explosion of diarrhea to deal with.

The stench had backed Dean off from trying to further kick his ass for just long enough to save him. By the time Florette had decided to do it anyway, some adults had called out from the direction of the schools, scaring Dean away. Cameron had scrambled to his feet and run home, limping, the diarrhea running down both legs as he went.

He had wanted to just throw away his pants and underwear, but his mother would have asked where the clothes had gone. There was no avoiding telling her he'd fallen, anyway, as scraped up as he was. His solution had been to rinse the clothes off first with a hose down by the boat dock, then put them in the washing machine before his mother could see or smell them. He had told her the truth about falling down—he just left Dean Florette out of the story.

It wasn't really a lie that way, was it? He *had* fallen down. If he told his mom Dean had knocked him down, she would want to call Florette's mother and make a big stink of it. She would complain to Kelvin, and Kelvin would want to know why he hadn't fought back. Cameron would be caught in the middle, like he always was.

His mother had always harped on him not to get into fights, to go tell an adult if another kid was picking on him. His father had scoffed at the idea and called him a sissy for not sticking up for himself. He had regularly called Cameron a mama's boy, said he would never be a real man, that they might as well have had a daughter.

Not wanting anyone to be angry with or disappointed in him, Cameron had mastered the art of telling half-truths. He didn't like to lie. He wasn't any good at it. Telling a lie just gave him something more to worry about getting wrong.

He paced his room, sweating and chilled at the same time, his stomach rolling and twisting, his heart thumping in his chest. How did he get so many things wrong when he tried so hard to do everything right? he wondered as he paced and fretted, feeling sicker and sicker. His intentions were always good—harmless, at least. But he seemed to screw up over and over, then had to work twice as hard to keep anyone from seeing his mistakes.

It wasn't fair. It wasn't fair at all. Someone as rotten as Dean Florette could go around doing all kinds of terrible things because he was just a terrible person, and no one expected anything better of him. Cameron tried to do everything right and suffered for it because everything always went wrong.

He stopped in front of a window and stared out at the backyard. The yard light on the end of the big garage had come on, spotlighting the space where Kelvin usually parked his Suburban. It looked like an empty stage awaiting the arrival of the star of the show.

Maybe he wouldn't come tonight. Maybe he was too busy. He had appeared on the six o'clock news, talking about the murder, promising he would solve the crime, threatening the person responsible, glaring at the camera. "*You can run, but you* CANNOT *hide!*"

Cameron almost jumped to the ceiling as a knock sounded on his door.

"Cameron?" his mother called. "I'm coming in!"

The door was opening before he could say anything.

"I'm going to set a place for you at the table," she said, coming in and going directly to his bed to smooth the coverlet he had messed up earlier. "I know you said you're not hungry, and I hate to have you eat late, but you cannot go to bed on an empty stomach. You're a growing boy, and you need your nutrition."

"But I don't feel good—"

"You don't feel *well*," she corrected him, coming to him and pressing her hand to his forehead. "I don't think you have a fever, but you're positively clammy. You need to put something in your stomach, even if it's just a little rice or some breakfast cereal or something. Anything. I swear you have these stomach problems because you don't eat regularly the way you should. I can't be with you every minute of every day, telling you when to eat.

"Did you eat your lunch today?" she asked, looking him hard in the eyes.

He shrugged away from her, frowning, tears pressing up behind his eyes. "I told you this morning I was sick at my stomach, and you wouldn't believe me!"

His mother gave one of her Big Sighs that told him she was exasperated with him.

"If I let you stay home every time you said you were sick at your stomach, you'd never go at all."

"That's not fair!" Cameron argued, his voice cracking badly.

Outside, headlights flashed past the window as Kelvin swung his Suburban into his parking place down by the big garage. Cameron's stomach cramped hard.

"You will come and sit down and have something to eat with Kelvin," his mother said. "Go splash some water on your face and comb your hair. And turn the fan on in your bathroom. The smell is terrible."

He went into his bathroom and did as he was told, his hands shaking as he cupped water to wash his face. How was he going to sit at the table and eat? Maybe they wouldn't even make it to the table. Maybe Kelvin would start yelling at him as soon as he came in the door. Cameron almost hoped so, just to get it over with, and yet, he couldn't bring himself to move. He stared at his reflection in the mirror until he thought he didn't recognize himself.

Who was he?

What was going to happen to him?

Would his mother send him off to military school like Kelvin wanted her to? She thought he didn't know, but he did. The idea terrified him. He was barely surviving junior high. How would he ever make it out of military school alive?

"Cameron!" his mother called sharply from his bedroom door. "Hurry up! Don't keep Kelvin waiting!"

"I'm coming!"

He took one last long look at the stranger in the mirror then left his room and walked down the hall like he was going to his death, thinking maybe he was.

TWENTY-SIX

*S*he killed a baby."

Hands tightening on the steering wheel, Annie relived the sickening jolt of shock that had gone through her when Nick greeted her with those words in Remy's driveway. More than an hour had passed since the revelation. They had tucked their son into bed and then sat down to share a rushed dinner of takeout Thai food in Remy's kitchen, Nick filling in the details of the story.

Dixon had dug into Genevieve's juvenile record and then cross-referenced with news stories from the archives of the local Houma papers. The murder of an infant by her teenaged mother had been big news thirteen years past.

The story was one that happened more than most people would ever care to know. A scared teenager had managed to keep her pregnancy a secret until it was too late. She had given birth in the bathroom at school. Two months later, the baby was dead. SIDS, the teenage mother had claimed. The coroner had disagreed strongly enough that charges had been brought. Fourteen-year-old Genevieve Gauthier had been found guilty of suffocating her baby daughter and had been sentenced to eighteen months in the Terrebonne Parish Juvenile Justice Complex on a negotiated plea of involuntary manslaughter.

Fourteen. Just two years older than Lola Troiano and Nora Florette, little girls who traded friendship bracelets and kept stuffed animals on their beds. Barely old enough to know how babies were made, Genevieve had given birth to one alone in a bathroom stall.

Everything about her story was upsetting and tragic. Annie had a thousand questions she wanted answered. Who was the father? What had been the circumstances of the conception? Was the pregnancy the result of kids having consensual sex, or had this been a case of rape or incest?

"It doesn't matter," Nick said. "It matters that a baby is dead. She killed her own child."

"You can't say it doesn't matter," Annie argued, twirling her fork in her pad thai. "The truth goes to motive."

"Don't talk like a defense attorney to me, 'Toinette," he said, stabbing a shrimp. "It doesn't matter to me *why* she did it. It matters to me *that* she did it. Now I know she's capable of murdering a child. She *has* murdered a child—*her own* child. And here we are, investigating the murder of another child—a child with problems, a child she's already told us wouldn't settle down last night while she was fighting a migraine headache. She's alone, she's frustrated, she's poor—"

"Is there a higher rate of stabbing deaths among children of the poor that I don't know about?" Annie asked snappishly. "'Cause this would be the first stabbing-because-I'm-poor case I've come across. But you've been at this longer than me, so—"

"Her circumstances had her backed into a corner," Nick pressed on. "There she is, stuck living in that shit hole, wanting a better life. What's holding her back? That child. She can't get ahead, she can't get away, she can't get a man. She blames the boy. She's already crossed the line to kill once. That makes it ten times easier to do it again."

"Well, first," Annie argued, "there's a big difference between suffocating an infant and stabbing a seven-year-old to death while he's fighting for his life. Second, that's a boatload of speculation as to her state of mind. I haven't seen any evidence that she didn't want her son, have you?"

"She was drinking and popping pills last night because she couldn't deal with his behavior."

"And I had a meltdown in the parking lot at school this morning because our son was having a temper tantrum. Does that make me a murder suspect?"

"*Mais* yeah," Nick insisted. "If he turns up dead, it does!"

Annie sighed and looked away, absently taking in the details of her cousin's kitchen, a spotless magazine spread of elegant cabinetry and Carrara marble. A far cry from the cramped, dingy closet of a kitchen in Genevieve Gauthier's shitty rented house on the edge of nowhere. A far cry from where Annie herself had spent her early life with her mother, in the apartment over the store and café at the Corners.

As young and pretty as Genevieve, Marie Broussard had never talked about wanting anything more than she had. She had never spoken of having dreams and aspirations for a fancier life. But then, Marie Broussard hadn't envisioned a life for herself at all, as it turned out, and Annie would never know why. No matter how many years passed, the ache of that loss was never far from her heart.

She didn't know enough about Genevieve Gauthier to make a judgment about her, though she knew Nick was right. They had to consider Genevieve as a possible suspect. A parent was, sadly, the most obvious suspect in the death of a child. But Annie had stood in the morgue and listened to the mother's soul-wrenching sobs that morning, crying over the body of the child she had carried and nurtured and struggled with, and struggled for, and the mother in her wanted to reject the idea. Had those cries been heartbreak? Despair? Remorse? Remembrance of another dead child?

"Have you asked her about that baby's death?" she asked. "Have you asked her did she kill KJ?"

"No. I just found out about the baby. It can wait 'til tomorrow. She isn't going anywhere."

"Because she's in the hospital with knife wounds," Annie pointed out.

"*C'est vrai.*" Nick nodded. "And now we have to wonder: Could those wounds have been self-inflicted?"

"That cut on her shoulder is deep. The knife chipped her collarbone. I can't imagine someone doing that to themselves."

"I don't reckon she planned it that way."

He got up from the table and pulled a boning knife from the wooden block on the kitchen island.

"Sharp knife, adrenaline pumping," he said, setting the stage. "She's just killed her son in a frenzy. She realizes the horror of it. She'd better make it look like they were attacked.

"She brings the knife down like this," he said, pantomiming with the boning knife, his right hand coming down at an angle across his left shoulder. "A sharp knife cuts like hot steel through butter. It would be easy to go deeper than she meant to. There's not much to her, little slip of a thing. That bone is right there just under the skin . . ."

"Who's to say she owns a sharp knife?" Annie challenged. "Cheetos and whiskey for supper. That's not exactly a chef's kitchen she's got going on there."

Nick put the knife back in the block and took his seat. "For the sake of this theory, we're gonna say she had a sharp knife."

"Where is it?"

"Bottom of the bayou, I should think."

"Well, I'm glad you've got it all figured out," Annie said irritably, shoving her plate away. "I'll just leave you to it then and go on my way and find this babysitter who seems to be missing for no good reason. Or do you think Genevieve stole her out of her bed and killed her, too?"

"Why are you getting mad at me?" Nick asked, annoyed. "I'm just following this thread through to the logical possibility. That's our job. It's not my fault if it turns out she killed her own child to free herself from a shitty life."

"You know my mother was poor and alone and overwhelmed, too," Annie said, "and she didn't stab me to death."

"No. She killed herself."

His words struck like a fist to the solar plexus. Annie gasped, shoved her chair back, and shot to her feet. Nick rose and took a step toward her, looking more exasperated than contrite.

"'Toinette, I didn't—"

"Don't you even think about touching me!" she snapped as he reached out.

He heaved a sigh, his thick shoulders rising and slumping as he set his hands at his waist. "'Toinette, I didn't mean—"

"I am half past sick of having to listen to the postmortem on what you said versus what you meant," she said, her voice trembling with emotion. "I'm leaving now. I have a twelve-year-old girl MIA, not that her mother seems to give a shit one way or the other.

"Oh, but then maybe Jojean Florette just up and killed her daughter!" she said, feigning amazement at the idea. "Seeing how she has to work two jobs while her husband is off in the Gulf of Mexico playing around on some oil rig. Anyone can see how killing her children would be the obvious solution to all her problems! I can't imagine why she hasn't done it already—especially the boy. I would have started with him, myself."

"Don't be ridiculous—"

"Don't follow me out," she warned, grabbing her handbag and heading to the kitchen door. "I might become hysterical and shoot you."

"*Bébé*, please . . ."

"Don't you *bébé* me. I don't want to hear it. I'm out of here."

She hit the screen door hard with both hands, wishing it was the old-fashioned wooden kind that would fly back and bang off the house. No such satisfaction from a modern screen door. She was so angry she felt like she might explode. Tears rose up like floodwaters behind a dam, pressing on her eyeballs, burning, blurring her vision.

It only made her angrier that she was about to cry. She didn't want to cry. She didn't want to overreact. She already wished she hadn't reacted at all. She should have just gotten up and left. "'Toinette!" Nick called behind her. *"Arrête, toi!"*

She didn't want to stop. She didn't want to go to him. She had no interest in hearing his apology. She kept her focus on her vehicle no more than twenty feet away now, wanting to run to it but not willing to look that desperate to get away.

As he put a hand on her shoulder, she shrugged him off and kept walking.

"You didn't let me finish," he said.

Annie glared at him over her shoulder.

"My point was that your mother didn't hurt you. She hurt herself."

"*That's* your point?" she asked, resting her hand on the door of the SUV. "That my mother didn't kill me, so she killed herself instead. So it's *my* fault my mother is dead?"

"*Mon Dieu!*"

"God isn't helping you out of this. So you just keep digging that hole. You'll be able to bury yourself upright."

"I did not say it with the intention of hurting your feelings."

"Oh, well," Annie said, opening the car door. "It doesn't matter to me *why* you said it. It matters to me *that* you said it."

He held up two fingers. The *missio*. The gladiator's symbol of surrender. Their symbol for the end of an argument. It didn't give her any satisfaction.

"I don't want to fight with you."

"We're not fighting," Annie said, climbing into the driver's seat. Nick moved into the open space and held the door open before she could shut him out. "You hurt me, and I'm angry with you. That's not a fight."

"*Bon*. I'm relieved to hear it."

She stared out the windshield at the inky blackness beyond the reach of Remy's yard light, working to compose herself. She didn't want to fight with him, either. She didn't want to be angry or upset or feeling the breath of any of the demons from her childhood.

"I'm sorry if I overreacted," she said, struggling for calm. "But this is hard for me, Nick. I will never know why my mother did what she did. I will never know if I caused it—"

"*Bébé*, you were just a child—"

"So? You've just posed a very sound theory that a child being a child might drive a young mother over the edge. I have lived with that notion every day of my life since I was nine years old. I can't look at Genevieve and not think of my mother, of what she went through and what it did to her."

The pain came in a wave. She couldn't stop it. The emotion forced itself out on a sob to alleviate the internal pressure. Tears spilled down her cheeks. Then Nick's arms were around her, and her cheek found his shoulder, and she wrapped her arms around his neck. He held her tight and whispered words of comfort. She clung to him and soaked in his strength. Just for a moment. Just long enough to remind her she wasn't alone, and she wasn't nine, and she didn't have to stay in that painful emotional place. She could put those feelings back in their box and hope that they would stay there for a while.

When the wave receded, she sat back and wiped the tears away with her hands. She found a tissue in the console and blew her nose. Nick slowly stroked a hand over the back of her head.

"Are you okay?" he asked softly, still close enough that his breath tickled her ear.

Annie nodded. "I'm sorry I was such a bitch."

"Hush. You're not a bitch," he said, leaning in to press a kiss to her cheek.

"Don't ever think I don't love you," she whispered, looking into his dark eyes.

He shook his head, smiling slightly. *"Non, cher,"* he murmured. "I don't ever think that."

"Please be careful tonight."

"I will. I wanna come home and slide into bed with my wife later."

"That's a pleasant fiction we probably won't get to realize tonight," Annie said. "But I'll be happy to look forward to it, just the same."

"Me, too." Gently, he brushed her hair back from her face. "I'm sorry this is hard on you, baby. I'm sorry you have to have those memories. But you know that can't stop us having to look down that road with Genevieve. Her story is not your story."

She took a slow, measured breath and released it at the same deliberate pace. "I know."

"Maybe if you can find this babysitter she'll be able to shed some light on the situation."

"Let's hope," Annie said, starting the car. "My fear is that's the reason she's missing in the first place."

THE QUESTION WAS whether Nora Florette was missing because of something she'd done or because of something she'd seen. Was she gone by choice or gone by violence?

Annie tried to sort out the threads in her mind as she drove back toward town. Genevieve had killed a baby thirteen years ago. Now her second child was dead. Nora Florette was her babysitter. Now Nora Florette was missing.

"She killed a baby . . ."

Genevieve Gauthier had killed a baby when she was little more than Nora's age. Had she meant to? Had she done it out of desperation or rage? Was she a person with a red line, and once the red line was crossed she was capable of things she otherwise wouldn't imagine doing? People could snap. Annie had seen it happen, had seen the results. Some people had a rage switch that, once flipped, rendered them capable of almost anything.

She also knew the challenges of being a new mother with a colicky baby, at the end of her rope, struggling to cope on too little sleep, buried under an avalanche of insecurity. Put that burden on a fourteen-year-old with few resources. Add the trigger point of suddenly realizing she had effectively ended her youth by having a baby.

After the initial rush of attention from others cooing over the new baby, her school friends would have moved on and gone back to their lives where making the cheerleading squad and getting a date for prom were the heaviest priorities. A classmate with a baby wouldn't fit in, wouldn't be fun, wouldn't be included. Had the dual pressures of isolation and responsibility been too much?

And here she was thirteen years later, isolated, alone, solely responsible for a difficult child . . .

Nick said Genevieve had been popping pills and drinking because she had a migraine and couldn't get her son to settle down. But the mix of those particular drugs didn't induce hallucinations or paranoia or cause people to become violent. Quite the opposite was true. Oxy and Xanax combined to create a sense of relaxation and euphoria. Adding alcohol to the mix should have made Genevieve more apt to fall asleep than to pick up a knife.

Her story of waking up at the sound of her son's cries was more in line with someone whose senses were dulled than someone jacked up into a killing frenzy. She had trouble getting out of bed, got tangled in the sheets, and fell—as a person with impaired motor skills might.

And even if Genevieve was some kind of murderous mastermind and had killed her son, how and when could she have gotten to Nora? And why would she? Dean claimed Nora had been home last night. It made no sense to think Genevieve could have done anything to her. Neither did it make any sense to Annie to try to cast Nora in some kind of villainous role.

Murder was almost always stupidly, tragically simple when it came right down to it. It almost always made sense. Motives could pretty much all be boiled down to fit in one of three categories: money, love, or pride. Even the rare killer who seemingly chose victims at random had a kind of logic to his choices when all was said and done. There was no logic in any scenario Annie could conjure up casting a twelve-year-old babysitter as the killer. Maybe if the boy had died in her care, but he hadn't. She would have had to go to his house in the middle of the night to do it. Nora, who was by all accounts lazy and irresponsible. Nora, who made bracelets for her friends and still slept with a teddy bear.

No. If Nora Florette was missing because of the murder of KJ Gauthier, it wasn't because she'd killed him.

Annie ran back through the timeline as she hit her blinker and turned west. Monday afternoon Nora had left KJ at home with no one to supervise him but Dean the delinquent. She went off with Lola Troiano to the Quik Pik, where she tried to shoplift a *Penthouse* magazine. As payment to Dean? A bribe for her brother for leaving him with a hyperactive seven-year-old—something she had done again the next day? Had Dean even bothered to stick around?

It bothered her to think of little KJ getting shuffled around like a stray puppy nobody wanted. It was easy to imagine him frightened and confused and feeling abandoned. The idea stirred Annie's maternal ire in a way that made her want to sink her teeth into someone. But who? The single mom who was trying her best to make ends meet? Jojean Florette for forcing the job of supervising a seven-year-old with ADHD on an immature twelve-year-old in hopes of teaching her responsibility? None of it had been done with bad intentions. People made their choices for their own reasons and just hoped for the best, refusing to imagine the alternative.

The only person with bad intentions in this story had been wielding a knife and had used it to deliberately kill an innocent child.

Annie slowed the car as she turned down the Florettes' street. Her last text from Jojean had been a curt *No* in answer to *Any sign of Nora yet?* The house was ablaze with light, upstairs and down. She wondered if any kind of concern had begun to creep into Jojean's psyche or if she was still choosing irritation over panic, mentally planning her next irate tirade to launch when her daughter walked in the door.

One more kid to interview, and if by the time she was done with Cameron Spicer there was still no sign of Nora, Annie would have to force the issue with Jojean. She wasn't going to let the night pass with no sign of this girl. If Nora had run away, if she had somehow gotten herself out of Bayou Breaux, every minute was putting her another mile out of easy reach. If something else had happened to her, if she was being held somewhere, every second counted.

The street took a dogleg left then right, connecting to the wider, smoother, newer Blue Cypress Trace, which led into the Blue Cypress development. Like Quail Run, where the Troianos lived, Blue Cypress was a neighborhood for upper-middle-class professional people, people who could afford to buffer themselves from their neighbors with broad expanses of green lawn; people with gigantic RVs and bass boats who wanted a dock in their backyard connecting them to the vast network of bayous and marshes and swamps at the edge of the Atchafalaya Basin.

No more than a block from the Florette house, driving from one neighborhood to the other was literally driving from one century to the next, from the side-by-side homes built in the 1940s and '50s to the quarter-acre middle-class estates of the new millennium. Annie remembered well the stink that had been raised when the real estate developer had come in and bought out the people who had lived along these banks when she was a kid—swampers and commercial fishermen and retirees—and razed their modest little homes to make way for progress and people willing to commute to jobs in Lafayette.

She pulled in the driveway of the first place on the left and cut the engine. The house was yet another brick Caribbean-style, the front entrance tastefully dressed up for fall with pumpkins and chrysanthemums. She didn't know the Spicer family, had no idea what Sharon Spicer—the only parent listed with the school as a contact for the ninth-grader, Cameron Spicer—did for a living. Jaime Blynn, who had an uncanny ability to remember students long after they'd left the elementary grades, had said she thought the Spicers might be new in town.

"Welcome to Bayou Breaux," Annie muttered as she pressed the doorbell.

TWENTY-SEVEN

I fail to see how this day could get any worse," Kelvin grumbled as he came into the kitchen through the laundry room, a dark scowl twisting his face. "I've got a murderer loose. I've got a media circus with my lead detective smack in the middle of it. I've got lawyers threatening to sue the Sheriff's Office.

"It's an absolute mess. It's a disaster. It's a word I won't use in polite company, that's what it is," he said. "I don't know why people can't listen and just do as they're told."

Cameron slid into his seat at the kitchen table, his head ducked, shoulders hunched, trying to make himself as small as possible. He watched from the corner of his eye as Kelvin washed his hands at the kitchen sink and dried them on one of Cameron's mother's dish towels—an act that would have gotten Cameron a scolding. His mother made no comment about it but took the towel as he finished and folded it smoothly.

"I'm sorry to hear it, Kelvin," she said in her most soothing voice. "Please sit down and let me get you something to drink. What would you like?"

"For people to follow orders and use common sense. That's what I'd like," he snapped.

He stood in the middle of the kitchen looking twice his real size to

Cameron, puffed up with anger and outrage. Dressed all in black with combat boots, his name on a brass plate pinned to his chest, brass stars on the collar of his shirt, he looked like a military movie bad guy, the evil commander of the special forces set to destroy the Resistance.

"I told Fourcade not to draw attention to himself, and what does he do? He gets into an altercation in front of TV news cameras! Now I have to clean up this mess! I've got to put together another press conference for ten P.M. to try to get control of the situation. Meanwhile, the Theriots' lawyer is already threatening to sue for false arrest and excessive use of force."

"Oh, my goodness. You poor man," Cameron's mom said, resting a hand on his arm and looking up at him with great sympathy. "You've had a terrible day! You need to take your seat and let me get your supper for you. I've got you a nice baked chicken breast and rice pilaf. Something not too heavy, as I was afraid you might have to work late tonight. Cameron is going to join you."

Cameron's stomach clenched as Kelvin's attention swung toward him.

"You didn't eat with your mother?" Kelvin asked.

"No, sir."

"Why is that?"

"I wasn't feeling well, sir," Cameron mumbled, bracing himself against the expected reaction. Kelvin was generally disgusted by Cameron's weak stomach. A weak stomach equaled a weak man. That was how Kelvin thought. That was how Cameron's father had thought as well. Cameron didn't see how he could help having a bad stomach. It wasn't as if he wished for one.

Kelvin took his seat, and Cameron's mom was instantly at his elbow with a heavy glass tumbler with an inch of amber liquid in it. Kelvin liked a whiskey in the evening. Cameron's mother disapproved of hard liquor, but she never said a word about it. Whatever Kelvin wanted was fine by her.

What was going to happen when Kelvin wanted him gone?

The sheriff took a sip of his drink, seeming to hold it in his mouth as he looked at Cameron. Cameron wanted to crawl under the table. He hoped if he could keep his head tilted down, Kelvin wouldn't be able to see the scrapes and bruises. Maybe he would be too preoccupied with his problems to notice—

"Look up at me," Kelvin ordered. "You look a man in the eye when you speak to him. How many times do I have to tell you that?"

"Yes, sir. I don't know, sir," Cameron mumbled.

Slowly he raised his head. His heart seemed trapped at the base of his throat, fluttering like a bird's wings. He tried to swallow it down, but it didn't budge. He thought he might throw up.

His eyes met Kelvin's. The man's gaze seemed to burn right into him like laser beams.

"What happened to your face?"

Cameron tried to draw breath but couldn't. Maybe he was going to faint, or better yet, die.

"Answer me when I ask you a question," Kelvin demanded, the edge in his voice growing stronger and sharper.

"I told you he shouldn't go out for sports," Cameron's mother said, putting herself between the two of them as she brought Kelvin his plate of food. "Sports are dangerous, and I love my son, but Cameron is not gifted that way. He should be allowed to excel at the things he's good at."

Kelvin slapped a hand down hard on the table, making the silverware jump. Cameron flinched like a whipped dog.

"Sharon, I am not having this discussion with you again!" Kelvin snapped. "If I've told you once, I've told you a hundred times: sports build character. The boy needs character. He needs to grow a spine and a set of balls and become a man. If he gets a little scraped and bruised in the process, so be it! He won't die from it!"

He didn't know, Cameron realized with a wild rush of relief. He didn't know Cameron was no longer in football. The lady detective hadn't told him. Cameron felt almost dizzy. He could survive the night.

"You coddle him to the point he might as well start wearing skirts," Kelvin said.

"As you said, we don't need to discuss this tonight," Cameron's mother said. "You have enough to deal with, Kelvin. I never should have brought it up. I'm sorry. I don't know what I was thinking. I don't need to add to your burden."

"No, you don't," Kelvin said, still angry. He glanced at his watch, frowning darkly, then finished his whiskey in a quick gulp.

"Sit down," he ordered. "I can't stand you hovering that way."

She wiped her hands on her apron and slipped onto the seat to Kelvin's right. With knife and fork clutched purposefully, he set to aggressively carving the chicken breast on his plate as if it were a twenty-pound Thanksgiving turkey.

"I understand you visited our victim in the hospital today," Kelvin said, cutting her a sideways look as he raised a bite of the chicken to his mouth. "Why was that?"

"I took her flowers on behalf of the auxiliary and offered condolences. Poor thing seems to have no friends or family in the area. I can't imagine why she moved here, knowing no one."

"She has an elderly aunt at Evangeline Oaks Assisted Living."

"Does she? She didn't mention that to me."

"Why would she? She doesn't know you. Does she?" he asked, shooting her another sideways look.

"Of course not," Cameron's mother said. "How would she know me?"

"She was a file clerk at Houma City Hall for a time."

"Was she? I don't know anything about that. I just took her flowers. To be kind," she said. "Did you know her then?"

"Don't be ridiculous. Of course I didn't know this girl."

"It's just a coincidence that she worked in Houma."

"A lot of people work in Houma. This one happened to have a relative in Bayou Breaux, and so she moved here. Much to her misfortune, as it's turned out."

"Yes."

"I would prefer you didn't see her again," Kelvin said. "We believe her to be a drug addict and a possible suspect in the death of her son."

"You think the mom killed the little boy?" Cameron blurted out. He would have grabbed the words with his hands and put them back in his mouth if he could have. It was stupid to draw attention to himself.

"It's possible," Kelvin said. "We don't know yet.

"I'm sure you mean well, Sharon," he said. "But the parish has social workers whose job it is to assist in these matters. If Miss Gauthier needs assistance, she can call on one of them."

"Yes, of course you're right, Kelvin," Cameron's mom said, getting up from the table and taking his empty whiskey glass. "Would you like something more to drink?"

"Coffee, if there's any made."

"I'll start a fresh pot. It'll only take a minute."

The doorbell rang as she started across the room. Kelvin pushed his chair back from the table and stood.

"I'll get it," he said. "Better if the two of you don't answer the door this time of night if you don't know who it is. I don't want you getting an unpleasant surprise."

ANNIE DREW BREATH as the doorknob turned, ready to introduce herself to Sharon Spicer or to be greeted by the boy she'd met in the park that afternoon. Then the door opened, Sheriff Dutrow filled the space, and her mind went blank with confusion.

"Detective Broussard? What are you doing here?"

"Um—uh— Am I at the wrong house?" she asked.

"I wouldn't know. Where are you supposed to be?"

"Is this 14 Blue Cypress?" she asked, looking right at the house number beside the door. "I'm looking for a Sharon Spicer."

Inside the house, a woman's voice called out. "Kelvin? Who is it?"

Dutrow ignored the question. His small, hard eyes were as dark and shiny as onyx in the muted yellow of the porch light. "What for?"

"I need to speak to her son, Cameron."

"Why?"

"Because I need to," Annie said, irritated. "Why are you here?"

"I own this house," Dutrow said with an undercurrent of belligerence.

"Okay. Now I'm really confused. The school gave me this address for Sharon and Cameron Spicer."

"Kelvin? Who is it?"

An attractive, auburn-haired woman peered around his shoulder. He shifted positions just enough to allow her a clear view.

"Sharon, this is Detective Broussard from the department," he said. "Detective Broussard, this is my fiancée, Sharon Spicer."

"Oh, office business?" Sharon Spicer said with a smile of relief. "I shouldn't interrupt. I'll leave you to it. Nice to meet you, Detective—"

"She's here for you," Dutrow said, giving her a long look.

Her smile faltered. "For me?"

"For your son, actually," Annie offered. "I need to ask him a few questions."

"Cameron?" she said, looking worried. "Questions? About what?"

"A friend of his from school is missing tonight. I'm hoping she might have said something to him about where she might have gone."

"A runaway?" the sheriff asked.

"Remains to be seen."

"I thought you were working the Gauthier homicide."

"I am," Annie said, swatting at a mosquito in front of her face. "The girl that's missing was Gauthier's babysitter."

"Oh, my goodness," Sharon said.

"I spoke with Cameron at the park today after school," Annie explained. "Before we realized Nora was missing. I know they saw each other yesterday after school. They're friends; they walk together. Maybe she said something to him—"

"You spoke with him in the park after school?" Dutrow repeated, his brow furrowing. "Today?"

"Yes."

"What time was this?"

It seemed an odd question, Annie thought. What difference did it make to him what time? What difference did it make to him at all?

"Around four o'clock," she said, swatting again at the mosquito.

"For heaven's sake, Kelvin," Sharon Spicer piped up, "invite the detective in before we're all eaten alive. I swear, this nasty, muggy weather has got to break before we all lose our minds with it!"

Dutrow stepped back and held the door.

The house was lovely, reflecting, Annie supposed, the taste of the woman living in it—traditional with feminine touches, a color scheme that was vaguely beachy and soothing, flower arrangements and framed artwork she couldn't imagine Dutrow noticing, let alone picking out. Everything was carefully arranged, down to the knife creases in the sofa pillows—also reflecting Sharon Spicer, Annie thought.

By this time in the evening Annie was usually in baggy sweatpants and a Ragin' Cajuns T-shirt, barefoot and braless with her hair up in a messy knot, makeup—what little she wore—gone. Sharon Spicer was still on duty. A new-millennium twist on the 1950s housewife, every auburn hair was in place, lipstick fresh, small pearl necklace at her throat. She was in a flowing skirt and blouse and wore an apron. She had probably greeted Dutrow at the door with a cocktail and sympathy for his long, hard day.

Not that there was anything wrong with that. The level of formality and sense of role-playing didn't suit Annie, but she could totally see Dutrow loving it. This was exactly the kind of woman he would order up as his perfect mate, and it was a role Sharon Spicer clearly enjoyed playing.

"May I get you something to drink, Detective?" she asked. "I have a fresh pot of coffee brewing. Or sweet tea, if you'd prefer."

"No, thank you, ma'am," Annie said. "I don't want to keep y'all from your evening. I'm sorry for the confusion. The school listed only Ms. Spicer as the parental contact for Cameron."

"Cameron is my son from my first marriage," Sharon explained, as if that absolved Dutrow of any parental duties. "His father passed away several years ago."

Just to make the point that her marriage hadn't failed, Annie thought. "I'm so sorry for your loss."

"Thank you," she said, then quickly shifted gears into mother mode. "You said you spoke to Cameron this afternoon. Why was I not notified?"

"It wasn't a formal interview," Annie assured her. "Just a conversation."

"And this conversation took place in the park," Dutrow stated. "The park between the two schools."

"Yes."

"Around four o'clock."

"Yes," Annie said, annoyed with his interruptions. Did he think he was showing off his interviewing skills? For what purpose? To impress the soon-to-be missus?

"Is Cameron here?" she asked.

Dutrow cut a hard look at his fiancée. "Call him."

"Kelvin—"

"Get him in here. Now."

Dutrow didn't raise his voice. If anything, he lowered it, but the tension was unmistakable. A muscle in the sheriff's jaw was pulsing. Sharon had gone a little pale. Annie thought there might have been tears in her eyes as she hurried from the living room.

"Do you think this babysitter might be involved in the murder?" the sheriff asked, turning toward her.

He had taken up what Annie thought of as his commando stance—feet apart, shoulders back, hands on his hips. Dressed for a SWAT raid, he was the opposite of his predecessor in almost every way—which was probably why Gus had picked him. After more than two decades of familiarity with Gus Noblier, Dutrow was someone to come into the office and crack the whip and make everyone toe the line, a reboot of the SO for the future. It might have been a good idea in theory.

"I don't know," she said. "I can't imagine she is. How could a twelve-year-old girl be mixed up in a murder? But I'm not a fan of coincidence, either. The mother is of a mind that the girl has run away but probably hasn't gone far. They had a blowout Monday. Chances are, that's all this is about, but at the same time, a child is missing. We can't just assume she'll be home by morning."

Dutrow nodded almost absently. His attention was on the muffled voices coming from deeper in the house.

"Cameron, get in here!" he barked so suddenly and so loudly, Annie startled.

The boy came into the room reluctantly, one arm across his stomach as if he was in pain, his shoulders rounded as if he wanted to shrink into himself and disappear. He looked like he'd been in a fight or run over by a truck, with scrapes and burgeoning bruises on his face, hands, and arms. His mother walked beside him with a hand pressed reassuringly to his back. The pair of them looked like they were going to their deaths.

"Hey, Cameron," Annie said, trying to offer him a friendly face.

"Looks like you had a little run-in after I saw you today. Should I be worried about the other guy?"

"Detective Broussard has some questions for you," Dutrow said, his voice curt and hard as he stepped too close to the boy. "You will answer her. Is that understood?"

"Yes, sir," Cameron mumbled, looking down at the floor.

"Eyes up and speak clearly!" the sheriff snapped.

The boy's chin began to quiver.

"Kelvin, please—" Sharon started.

He cut her off with a look.

"You will answer the detective's questions," he said again. "And then you'll answer mine."

Tears welled in the boy's eyes. Annie could feel his misery from ten feet away.

"Is there something going on here I should know about?" she asked, looking to the sheriff.

"A family matter," Dutrow said. "It doesn't concern you or what you need. Ask your questions."

Annie wished she could ask him to leave the room, but she knew that wouldn't fly. There was nothing to do but get it over with. Though maybe if she could drag it out she could defuse the tension . . .

"Maybe we could sit down," she suggested.

"He can stand," Dutrow insisted. "Get on with it, Detective Broussard."

Annie took a long breath, just to make Dutrow wait, hoping he would hear the echo of his own assholishness hanging in the air, knowing he wouldn't. Men like Dutrow never heard themselves as wrong or even mistaken. His was the voice of truth and judgment.

"Cameron," she began, "I went to Nora's house after I saw you and Lola and Dean in the park, and she wasn't there. No one seems to know where she is. Has she, by any chance, been in contact with you today or this evening?"

"No, ma'am."

"I don't want you to worry that she's going to be in any trouble or that you're going to get in any trouble because you told me," Annie said. "We need to find her. That's the only important thing here. I know she had a fight with her mom and that they're not getting along, but now her mom is worried sick about her," she lied. "All she wants is for Nora to come home.

"Did she say anything to you at all about running away from home?" she asked.

He didn't make eye contact. His gaze darted up and down and side to side like a hummingbird unable to land.

"Cameron!" Dutrow barked.

The boy flinched like a frightened animal. "S-she s-said she ought to," he mumbled.

"She said she ought to run away?" Annie asked. "When was this?"

Cameron sniffled and rubbed his nose with the back of his hand. "Y-yesterday."

"Did she say where she might go?"

He shook his head.

"Who is this girl you're talking about?" Sharon asked.

"Nora Florette," Annie said. "She lives not far from here."

"Florette," Sharon repeated, using the same inflection Jessica Troiano had used—flat with an undercurrent of annoyance.

"You know the family?"

"Oh, yes." She turned to her son, clearly perturbed. "What are you doing hanging around with that girl?"

"Nothing! I wasn't!"

"Clearly you were! Don't lie to me, Cameron."

"I can't help it if we walk the same way to school!" the boy whined.

"Oh? And it's not your fault you were hanging out in the park with her either, I suppose?"

"I don't even like her!" Cameron said, his voice cracking. "She's stupid and annoying!"

"Ms. Spicer," Annie interrupted. "What's your objection to this girl?"

"She is not the kind of young lady I want around my son," Sharon said with self-righteous indignation. "She's fresh and immature and a thief. She stole a trinket box from this house when she had no business being here in the first place. Cameron is not allowed to have friends over without an adult present. And her *mother*—"

"Is irrelevant," Dutrow announced impatiently. "Cameron, do you know where this girl is?"

"No, sir."

"You had better not be lying to me. You are not going to enjoy the consequences of that, I guarantee."

"I'm not lying!" Cameron wailed. "I'm gonna throw up!"

"Oh, for the love of God," Dutrow grumbled, disgusted.

The boy doubled over, holding his stomach, sobbing. Sharon started to reach out to him but stepped back at the sheriff's expression.

Annie watched the silent exchange with anxiety. She had been called to many a domestic dispute over the years, had acted as referee and buffer, diplomat and defender. She didn't have those options here. The male with the simmering rage issue was her boss. Kelvin Dutrow was the absolute power in Partout Parish. Only the governor of Louisiana had more power than a parish sheriff. Dutrow didn't have to listen to her or fear her. If he didn't like the tone of her voice, he could fire her on the spot. And yet, her instincts were telling her to find a way to intervene.

"I think we're done here, Detective," the sheriff said, as if he was reading her mind. "If this girl has run away, you have an investigation to organize."

"The Florettes live inside the city limits," Annie said. "It's not our jurisdiction."

"Then you'll have to coordinate with the Bayou Breaux PD. Keep me apprised. I'll reach out to Chief Earl and offer the full support of the Sheriff's Office in any search efforts."

Annie looked at Sharon Spicer, who had taken the moment of her fiancé's distraction to go to her son and comfort him.

"Yes, sir," Annie murmured. She dug a business card out of her pocket and placed it on the coffee table. "Ms. Spicer, if you'd care to lodge a formal complaint about the item you believe Nora stole, please feel free to call me."

Dutrow snatched up the card and stuck it in his pocket. "She knows who to call on. I'll show you out."

Annie hesitated, her mind scrambling for some excuse to stay, some extra question to ask, some *Columbo* moment of "just one more thing."

"Cameron, does Nora carry a backpack to school?" she asked. Dutrow huffed an impatient sigh beside her.

"I guess so," the boy mumbled, looking confused. "Everyone does."

"Did she have it with her going home yesterday?"

"I don't know. Maybe."

"He doesn't know," the sheriff grumbled, herding her toward the front entry.

"Is there some reason Cameron shouldn't have been in the park today?" Annie asked quietly as they went.

"It doesn't concern you," Dutrow replied.

"Sheriff," she said as he opened the front door and held it. "I think you should know that Cameron is getting bullied at school. Verbally and physically, I think. He may need someone to intervene for him."

"Cameron needs to learn how to take care of himself," Dutrow said without sympathy.

"But, sir—"

He held up a hand to cut her off. His expression was carefully blank, but Annie could feel the tension in him. It rolled off him like heat from a furnace. "My family is not your concern, Detective. Do you understand me?"

"Yes, sir."

"You would do well to put your worry to your own family situation."

"Sir?" Even as she asked, a chill ran down her back.

"Your husband is hanging on to his job by a thread after that stunt he pulled tonight at the hospital."

"Stunt? That was an ambush—"

"I don't want to hear it," Dutrow snapped. "Every time I turn around I've got another fire to put out, and the source of the blaze is named Fourcade. It seems to me my life would be a lot easier without him in it."

"You'd lose the best detective you ever had."

"I think I'd make do."

"He wouldn't be the only one to go."

"I think you overestimate your husband's popularity. Unless you're only talking about yourself, in which case, you had ought to be more prudent. You have a child to consider, don't you?"

Annie stood mute, knowing any of the dozen things she wanted to say would only make the situation worse. Dutrow held all the power, and he knew it, and he enjoyed it. She could see it in his eyes. The pleasure he derived from rendering her helpless had a creepy, almost sexual aura that made her skin crawl. And now she was going to have to surrender and leave, and he would go back inside the house and exert that power over a sobbing fourteen-year-old who wasn't living up to his standard of manliness.

The words she wanted to say congealed into a thick lump in her throat. The frustration felt like scalding steam inside her head.

"You have a job to do, Detective," Dutrow said coolly. "You'd best get on it."

He shut the door in her face before she could say, "Yes, sir."

Feeling sick with anxiety, Annie went back to her vehicle and sat behind the wheel, not quite able to get herself to start the engine. In her mind's eye she could see Dutrow swaggering across the room to tower over Cameron while the boy's mother stood helpless.

Even as she thought it, Dutrow pulled back the drape at the front window and looked out at her.

"Asshole," Annie muttered, starting the car.

There was nothing more she could do here. If she couldn't help Cameron Spicer, she would try to help the child she could. Slowly, she backed out of Dutrow's driveway and headed toward the Florette house.

TWENTY-EIGHT

Kelvin watched the headlights of Broussard's vehicle pull back and then swing around and point east. The headlights became taillights as she drove away.

He didn't like that she had come here. He didn't like an employee intruding into his personal life. He didn't like anyone catching him off guard. He was a careful man. He liked the word *meticulous*. He was meticulous in all things—in his appearance, in his manner, in his business dealings. He allowed people to see only exactly what he wanted them to see, painstakingly crafting and orchestrating his image. Every aspect of his life was carefully thought out and planned to the last detail. He did not like deviations from his plan. He did not like surprises.

Angry and embarrassed, spoiling for a fight, he walked back into the family room. Cameron sat on the ottoman, bent over with his head in his hands, crying. Sharon stood beside him, stroking his back. She looked up at Kelvin, pale and wide-eyed. Afraid.

The look sparked a certain satisfaction inside him, a certain excitement.

"Kelvin," she began.

"Cameron," Kelvin snapped. "Go to your room and stay there."

Sharon drew a shaky breath and tried again. "Kelvin, please. If we could just sit and talk about this as a family—"

"As a *family*?" he scoffed.

"Yes, I—"

"Cameron!" Kelvin barked. "Go to your room. *Now!*"

Cameron looked to his mother, uncertain as he unfolded himself from his seat.

"Cameron, go," Sharon said, her voice soft and shaking.

Reluctantly, Cameron backed toward the hall.

Kelvin lunged at him, shouting, *"GO!"* and the boy turned and ran.

"Kelvin," Sharon started again, reaching out toward him with a trembling hand.

He grabbed hold of her by the forearm, suddenly, forcefully, shocking her. Her eyes went wide and filled with tears. She tried to stifle a whimper as his grip tightened.

"How long have you been lying to me?" he demanded.

"Please don't make it sound like that!"

"How long?" he asked again, drawing her closer, squeezing harder.

"I'm sorry!" she sobbed.

He yanked her up against him and screamed in her face. *"HOW LONG?!"*

"Ten days," she confessed, crying. "I-I just hadn't f-found the right t-time to tell you—"

"*Tell* me?" He jumped on the word. "*Announce* to me?"

"You've been so busy," she rushed on. "I didn't want to trouble you with—"

"—the fact that you went behind my back and made a decision to defy me? When were you going to tell me? Were you just going to wait until I showed up at a practice or a game, and he wasn't there?"

"Kelvin, please," Sharon whimpered. "You're hurting me."

He adjusted his grip on her forearm and tightened it like a vise. "Were you going to let the coach tell me after I'd shown up to make a fool of myself?"

"No!" she cried. "Honestly—"

"*Honestly*? There's a word! You been lying to me for how long, and you use a word like *honestly*? That's rich, Sharon. You made this executive decision to let the boy quit ten days ago and you just kept letting me go on about it. Was that funny to you?"

"It wasn't like that! Cameron was getting hurt! You weren't listening!"

"We made a decision that he would stick this out," he said quietly. "We talked about it, and that was the decision—that he would stay in the program," he said. "*You* made the decision to let him quit."

"I'm his mother. I have to protect him!"

"From me?"

"Kelvin, please!" she pleaded again. "You're hurting me!"

He didn't care. No, that wasn't right. He was glad to hurt her. She had hurt him, embarrassed him. She deserved to hurt. Besides, it was just her arm. It wasn't like he was striking her. It wasn't like he was beating her with a fist. He had every right to be angry.

"You want me to marry you," he said. "You want me to be your husband and be a father to your son—to *another man's* son. You want to be the wife of the sheriff, yet you defy me and lie to me and tell me you have to protect that boy from me?"

"Kelvin, please don't! I love you!"

Kelvin shoved her away in disgust. She stumbled and fell to the floor, banging a knee on the coffee table on the way down.

"You lie to me, you make me look a fool in front of an employee," he said. "You teach your son to lie to me. What kind of family values is that, Sharon? Huh? Have you no respect for me? If you don't respect me, if your son doesn't respect me, why would I marry you, Sharon?"

"Kelvin, *please!*" she cried.

He leaned down over her and shouted, "I am a pillar of the goddamn community!"

She was sobbing now but trying to cover it up. Gathering herself into a ball, she cradled her arm against her body. Kelvin stared at her, disgusted with her, disgusted with himself. He was a man of impeccable self-control, and she had made him momentarily lose that control.

"Look what you made me do," he said, shaking his head.

He rubbed the back of his neck and sighed and checked his watch.

"I shouldn't have pushed you," he said at last. "That wasn't gentlemanly."

She looked up at him, wary, as he reached out a hand to help her up.

"I stumbled," she said as she took his hand and got to her feet. "I'm s-so s-sorry, Kelvin. I sh-should have told you about Cameron. It's just that I—"

"You taught your son to lie to me," Kelvin said calmly. "You conspired with your child to defy my wishes, and then covered it up."

"I'm s-so s-sorry!"

He shook his head again and turned toward the hallway.

"What are you going to do?" Sharon asked, following at his elbow as he left the room.

"I'm going to teach your son not to lie to me."

"Kelvin, no. Please!" she begged, snatching at his shirtsleeve. "This is my fault! I made the mistake."

"Yes, you did," he said.

He stopped a few feet short of the boy's bedroom door and looked down at her with her tear-wet face and smeared makeup. The pretty paint was coming off, exposing the truth, he thought.

"And now your son will pay for it."

CAMERON PACED IN his room, terrified. His head was pounding with the effort to not cry out loud even as tears poured down his face, and his breath caught in his throat, and his nose ran like a faucet. He could hear his mother crying—*Kelvin, please! You're hurting me!* He could hear Kelvin shouting—*I am a pillar of the goddamn community!*

It's all my fault. It's all my fault. Everything is always all my fault.

His stomach rolled and twisted. When he heard his mother cry out in pain, he rushed to the wastebasket by his desk and threw up.

Why was he such a loser? Why did he always screw things up? Now his mother was being hurt, and it was his fault, and he couldn't do anything to help her. If he had been bigger and braver, maybe he would have rushed back to the family room and done something to help. But he was weak and clumsy and scared to death of Kelvin, and so he allowed his mother to be injured.

"You should just go kill yourself and be done with it."

Maybe he should, he thought as he looked out the window at Kelvin's Suburban sitting in the puddle of light at the end of the big garage. Maybe everyone would be happier if he was gone. At least he wouldn't be able to mess up anymore, and he wouldn't have to be miserable and afraid and angry all the time.

The sound of his mother's voice startled him back into the moment.

"No. Kelvin, no! Please! Please don't hurt him! He's just a boy!"

In the next second Cameron's door flew open and Kelvin filled the doorway. He looked huge, puffed up like the Incredible Hulk. His face was like stone.

Cameron braced himself to be yelled at, but when Kelvin spoke, his voice was normal, almost quiet.

"I want your phone and your iPad. Now."

Cameron stared at him, frozen in panic, the images he'd drawn in his iPad flashing through his head like a movie on fast-forward. If Kelvin looked at them, he'd be furious. He'd be screaming for Cameron to be shipped off to military school or to an insane asylum or maybe even jail.

"Are you deaf?" Kelvin snapped. "Get them. Now."

"Cameron, do as he says," his mother pleaded. She clutched at the doorjamb as Kelvin stepped farther into the room. Her face was wet from crying, and her eye makeup and lipstick had run and smudged so she looked like she was melting.

"Now!" Kelvin shouted.

Cameron jumped and scurried to grab his cell phone off his desk. He clutched it in his hand as he stared at his iPad, wishing it would vanish.

"There will be consequences to your actions," Kelvin said, reaching in front of him and snatching up the iPad. "Give me the phone."

Cameron held out the phone reluctantly, and the sheriff grabbed it from his hand.

"You do not ever lie to me," Kelvin said. "Do you understand me?"

"Yes, sir," Cameron mumbled.

"Not for any reason. Not even if your mother condones it. Do you understand me?"

"Yes, sir."

"You can be without these for a month."

A month!

"But, Kelvin," his mother said. "A month? He uses the iPad for his schoolwork."

"He'll have to make due." Kelvin turned and thrust the devices at her. "Take these and go to the bedroom, and stay there."

Her eyes went wide and shiny with new tears. "Kelvin, what are you going to do?" she asked in a small, trembling voice.

"I'm going to teach him a lesson he will not forget, and he will never lie to me again," Kelvin said, shutting the door in her face.

As the door latched and locked, Cameron stood paralyzed, his heart racing in the bottom of his throat. He thought if he threw up his heart would come shooting out of his mouth and land on the bed, flopping like a fish as it died.

Kelvin turned toward him, a frown bending his mouth. The look in his eyes was cold and hard.

"You're a young man now, Cameron," he said quietly. "A man lives by a code of honor. You don't seem to understand that. You still behave as a child when it suits you. You lied to me like a child, like you thought somehow I would never find out the truth. I will *always* find out the truth, Cameron."

"Yes, sir," Cameron mumbled, tears rising in his eyes as Kelvin took a step closer.

"And if you're gonna behave like a child, then you're gonna be punished like a child," he said, unbuckling his belt.

Panic ran through Cameron as he watched the sheriff slide his belt free of the loops on his pants.

"Take your pants down and bend over."

The humiliation was almost the worst part of it. Almost. He was fourteen, not four. To have to pull down his pants in front of anyone, especially this man, embarrassed him and made him feel weak and helpless.

He had never been whipped before. His father had spanked him when he was little, but it hadn't been like this. Just a few swats with his hand and it was over, leaving him with a stinging bottom and a lasting lesson not to misbehave in the same way again. He had learned not to anger his father, to try to stay out of his way. For the most part, his father had lost interest in him.

This was different. This was cruel. The belt burned and stung and cut as Kelvin applied it with force. And every time Cameron cried out as leather met flesh, his mother cried out in the hall outside his bedroom door.

It's all my fault, he thought. It was always his fault just because he'd been born, because he'd never been the son anyone wanted, because he couldn't do anything right.

"You should just go kill yourself and be done with it," Dean Florette had told him.

Maybe Dean was right.

TWENTY-NINE

I s she dead?" Dean Florette asked, his small eyes bright with morbid excitement.

"Go get your mother," Annie ordered.

She had no patience left for nonsense. It was past ten o'clock. Her nerves were rubbed raw. The day had begun with the murder of a child. She'd just had to walk away from a situation where her gut told her a child might be in some kind of emotional jeopardy. And a twelve-year-old was missing from a home where no one seemed to care.

"Go!" she snapped.

The smirk fell from Dean's battered face. He ran back toward the kitchen, calling for his mother.

Annie invited herself into the house and stood just inside the front door, taking in life in the Florette household. Taylor Swift was belting out a song upstairs. The television was blaring *Family Feud* in the living room. An elderly man with thick glasses and cotton-candy hair sat expressionless in a recliner, watching the TV and smoking a cigarette. He didn't spare Annie a glance. A toddler she hadn't seen before was asleep on the sofa with a pacifier in her mouth. In the dining room, someone had dumped a basket of rumpled laundry on the table.

Dean came shooting out of the kitchen, flipping Annie off as he ran past and thundered up the stairs, out of sight. Jojean emerged from the kitchen, scowling, drying her hands on a dish towel. She was followed by a younger, pregnant version of herself, a twenty-something sour-faced young woman with a shaved head and tattoos on both bare arms.

"You still haven't heard from her?" Annie said without preamble.

"No. I told you I'd call you."

"Mrs. Florette, we need to call the police—"

"I'm not calling the police," Jojean said stubbornly, crossing her arms over her ample chest. "It's not that late. She won't stay out all night. That girl is afraid of her own shadow. She'll be home by midnight. Mark my words. She's just trying to worry me."

"Yeah, well, that doesn't seem to be working," Annie said. "I have to wonder why that is."

"What's that supposed to mean?"

"It means maybe you're not worried where she is because you know where she is. Maybe you're not worried she's not coming home because you know she's not coming home."

Jojean wadded the dish towel into a ball, her stubby fingers digging into it. "What are you saying? Are you saying you think I did something to Nora?"

"I don't know what else explains your attitude, to be perfectly honest," Annie said. "Maybe we ought to be having this conversation at the Sheriff's Office."

"You listen to me, little Miss High-and-Mighty," Jojean said, advancing on her, her forefinger pointed to wag in her face. "I don't have an attitude. You're the one with the attitude. Coming in my house, telling me you know more about my kids than I do."

Annie stood her ground. "You haven't laid eyes on your daughter in two days."

"She was here last night. Just because I didn't see her doesn't mean she wasn't here."

"Let's just see about that," Annie said. She turned and marched to the foot of the stairs and hollered up in the tone of the Florettes. "Dean Florette, come down here this minute!"

She glanced back at Jojean. "Is your other daughter home? What's her name again?"

"Nicole," the pregnant one answered. Earning a dirty look from Jojean.

"Nicole! You too!" Annie shouted. "Right now, before I come up there and haul your ass down!"

Dean came first, grudgingly, stomping hard on one stair tread and then the next, his mouth set in an almost comical frown. His sister followed just behind in skimpy baby-doll pajamas, her hair up in a messy pile on top of her head.

"Dean, when did you last actually see Nora with your own two eyes?" Annie asked.

"I told you, she was here last night," he said.

"I know what you told me. I asked when did you actually see her last? You said she was in the bathroom and hogging the phone. Did you actually see her?"

He frowned harder.

"'Cause I been talking to her friends," Annie went on, "and none of them had a call from her last night. So, if she was here and she was on the phone, who was she on the phone with?"

Dean frowned harder.

"Has she got a boyfriend no one here is telling me about?" Annie asked, scanning the faces in the room.

"She's twelve," Jojean said. "She ain't got no boyfriend at twelve."

"Really?" Annie said. "She was stealing a *Penthouse* magazine at the Quik Pik for herself?"

"That was just a stupid kid thing," Jojean said.

"Was she stealing that for you, Dean?" Annie asked. "Was that how she paid you for dumping KJ Gauthier here after school so she could run off with Lola?"

"She didn't bring me no magazine!" Dean said.

"Well, she got caught, didn't she?"

"I don't know what you're talking about!"

Annie looked to Nicole, who clung to the newel post, chewing on a thumbnail. "What about you? Did you see Nora last night? This morning?"

The girl started to shrug but thought better of it as Annie stared her down. "No."

"That was you on the phone last night, not Nora?"

"I guess."

She turned to Dean again. "You saw Nora after school yesterday, then what?"

"I don't know. I didn't come straight home."

Annie heaved a sigh, trying to put together the timeline in her head. "She brought KJ here. Genevieve must have been the last person to see her when she picked him up after work."

Jojean dropped her dish towel and pressed a hand across her mouth.

"What?" Annie asked.

"She wasn't here," Jojean said, her voice uncharacteristically soft. "When Genevieve came to pick up KJ, Nora wasn't here. She called me and complained. I said it wasn't a big deal. It wasn't like he was left alone. There's always people here. What difference did it make if it was Nora?"

"Shouldn't you be out investigating that murder?" the pregnant woman piped up belligerently. "Instead of harassing our family?"

"What makes you think I'm not investigating a murder?" Annie asked. "Nora could be dead in a ditch for all y'all seem to care."

"Don't say that!" Jojean snapped. For the first time Annie thought she might have caught a glimpse of worry in the mother's eyes.

"Why not?" she challenged. "I hear you dragged Nora out of the Quik Pik by her hair on Monday."

"Who told you that? That horrid little Troiano girl—"

"She's been threatening to run away from home for days—weeks, probably—and who can blame her?" Annie went on. "Her friends tell me she talked about it all the time. She told you she'd never speak to you again. Maybe you're just as glad. From what I've seen, you've got a house chock-full of mouthy females. All the better to have one less, right?"

"Shut your mouth!" Jojean shouted. "Who do you think you are—"

"I'm the only one seems to give a rat's ass. That's who I am. Your twelve-year-old is gone and you won't even bother to call the police!"

"She's coming home!" Jojean insisted, though tears had begun to well up in her eyes. "She's just doing this to scare me! She's gonna walk in that door any minute!"

"And what if she doesn't?" Annie demanded. "What if she's raped and murdered and thrown in a bayou?"

"Stop it!"

"What if she's tied up in a car trunk on her way to New Orleans to be sold as a sex slave?"

"Stop it, goddamn you!" Jojean cried, rushing at Annie, her arms raised as if to strike her.

Annie caught her by the wrists and shouted in her face, "What if she doesn't ever walk in that door again?"

"Then it's my fault!" Jojean cried.

The last of the hard shell cracked and split, and the emotion came pouring out. She pulled back out of Annie's grasp, reeling as if she'd been stunned.

"It's all my fault!" she cried again. "She said she'd run away. And I told her I didn't care."

Sobbing, she sank down to her knees on the floor, dragging an armload of laundry off the table as she went. She buried her face in the clean, rumpled mess as she cried.

"Look what you done!" the pregnant one shouted at Annie as she knelt awkwardly to comfort Jojean.

Dean stared at the scene with morbid fascination. "Do you really think she's dead?"

Nicole sat down on the steps and hugged herself as if she'd gone suddenly cold.

Feeling drained and terrible, Annie pulled her phone out of her pocket and went outside to call the police.

THIRTY

The lightning appeared on the southern horizon as a soft white glow behind the clouds. Miles away yet. According to the weather report on his phone, the storm was still out over the Gulf, but moving north. Damned weather. Nick hoped it would stall out or take its time, at least. For now he had some moonlight to navigate by.

Standing in the back of the boat, he used a pole to propel it forward soundlessly across the black water.

He had built the pirogue himself from cypress and marine plywood, just like his papa had taught him when he was a little boy and the family had lived the swamper's life on a house barge on the edge of the Atchafalaya Basin. Nick had painted the boat green and red—the traditional colors the old fishermen back in the day had used to distinguish themselves from the sports who came to play on the weekends at their fish camps. As if there could ever have been any confusing the two—the sports coming with their fancy aluminum and fiberglass boats tricked out with sonar fish finders and whatnot.

Now aluminum *bateaux* and fiberglass pirogues were the norm, and practically every Cajun man alive had a bass boat with two outboard motors. But since he didn't have to make his living on the water, and his idea of water sport didn't involve noise or speed, Nick had the luxury of embracing tradition.

Building the pirogue had been a labor of love to preserve his sanity when he had first come to Bayou Breaux, psychologically battered from the demise of his career in the New Orleans PD. Navigating the bayous calmed him and centered him. As shallow and delicate as a milkweed pod, the pirogue skated across the water, skimming over the duckweed and water hyacinth, deftly slipping between the cypress trees. It was the perfect craft for navigating the shallows where bigger boats could never go. Perfect for his mission this night.

He knew these waterways like the back of his hand, knew he could launch from a particular spot on Pony Bayou, slip around behind Blue Cypress Point, and connect to the nameless little backwater across the road from the home of Genevieve Gauthier in a matter of half an hour with no one the wiser. This time of night, no one would see him save the creatures of the swamp. As much as he likened Roddie Perez to a reptile, none of the snakes or gators would bother to warn him trouble was coming.

He sank the pole into the mud and pushed, working the muscles of his shoulders and back and arms. The pirogue shot forward, and he automatically adjusted his weight over his feet as the boat rocked beneath him. It was all as natural to him as breathing.

Inhale. Focus. Calm. Exhale. Focus. Calm . . .

He cleared his mind of the noise and clutter and contentiousness of the day to connect with the only world that truly made sense to him. He breathed deep the warm, humid air, the smell of water and mud and lush vegetation. He listened to the sounds of the night—the singing of frogs, the chirping of crickets, the splash and slap of a fish breaking the surface. Birds chattered their disapproval of his presence as he brushed past a tangle of willows and hackberry saplings. And in the distance, the rolling growl of thunder echoed the throaty purr of an alligator on the bank.

I go to nature to be soothed and healed, and to have my senses put in order. He had used the John Burroughs quote as a mantra since he had first read it as a teenager.

Ironically, it was the chaos of the man-made world that provided him a vocation and a living, but it was nature that fed his soul.

He had left Remy's, gone home, and grabbed an hour's fitful sleep to at least in part recharge his energy for what he suspected would become a long night, if they were lucky. His mind had refused to clear, scenes from the day tumbling through his head like colored glass in a kaleidoscope, always coming to rest on the image of the Gauthier boy dead on the floor in a pool of blood, that image just one click away from the image of Justin asleep in bed with his teddy bear.

He loved his son, loved being a father. He welcomed and embraced the responsibility that came with being a parent. Not every parent did. For some, it came as an unwelcome surprise, something they had failed to consider during the nine months of waiting for their child to come into the world.

He saw it all the time with girls too young to be mothers. They wanted someone to love, someone to love them, and blocked out the notion that parenting was a job until it was too late. Genevieve Gauthier might have been one of those girls. She had been nineteen or twenty when KJ was born—not a child herself, but young and single. Did she regret the choices she'd made? Had she resented the result of those choices?

Annie was right, though. They had no evidence Genevieve didn't want her son. She had no record—neither official nor anecdotal—of abusing the boy. Nick had stood there in the morgue that morning and listened to Genevieve's sobs, too. But he also knew that grief and guilt were not mutually exclusive. People who murdered family members and loved ones were often very remorseful after. A grievance that built to a head and exploded in a moment led to a lifetime of regret, but regret didn't change or excuse what could never be undone.

If that was the answer the evidence led them to—that Genevieve had killed her son—it wouldn't come as a shock. Not even to Annie, as much as she didn't want it to be true.

The idea rubbed raw the wounds that had never completely healed for her after her mother's death. Without an answer to the fundamental question of why her mother had taken her own life, Annie had never found a way to completely close those wounds. Because of that, a part of her would always be that abandoned little girl. Just as a small corner of Nick's heart would forever be a seventeen-year-old boy feeling heartsick and impotent at the loss of his sister and the disintegration of his family.

He kicked himself for not thinking about that. The fact that as investigators they had to consider the possibility of Genevieve's guilt didn't excuse him so carelessly running over his wife's feelings. He would sooner have cut himself to the bone as hurt her, even unintentionally. His strongest instinct was to protect her from harm.

He had never imagined himself as a husband or father before Annie. He couldn't imagine himself as anything else since. Their life together meant everything to him. Before their summer had gone to hell with Fanchon's stroke and his involvement in the Theriot case, they had been talking about having another baby, expanding their family now that Justin had started school. Now they couldn't go a day without an argument, and his job was hanging by a thread.

Maybe when these cases were cleared they could go away. They could take Justin and go down to the Gulf for a few days of solitude and get themselves back on the rails.

Once these cases were cleared . . .

He checked his position, sank the pole down into the mud, and pushed the pirogue forward.

The lights were on in the Gauthier house as he steered to a vantage point on the far side of the road. He sidled the boat up parallel to the bank and tied off on a young tree only as thick as his forearm. Anyone on the road would pass within a dozen feet of him and be none the wiser. Hidden from easy sight by nature's lace of scrub and young trees hung with vines, he would have been hard to spot in daylight. At night, dressed in black head to toe, his face smeared with black grease, he was as close to invisible as he could be.

He dug into his backpack for his phone and, holding it inside the bag to hide the light, texted a message to Stokes. He checked his sight lines and settled in to wait.

Across the road, Ossie Compton sat in his cruiser in the Gauthier driveway, silhouetted from one side by the porch light and from the back by the light over the door on the ramshackle garage.

At the property next door, the only light visible in Roddie Perez's house was the flickering, ever-changing light from the big-screen TV in the front room.

A set of headlights appeared down the gravel road, coming from town. When the car was within fifty yards, the deputy driving the cruiser hit the roof lights—ostensibly to signal his counterpart in front of the Gauthier house. The lights rolled, red and blue as the car turned in at the Gauthier driveway and pulled up just to Compton's left.

The deputies got out of their respective vehicles and stood leaning against their open car doors, talking. From where he sat, Nick could hear the sounds of their voices, the tones and inflections, but couldn't make out what they were saying. He pulled his night-vision binoculars out of his backpack and trained them on Roddie Perez's dining room window, letting his eyes adjust to the green glow as he waited.

The plan was a gamble, but one with not much of a downside, other than loss of sleep. Finding Perez with the slumlord Carville at Club Cayenne had rubbed Nick's instincts the wrong way. Bad enough having a scumbag, drug-dealer ex-con living next door to a victim, but tie that character to a piece of shit like Roy Carville, landlord and flesh merchant, and that was a recipe for nothing good at all.

It could have gone down just the way Nick had suggested to Carville. Tired of waiting for his rent, wanting to coerce Genevieve into taking her clothes off for his profit, Carville might have tapped Perez to scare the girl. Perez might have gone in through the boy's window, waking the child, and the situation spiraled out of control . . .

But why would he go to the trouble of climbing in the boy's window? Surely, Carville had keys to the house. Why not go in through a door and make it look like a break-in after the fact? And why would Perez not have then killed Genevieve, too, if there had been any chance of her pointing the finger at him for murdering her son?

Nick didn't like the loose ends, but even as he questioned them, Roddie Perez stepped up to his dining room window and looked out in the direction of the Gauthier house.

Setting down the binoculars, Nick reached into his backpack again and sent a text to Ossie Compton. Seconds later, Compton and the other deputy slammed the doors on their cruisers and went up to the house. They took down the yellow barrier tape from the front door slowly and carefully, folding it up neatly, as if they were planning to reuse it.

Roddie Perez watched them from his dining room.

Nick watched Perez. At twenty-five yards he cut a distinguishable black-and-white shape in the field of green light. He wore a white undershirt. His pants were several shades darker. He held a pair of binoculars to his eyes. That was as much detail as Nick could make out.

The deputies went inside the house and through the residence, turning out the lights, reappearing on the front porch less than five minutes later. Compton stepped back inside, and the porch light went out. The pair sauntered back to their vehicles like men in no particular hurry to go anywhere. Compton drove out first. The second car made a lazy U-turn half on the lawn and half on the driveway, and followed.

Perez remained at the window, watching as the taillights of the cruisers grew smaller and smaller on the way back to town. Then he backed out of sight.

Now the wait began.

The thunder rumbled closer.

Would Perez take the bait?

He wasn't stupid. A lifetime of criminal behavior had sharpened his sense of animal cunning, at the very least. Already a two-time loser on felony convictions, he was liable to be especially wary of a trap. But he wasn't a genius, either. And if he had for any reason left any trace of himself in Genevieve Gauthier's home, this was his window of opportunity to get it back or erase it.

Then again, he had to know that if they had anything on him already Nick would have gotten his search warrant and Perez would have been sitting in jail tonight instead of sitting in his easy chair watching his big-screen TV. He would know there would be no drugs left in the house for him to steal, if that might have been a motivation—unless he knew Genevieve had a secret stash somewhere the crime scene people wouldn't have looked.

Entirely possible, Nick conceded, based on his low opinion of Keith Kemp. Stokes had supposedly kept his eye on the CSIs after Dutrow had thrown Nick out of the house, but Stokes was only as diligent as he wanted to be. He generally had no objection to the crime scene unit doing what he thought of as tedious scut work. Over the years, he had consistently expressed his impatience at Nick's obsessive attention to detail at a scene.

Left to his own devices, Stokes was an average detective at best and lazy at worst. Supervised and motivated, he could rise to the occasion. Which had he been last night while Nick had been outside pacing in the yard?

Impatient with his own paranoia, he dismissed the question. He had walked the scene himself that morning before heading to the hospital. If anything had been overlooked by Kemp or Stokes, he should have caught it himself then.

He thought back to the night before, calling Kemp on not picking up the tangle of colored thread he had seen on the carpet, his irritation with the man stirring anew. Kemp, who had been a cop himself, should have known better.

Nick called to mind the photograph he had seen on Dutrow's wall of fame—Dutrow and Kemp in uniform, teaching self-defense to women. He wondered when and why Kemp had made the switch to working crime scenes. He wasn't old enough to have reached retirement and make a second career as a CSI. He certainly didn't seem like the kind of detail-oriented, science-minded individual to make that choice out of love for the job.

He and Dutrow had to have been tight friends for Kemp to follow him to Bayou Breaux to work a job as unsworn personnel.

That thought raised another question. Since Dutrow had created the crime scene unit from scratch and could staff it as he wished, why hadn't he hired Kemp on as a deputy and given the unit to him? Why would Kemp have left the Houma PD, where he had to have built years toward a pension?

The sound of a truck engine roaring to life broke Nick from his musings. Perez rolled out of his driveway and turned toward town. Nick hunkered down in the pirogue as the four-by-four crept past, the big tires crunching over the gravel and crushed shell. It stopped and idled at the end of Genevieve Gauthier's driveway. Thirty seconds . . . sixty seconds . . . ninety seconds . . . Nick stayed still, his breathing shallow, listening for any indication Perez was leaving the vehicle.

Finally the truck inched forward, slowly picking up speed as it headed toward town.

Nick sat up and watched the taillights disappear, then reached into his backpack and texted Stokes: *Perez headed your way.*

Headed where? Back to Club Cayenne? On to some other dubious meeting? The deputies on the drug task force claimed Perez had been keeping his nose clean, but Nick's gut told him the con was getting money from somewhere, and it probably wasn't honest labor. The big TV, the laptop computer, the tricked-out four-by-four, all spoke of disposable income.

Stokes texted back: *Tailing.* Just minutes later, Nick's phone vibrated, Stokes's name appearing on the screen.

"Coming back your way, Nicky. He just drove around a couple blocks. He's sniffing for a trap."

"Did he make you?"

"I don't think so. If he did, he didn't react."

"Hang back and wait for my signal."

"Roger that, boss."

Even as Nick ended the call, he could hear the distant approach of a vehicle between rumbles of thunder drawing ever closer. He slid down once again, crouching low in the pirogue. Once again, Perez slowed the truck as he came past the Gauthier house, then drove on by.

"*Merde* . . . Come on, you ugly son of a bitch," Nick murmured, watching as the four-by-four turned in at Perez's own driveway.

The first fat raindrops began to fall. Lightning crackled across the sky.

The truck's headlights and taillights went dark, and the truck sat idling. Three minutes . . . five minutes . . , The rain came a little harder.

Perez was thinking about it, weighing his options.

Ten minutes . . .

The lightning and thunder came closer together. The rain came harder still. Nick paid no attention to the elements. He made no move to cover himself. He kept the binoculars raised to his eyes, watching, trying to will Perez to move.

Fifteen minutes . . .

The truck shifted gears and, without turning on the lights, backed out of the driveway and turned north again. It rolled past the Gauthier driveway and then backed in, backing all the way to the garage area.

The driver's door opened and closed. Through the night-vision binoculars he could see the blurred figure rush toward the back door of the house.

Nick texted Stokes and then waited until he caught a glimpse of the briefest flash of light inside the house. Then he slipped from the pirogue and crept up the bank. Staying as low to the ground as he could, he dashed across the road. The rain was coming in earnest now, providing an extra layer of cover in between flashes of lightning as bright as day.

If Perez saw him—*when* Perez saw him—what would he do? Run or fight? Breaking and entering was a felony. Burglary was a felony. Assaulting a law enforcement officer was a felony. He would be going back to Angola—one of the worst hellholes of a prison in America—for the rest of his time on earth.

His best bet would be murder. If he could kill Nick and make a run for it, he would have a slim chance of escaping. If he was apprehended, he would get the death penalty, but plenty of men who had endured sentences in Angola would have gladly taken that option.

Soaked to the bone, Nick ran along the north side of the house, crouching below window level, weapon drawn and ready. As he reached the back of the house, he pressed against the clapboard siding and slowly peered around the corner, leading with his gun. As the lightning flashed, he had a clear view of the back porch and, beyond that, Perez's truck.

The screen door swayed in the wind, half-open. Nick made a dash for the porch, praying whatever Perez had gone in for was keeping him deeper into the interior of the house. Making entry would be his most vulnerable moment.

And then he was up the steps and into the tiny, cramped kitchen. A bright burst of lightning illuminated the kitchen and the dining room and front room beyond. No sign of Roddie.

Thunder boomed hard enough to rattle the old windows. Staying along the perimeter of the room, Nick made his way to the hall that led to the bedrooms.

Stokes should be in the yard by now, he thought, blocking Roddie's truck from its escape route.

The beam of Perez's flashlight bobbed in the room at the end of the hall—Genevieve's bedroom.

Nick moved quietly on the balls of his feet, his Glock out in front of him, aimed chest-high.

"Goddamn it!"

The curse was followed by the sound of something metallic hitting the wood floor in the bedroom.

Nick crept closer to the half-open door, taking in the sounds of mumbling and rummaging. What was he looking for? Drugs? Money? Would he risk life in prison for the meager few bucks a girl like Genevieve might have stashed in her underwear drawer?

Glass bottles collided. Something else fell to the floor.

Perfume bottles, Nick thought. The clutter a woman kept on her dresser.

Genevieve's dresser was through the door and to the left.

He moved into the doorway—the door acting as a shield—and peered around the edge of it.

Lightning brightened the room, showing Perez standing on the dresser, his flashlight sandwiched between his cheek and shoulder as he reached into a cold air return vent high on the wall.

"Whatcha got there, Roddie?" Nick asked, stepping into the room, flicking on the ceiling light.

Perez swung around, wide-eyed and open-mouthed. The flashlight fell off his shoulder, and he grabbed for it with one hand and then the other like a drunken juggler. Catching one end of it, he hurled the thing in Nick's direction, losing his balance in the process. The flashlight fell wide of its target as Perez slipped and slid in a crazy, scrambling tap dance on the dresser. One foot stepped into space, and down he went, hitting the floor with a bone-jarring thud.

"I'll tell you whatcha got, Roddie," Nick said, standing over him, pointing the gun down at his face. "You got the right to remain silent."

THIRTY-ONE

"I think I got a concussion," Perez complained, squinting hard. "Y'all gotta take me to the emergency room."

He sat slumped over on a straight chair, his hands cuffed behind his back. Outside the bedroom window, the rain was still coming down in sheets. A cruiser sat in the driveway, waiting for the storm to let up before they loaded Perez to take him to jail.

"Don't you have to have a brain to get a concussion?" Stokes asked. "I don't see much evidence of that."

"Ha-ha," Perez said. "You're a laugh riot, you are. You won't be laughing when I sue your ass for negligence."

"That joke's on you, asshole," Stokes said. "I'm a cop. I ain't got a pot to piss in nor a window to pitch it out of. Go on and waste your own money suing me. You're gonna die in prison just the same. Here you are, Mr. Two-Time Loser, breaking and entering—"

"It ain't breaking and entering," Perez argued. "I had a key, and I had permission from the landlord."

"*Mais* yeah, try selling that story to a judge," Nick said. "Your good friend Mr. Carville sent you in here for what purpose?"

Perez gave him a look of disgust. "I have got *nothing* to say to *you*."

Nick ignored him, his attention on the small electronic device in his gloved hand, a black sphere about the size of a Ping-Pong ball. "So planting cameras in the bedrooms of female renters is Carville's idea? And you're just an accessory?"

"Stick it up your ass."

"If it's Carville's idea, then you'd be off the hook for the felony," Nick lied. "If we believed you. Me, I don't see any reason to believe anything that comes out your mouth, Roddie."

"Go fuck yourself, Fourcade. I don't know nothing about these cameras. I got nothing to do with any of it."

Cameras, plural. *Any of it*. Any of what? As if Nick couldn't guess.

"You're just the errand boy, you are?" he asked. "So when I get my search warrant for your house and seize your computer, I'm not gonna find video of Genevieve Gauthier dressing, undressing, having sex?"

Perez said nothing.

"I'm not gonna find you had a camera in her bathroom, too, recording her taking a shower, shaving her legs, sitting on the toilet?"

The con scowled harder.

"My, my, Roddie," Stokes said, shaking his head as he walked back and forth, his arms crossed over his chest. "I never pegged you for the kind of perv that likes to watch people wipe their asses. You've slipped a notch in my esteem."

"What else are we gonna see when we download these cameras?" Nick asked. "We gonna see you beating the shit out of this girl? Have we hit the jackpot here? 'Cause I would love nothing better than to wrap this all up tonight and put a big red bow right around your neck."

"I never touched that girl!" Perez shouted.

"You better hope not, Roddie. 'Cause if there's video of you doing harm here, if there's evidence of you touching a hair on the head of that little boy, I will make it my personal crusade to see that the state of Louisiana dusts the cobwebs off ol' Gruesome Gertie to light you up like a goddamn Christmas tree."

"I never laid a hand on that brat!" Perez snapped. "Y'all can look right at that mother, you want to see who abused that child."

"You saw that happen?" Nick asked.

Perez looked away, done talking.

"Get him out of here," Nick said to Stokes. "I'm done looking at him for tonight. And get a judge out of bed. We need a search warrant for his house."

"Let's go, Roddie," Stokes said, reaching out to take Perez by the arm.

Perez shrugged him off as he got to his feet. "I don't need you touching me."

"Consider it foreplay for your body cavity search."

Nick followed them out of the room and down the hall. Kemp was coming in the front door as they reached the living room, a sour look twisting his mouth as he shook himself like a wet cat.

"Why am I out here in this shit hole again?" he asked, shrugging out of his rain slicker and dropping it on the floor, glaring at Stokes and Perez as they went out the door.

"Turns out you missed a few things," Nick said, holding up the spy camera.

Kemp squinted at the device. "What is that? Is that a camera?"

"Yeah, genius, that's a camera and you failed to find it."

"Well, we didn't go crawling through the air vents."

"Then how do you know where it was?"

"Where else would it have been if it wasn't in plain sight?"

"In a piece of furniture, in a lamp, in a clock, in the ceiling light, in the air conditioner that doesn't fucking work." Nick rattled off the possibilities.

"You didn't find it, either," Kemp pointed out.

"Would have been hard for me to see it from the yard," Nick said. "I had been asked to leave, if you recall. To keep from upsetting your delicate sensibilities."

"And you can leave again," Kemp said, pulling on a pair of black latex gloves. "I don't need your supervision."

"You're gonna get it whether you want it or not," Nick said, standing just a little too close. "I want that room taken apart, and the bathroom, and the boy's room, too. And this time I will stand there and watch you do it until I'm satisfied."

"What-the-fuck-ever," Kemp snarled as his underling came through the door. He barked at the kid, "Go get the tool kit! And evidence bags. And hurry the fuck up! Bring it to the back bedroom."

"Yes, sir!" The kid spun around and went back out into the rain.

"So you gave up the badge so you could boss a pimply-faced kid around and dig through other people's stuff in the middle of the night?" Nick asked.

Kemp gave him a look and stepped around him, heading for the hall.

Nick followed. "Interesting career choice."

Kemp said nothing.

"You were in a uniform down in Houma. Why'd you give it up?"

They walked into the bedroom, and Kemp stopped in the middle of the floor, looking up at the gaping hole of the air vent above the dresser as if he expected something to come crawling out of it.

"There you were," Nick said, "working side by side with your good buddy Dutrow, putting in the years toward a pension, and then . . . what? What happened?"

"I don't see how my life choices are any of your business."

Kemp went to the window, bent down, and peered at the ancient air conditioner, poking at the broken louvers of the front grille. Muttering, he pulled a Leatherman tool off his belt, sorted out the Phillips-head screwdriver, and went to work to loosen the front panel. He cut a sideways glance at Nick.

"How'd you find out about these cameras?"

"The landlord was a little too eager about getting the house back when I spoke with him. And there he was, sitting at the bar at Club Cayenne with Roddie Perez, career criminal and next-door neighbor of Ms. Gauthier. A curious choice of friends, I thought. So we set a little trap. Mr. Perez is not half as clever as the average rat."

"Lucky."

"How long have you known Dutrow?" Nick asked.

"What's it to you?"

"Just curious," Nick said, drifting closer. "The two of you must be tight. You followed him up here."

Kemp heaved a sigh, irritated. "He offered me a job. I took it. Mystery solved. You should be a detective."

"You already had a job. Did you have a problem with that one?"

"People change jobs, Fourcade."

"Mm-hmm. Not without reasons. Did you have a beef with someone higher up the food chain?"

"No."

"You were in a uniform, then you weren't. You worked crime scenes down there for what—eight or nine years? Banking up the seniority, and then, boom, you up and leave . . ."

Kemp shot him a look as he pocketed the screws from the AC panel. "So what? Weren't you some hotshot detective down in New Orleans before you cracked up? Now here you are."

Nick didn't turn a hair. Kemp's jab wasn't far from the truth. It was all ancient history now anyway, not that it had ever mattered much to him what people thought.

"Did you mean to imply you had some kind of breakdown?" he asked. "Maybe you had that badge taken away?"

"What? NO!" Kemp overreacted, surprised to have that particular table turned right back around on him.

"Do you know this woman?" Nick asked, changing subjects before Kemp could regain his mental balance. "The mother. Ms. Gauthier. Do you know her?"

"Why would I know her?" Kemp returned defensively, working to pry the rusted front panel off the air conditioner.

"Why wouldn't you?" Nick challenged. "She worked in Houma. You worked in Houma. You were a cop. She has a record. Maybe you arrested her, yeah?"

"Maybe I arrested the Queen of England. It was years ago. Who remembers shit like that? I've arrested more people than I can count."

"No matter," Nick said, stepping closer as the panel came free and Kemp stumbled backward. "Dutrow said he'd call Houma PD and get me the original arrest report. Dixon couldn't find it the usual way. Odd, that."

"You're a regular goddamn Chatty Cathy, pulling your own string,

Fourcade," Kemp groused. "Why don't you shut the hell up and let me do my job?"

"Right," Nick said dryly as he leaned down and plucked another camera the size of a Ping-Pong ball from inside the shell of the air conditioner. It had been situated just behind the broken louvers, pointed at Genevieve Gauthier's bed. "Because I'm sure you're so much more efficient working in unsupervised silence."

"Jesus, you're an asshole."

"I prefer to think I'm thorough," Nick said as Kemp's underling hustled into the room, dripping wet, out of breath. He dropped the toolbox on the floor. Nick dug into a pocket on the leg of his pants and pulled out an evidence bag to drop the camera in. He handed it to the kid.

"Mark that, and have a care," he said. "I don't want anything messing up what's stored in the memory. God only knows who we'll see on that video."

The kid looked at him wide-eyed then glanced at Kemp, who nodded grudgingly.

"Might we see you in the movies, Keith?" Nick asked, looking at Kemp, shifting a little closer to him just to irritate him. "Reuniting with an old flame from Houma? Is that why you didn't find these cameras the first time you processed this scene?"

"I told you, I don't know this woman."

"Actually, no, you didn't. You said, 'Why would I know her?' That's not the same thing."

"Well, I'm telling you now. I don't know her," Kemp snapped, his hands fumbling as he tried to hook his Leatherman tool back on his utility belt. "Seriously, fuck the fuck off, Fourcade."

"Maybe you met her teaching that self-defense class with Dutrow, yeah? The timing would have been about right."

"I don't know what you're talking about."

"Come on, Keith, don't be modest," Nick cajoled. "You were big news in Houma. You made the Houma *Courier*."

"What the hell are you doing?" Kemp demanded. "Why would you know anything about that? Are you investigating me?"

"That is what I do."

"Because I'm from Houma?" he said, his face turning a deeper shade of red. "Lots of people are from Houma, Fourcade. There's thirty-four thousand people in Houma. Are you investigating all of them?"

"Now you're just talking foolish, Keith," Nick said calmly. "That would be a waste of my time. I'm only investigating the ones that recently moved to Bayou Breaux. Maybe Genevieve Gauthier is the reason you don't have a badge anymore, yeah?"

He was just poking a stick at a snarling dog to irritate him, to aggravate him. Kemp rose to the bait like a champ and lunged toward him, fists balled, face contorted, ready to scream.

Unflinching, Nick raised a finger and wagged it in his face.

"Don't you touch me, Keith," he said quietly. "I warned you about that once already. Me, I don't like to repeat myself."

Kemp held himself rigid, just inches away. Small white bubbles of spittle gathered in one corner of his mouth. "I can't wait for Dutrow to get rid of you, you coonass son of a bitch."

Nick chuckled low in his throat and smiled like a predator. "You think that would save you from me if you did this thing, Keith? Clearly, you don't know who I answer to, and it sure as hell ain't Kelvin Dutrow."

Kemp said nothing. Nick held his gaze steadily, letting what he'd said sink in, savoring the smell of anxiety.

"I can't leave you alone for five minutes," Stokes complained. Nick could see him from the corner of his eye, filling the doorway.

"I thought you went with Perez," Nick said, not moving. Kemp took half a step back.

"A deputy can book him and show him to his accommodations," Stokes said. "It's past my bedtime."

"Then let's get this job done, Sleeping Beauty," Nick said, walking away from Kemp at last. "This day's been long enough."

THIRTY-TWO

Annie woke from a fitful sleep to the sound of running water. Rain. No. The shower. Nick was home. She turned on the lamp on his nightstand, fluffed up the pillows, and sat back to wait for him. She was exhausted but too agitated to relax. The events of the evening played on a continuous loop in her mind. Jojean Florette sobbing on her knees. Dean watching in morbid fascination. The look in his eyes as he asked, "Do you really think she's dead?" Dutrow.

That scene bothered her as much as any. The tableau in Dutrow's living room: Dutrow standing like a drill sergeant as his fiancée begged on behalf of her sobbing child.

A sick sense of dread rolled in the pit of Annie's stomach.

The sound of water ceased. Moments later, Nick emerged from the bathroom, naked, rippling muscle, wet hair slicked to his head. He frowned seeing she was up.

"Hey, *bébé*, I didn't want to wake you," he murmured, sliding into bed beside her, leaning back against the pillows.

"You didn't," Annie said, curling up against him, her head finding the hollow of his shoulder, her legs twining with his. He wrapped his arms around her and kissed her forehead, and she sighed as some small amount of the tension left her body. "Not really," she added. "Did you get your guy?"

"Mm-hmm. Perez and the landlord had cameras stashed in her bedroom and bathroom. I haven't looked at any of the recordings yet, but it's not hard to imagine what's on there. They were probably selling it on the Internet."

"Gross."

"It could be worse than that."

"Oh, my God," Annie murmured, looking up at him. "Do you think they recorded the murder?"

"No. There were no cameras in the boy's room. But Perez suggested she abused her son. And he said it like he had firsthand knowledge of it."

"I really hope that's not true."

Nick made no comment. They had already had this conversation. He was fully ready to accept that Genevieve might have killed her child, and he wouldn't waste any emotional energy hoping otherwise. The truth would be the truth. No sense wishing for something else.

He breathed in the scent of her hair and sighed. "What time did you get home?"

"About half an hour ago."

"Did you find the babysitter?"

"No. And I had to browbeat the mother until she broke down. She didn't want to believe anything bad might have happened because then she would have to blame herself. She hadn't seen her daughter for two days, but somehow that wasn't her fault. That Jojean Florette is a piece of work, but still, I couldn't help but feel mean as a snake for doing that to her."

"Florette?"

"Yeah. The babysitter is Nora Florette. The twelve-year-old—"

"Where do they live?"

"On the south side of town. The last street in the PD's jurisdiction. I had to bring them in. Technically, it's their case, but I'll work with them since I've got the jump on interviewing friends and family. Why?"

"The Theriots live on the other side of the line, in Blue Cypress."

"Is Dean Florette on your list of suspects?" Annie asked, only half joking.

"Is that the father?"

"No. That's the fourteen-year-old prospect for long-term incarceration," she said. "Did you talk to him? He's a short, mean-eyed, mouthy little shit. Of course, that describes most of the Florettes, to be honest. The father keeps himself absent as much as possible. He works on a rig in the Gulf. His daughter is missing and he asked me was it really necessary for him to come back to help search for her." She shook her head. "He doesn't want to take this seriously, either. People are endlessly disappointing."

"I recognize the last name," Nick said. "Stokes and Dixon talked to the neighborhood kids at the time of the assault. They all run together, in and out of each other's houses. Some are friends of the older Theriot girl. No one stood out, as I recall."

"So, for sure the Florettes know the Theriots?" Annie asked. She sat up straighter, turning to face him, the anxiety stirring inside her anew.

"What?" Nick asked. "Do you seriously think this boy could be a suspect for the Theriot assault?"

"I hate to think that," Annie said, "but he tried to put his hands on a girl in the park yesterday. She told me he does that kind of thing—tries to touch girls' breasts. He already has a taste for pornography. He's a bully. He has a tendency toward violence. No one told you any of this?"

"No."

Annie sighed and ran her hands back through her hair. She had been wrapped up in dealing with Tante Fanchon's stroke and recovery while Nick had been in the thick of the Theriot case. She would have been the one to interview the kids had she been there. Dixon had adequate interviewing skills, but it was too easy to imagine Stokes having no patience talking to kids, not taking them seriously.

She thought back to the scene in the Florette home just hours past. Dean asking, "Do you really think she's dead?"

"And it's this kid Dean Florette's sister that's missing?" Nick asked.

"She was in the park after school on the day of the murder. No one

has seen or heard from her since. She wasn't at the house when Genevieve picked up her son. Genevieve complained to Jojean about it. Jojean just blew it off. Dean first told me Nora was home in the evening,
but she wasn't."

Had he lied to throw the timeline off, or had he just been mistaken?

She rubbed a hand across the increasing tension in her forehead. "I
thought this case couldn't get much worse . . ."

"Is there a chance this girl just ran away?" Nick asked.

"Yes. Absolutely. She had threatened to run away more than once.
She had a big fight with her mom a couple of days ago. Do you think
I'm overreacting?"

"No," he said, reaching out to tuck a lock of hair behind her ear. "A
twelve-year-old girl has been missing for more than a day. That's cause
for alarm no matter the reason. Did it look like she might have taken
anything with her? A handbag, clothes?"

"A backpack," Annie said. "She usually carried a backpack to school.
It's not at the house."

"So she brought the Gauthier boy to her home after school and hasn't
been seen or heard from since?" Nick said.

"And later that evening the boy was murdered," Annie pointed out.
"I realize the two things may not be related at all, but that comes pretty
close to the *C* word for me. The odds of the two things being coinciden-
tal seem pretty long.

"Our assumption has been that the boy's murder was a crime of
opportunity in the commission of an attempted burglary or that Genevieve was either the actual target or the cause of her son's death," she
said. "But what if it's related to the disappearance of the babysitter?"

Nick said nothing for a moment as he considered the possibilities.
Finally he said, "Genevieve says the girl wasn't there when she picked up
her son. Were there other people at the house? What do any of them have
to say?"

"The household is chaotic, to say the least," Annie confessed. "People
come and go. Jojean wasn't there at the time. Who knows where Dean
was? I don't know who else might have been there."

"You'd better find out."

"Are you suggesting Genevieve might have done something to Nora? Why?"

He shrugged a shoulder. "Why'd she kill her own baby when she was fourteen? If she's capable of murdering one child, is she not capable of murdering another?"

"So she's gone from potentially losing her temper and killing her son to being a serial killer?"

"I didn't say that. I'm saying you have to be open to all possibilities, 'Toinette. You can't dismiss a theory just because you don't want it to be true. You know as well as I do, sufficiently motivated, people are capable of damn near anything."

He was right, of course. They didn't get to pick and choose killers and motives. Their only goal was the truth, no matter how ugly it might be.

"Who's the lead for the PD?" he asked.

"Harlan Hanks. He thinks I'm an alarmist because I wanted an Amber Alert issued."

"Did he do it?"

"Eventually. He knows the family and was of the 'Oh, she'll get scared and come home' school of thought. I swear to God," she muttered. "We're investigating the brutal murder of a child and people still want to believe nothing bad happens in a small town—even the cops.

"Chief Earl finally lit a fire under his ass—prompted by Dutrow, who is probably planning their joint press conference for tomorrow as we speak," she said sarcastically. "I guess that's the upside to having a raging narcissist for sheriff. Any time two or more cameras can gather in his name he's right there, Johnny on the Spot."

"You talked to Dutrow?"

"Yeah. That was the weirder part of the evening, if you can believe that. I went to the address of one of Nora Florette's friends, and Dutrow answers the door. Turns out the kid is the son of his fiancée, and One Big Happy they are not."

"Why do you say that?"

"He wasn't pleased with me showing up. There was already something going on between the three of them—something to do with the son and where he was supposed to be after school. I had seen the kid at the park, and when I made mention of it, it was like I lit a stick of dynamite. I could see Dutrow getting angrier and angrier. The boy was terrified of him. The fiancée, too," she said, her own anxiety level rising again with the memory.

"I've been to a thousand domestic calls, Nick. You have, too. You know that feeling—like if one person says the wrong thing, the whole place is going to go up in flames. I didn't want to leave," she confessed. "I had that sick feeling that the minute I was gone . . ."

"You think he's abusive?"

"Emotionally, psychologically, verbally—absolutely. Physically? I don't know, but I wouldn't bet against it."

"Does that surprise you?" Nick asked. "He's rigid, controlling, manipulative, can't abide anyone who doesn't toe his line. The guy probably starches his underwear."

"I guess it's one thing to think of a boss that way," Annie said. "I never thought about him as anything else. I don't know him. I don't want to know him after tonight. And he certainly wishes he didn't know me.

"He couldn't get me out of there fast enough. When I tried to talk to him about the boy getting bullied at school, he told me I would do well to put my worry to my own family situation."

"He threatened you?" Nick came to attention at that, leaning toward her, his dark gaze on her like a pair of lasers.

"He told me your job is hanging by a thread and that I should think of my child."

"*Fils de pute!*"

He snapped the sheet back and got out of the bed to pace beside it, his rage instant. He had to move or explode. He swore a streak of hot, virulent French, cursing Kelvin Dutrow and most of his ancestors. To threaten his family was the worst possible offense.

"Please don't do anything rash, Nick," Annie said calmly. "He's spoiling for an excuse to fire you."

He cut her a look that would have made grown men scurry backward. "This *putain* threatens my wife and child, and I'm not supposed to do anything? *Putain de merde!*"

Annie moved to the edge of the bed and reached out to catch him by a rock-hard forearm. "Please don't make me regret telling you."

He shook his head, though she suspected the conversation he was responding to was one inside his own mind. *Kill Kelvin Dutrow? Don't kill Kelvin Dutrow . . .* He stayed in place but shifted his weight back and forth, left and right, too angry to be still.

"The last thing you want is him taking you off this case," Annie said. "You lock that temper in a box. Think of that poor little boy lying dead in the morgue. He needs you. *I* need you," she added. "Justin needs you. I don't want him visiting his papa in jail."

He took a deep breath and visibly worked to calm himself, though his frown remained dark.

"You wouldn't bail me out?" he said at last.

"I don't know," Annie teased gently, stroking her hand slowly up and down his arm. "You know I've been saving up for a new washer and dryer . . ."

He didn't always let her talk him out of his temper. He probably didn't want to now, but they'd been up and working this case for over twenty-four hours . . .

"That's harsh," he said, wincing a little. "Left to rot by my own wife in favor of a household appliance. You're a hard woman, 'Toinette."

Annie got up on her knees and hugged him. "I would gnaw my own arm off for you," she whispered. "I just don't want to have to."

"It's not okay, what he said to you," he insisted.

"No part of tonight was okay," she returned. "The most powerful man in the parish is potentially an abusive monster, and the only person who can do anything about him is the governor, who probably can't find Partout Parish on a map."

"No," Nick said. "If that's what Kelvin Dutrow is, he'll do himself in, one way or another. We just have to be patient."

Annie rolled her eyes. "Oh, well, your strong suit, Mr. Hanging by a Thread."

"He won't fire me. I'm too useful as a scapegoat."

"Don't be so sure. Especially now. Now he doesn't want me around,

either. I saw something he didn't want me to see, and he knows if he
fires you, he gets a twofer."

"You told him you'd quit?"

"Of course!" she declared, scooting back to her spot in the bed. "I'm
supposed to keep working for the giant asshole who disrespected my
husband and threatened me? I don't think so!"

Nick slipped back into bed and reached for her, drawing her back to
their default position: her head on his shoulder, her body melted into
his, his arms around her, their legs entwined.

"Do you have any idea how much I love you?" he whispered into her
hair.

She pressed a hand to his chest and felt his heart beat, steady and
true. "Will you still love me when we're homeless and living in my car?"

"Even then," he promised. "Dutrow's fiancée, what's she like?"

"Proper," Annie said on a yawn. "Head of the Junior League type.
Exactly what you would expect, I suppose. I imagine she thought he was
quite a catch, and vice versa."

"She went to see Genevieve Gauthier in the hospital today."

"What? Sharon Spicer? Why?"

"She brought flowers. Ostensibly from the hospital auxiliary."

"That's a little weird. She just happened to be there to bring flowers
to a crime victim in a guarded room? Who let her in?"

"Young Prejean."

"Oh, that boy . . . ," she said on a sigh. "Bless his heart. The short
sperm won the swim meet there. Go figure. Did Genevieve say anything about it?"

"No. I didn't ask. It didn't seem important at the time. Do you know
where she's from—this Spicer woman?"

"Uh . . . Houma," Annie said, remembering Dean Florette's nasty
nickname for Cameron: *Houma Homo.* "Do you think they know each
other? I wouldn't say they probably ran in the same circles."

"Genevieve worked at the Houma City Hall for a while. Their paths
might have crossed. Me, I don't like coincidence," he said. "Genevieve
worked in Houma. She's got a record. Dutrow is from Houma. Kemp

is from Houma. This fiancée is from Houma. There's too damn many people from Houma in this to suit me, that's for true."

And they had all come to Bayou Breaux dragging their life's baggage with them, Annie thought as the day's fatigue pressed down on her.

"And they're all around this poor dead child," Nick murmured. "A little child who didn't live long enough to do anything wrong."

There was nothing more innocent or uncomplicated than a child. The idea that a child might have died because of the complicated entanglements of the adults in his life was always an especially hard pill to swallow. For the people working to solve the murder of KJ Gauthier, there was no opportunity to protect the child. They could only seek justice after the terrible fact.

That truth was a tough ongoing internal struggle for Nick, who took everything to heart. There was a tender part of him buried deep inside that would always be a seventeen-year-old boy who hadn't been able to protect his beloved sister, who had watched his family disintegrate because of her murder. There was a part of him that would always be a young detective trapped in a corrupt department that hadn't been able to get justice for a fourteen-year-old runaway. Those experiences were woven into the fabric of who he was.

Most cops developed mechanisms to protect themselves, at least somewhat, from the emotional ravages of the job. Nick had never been able to do that. He didn't really try. His empathy for victims made him very good at what he did, but it took a hard toll.

"Pauvre 'tite bête," he murmured.

Poor little thing . . .

Annie leaned up and kissed his cheek, dark with the beard stubble he hadn't taken the time to shave. "Please try to get some rest."

"I will," he said, but he didn't meet her eyes.

He looked away as he reached out to turn off the lamp. Annie knew sleep would be slow in coming—for them both—and it would be plagued with images of a dead boy lying in his own blood.

THIRTY-THREE

He couldn't sleep. The pain burned and throbbed. The shame and self-pity and depression came in relentless waves, one on top of the other, over and over and over, making him feel worse and worse and worse. He had cried until it felt like his eyeballs would pop out of his head. Even once his eyes were burning and dry, he cried silently into his pillow. His throat was raw, and his head felt huge and heavy.

As if the beating hadn't been bad enough, his mother had come to him afterward—after Kelvin had left—and insisted on taking care of his wounds. He was supposed to be nearly a man, and he'd had to lie on his stomach and suffer the embarrassment of having his mother wash his butt and put antibiotic ointment on his cuts while she cried for her "little boy."

He didn't want to be a little boy.

He wasn't anything he wanted to be. He wasn't anything anyone wanted him to be. He was nothing but a loser.

He wanted to be strong. He wanted to be an athlete. He wanted girls to like him and for him to like girls. He wanted not to always be afraid. He wanted not to be a freak. He wanted not to be a screwup and a disappointment.

He wanted not to be.

Kelvin was going to look through his iPad and see his drawings and the things he wrote about, and he would never want Cameron for a son. He would never want him anyway. *Some other man's child.* It was just stupid to hope otherwise. And why would he hope, anyway? Kelvin Dutrow couldn't stand the sight of him. Kelvin Dutrow had beaten him like he was the lowest, most worthless animal on the earth, and he enjoyed doing it. That was the man his mother wanted to marry.

And she still wanted to marry him. She had rambled on and on about how she might be able to make amends and get Kelvin to take her back. If only she did this differently or that differently.

Slowly, painfully, Cameron eased himself off his bed. It hurt to move. Even just the slightest brush of his pajama bottoms felt like fire against his raw skin. He wouldn't be able to sit down for days. He wouldn't be able to go to school—at least he hoped his mother wouldn't make him. He could only too well imagine his shame and embarrassment if the kids at school figured out what had happened to him. He would rather die.

Everyone was going to wish he had anyway.

Barefoot, he shuffled out into the dark hall, not even able to walk like a normal person. The house had been silent for a long while. His mother must have finally fallen asleep by now.

He stood at the door that went to the patio and stared out at the shimmer of the landscape lights reflected across the surface of the swimming pool. The storm had passed, but rain was still falling, a gentle shower he imagined might feel good against his skin.

He slipped out the door and stepped onto the wet concrete, wanting it to be cool, but it wasn't. The air was still warm and heavy, like steam in the shower. It felt like inhaling velvet. He wondered if this was what it would feel like to breathe in water.

As the rain slowly soaked his hair and pajamas, he stood at the edge of the pool and stared down at the rippling glow of the pool lights across the pale blue bottom. It looked inviting, soothing. All he had to do was just step off the edge and the water would welcome him, surround him. All he had to do was just take a deep breath and feel no more pain.

* * *

SHE COULDN'T SLEEP. The pain in her arm burned and throbbed. The shame and self-pity and depression came in relentless waves, one on top of the other, over and over and over, making her feel worse and worse and worse. She had cried until she couldn't cry anymore. Her tears had soaked one pillow and then another. Her throat was raw, and her head was throbbing.

How had everything gone so wrong when she worked so hard to make everything right? She followed every rule. She did everything she could think of to make a nice home, to be a good cook, to be of service to her community. These were the things that were important to her: to be a good wife, to be a good mother, to be respected by people she respected.

From the time she was a little girl, she had watched her mother do the same—make a nice home, raise a nice family. Somehow Sharon had managed to fail—not once, but twice.

Her first husband, William, had been a businessman, successful until he'd had a couple of setbacks. Sharon had supported him in every way she could. Even when they had struggled financially, she had kept up appearances and maintained a successful demeanor to their friends and to their church group. Even as he had grown bitter and started drinking in private, she kept up the charade.

He should have appreciated her efforts, but instead, he had begun to resent her. He mocked her at home, and occasionally in front of others when he was feeling particularly mean. And he had turned his moods on Cameron, picking on him, belittling him.

She had grown to hate him, but she hadn't left. Women in her family didn't leave their marriages. What would the neighbors think? Even as that thought went through her head, she berated herself for it. She had subjected herself and her son to the abuses of a cruel man for what? So people who didn't matter would believe the lie of her façade.

It had been a relief when William died. She never would have admitted it, of course. She had dressed in black and cried at the funeral, but the tears were more of relief than grief. And the grief had been more for the years wasted than the years they would never have. She had been more than happy to start her life over.

She had thought things would be different with Kelvin—a man of the law, a man with ambition and character. She had set her mind to catching him, showing him she would be the perfect wife, someone he would want to present proudly in his public life. She had succeeded. And when the opportunity had come for him to take the job of chief deputy for Partout Parish—an obvious stepping-stone to becoming sheriff—she had been so proud.

In her quiet moments, when doubts crept in, she told herself it didn't matter that he wasn't overly loving toward her. That just wasn't who he was. He was respectful, a gentleman, and besides, she'd never been one to dream of a romance novel hero for herself. That wasn't realistic. A marriage was a partnership built on more important things than physical passion. So, if she sometimes felt like she was just a prop for him, she tried very hard not to let that hurt her feelings. He was the star. She expected to be a supporting character.

That was her role—to support her man. And if he was sometimes cold and demanding, well, he was under a great deal of pressure. He was a very important man in the community now. All eyes were on him. He even talked sometimes about having bigger ambitions one day. Running for Congress, perhaps. And once he was established and they were truly settled, then maybe he would be more attentive to her and to Cameron.

But it had been clear from the start that Kelvin wasn't fond of Cameron. He had wanted to send Cameron off to military school, and Sharon just hadn't been able to abide the thought. Yes, maybe she coddled the boy, but he was her only child, and he hadn't had it easy. He had never been what his father wanted in a son. Though he was quite bright, he had always been a little awkward, both physically and socially. He had trouble making friends. But he wanted so badly to do everything right it made her heart ache.

Since the beginning of her relationship with Kelvin, Sharon had stressed to Cameron again and again the importance of doing what he was told, of not being a bother or an embarrassment to Kelvin. And he had tried so hard.

He had taken to watching true crime shows on television to learn about police work and to come up with questions to ask Kelvin. Even though he was a city kid, he had learned to row the little boat Kelvin had bought for him. The two had gone out fishing in Kelvin's boat once, as well. And though the job of gutting the fish had made Cameron throw up, he had stuck it out and finished. Sharon had been so proud of him, she'd taken his picture holding up one of the fish, his other hand held high in victory, encased in Kelvin's too-large protective steel-mesh glove.

The memory of Cameron's beaming smile in that photo brought tears to her eyes now. Her poor, sweet boy. Never had she imagined Kelvin would become physically abusive. As she stood in the hall outside Cameron's room, just the sound of the beating had made her hysterical. And seeing the damage that had been inflicted had made her physically ill.

What had she done? In her effort to have the family she wanted, she had put her own child in jeopardy. It was her fault. All of it. She should have found a way to dissuade Kelvin from the idea of putting Cameron in football. She should have found a way to save Cameron from playing. She should have gotten him a doctor's note or enrolled him in some activity that conflicted with the football schedule. She should have found a way to break it to Kelvin that she had allowed Cameron to quit that wouldn't have left him feeling ambushed.

She couldn't blame him for getting angry, really. He was a proud man, and he had been embarrassed in front of one of his own detectives. Of course he'd been angry. He was a man who didn't lose control of his temper or anything else. He probably hadn't even realized he was hurting her when he twisted her arm. He would probably be embarrassed and remorseful.

She would have to find a way to make that easy for him, a way to smooth things over and make amends. She would make sure it never happened again.

Maybe if Cameron could just go stay with her parents for a few weeks. Through the holidays, maybe. Time for Kelvin to cool off and for them to reboot their relationship. Cameron would probably be relieved. He hadn't made many friends here. And when he came back, they could all start over. She would just have to figure out how to make it work with his school credits.

Slowly she sat up, touching her mussed hair, taking a shaky breath. She felt a little more in control with a task to strategize. Making a plan required structure and careful thought. These were things she was good at.

She got out of bed, her sore arm cradled against her body. She was still dressed, her clothes creased and wrinkled. A glimpse in the mirror above her dresser confirmed her fear that she looked a mess, like something from a horror movie. At least she didn't have to worry that Kelvin would walk in and see her.

She needed an ice pack for her arm and perhaps a cup of chamomile tea for her nerves, she thought as she went out into the hall. She would check on Cameron. She hoped that he was sleeping. She had given him a pain pill she had left over from a trip to the dentist, hoping it would help him sleep through the night.

The house was so quiet. It was her dream house, really. The perfect size and style, everything shiny and new. She especially loved the patio and pool. She envisioned entertaining out there under the patio cover. It was so pretty and magical at night with the landscape lighting. She had the gardener set the timer so the low-voltage lights and the pool lights ran all night. Maybe it was frivolous, but she allowed herself that. She had told Kelvin it made her feel more secure to have the lights on at night, and he had accepted that as a sound safety precaution.

She glanced out the bay window as she walked into the kitchen and startled at the sight of a figure standing by the pool. Then a motion-sensor light came on and she could see it was Cameron, standing in the rain in his pajamas at the pool's edge.

"Cameron?" she called as she stepped out of the kitchen door. "Cameron? Sweetheart, what are doing out here? Oh, my goodness! Come in out of the rain!"

He didn't move as she hurried up to him. He just stared down into the water, rain dripping from his nose and chin. Perhaps the painkiller had been too strong for him. Or maybe he was sleepwalking, as he had when he was younger.

She touched his face and took him by the arm. "Are you all right? Darling, come inside. You're soaking wet."

"I don't want to be here," he said softly as he started to cry. "I don't want to be here."

Her heart broke for him, and for herself as she wrapped her good arm around her child, and they cried together in the rain.

SHE COULDN'T SLEEP. The pain in her shoulder burned and throbbed. The shame and self-pity and depression came in relentless waves, one on top of the other, over and over and over, making her feel worse and worse and worse. She had cried until she couldn't cry anymore. She had asked for more pain medication. It had yet to kick in.

She wanted to be numb, or unconscious, or dead. What a stunning clusterfuck she'd made of her life. This was her second night in the hospital, though she didn't really remember much about the night before. Just as well. What little sleep she'd had tonight had been plagued with images of KJ lying broken on the floor in a sea of blood, or KJ lying cold and pale on the stainless steel table in the morgue, his body washed clean, the knife wounds just small, straight cuts that didn't look like anything anyone would die from.

A song came to mind as she relived the memory, the melody playing in her mind like a soundtrack to a movie. The Band Perry. "If I Die Young." It was a pretty song. A simple country song. She had always liked the melody without ever really thinking about the lyrics. *If I die young . . .*

A Dr. Benton had come to check on her late, asking if she remembered him, but she couldn't say she did. She had managed to eat some dinner and drink some ginger ale, and so he had removed the IV from her arm. He said he thought she would be released the next day.

The idea terrified her. Where was she supposed to go? Back to the house? She couldn't. She couldn't go back there. No. Not ever. But she had nowhere else to go. She didn't have money for a deposit on a new place. She didn't have money for a hotel. She didn't know anyone who would take her in.

She was afraid to ask Clarice. People at Evangeline Oaks raised their eyebrows at her as it was. How was Clarice Marcel her aunt? She was too old. Genevieve was too young. Why were there no older pictures of her in Clarice's apartment if they were so close? Why had she never come to visit before moving to Bayou Breaux?

"Aunt Clarice, my ass," she had once heard Mavis Parsons say behind her back.

But Clarice Marcel had not always lived at Evangeline Oaks. For all anyone knew, Genevieve might have visited all the time. And plenty of people called someone aunt or uncle without being blood kin. No one ever thought about that when they looked at her helping the old woman and taking a little money on the side for doing errands and whatnot.

People always thought the worst of her, anyway.

They weren't always wrong.

She didn't have much to be proud of in her life. Her mother had always told her she would never amount to anything. So far, despite Genevieve's best efforts, her mother was right.

Gingerly putting weight on her bandaged feet, Genevieve eased herself off the bed. Restlessness and anxiety stirred through her like the ache from a fever. She needed to move. Her body felt big and awkward, like it wasn't her own, making movement clumsy and slow.

The room was lit by the television, playing an infomercial without the sound. She didn't want to hear what was being said. There was too much inside her mind as it was. She only wanted the visual company of the tiny two-dimensional people on the screen. They made her feel less alone.

She made her way to the window and stared down at the hospital entrance. It had rained, but the rain had stopped, leaving the pavement wet and shiny in the little puddles of light. The white statue of the Virgin Mary basked in the glow of amber up-lights, her back to Genevieve. That seemed fitting, all things considered.

Where will I go? What will I do? she wondered. Like Scarlett O'Hara in *Gone with the Wind.*

Frankly, my dear, no one gives a damn.

That was the truth. She had nothing and no one. She thought of the people who had come to see her today—the detectives, who only wanted her story; the sheriff's fiancée, who only wanted to feel superior because she'd done a kindness for someone less fortunate; her boss and his wife, the perfect couple, doing their Christian duty. It wouldn't have mattered to any of them if she had died.

The only person she had ever really mattered to was KJ. He needed her. All day, every day. He needed her to feed him, to clothe him, to take him to school, to kiss his boo-boos and put him to bed. She worked to earn a paycheck to take care of him. Nothing was for her—not time, not money. Her life was all about her child. And now her child was gone.

What purpose did she serve?

The idea of starting over was by turns daunting, exciting, terrifying, exhausting.

Would people feel sorry for her because she'd lost her child? Or would they blame her for living when he had died? What would they have been thinking if she had died, too? That she was unlucky? A victim? A loser? A heroine? The brave mother who died protecting her child?

It would have been the first time anyone had thought anything good about her—if she had died.

She stared out the window and sang the song.

"If I die young . . ."

THIRTY-FOUR

Nick didn't sleep. Not really, not in any restful way. He closed his eyes and tried to meditate with limited success. *Inhale. Focus. Calm. Relax. Exhale. Focus. Calm. Relax. Inhale . . .* Breathe in through the nose, out through the mouth, counting the seconds—four seconds in, four seconds out . . .

His brain was too busy to rest, trying to sort and make sense of all the information he had taken in from the moment he'd walked into the crime scene at the Gauthier house to the last words he'd had with Annie before she'd fallen asleep—that there were too many people from Houma in this to suit him.

Gus had brought Dutrow up from Houma PD to take the chief deputy position. Dutrow had brought Kemp up to run his crime scene unit. And Dutrow's fiancée and her son had followed. There was nothing strange in any of that. But about the same time, Genevieve and her son had moved from Dulac, just outside of Houma, into Roy Carville's shitty rental house on a bayou with no name. She had settled for a job beneath her skill set on the excuse of working near a woman who may or may not have been a relative.

Genevieve, who had killed a baby years ago. Genevieve, who may have had a drug problem. Genevieve, who had a police record from the department where Dutrow and Kemp had worked—where Keith Kemp had turned in his badge to take a job for which he seemed to have no passion.

Annie stirred restlessly beside him and made a small sound of distress in her sleep. Nick shifted positions, wrapped an arm around her gently, and pressed a soft kiss to her temple, and she sighed and settled again. He wanted her to sleep. The last few months had taken a toll on her. She'd lost weight. She looked pale. He would have wrapped her up in cotton wool and kept her home if he could have, but she would never have it.

She wanted him to sleep but knew he wouldn't. She worried about him getting too emotionally involved in the case, and yet she knew that was what drove him. She had fallen in love with that very trait early on in their relationship. She wanted to keep him safe from his own obsessive tendencies, but she wouldn't be surprised to find him gone when she awakened.

The rage burned inside him all over again at the thought of Dutrow trying to frighten and intimidate her. It was one thing for the sheriff to try it with him, but to do that to a woman or a child? No. That was not acceptable. And for Dutrow to pull that with Annie? Nick would have happily beaten the man into a hospital bed.

Too restless now to even pretend to sleep, he slipped from the bed, went into the bathroom, and dressed quickly and quietly in the fresh clothes he had hung on the back of the door before his shower. Barefoot, he padded silently out into the hall and down the stairs.

The air that greeted him as he left the house was thick and warm. The eastern horizon was a soft charcoal gray beneath the last of an indigo night sky. Fog lay low over the water, drifting like smoke among the cypress trees. The night hunters would be finding their way back to their dens and nests, but it would be another half hour before the songbirds would begin to greet the day. Peace had settled in a temporary hush over the basin. Nature's held breath before the new day could begin.

Puddles from last night's storm dotted the gravel drive. Lingering raindrops in the Spanish moss that draped the big live oak in the side yard caught the glow of the headlights as Nick started the Jeep.

The no-frills vehicle had been Annie's before they had met—and someone else's before that. At some point it had gotten tricked out with a police radio. Nick preferred the Jeep to any of the unmarked vehicles in the SO's yard.

He flipped on the regular radio to catch the latest news and weather as he turned out of the driveway and headed toward town. The news was of the murder, and of the missing girl, and of the "altercation" in front of Our Lady that had resulted in the arrest of Bobby Theriot. Nick's name was mentioned, along with a brief litany of his checkered past. Dutrow would be unhappy. No one was supposed to get more media attention than himself.

The weather report centered on a freshly named tropical storm spinning in the Gulf, which might have been the reason Nora Florette's father had balked at the idea of coming home. If the weather had already begun to amp up where his rig sat, miles offshore, flying became a dicey proposition. Helicopters and hurricanes didn't mix well, though it wouldn't have been enough of an excuse for Nick had his child been missing. He would have moved heaven, earth, and sea to get back.

Clearly, the Florette family preferred to think this girl was crying wolf, disappearing to punish and scare them. Maybe they thought that because she'd done it before. Harlan Hanks, the detective from the PD who had wanted to drag his feet, knew the family, Annie said. Personally or professionally? Nick wondered. Either way, a twelve-year-old girl had been missing for more than a day. She was the babysitter for a murdered boy. She was the sister to a budding sexual predator, according to Annie.

Nick didn't like the Florettes' proximity to the Theriot house, though no one had made mention to him any concern over this Florette boy— not his detectives, who had interviewed the kids, nor the Theriots themselves. His focus had been on chasing down the phantom lead of a drifter having been seen in the area in the days leading up to Vanessa Theriot's assault. Nothing had panned out, much to the dismay and frustration of both the family and law enforcement.

Nick would want to go back over the interviews with the neighborhood kids. But his immediate attention had to be on the Gauthier murder.

A mile south of town, he took a right onto a blacktop road and drove toward the just-pinking dawn. The properties on either side of the road were tidy hobby farms with white or stained-dark fences, brick houses, and big metal-sided sheds for RVs.

The lights were on in the horse barn on the property where Nick turned in, a place divided into paddocks, studded with gnarled old live oak trees reaching their twisted branches out to provide islands of shade. He parked at the end of the barn and walked down the wide center aisle, greeted by the nickers of half a dozen quarter horses hanging their dainty heads over their stall doors.

"Well, if it ain't the star of stage and screen, Nick Fourcade himself!"

Gus Noblier came out of the feed room pushing a cart full of whatever horses ate for breakfast. Dressed in jeans and a plaid western shirt, he was a big, rawboned man with a belly that advertised his love of rich food. His color was healthier since he'd left the Sheriff's Office, but his crew cut was more silver than steel now.

"Saw you on the news last night," he remarked, giving Nick a look. "Twice. Winning friends and influencing people, as usual. 'Get that fucking camera out of my face' was my personal favorite moment."

He shook his head in amazement. "How you ever got that sweet girl to marry you, I will never know. How is Annie?"

"She's well," Nick said. "It was a tough summer."

"I heard her *tante* had a stroke. Is she all right?"

"Better, yeah, but that was hard on Annie."

Gus shook his big head. "I'll tell you what, son: it sucks getting old. There ain't no upside, except it beats being dead—or so I think. I'm gonna be seriously pissed off if I get to the other side and find out being dead is the best time of my life and that I gave up cigarettes and fried food for no good reason."

Nick arched a brow at Gus's belly. "When did you give up fried food?"

"Oh, you're a smart-ass comedian now, too? You gonna take that act on the road or what?"

"I might have to."

"Did Dutrow fire you?"

"Not yet, but the day is young."

"You gotta keep that coonass temper of yours in check," Gus said, wagging a finger at him. "How many years have I been telling you that?"

"Too many."

"And you are too goddamned hardheaded to learn."

He scooped up a measure of sweet feed from the cart and dumped it in the bin of the first horse on the row. It smelled of molasses. The horse dove into the food with murderous intent, its ears pinned flat to its head.

"I suppose you didn't come here for a lecture or to hear about my arthritic knees, did you?" Gus asked, moving the cart to the next stall.

"No. Have you heard from Dutrow?"

"No. Why would I? He's running his own show. He doesn't need my help, I'm happy to say. He's shaking things up, making people take notice. Looks to me like he's got it all under control—except for you, of course."

"You can't think that YouTube showboat bullshit is a good thing," Nick challenged, though he knew exactly where this conversation would go. They'd had it already, more times than he cared to remember.

"Can't I? He's made a name for himself. He's already got the attention of all the people he needs to impress. It took me years to do that."

"Because you earned it."

Gus shrugged off the comment and pushed the cart to the next stall. "Let's not reinvent history. I was just as full of shit as anybody. I just didn't have social media to help me craft my image. I had to do it the old-fashioned way—kissing babies and eating rubber chicken dinners. Dutrow is the modern model of a political animal."

"You say that like it's a good thing."

"It's a necessary thing," he said, moving on to the next horse.

"How well did you know this guy before you brought him on?" Nick asked.

"Personally? Not at all. I know the chief down in Houma—Owen Irvin. Known him for years. Owen talked Dutrow up, said he was ambitious, squeaky clean, cut out for leadership—exactly what I was looking for." He scooped up another measure of grain. "Why? Is he cramping your style? As if I need to ask. I told him to give you a wide berth or stock up on antacids.

"I suppose he didn't take my advice, either," he groused, dumping the feed. "Why would anybody listen to me? I only survived that job for twenty years despite the best efforts of all my enemies."

"Did it occur to you that Dutrow had probably been angling for Owen Irvin's job and the chief just wanted rid of him?" Nick asked.

"Of course. And that suited me fine, didn't it? I handpicked my successor, and by all accounts except yours, he's doing a bang-up job. What's your problem with him now—besides you never wanting to yield to authority?"

"He's an asshole."

"You been on the record with that opinion for quite some time now," Gus said. "I don't think that's why you're in my barn at the crack of dawn. What's this really about?"

Nick blew out a sigh and looked out the end of the barn at Gus's little post-retirement sanctuary. The yard was well-tended, neat as a pin. A pair of Brittany spaniels wove in and out of the banks of red and white flowers around the brick house, their noses to the ground. Gus's fire engine red Ford F-350 dually truck sat in the driveway, spotless.

He was enjoying his life after having been the most powerful man in the parish for nearly two decades. He had his horses and his bird dogs and his bass boat. He helped his wife with the gardening and took her out dancing every Saturday night. He had grandkids to indulge. While he had been very adept at the political gamesmanship required for attaining and hanging on to office in south Louisiana, and he had been very successful at the job itself, the job had never defined Gus Noblier. He was the same man with or without the badge. When he had decided to walk away, he had done so without a glance back.

Nick couldn't envision Kelvin Dutrow ever doing that. It seemed to him that every second of every day Dutrow worked to craft and maintain an image. It was all calculated, from the part in his hair to the crease in his trousers. He orchestrated every minute of his day like it was an elaborate stage production. Last night, Annie had gotten a glimpse of what might exist behind the curtain, and Dutrow hadn't liked that at all.

"You don't have to like him," Gus said. "Hell, there can't be but five or six people in the world you can stand to tolerate at all. You just have to work with him—or around him."

"He threatened Annie last night," Nick confessed.

Gus's face momentarily went blank, as if the news came as such a shock that it briefly shorted out his brain. "He what?"

"She saw something he didn't want her to see, and he made it very clear that she'd do well to forget about it."

"The hell!" Gus exclaimed, genuinely shocked. "What'd she see?"

"A domestic situation between Dutrow, his fiancée, and her son. Annie said they were scared to death of him."

"No," Gus scoffed. "She had to have misread that."

"She didn't misread anything. She's been on a thousand domestic calls. She knows what she's looking at. And it's no stretch to think it, either," Nick said. "He's a controlling, manipulative bully."

"Well, now," Gus said, shifting from denial to rationalization. "People have said worse than that about me, for God's sake."

"We're not talking about you," Nick said. "There were no red flags of any kind with this guy in Houma?"

"No! I'm telling you, squeaky clean. Commendations out the wazoo. You're barking up a wrong tree here because you don't like the guy. Do you really think I'd bring the man on board if I had any doubts about his character?"

"No, but then, maybe you liked the package well enough you didn't bother to look too close under the hood."

Gus chucked the feed scoop down into the cart, his face flushing red, just like old times. "You have got a hell of a cheek on you, Fourcade! I gave you a job when no one would touch you with a goddamn barge pole, and you're questioning my judgment bringing in a man with a wall full of awards?"

"I'm saying there's more to any man than meets the eye, and you know that, too."

"Why are you on about this, anyway? Don't you have a murder to solve?"

"A murder related to a woman who used to work in Houma, as it happens," Nick said. "A woman with a police record and a missing arrest report."

"Oh, my God. And you're gonna somehow try to twist this all around until Kelvin Dutrow is a suspect? Because he rubs you the wrong way?"

"I never said he was a suspect," Nick said. "And my relationship with him has got nothing to do with it."

Gus rolled his eyes. "Oh, no. I can see you're as impartial as ever. You don't like Dutrow. He offends your delicate investigative sensibilities. Now you've got it in that thick Cajun head of yours he insulted your wife—"

"He threatened her!"

"And you want to kick his ass!"

"*Mais* yeah!" Nick barked, letting his temper slip. "For that? Yeah! Me, I want to take him apart for that. He can do whatever he will to me, but to my wife? No. Hell no!"

Gus nodded in a way that seemed more in confirmation of his own thoughts than in validation of Nick's. Nick clenched his jaw and walked away, frustrated with himself for falling into the trap. Now he looked like a fool and sounded like a hothead.

Gus moved his cart and fed the next horse, and the next, unconcerned. He finished his chore, parked the cart, and wiped his hands on his jeans.

"It's a bad one, this murder, yeah?" he said quietly.

"*Oui,*" Nick murmured. He reached out and touched the velvet nose of a blaze-faced horse with bright, curious eyes. Its flared nostrils sniffed then blew a warm breath across his hand.

"Any suspects—other than your sheriff?"

"I never said he was a suspect for the murder," Nick snapped.

"Don't sulk," Gus ordered. "It's not all about you."

Nick cut him a look and started to pace. "The mother is as good a suspect as any. She killed a baby when she was fourteen. She's abusing alcohol and opioids. She had an arrest for a DUI eight or nine years ago—would have been about the time she got pregnant with her son—and that may have had a drug charge attached, but it went away. I need to know more about that. Did she flip on somebody? I don't know. There's something hinky about it. Differing versions of the charges, depending on where you look. Dixon hasn't been able to get her hands on the original arrest report. I asked Dutrow to reach out to his old department and get it for me. He tried to blow me off, but I insisted. Best-case scenario: I don't think he'll bother. Worst-case scenario: he doesn't want me to see it."

"He's got bigger fish to fry," Gus said dismissively. "He's not gonna use his time to track down some moldy old arrest report on a DUI—"

"That might turn us in a direction in a murder investigation?"

"That seems like a big stretch."

"Oh, well, then why fucking bother, right?" Nick said sarcastically. "Let's only look at obvious explanations for someone killing a child—oh wait! There aren't any." He threw his hands up in the air. "Oh, well."

Gus scowled. "Bitchiness does not become you, Nick."

"Apathy does not become you, Gus," he returned. "I get that you're happily off the job, and you have so many better things to do now, like shovel horse shit and prune the azalea bushes. And maybe your old friend Owen Irvin, he won't bother to take your calls anymore 'cause he's out celebrating being rid of the arrogant prick heel-biter he foisted off onto Partout Parish. The guy you're all too happy to paint as the second coming of Jesus H. Christ just so you can retire.

"But never you mind, Gus," he said bitterly. "It's just a dead seven-year-old child. Thanks for nothing."

Fuming, he started for the Jeep. He maybe shouldn't have expected more. Gus Noblier had always been both practical and self-serving by nature. But he had also been like family. Nick didn't care to think it, but subconsciously he may have wanted that support as much as he wanted anything when he'd pulled into Gus's driveway.

"Oh, hang on," Gus called as Nick reached for the door handle. "Turn your high horse around and come back here. I never said I wouldn't make a phone call, for God's sake, you hotheaded, temperamental Frenchman."

Nick turned and looked at him, making him wait.

"Come on," Gus urged. "Let's go in my office. I need a cup of coffee . . . and a bottle of Excedrin for the pain in my ass."

His office was a tack room with a large, old oak desk and a kitchenette on one end. One wall was lined with well-oiled western saddles; another hung with bridles. A shelving unit held piles of saddle blankets and other assorted horse paraphernalia.

Gus poured them each a cup of strong black coffee from an ancient Bunn coffeemaker on the counter of the kitchenette as Nick took a seat at the desk.

"Write down what you need," Gus ordered, setting down the thick ceramic mugs on the desktop. He eased himself into his leather-padded chair. "What'd you do with Bobby Theriot last night?"

"Booked him as a drunk and let him sleep it off," Nick said as he jotted down the information on a notepad.

"He assaulted you on live television."

"And you think there might be somebody in this town didn't think I had it coming? Or that I wasn't in the wrong for subduing him?" he asked, glancing up at his old boss.

"Dutrow thought we should charge him with assaulting an officer. Mark that on your calendar. The one and only time Kelvin Dutrow ever stuck up for me," he said with a chuckle.

"Are you getting anywhere with their daughter's case?"

"No. Maybe," he corrected himself. He didn't know which would be worse, having another lead turn out to be nothing, or having this particular lead come to fruition—a child sexually assaulted by another child.

He looked over what he'd written. GENEVIEVE GAUTHIER, the dates in question, the questions he wanted answered. At the bottom of the page, he added the name KEITH KEMP.

"What's that last bit?" Gus asked, reading upside down as he sipped his coffee.

"Kemp is the man Dutrow brought up from Houma to run his brand-new shiny crime scene unit. He used to be on the force down there. They worked together. I want to know why he isn't still carrying a badge."

"People change jobs."

"Mm-hmm," Nick said with no conviction. "This is the kind of guy who would have gotten off on writing tickets, clubbing suspects, and running lights-and-sirens down the road. He couldn't give two shits about crime scene investigation. But here we all are in Partout Parish with a brand-new crime scene van."

"Joining the modern era of police work," Gus said. "That unit will bring in revenue for the parish."

"Whatever," Nick said, getting to his feet.

Gus turned the notepad around and glanced at the list. "And I suppose you need this ASAP."

"You can finish your coffee first."

"That's big of you."

"De rien," Nick said with half a shrug. "Don't mention it."

He took a swig of his coffee and set the mug back down. *"Merci*—for the coffee and for the help. I gotta go see if I can solve this thing before I have to file for unemployment."

THIRTY-FIVE

Annie pulled in the driveway at 14 Blue Cypress and cut the engine, sitting for a moment, scanning the front of the garage, spotting the security camera. Dutrow would be the kind of man who spied on his family, she thought.

Never mind the Roy Carvilles and Roddie Perezes of the world, uploading the private moments of strangers for sleazy instant porn. Kelvin Dutrow would be the kind of twisted, controlling creep who watched to make sure his fiancée wasn't secretly eating Snickers bars and drinking Coca-Cola while watching *The View*. He'd be spying on her to make sure she was starching his shirts herself and not sneaking bags from Alouette Dry Cleaners into the house.

His black Suburban had already been parked in his reserved spot in front of the SO when Annie had driven past at seven twenty-five. He might have spent the night there for all she knew. He could have been sitting in his office right that minute, drinking his coffee and watching her sit in his driveway via an app on his cell phone. Except that he had to be very busy this morning with the media. Between the Gauthier case, the fiasco at the hospital with Bobby Theriot, and coordinating the search for Nora Florette with the BBPD, he shouldn't have time to sit around stalking his fiancée.

Annie hoped so, at least. Otherwise, she was going to have to start considering other lines of work. Slushy machine attendant at the Quik Pik, under-endowed dancer at Club Cayenne . . .

She walked up the sidewalk to Sharon Spicer's front door, taking in the careful arrangement of festive fall décor. Life was all about appearances for people like Kelvin Dutrow and his fiancée. The right house, the right clothes, the right car, the just-right wreath for the front door. But it was all just a pretty house of cards if the foundation wasn't rock-solid.

Annie checked her watch as she rang the doorbell. Seven thirty-seven—by design, way too early for a social call. People were easier to read when they were caught off guard. They were more apt to trip up if their inclination was to lie. There was no lead time for them to get their story straight. There was no time to arrange the pretty curtains over a false façade. She rang the bell a second time to create a sense of urgency.

A muffled call came from somewhere inside: "I'm coming!"

Sharon Spicer appeared at the sidelight a moment later, her expression a mix of concern and consternation. She was already dressed in a loose, calf-length khaki linen skirt and a long-sleeved crisp white blouse that tied at the waist. No sloppy sweats for Sharon.

"I'm sorry to disturb you so early, Ms. Spicer," she said as Sharon cracked open the door. "I have some additional questions I'm hoping you can help me with. May I come in?"

"I really don't see how I can be of any help, Detective," Sharon said with the faintest of polite smiles, ready to close the door.

"That's what people always think," Annie said. "But sometimes it's the smallest, most seemingly insignificant detail that turns an investigation in the right direction."

"I really don't—"

"I won't take much of your time," Annie promised earnestly. "We're trying to put together a timeline that's as detailed as possible to account for Nora Florette's whereabouts right up until the time she went missing."

"I thought you said last night she had run away," Sharon said, annoyed that she was being forced to have even another few sentences of conversation.

"She may have," Annie conceded. "The thing is, whether she's missing by choice or by some other means, she's a child, and she's in danger. I'm sure as a mother you can imagine the panic of having your child missing."

Outplayed, Sharon frowned. She couldn't deny Annie's statement without coming across as a heartless bitch. What kind of mother would condemn another mother to that kind of suffering?

She flinched as a teakettle suddenly blasted out a shrill note somewhere deeper in the house.

"Oh, feel free to take care of that," Annie said.

Making a small sound of frustration, Sharon turned and hurried toward the kitchen, leaving the door ajar. Annie followed her inside.

"Sorry if I'm interrupting your breakfast," she said. "Investigations don't let us keep banker's hours, I'm afraid. But I'm sure you know that from dealing with the sheriff's schedule."

"I was just fixing myself a cup of tea," Sharon said, turning off the burner and silencing the kettle.

Her Southern manners would never allow her to make just the one cup. Annie could see that thought process waging war in her head as she stared at the single delicate china teacup sitting on the counter. An heirloom, no doubt, handed down from mother to daughter for three or four generations.

"Would you like a cup?" she asked at last, holding herself stiff in the hope that Annie would decline.

"That would be lovely," Annie said. "Thank you."

She watched as Sharon Spicer reached up with one hand to open a cupboard and take down first a saucer and then a cup. She kept her other arm pressed close across her stomach.

"I hope English breakfast is all right," Sharon said. "I ran out of Earl Grey just last night. I have to go to the store today. It's always something, isn't it? Do you care for milk? Sugar?"

Nervous chatter. Her hand was shaking a little as she poured the water. She used both hands to open the packets of the tea bags but kept her left arm close to her body even then, not wanting to move it any more than she had to.

"Just tea is fine, thank you," Annie said. "How did you hurt your arm?"

"My arm? I don't know what you mean."

"You don't seem to be using your left arm. I didn't notice that last night. Did something happen?"

"Oh, it's nothing," Sharon assured her with another brittle fake smile. She raised the arm as if to show it still worked. "I just . . . I tripped and I took a fall, and I wrenched it a bit. It's nothing. Just clumsiness on my part," she said with a forced laugh. "Trying to hurry to get things done."

Her respiration was too quick. A flush came to her otherwise pale face. She hadn't managed to put her makeup on yet, not that it could have done much to hide the fact that her eyes were puffy and glazed from crying.

Son of a bitch, Annie thought, anger stirring. *That son of a bitch.*

She took her cup and followed Sharon to the table that sat in an alcove looking out on a small swimming pool.

"Isn't that the way?" Annie said with a friendly smile, as if she was just a neighbor over for a morning visit. "There aren't enough hours in the day. I know I'm always rushing around the house, trying to get three things done at once. I have a son, too," she said. "He's five. He just started kindergarten. That's almost more than I can manage. You have a teenager. You must be so busy."

Sharon nodded, touching her hair self-consciously. She had run a brush over it, but it wasn't the perfectly coiffed and starched helmet of the day before.

"It's all about managing your time," she said. "I keep a very strict schedule with Cameron's school activities, and Kelvin, of course, has a very demanding schedule."

"And you volunteer as well, I understand," Annie said.

"Of course. Community service is so important. I've become involved with the PTA—"

"Is that how you know Genevieve Gauthier? Through the PTA?"

Sharon faltered. "No. Um, no. I don't know her at all."

Annie feigned confusion. "Really? I understood you went to see her in the hospital yesterday."

"Oh, well, I belong to the hospital auxiliary. I just took her some flowers and expressed condolences on behalf of the auxiliary."

"That was kind," Annie said. "I thought maybe you knew her somehow, through the school, or from Houma. I understand she used to work in Houma, and you're from Houma. Obviously, that's where you met Sheriff Dutrow."

"Yes. He was in the police department. I worked there as a secretary. That's how we met."

"Genevieve worked in City Hall for a time," Annie remarked.

"Did she? I didn't know her."

"Funny how you all ended up here in little Bayou Breaux."

"Isn't it?" Sharon took a sip of her tea, burning her tongue and then trying without success to set the cup back down without rattling it against the saucer.

"You said you have questions about this Florette girl?" she asked. "Honestly, I haven't seen or heard a thing about her since summer. The one time. That was all. That was enough. She's very fresh. No manners at all. I told Cameron I don't want him having anything to do with that family. They just aren't the kind of people I want him around."

Annie nodded. "I don't blame you. The Florettes have a chaotic family situation, to say the least. But I can see that it would be difficult for Cameron to avoid them, just based on proximity. They all walk the same way to and from school. Is Cameron home?"

"He's sleeping in," Sharon said. "He isn't feeling well today. He has a delicate stomach."

"Oh, that's too bad. I'm sorry he's not feeling well. I hope I didn't make a problem for him last night," Annie said. "I got the impression Sheriff Dutrow expected him to have been somewhere other than the park after school. I didn't mean to get him in trouble."

"Oh, no." Sharon waved off the notion, but she looked away as she did it. Her right hand went to her throat to worry at the simple pearl necklace she wore. "That was just a misunderstanding."

"He seemed upset."

"Oh, well." She forced a laugh. "You know how men can be. Kelvin is very regimented about the order of things—"

"*Cameron* seemed upset," Annie corrected her. "He seemed afraid."

She inhaled sharply, as if startled. Annie had no doubt that on a better day, with better preparation, Sharon Spicer would have fended off all emotion and kept her perfect image squarely in place. But in this moment, caught off guard, she was vulnerable.

"Is Cameron afraid of Sheriff Dutrow?" Annie asked gently.

"No, no! Don't be silly!" She laughed, shaking her head. "He's just not used to Kelvin yet, that's all. Cameron is a very sensitive boy. It's taking them a while to find their footing, so to speak."

Annie said nothing for a moment, her gaze steady on the woman across from her. Sharon shifted nervously on her chair and looked out the window. She was probably wishing she had never answered the door, or wishing she could be beamed up into space by aliens. Anything to escape this line of conversation. Unconsciously, she touched her injured arm.

"Does Cameron have reason to be afraid of him, Sharon?" Annie asked softly. "Do you?"

Sharon shot to her feet, the panic clear in her eyes, though she tried to cover it with outrage. "That's ridiculous! Why in the world would we be afraid of Kelvin? He is a fine man! He is a fine, upstanding leader in this community! I can't believe you would even ask such a thing!"

"I'm sorry if I misread the situation—"

"You certainly did! Now, I'm sorry to rush you, Detective," she said curtly, "but I really have to get on with my day. I have to ask you to leave."

She turned too quickly in her haste to get away from Annie's scrutiny. Her china teacup flew off the saucer and shattered on the tile floor. Crying out in dismay, Sharon dropped to her knees, scrambling to pick up the shards, cutting a finger in the process.

"Oh, no!" she cried as she looked at her hand and the blood dripping onto her crisp white blouse.

Annie hurried to the sink to wet a paper towel.

"Here," she said, handing the towel to Sharon. "Put pressure on it."

Carefully, she picked up the bits of broken cup and set them on the counter next to the sink, unsure of where the trash can might have been hidden in the picture-perfect kitchen.

"That was my grandmother's!" Sharon sobbed. "They don't make that pattern anymore!"

Annie's heart broke for her. Sharon Spicer was a woman for whom image was everything, and here she sat on her kitchen floor, in front of a stranger, bleeding, crying over a teacup, her whole body shaking with emotions she didn't dare let go.

Annie knelt down in front of her and reached out to put a hand on her arm.

"Sharon," she said softly, "it doesn't matter who he is. It's not okay for him to hurt you. It's not okay for him to hurt your son. If that's what's going on—"

"No!" Sharon snapped. "No no no no!"

Struggling, wincing in pain, she got to her feet and turned around in a circle like a caged animal looking for a way to escape.

"Sharon—"

"You don't know anything about us!" she shouted. "How dare you come into my home and-and judge me, and judge my family—"

"I'm not judging you at all," Annie said. "I just want you to know, if you need help, I can help you."

"I don't need your *help*." She all but spat the word. "You come into my home and insult me that way—"

"Honestly, that is not my intent."

"I have half a mind to call Kelvin and report you! You need to leave right now!"

Annie moved to stay in front of her, trying to make eye contact, to connect emotionally. What a clusterfuck she'd have on her hands if Sharon called Dutrow. And that threat was very real, she knew. It wasn't at all uncommon for the abused woman to take the side of her abuser, trying to deny her situation, trying to win points with the man who hurt her.

"Sharon—" She reached out a hand only to have it batted away.

Sharon was hyperventilating now, on the brink of full-blown panic. She gasped a breath and shouted, "GET OUT!"

"Sharon, let's sit back down so you can catch your breath—"

"GET OUT OF MY HOUSE!!!"

Wild-eyed, Sharon lunged forward. Shocked by the outburst, Annie stumbled backward, slamming into the counter.

"GET OUT OF MY HOUSE!!!"

As her emotions coursed through her like a flash flood, Sharon Spicer lashed out physically, striking before Annie could think to defend herself. Her half-made fist connected like a hammer, hard enough to hurt, catching Annie on the side of her nose and smashing her upper lip against her teeth. The taste of blood was instant.

Sharon gasped in shock at what she'd done. She backed away quickly, looking at the hand she'd used to strike Annie as if it was not her own.

"Oh, my God! Oh, my God! I'm so sorry!" she said, gasping, tears rising, terrified of what she'd done and of the emotion that had driven her to do it. "I'm so, so s-sorry!"

She reached out toward Annie with her injured hand, blood from her cut finger dripping on the floor.

Annie touched her swelling lip gingerly with one hand and waved off Sharon Spicer with the other.

"It's all right," she said. "You're upset."

"I've never done anything like that in my life!"

"Emotions sometimes overwhelm us," Annie mumbled, fingering a tooth. "Don't worry about it. I'm fine."

She went to the sink, wet another paper towel, and pressed it carefully to her lip. Sharon stood watching, trembling.

"Please don't tell Kelvin," she begged. "I didn't mean to do that. I just— I don't know what happened! Please don't tell him. Please don't!"

"I won't tell Kelvin," Annie promised, perversely glad to have a bargaining chip. "Your secret is safe with me."

THIRTY-SIX

The protection of our children and families is of paramount importance to the Partout Parish Sheriff's Office," Dutrow said. He paused to look right and then left, giving all cameras the opportunity for a profile shot. "I'm a family man myself. I cannot abide the thought of harm coming to a child under my watch. That is why I'm here this morning with Chief Earl to announce that the Sheriff's Office will offer full support to the Bayou Breaux Police Department in the search for this missing girl, twelve-year-old Nora Florette of Bayou Breaux."

He pointed to the blown-up school photo of the girl that was being held by Chief of Police Johnny Earl, who was standing beside him on the front porch of a house that needed paint.

"A joint agency ground search will be getting under way shortly. I've called in our drone team to lend support from the air, and we'll be bringing in our search dogs. Our mounted patrol and water search-and-rescue team have been alerted should the search area expand beyond the city limits. We need to bring this young lady home to her family."

Nick paused just long enough to take in that much of the press conference on the TV in the break room as he poured himself a cup of strong coffee. He was glad for Dutrow to have the distraction of horning in on Johnny Earl's media spotlight. The sideshow would keep him out of Nick's hair, at least for part of the day. He would have to make the most of that time.

He hoped to hell Gus would have already put his call in to Owen Irvin at the Houma PD before he had to load horses up for the search. There was no way in hell Keith Kemp wasn't going to go to Dutrow about what had transpired at the Gauthier house the night before. He might have already done so. It seemed clear to Nick the two had already had a conversation about his possible exit from the department. *"I can't wait for Dutrow to get rid of you . . ."*

Despite the reassurance he'd tried to give Annie, his usefulness as a scapegoat was not going to outweigh the trouble he would be in if he found something on Kemp, and Dutrow would choose his friend over his resident pain-in-the-ass detective.

They seemed an odd pair, Nick thought as he took his coffee and headed back down the hall toward the bullpen. Dutrow, so controlled and so controlling, so by the book. Kemp struck him as more of an opportunistic animal, not smart but cunning. He was more of a coyote to Dutrow's police dog. They didn't seem to have much of anything in common, yet here they were. Dutrow had whistled, and Kemp had come running.

"I got your porn site set up, boss!" Dixon called as Nick walked into the bullpen.

"Damn, Winn-Dixie!" Stokes said, swiveling around on his chair. "You been working on that all this time and you didn't hook me up?"

Dixon rolled her eyes. "Well, I just figured Pornhub is probably your home page, Chaz, so you don't really need my help."

Stokes gave her the squint eye. "You been looking at my screen saver?"

Nick cut him a glare. "I catch you looking at porn in here, you won't have a willie left to whack off. My office, both of you. Now."

"It's a joke!" Stokes called.

"It's not funny. I'm in no mood for your juvenile sense of humor."

They followed him down the narrow hall and into his office, where the kitten was on the floor playing with a wadded-up piece of paper, batting it with his paws and chasing it around the room. At the sight of the people, it flattened its ears and dashed sideways like a crab, going for the cover of the desk.

"Did you have any trouble cracking into Perez's laptop?" Nick asked.

He had called Dixon in to work in the middle of the night, setting her to the task of finding out what the cameras in the Gauthier house had recorded. She had focused not on the cameras themselves but on Roddie Perez's laptop, in search of not only the recordings but anything that might show how and where the recordings might have been uploaded to the Internet with the intention of making money.

"His password is one, two, three, four," she said. "We're not exactly dealing with a mastermind here."

She took a seat in Nick's chair, waking up his computer with a wiggle of the mouse. She looked like she'd been up all night. Her short red hair stood up from too many finger combings. Her eyes were bloodshot but still bright with the energy she drew from the challenge of the puzzle she had set out to unravel.

"He has files with hours and hours of what was recorded on the cameras in the Gauthier house—and several other houses, by the way."

"No surprise there," Nick muttered. "Every property Carville owns is being searched today."

"I haven't gotten through it all yet. That will take a while. I went directly to the stuff he had uploaded to the porn site. Most of what's recorded is everyday stuff—Genevieve getting up in the morning, dressing, getting undressed at night, masturbating. People get off on that, I guess. I fast-forwarded through most of it for the sake of time. I didn't see how any of that would be relevant to the murder investigation with regards to finding any suspect other than Genevieve herself."

"Unless a subscriber to the website became fixated on her," Stokes suggested, "and somehow found out where she lived. We could be looking at Carville or some crony of his. I wouldn't put it past him to share her address."

"Let's pursue that," Nick said. "Carville's circle." Nick turned to Dixon again. "Did she look high in any of it?"

"Yeah. In some of it. Like I said, I fast-forwarded through most of the everyday stuff. I downloaded what looked to me to be most pertinent pieces onto this thumb drive for easy access," she said, plugging the drive into the computer.

"Did she have any visitors?" Nick asked.

"One so far."

Dixon opened the file, and the monitor came alive with the grainy black-and-white images of Genevieve Gauthier and a white male undressing each other at the foot of her bed.

Jeff Avery.

"There's a shock," Nick muttered sarcastically.

"Screwing the boss," Stokes said. "It's a cliché for a reason."

"Go pick him up," Nick said. "He can come to our house for a chat this time."

He turned again to Dixon as Stokes left the room. "I want Genevieve Gauthier's bank records. I want to know if she's been making any deposits other than her paycheck, anything that might look like a payoff. Mr. Happily Married Man here is ripe for blackmail, and blackmail is as good a motive for murder as any."

"Will do," she said, vacating his chair.

"Did you find that old arrest report from Houma PD yet?"

"Not yet."

"How is it not in their system?"

"Well," Dixon said, "the easy answer is someone got rid of it. The question would be, why?"

And who, Nick thought, taking his seat. He frowned at the video still playing on his monitor.

"I did speak to someone at the Terrebonne Parish DA's office," Dixon said. "He told me if the court records don't show the drug charge, then there was no drug charge, period. They didn't cut a deal with her."

"And they don't have a copy of the original arrest report?"

Dixon rolled her eyes. "If they do, I'm sure they'll get right on that for me, lowly peon from another parish."

Nick waved her off. "Go see about her bank records. And her cell phone records, too."

"I'm already on the phone records. We should have them this morning."

"Good. Is there anything else on this drive I want to see?"

She leaned over and gave the mouse a couple of moves and clicks. "I don't think *want* is the right word. It's from the night of the murder."

The scene was from the bathroom camera. Genevieve, not sober, trying to deal with her son at bath time. KJ fussing and whining. Genevieve arguing with him, grabbing him roughly by the arm, shaking him. The boy sobbing. Genevieve sobbing.

It was hard to watch. There on his screen was the boy Nick had only seen as a corpse, alive, breathing, having a tantrum. Being a child. And his mother, struggling to handle him, no one to help her, living in a shit hole, drugging herself to cope. Losing her temper. Resorting to violence.

In the end, the boy wrenched out of her grasp and ran from the room, and Genevieve sank down onto the floor next to the bathtub, crying.

Hours later, KJ Gauthier would be dead. Stabbed to death. And his mother would run the wrong way down a road to nowhere, looking for help that would be way too late in coming.

He clicked his way out of the video and went to his photos from the crime scene. He looked them over one by one. The surreal portraits of a dead boy. What might have been a partial shoe print in blood—a running shoe, he guessed. Not enough of a print to draw any conclusions as to size or make. What might have been a partial handprint on the wall.

Could he see Jefferson Avery stabbing a little boy? Why would he? What would be the point? Even if Genevieve had been blackmailing him, threatening to tell his proper wife and the mother of his beautiful children about the affair, why kill the boy? Why kill the boy and leave Genevieve alive?

He couldn't see Jeff Avery as a killer. Avery was an average man with a desk job and a wife and kids. The extent of his secret life was a sweaty tumble with a girl from work, and guaranteed, he would be mortified to see the video. He was probably at that very moment trying not to shit himself at the idea of being formally questioned by a couple of hard-ass detectives. He couldn't see Jeff Avery choosing to murder anyone.

Murder was generally depressingly simple. Person A hated Person B bad enough to want them off the planet. Motives were basic. Money, sex, drugs, revenge. But why did anyone kill a child?

Child predators killed children because they liked it.

He had one dead child and one missing child. But they were different in every way—different ages, different sexes, one from town, one from the country. The only thing they had in common was each other. So why would someone want either of them dead, let alone both of them?

Genevieve said Nora had not been at the Florette house that night when she picked up KJ. Hours later, Genevieve was high and fighting with her son. Hours later, KJ Gauthier was dead.

Who killed a child?

A parent.

Suddenly, the kitten launched itself up his leg from under the desk. Nick gently extricated the tiny claws from his pants leg and cradled the animal in one hand. The kitten curled up against him and began to purr. He closed his eyes and concentrated on the feeling of the vibration against his chest. This was what innocence felt like—to have absolute trust for no good reason. He could have killed the creature with one hand, but it pressed against him in absolute contentment. Like a child.

"Hey, Nicky!"

Stokes's voice pulled him back to the moment.

"I got Avery in the box."

Sighing, Nick set the kitten in his in-box and got up, dusting the cat hair off his tie.

"Let's go scare the hell out of him."

"MAN, HE ABOUT ran backward when he saw I was taking him into the jail," Stokes said, chuckling.

They stood in the darkened observation room adjacent to where Jeff Avery waited impatiently, watching him through the one-way glass. He couldn't sit still. He moved and shifted and fidgeted. He got up to pace and sat back down.

"Why was I taking him there? Why couldn't we just go into an office? What about the Sheriff's Office? He's suddenly remembered they go to the same church," Stokes added in an aside.

"Surely, there must be some mistake, Officer," he said in his mocking-white-people voice. "I'm a white dude who goes to Calvary Baptist with Sheriff Dutrow. No jail for me!"

"Ass-pucker level: eight," Nick remarked.

"At least. The first thing he wanted to do when we got in the building was run to the men's room. I wouldn't go in there for a while if I was you. Just sayin'."

Avery got up again, checked his watch, rolled up the sleeves of his blue dress shirt, and paced a little more.

"Take the monitor in," Nick said.

He flipped on the speaker and watched as Stokes wheeled the cart with the monitor and laptop into the interview room.

"What's taking so long?" Avery demanded. "I'm a busy man. I can't be this long away from my office. I have an inspection to prepare for. Where is Fourcade?"

"He'll be along directly," Stokes said, plugging in the equipment, setting everything up just so.

"I don't understand why he still has a job," Avery went on. "I saw him on the news last night tackling the poor father of that autistic girl. I don't understand why Sheriff Dutrow hasn't fired him. He's incompetent and unhinged!"

"I'd keep that opinion to myself if I was you," Stokes counseled. "Don't antagonize him. Nicky doesn't take that well. That will *not* work out for you."

Avery looked alarmed. "What's that supposed to mean?"

"I'm just sayin'," Stokes said, going for the door. He tipped his porkpie hat and flashed a big white grin. "Good luck to you, Mr. Avery!"

He left Avery and came back to the observation room chuckling. "Poor guy's sweating like a whore in church."

"'Nothing is more wretched than the mind of a man conscious of guilt.'"

"Translating your fancy philosopher: Married guys—keep it in your pants!"

Nick's phone vibrated. He checked the screen. Dutrow. And so the countdown began, he thought. Ignoring the call, he scooped up his props.

Avery jumped back as Nick opened the door and walked into the small interview room, his expression sober and dark. He placed a thick file folder on the small table along with a pack of cigarettes and a lighter.

"Mr. Avery," he began quietly. "I'm disappointed to have to see you again."

"You know I'm here voluntarily," Avery said defensively.

Nick arched a brow in amusement. "Are you?"

"And I certainly don't see why we have to be meeting in the jail, for God's sake!"

"Well, it's convenient, isn't it?"

"For who?"

Nick just looked at him, expressionless, letting the implication make itself.

Avery turned a little gray.

"I don't know what I'm doing here at all," he said. "I don't know anything about what happened to Genevieve. I've told you that. That hasn't changed."

"You don't know what I know."

Nick pulled out a chair, sat down, and tapped a finger absently on the file folder. The sound was like the steady *drip, drip, drip* of a faucet in the otherwise quiet room.

Avery's eyes fixed on the folder. "I would sooner deal directly with Sheriff Dutrow."

"Would you?"

"I find your manner unnerving, to be frank. And I know Sheriff Dutrow from our church—Calvary Baptist. I would be more comfortable speaking with him."

A slow smile spread across Nick's face. He held Avery's gaze as if in a tractor beam.

"Well, you see, Mr. Avery, I don't care what you want, and I don't care about your church. Me, I believe organized religion was created as a panacea for the masses and a way to control the population of any given kingdom.

"People are easily manipulated by the notion of an omnipotent entity and the robed men who allegedly enforce his rules on the common folk," he said. "Curiously, in my experience, this seldom prevents anyone from doing exactly the thing they desire most, no matter how egregious. They can always repent and start over; therefore, sin is conveniently without actual consequences."

"You don't believe in heaven and hell, then?" Avery asked. "Hell is a mighty powerful consequence."

"Does one have to belong to a religion to believe in an afterlife? No, I think not. But if you need the threat of burning in eternal damnation to do the right thing, you don't lack religion, Mr. Avery. You lack morality. Churches are just chock-full of people who preach and pray on Sunday and sin every night of the week. Which brings me to my case in point."

He rose from his chair and went to the cart. "You should come around here, Mr. Avery," he suggested. "So you can have a better view."

"View of what?" Avery asked, coming closer cautiously.

"I call this Exhibit A," Nick said, clicking the Play icon to start the video. He turned the volume all the way up.

"*A*," he said, stepping back and crossing his arms, "for *adultery*."

He watched Jeff Avery's face as his expression went from confusion to apprehension to a sick realization as he watched the video.

"Oh, my God," he murmured, his face going pale and then flushing red. "Oh, dear God."

"See?" Nick said. "Now you ask forgiveness, and all is well. That doesn't work for me, but then, I have always had a punitive streak in me."

"Turn it off!" Avery shouted as the voices from the video moaned and panted and called out.

"And there you are, taking the Lord's name in vain while breaking a commandment," Nick pointed out. "That's gotta be double strikes against you, yeah? I don't know about the Baptists, but that would have been a whole lotta Hail Marys for me back in the day. That's for true."

"Please. Turn it off," Avery begged, turning his back to the monitor. He was breathing like he'd run a hard mile.

"Why?" Nick asked. "Are you ashamed?"

"Yes, of course I'm ashamed!"

"Cheating on that pretty wife, those beautiful children."

"It only happened once! I didn't mean for it—"

"You look pretty purposeful here to me, Jeff," Nick said over the impassioned grunts and groans coming from the speaker. He sat back against the edge of the table, shook a cigarette from the pack next to the file folder, and took his time lighting it.

"Jesus Christ, make it stop!" Avery shouted. He wheeled around and shoved the cart, no doubt meaning to tip it over dramatically. But it simply rolled away and bumped harmlessly into the wall beneath the one-way glass.

"Where did you get that video?" he demanded.

"Mmmmm," Nick hummed, taking a long drag on his cigarette and blowing the smoke up at the ceiling. "Now, here's the part you're really not gonna like, Jeff. This video is playing On Demand all over the globe on multiple Internet porn sites."

Avery's face went ashen with panic. "What? No!"

"'Fraid so. Me, I don't see the appeal of watching such things, but apparently a great many people do. Genevieve's landlord, he had cameras hidden in the bedroom and bathroom. On the upside, you might be able to sue him for a cut of the proceeds. Get yourself a screen credit, at least."

"Oh, my God, this is a disaster!" Avery cried, clamping his hands around his head as if to keep it from coming off. He didn't seem to know if he should stand or sit or collapse. The underarms of his shirt were soaked dark with sweat. "This is fucking horrible! I'll lose my job for this! Janine will leave me!"

"But if you hadn't gotten caught, all would be well, yeah?"

"No! I regretted it immediately. It was *never* going to happen again."

"How did it happen in the first place?"

"Her car wouldn't start. I gave her a ride home. She was depressed because of the car and her finances, and she started to cry—"

"And you happened to be in her bedroom at the time? How strange."

"I just wanted to comfort her. I felt badly for her. She's a sweet girl, and she's had it rough, and one thing just led to another . . ."

"Where was KJ?" Nick asked.

"He wasn't there."

"Where was he?"

Tears rose in Jeff Avery's eyes as he struggled with the weight of his guilt.

"At a sleepover," he said quietly, his voice thick. "At my house."

"So," Nick said, "while your devoted wife was looking after the boy, you were busy fucking his mother."

"Don't say it like that!"

"Why?" Nick asked, pushing to his feet, walking into Jeff Avery's space. He backed him up against the wall and spoke just inches from his face. "Is that too ugly for you, Jeff?"

"Yes," Avery whispered.

"You're a piece of work, you are, Mr. Happily Married Man."

He backed away, disgusted, and Avery seemed to slump against the wall.

"When did this happen?" Nick asked.

"Last Friday."

"Genevieve, did she think it might happen again? Did she want that? A relationship?"

"I told her it couldn't happen again. I told her it wasn't right. I have a family. She has her son . . ."

And now she doesn't, Nick thought, shaking his head. No matter the intent Jeff Avery put to it, he was a man in a position of power, a man in a position to make Genevieve Gauthier's life exponentially better, and he had given her the brief hope that could happen, and then he'd taken that hope away. Because she had a child.

"Does my wife have to hear about this?" Avery asked. "I don't want to hurt her."

"Oh, you've already done that," Nick said. "You think she couldn't smell that on you last night at the hospital? And yet she went there to be kind to your mistress—"

"She's not my mis—"

"You can only hope she'll be that forgiving to you." He stubbed out his cigarette and sighed. "You're free to go, Mr. Avery. Being an adulterous ass is not against the law. It will, however, fuck you in divorce court. Detective Stokes will take you back to your office."

THIRTY-SEVEN

Annie's lip was throbbing, and her nose felt askew. She looked at herself in the visor mirror as she sat in her car across the street from the Florette house. She was beginning to look like a Picasso painting, she thought, though she had carefully felt her nose and determined it wasn't broken. The swelling made it look worse than it was. She was probably going to get a black eye out of the deal.

It wasn't the first time, nor would it be the last. She'd had worse on the job, having been drugged and shot and pushed down a staircase, among other things, over the years. A little punch in the face by the sheriff's fiancée was nothing. She was more concerned with what to do about Sharon Spicer.

There wasn't a doubt in Annie's mind that Dutrow had hurt her, but she had no proof. As she had regained her composure, Sharon had pulled the protective curtain around her and shut Annie out entirely. She had politely refused to talk about what might have happened the night before. She had politely refused the suggestion of getting her arm checked out by a doctor. She had politely refused to allow Annie to speak to Cameron.

None of her behavior came as a surprise to Annie—with the exception of that right hook to the kisser. Women like Sharon, who prided herself on her position and her self-control and her image, had an especially difficult time admitting abuse and asking for help. She feared the embarrassment of having people know her perfect life was nothing but a beautiful shiny apple with a rotten core. She probably feared what she stood to lose—her home, her standing, financial stability. She had undoubtedly already rationalized her fiancé's behavior in order to cope.

It was a difficult thing to stand by and watch, made doubly so by the fact that the perpetrator was the sheriff. Annie's stomach turned at the prospect of having to take action. Kelvin Dutrow was the most powerful man in the parish. He could end her career. He could end her husband's career. But he couldn't be above the law, not even if he *was* the law.

She could see him standing on the Florettes' front porch, the center of attention for the news people gathered there on the lawn. Asshole. This wasn't his case—unless, of course, he decided to take it away from the Bayou Breaux PD, which was entirely possible. The SO had greater resources, more manpower. The case was another chance for attention for a man who seemed to feed on the media spotlight like a vampire on blood.

Chief of Police Johnny Earl stood beside him, looking distinctly unhappy as his counterpart ranted and gesticulated for the cameras.

Annie put on her sunglasses and a baseball cap, tugging her ponytail through the opening in the back. She wanted to attract no attention to herself, not from the press and certainly not from her boss. She crossed the street, skirting around the crowd gathered on the Florettes' lawn, keeping her head down.

Two drones buzzed loudly overhead like small mechanical pterodactyls. Controlled by a pair of deputies decked out in tactical squad gear, they swooped and dashed and hovered where the press could see them. The sheriff's latest toys, they would be deployed for the search, able to quickly and easily cover more ground than humans could in twice the time.

A handler with a pair of bloodhounds cut a path through the crowd and went up the porch steps to stand to Dutrow's left, the dogs baying their excitement. Annie wondered how effective they would be considering the torrential rains that had fallen since Nora Florette had gone missing. It would all depend on where the girl had gone and how she had gotten there, she supposed. If she'd gotten in a car and been taken out of the parish, no dog was going to find her.

The sheriff opened the press conference for questions. Annie stood off to the side, listening to the cacophony of voices, picking out the loudest.

"Sheriff, two crimes against children in a matter of days, and the Theriot case remains unsolved. Are children safe in Partout Parish?"

"Sheriff Dutrow, is it true this girl was a babysitter for the murdered Gauthier boy?"

"Is the Gauthier woman a suspect in either case?"

"Is it true that Genevieve Gauthier killed a baby?"

"I can't comment on that," Dutrow said.

Oh, shit! Annie thought. How had anyone dug up that detail? Genevieve's juvenile record was sealed. It was one thing for someone in law enforcement to have access to it, but for someone outside that closed world to get that information . . . Although, south Louisiana was a small place with a long memory. Thirteen years might have been enough to cover most news in a foot of dust, but the murder of a baby by its teenaged mother would have stuck with people who had known about it at the time.

"In light of his actions last night," another reporter called out, "is Detective Fourcade still on the case?"

Annie held her breath.

"Thank you! Thank you all!" Dutrow called out to the crowd. "That's all the questions we have time for now. We've got crime to fight!"

Annie let out her breath, put down her head, and walked around the side yard to the back of the Florette house. The grass had been worn to dirt in spots and was littered with bikes and trikes and toys. A swing set stood to one side of the yard, ruts carved into the ground beneath the swings. A trampoline took up the other side.

She went up the back steps and into the house through a back porch that had been converted into a laundry and storage room bursting at the seams with shelves crammed with stuff of all kinds—giant cans of tomatoes, clothes, piles of magazines, boxes of lightbulbs, empty Mason jars, plant pots, Christmas ornaments, toys. The floor was a minefield of dirty laundry piles, shoes, and rain boots.

In the kitchen a couple of women she hadn't seen before were busy cooking. No one had ever died of hunger during a family tragedy in south Louisiana. The answer for literally every catastrophe was for friends and neighbors to cook food and surround those suffering.

The smell of onions and bay leaves perfumed the air in clouds of steam rising from a pot on the stove. Just the idea of gumbo made Annie's stomach grumble. She had been too tense for breakfast before speaking to Sharon Spicer and too anxious after to think of it.

Jojean sat at the dining room table, looking like she'd been up all night. She looked smaller, weaker, diminished by the stress and the helplessness. The pregnant woman from the night before—Jojean's youngest sister—sat to her right. Tiffany, the niece with the baby, stood in the living room, baby on her hip, cell phone sandwiched between her shoulder and her ear, as she looked after three toddlers that Annie could see. The sounds of a cartoon emanated from the television.

"Jojean, how are you holding up?" Annie asked, taking the seat to her left.

"She didn't come home," Jojean said. Her eyes were full of anguish and the strange kind of surprise that hits victims over and over—the shock that something terrible had struck them like a bolt out of the blue. "I thought sure she would come home. I truly did."

"I know," Annie murmured, resting a hand on the woman's arm. "We're doing everything possible to find her and bring her home to you. Is your husband coming back?"

"There's a storm in the Gulf," she said. "They can't fly. So I get to do this without him, too," she added, the sharp taste of bitterness turning her mouth.

"It's good that you have so much family around," Annie said. "You have a lot of people here supporting you. Let them help you."

As she got up to leave, Jojean reached out and caught her by the wrist. "That storm is coming this way. Do you think you'll find Nora before it hits? I can't think of her out in a storm."

"We'll do our best," Annie assured her, thinking that Nora Florette—if she was out in the elements—had already been through two storms in the time she'd been missing.

She left the house the same way she'd gone in—through the

gumbo-scented kitchen and the *Hoarders* laundry room. As she walked out onto the back stairs, she spotted Dean Florette on the roof of the garage, chucking rocks up at one of the drones as it hovered overhead.

"Hey! Knock it off!" Annie yelled.

"Suck it!" he yelled back, throwing another stone.

"Dean Florette!" Annie shouted, hustling down the steps. "Get down here right now or I'll have a deputy come up there and pitch you off. And I'm not gonna care if you land on your feet or your head. You are just one smart-ass remark from me hauling you to jail!"

She hoped to God the press out front were too preoccupied with the Dutrow circus to hear her.

"Get down here right now!" she yelled.

Dean cast a glance toward the street, where half a dozen law enforcement vehicles were parked, and decided not to call her bluff. He scrambled down the slope of the roof, dropped onto the trampoline, and flipped over the edge to the ground.

"How boys live to maturity is beyond me," Annie muttered, watching him get up, tugging his sweatpants up and his T-shirt down.

The sun hadn't been up two hours and he was already dirty—or maybe he had started the day that way. His face was a puffy red mess courtesy of Lola Troiano and her soccer ball.

"I don't have to go to school," he announced.

"I suppose not," Annie said. "But you can help with the search."

"Why?" he asked, looking offended at the notion. "I don't want to find her."

He looked up at the drones flying over. "All this fuss for Dead Nora."

A chill ran down Annie's arms. "Why do you call her that? Because you wish she was dead or because you know she's dead?"

He shrugged, disinterested, picked up a baseball off the ground, and tossed it up in the air. Annie reached up and snatched it before he could catch it again.

"I grew up with boy cousins," she said. "You can't faze me, Dean. Answer my question. Why'd you call your sister Dead Nora?"

"She's been gone two days," he reasoned. "Two days without hearing her big mouth. She must be dead. Where else would she be?"

"I don't know. There's nowhere she might go to hide? No friend she might stay with?"

"She doesn't have any friends."

"That's not true. Lola Troiano is her friend. Cameron Spicer is her friend."

"The Houma Homo," Dean sneered. "Mama's boy. Scared of his own shadow. What good is he? He wouldn't know what to do with a girl if he had one."

"And you would?" Annie asked, instantly regretting it as she remembered Lola's remark about Dean hoarding pornographic magazines. He was getting his lessons in human sexuality from the pages of *Penthouse*. "Don't answer that. I'm depressed enough with the state of the society as it is.

"I heard Nora got in trouble for going to Cameron's house this summer."

Dean swiped the baseball out of her hand and threw it against the side of the garage. "Yeah," he answered. "His mom is a scary bitch! She came here screaming and yelling how Nora stole some stupid box, and she was gonna tell the sheriff.

"I thought she was gonna pop my mom in the mouth!" he said, excited at the memory. Then he looked at Annie and squinted. "What happened to your face?"

"Nothing," Annie muttered. "Did Nora ever go back there again?"

"Only if she was stupid," Dean said. "That lady would have killed her."

THIRTY-EIGHT

P lease try to eat something, Cameron," his mother said.

She buzzed around the kitchen, busy, busy, busy. Put away a coffee cup, water a plant, neaten a stack of mail, make a note on her list of things to do . . . Cameron watched her flit from one stupid thing to the next to the next, an anxious feeling churning in his stomach. His mother was always very purposeful and efficient, but this was different. Her movements were too quick, her eyes were too bright. She held her left arm across her stomach like it hurt.

"I'm not hungry," he said. "My stomach hurts."

"Your stomach hurts because you haven't put anything in it," she said, going to the refrigerator. "We have yogurt. You should eat yogurt. The cultures will rebalance your digestive system."

She pulled out carton after carton after carton of yogurt and lined them up on the counter.

"We have vanilla and strawberry and black cherry and pineapple and— Don't eat the pineapple," she cautioned, putting that one back. "Pineapple is too acidic for you. We have blueberry and peach. You like peach. Eat the peach. Yogurt will settle your stomach, and that's one of your five servings of fruits and vegetables for the day."

She turned and looked at him with a strange, forced smile, and

Cameron felt afraid. She was acting like a pod person from *Invasion of the Body Snatchers*.

She wouldn't know what that meant if he told her, and she'd be furious to find out he had watched the movie without permission. He wasn't allowed to watch horror movies because his mother equated them with the occult and devil worship—even if they were about aliens from another planet.

He held himself very still and waited for her to open her mouth and make that weird inhuman screaming sound like the pod people in the movie.

"Cameron, did you hear me?" she asked. "Cameron!"

"I don't like yogurt," he said in a small voice.

"What? That's nonsense! You'll eat it, and it will help settle your stomach!"

"Yes, ma'am," Cameron said, cringing a little at the sharp tone of her voice.

She closed the refrigerator door and then got a towel and polished away a fingerprint marring the finish on the stainless steel.

"I have so many things to do today," she said. "Are you all right to stay home alone?"

"Yes, ma'am," Cameron answered, not sure he was all right at all.

He was afraid, to be honest. He felt so strange, so small and lost within a body that didn't feel like his own. His butt felt huge and on fire. Even the brush of his old sweatpants against his skin was painful. And he was stiff and walking awkwardly, like some kind of robot. He couldn't sit down. He was too tense to lie down.

I don't want to be here . . .

The line kept whispering through his brain like a secret. He kept thinking about standing on the edge of the swimming pool as the rain soaked his clothes. What if his mother hadn't come out to get him? What if she left and he felt that way again?

"I have to go to the school and speak with the principal," she was saying as he struggled to tune back into the moment. She set a bowl and a spoon next to the half-dozen jars of yogurt on the counter. "And it's going to be a zoo with everyone preoccupied with finding that horrible

Florette girl. And I just know in the end they'll find she went off with some boy. It would serve her right if something happened to her."

She went to another cupboard and got out a juice glass and put it next to the bowl.

"Do you want apple juice or white grape juice?" she asked. She didn't wait for an answer before she got out the jar of apple juice and poured it, then put the jar back and went through the whole ritual of wiping the fingerprints off the refrigerator door again.

"I have to speak with the principal and let him know you'll be going to spend some time with your grandparents."

A jolt went through Cameron like he'd been blasted with a Taser. "What?"

His mother looked at him with an expression of strange, cold pity. "It's for the best, darling."

"You're sending me away?" he asked, his voice sounding small and young.

"Just for a short time," she said, smiling. "Until the holidays, I should think. We just have to give Kelvin some time. He's upset and angry and embarrassed—"

"But it's not my fault!" Cameron cried. "I try so hard!"

He tried and tried, but nobody liked him—not Kelvin, not the kids at school, now not even his own mother. He tried to be everything everyone wanted, but he failed again and again and again. And he tried to be so careful not to make a mistake, not to upset his mother or draw the attention of her fiancé. And when he made a mistake, he did his best to fix it before anyone could even find out, but still this was happening. His mother was going to send him away.

"I don't want to go to Grandma and Grandpa's!" he cried.

"Would you rather go to military school?" his mother asked sharply. "Because *that* is where Kelvin wants to put you!"

Put you, like he was a piece of property or an unwanted dog or something.

"You told me last night you don't want to be here!" his mother said, her voice getting shriller and shriller.

That wasn't what he had meant, but he couldn't tell her. He couldn't tell his mother that he didn't want to be in this life—not just here at this house but in this life at all. Who knew what she would do then—probably ship him off to an insane asylum.

"You don't want me," he said, tears welling up in his eyes.

"Now you're just being overly dramatic and completely unfair to me," his mother said. "I'm trying to repair the damage, Cameron. I'm trying to salvage our situation. I never should have let you quit football. That's my fault. Now I have to fix this. I need time alone with Kelvin to repair the damage. He's a proud man, and we've wounded his ego. We lied to him. Who could blame him for being angry? I have to fix this! What else would you have me do, Cameron?"

Love me, Cameron thought. His pulse began to roar in his ears so that he couldn't really hear her anymore, but she kept talking anyway. As usual, not paying any attention to what was going on inside him. He could feel his sense of self growing smaller and smaller until he was terrified he would fall from his perch in the eye socket of this shell of a body and disappear into the black abyss within. How could she not see that? It was happening right before her eyes.

But at the same time his mother's eyes were getting bigger and bigger, the look in them wilder and wilder. Maybe her true self had already fallen into the blackness inside her, and this wasn't really his mother at all. The idea frightened him even more. If this wasn't really his mom, who would save either one of them?

Cameron wondered if she would hit him the way she had hit Detective Broussard.

He had seen her do it. He had heard her screaming at someone to get out, and he'd been terrified that it was Kelvin, come back to kill them both. Surely, Kelvin had looked at all the stuff on Cameron's iPad by now, and he wouldn't want them around. He had guns. He had all kinds of guns and other weapons—knives and clubs and Tasers. And he was the sheriff, so he would get away with it. He would make it look like a lunatic did it, or like he had been defending himself. Then he'd be rid of them, and he'd be glad because he had never wanted Cameron in the first place.

Cameron had crept into the hallway to see for himself what was going on in the kitchen, to find out if he should expect to be shot or stabbed. Shot, he hoped. That was quicker. He didn't want to know what it felt like to get stabbed over and over until all his blood ran out of his body. But what he had seen was his mother, ranting, screaming, out of control, attacking the detective.

It scared him sick to see his mother that way. She was the most in-control person he knew. No matter what happened, she was calm and had an answer and a plan. She always had a plan. To see her wild-eyed, screaming, hitting a detective right in the face—Cameron didn't know who that was. The one person he had always counted on had vanished in an instant, replaced by an angry, violent stranger.

He was crying now, just standing there like a dope, barefoot in the kitchen, bawling like a baby. And then his mother was there, standing right in front of him, reaching out to touch him, to reassure him, to give him comfort.

"Don't cry, sweetheart," she whispered. "Please don't cry. Mama will fix everything. I always have. I always will."

And then she was gone. And he wasn't sure she'd ever been there at all.

THIRTY-NINE

With the reporters' attentions divided with the need to cover the search for Nora Florette, Nick expected the number of them hanging around the hospital entrance to have dwindled considerably, if not vanished altogether. Genevieve Gauthier was yesterday's news. A possible child abduction had a much greater sense of urgency about it. There was a chance the child was still alive, that terrible things might have been happening to her in real time, and she could yet be found alive and returned to her family. KJ Gauthier was dead on a slab.

But as he drove past the statue of Mary, he could see reporters and photographers and videographers lying in wait near the main entrance, at least as many as the night before. News of Genevieve's pending release had leaked.

He swore under his breath as he parked the Jeep. He could have—probably should have—parked around the back and gone in through a service entrance. But he had a perverse need to hear what they might shout at him today. Better to know than not know.

He kept his head up and his mouth shut as he walked toward the main entrance.

"Detective Fourcade!"

"Detective Fourcade!"

"Is Sheriff Dutrow keeping you on the case?"

"What happened to Bobby Theriot?"

"Is it true Genevieve Gauthier killed her own baby?"

Who had leaked that information? Who else knew? Dixon, himself, Annie, Stokes, Dutrow . . . Anyone from Genevieve's past life. Genevieve's court records might have been sealed, but the story would live on forever in news databases and the memories of people who had known at the time.

"Is Genevieve a suspect in her son's murder?"

"What was the raid on her house last night?"

"Is there any evidence connecting the missing babysitter to the murder?"

"Genevieve is being released today. Where will she go?"

"Will she be arrested for her son's murder?"

"Is she the only suspect in the murder?"

A pair of uniformed deputies stood at the hospital entrance to prevent the mob from following him inside. He passed them without a word, his brain busy prioritizing the questions and the choreography of the interview. He would let Annie ask her questions first, easier, gentler questions. There was no way to soften *Why did you kill your baby?* Chances were good he would lose what trust he had built with her as soon as the question was asked.

Annie was waiting for him in the second-floor conference room, sitting at the table with a bag from Po' Richard's and a fat lip.

Instantly, his blood pressure jumped to the red zone. "What the hell?!"

"I'm fine," she said. "Don't freak out."

"I'm not freaking out! Who did this to you? I'll beat his ass!"

"That's calm and reasonable."

He caught her chin gently in his hand and turned her face this way and that. The swelling went up the side of her delicate upturned nose and halfway across her cheek. The first faint shades of a black eye had begun to rise beneath the skin.

"Who did this?" he demanded.

"Dutrow's fiancée, Sharon Spicer."

"*Mon Dieu!* I thought you said she was a proper lady!"

"Even ladies have their limits. I went back to her house this morning, hoping I might get her to talk."

"She struck you?"

"I backed her into a corner, psychologically speaking," she said. "She lost it, and she lashed out, and she caught me."

Nick scowled, gently pressing his thumb to the swollen flesh of her cheek. "You should get an X-ray."

"I'm fine," Annie insisted. "She's a PTA mom, not Mike Tyson."

"*Mon Dieu . . . ,*" Nick muttered again. "And you were worried about *her* being abused."

"She *is* abused," Annie said. "Please sit down. I brought you a sandwich."

"I can't eat now," he said, though he obliged her in pulling out a chair and sitting close enough that he could touch her. She turned her hand over on the tabletop and twined her fingers with his.

"Her left arm is messed up enough that she isn't using it," she said. "Like maybe somebody wrenched it good and hard. And she wouldn't let me see her son at all. She said he was sleeping in because he has a bad stomach. For all I know, the kid is dead. And all this is courtesy of our boss."

"She won't file a complaint?" Nick asked.

"She won't even admit it's him that hurt her. She's got too much riding on her fiancé being a pillar of the community. If he's not that, she loses everything."

"There's not much you can do, then. You can't prove she's a victim, and you can't prove he's victimizing her or the boy. People have to want help."

"If I could get the son alone," she said, "I think I could get him to talk to me."

"You want to put a child in that position?" Nick asked. "Ask him to tell you his mother's deepest secret, the thing that makes them both so ashamed they would rather live with the consequences of their silence?"

"He might welcome the chance."

"Or fear it."

"I can't let it go, Nick," Annie said. "I can't know he's an abuser and just turn a blind eye. But if he catches me talking to Sharon, he'll fire me so fast my head will spin. And what will he do to her?"

"Then there's naught to do but wait. You didn't haul her in for assault. You let her know she can trust you. Give her time."

"I hope we have time. The press is asking for your head, if you hadn't heard. Dutrow might just be all too happy to give it to them."

Nick pushed to his feet and drew her up with him. "Then let's go do our jobs while it's still on my shoulders."

GENEVIEVE WAS SITTING on a chair by the window as they walked into her room, the sunlight casting an angelic glow around her. From this angle, she was beautiful, her profile delicate, her hair a soft cloud of dark waves. Then she turned to face them like something from a horror movie, her left eye still nearly swollen shut, the flesh around it the color of a ripe plum.

"They're down there because of me, aren't they?" she said, turning and looking out the window again.

"The reporters?" Annie asked. "Yes. They're here because of you."

A wry smile turned the corner of her mouth. "I always wanted to be famous. This wasn't quite what I had in mind."

Slowly, she rose from the chair, adjusting her hospital gown with her free hand as if it was a party dress. Nick moved to help her back to her bed, and she took his arm and gazed up at him like he was her date for the prom.

"They tell me I'm being released today," she said. "Released to where? I can't go back to that house."

"No," Annie said, pulling back the blanket and smoothing the wrinkled sheets, "you don't have to go back there ever again."

"The house is still a crime scene," Nick said, steadying her as she got back into bed. "We've arranged for you to go to a women's shelter here in town—unless you have friends you can stay with."

"I don't have any friends."

"That's not true, Genevieve," Annie said. "I spoke to Jaime Blynn this morning—KJ's teacher. She wants you to know there's a GoFundMe page up online for you and that people have already donated about twelve hundred dollars to help you cover your medical bills and funeral expenses."

"What? For me?" Genevieve said. She looked almost suspicious, as if she was waiting for a bad punch line. "People are doing that for me?"

"Yep. You have friends you don't even know."

"I don't know what to say," she admitted. "No one has ever done anything for me before."

Three days before, she had been a drug-dabbling single mother of questionable background, behind on her rent, and desperate enough to have seduced her married boss. Today she was "famous" with the sympathy of a community she didn't know pouring into a GoFundMe account. All because someone had murdered her child.

"Genevieve," Nick said quietly, "we have a few more questions we have to ask you for the investigation."

"Do you have any suspects yet?" she asked, looking from Nick to Annie and back.

"None that stand out," Nick said. He glanced at Annie. "Detective Broussard?"

"Genevieve," Annie began, "Nora Florette has gone missing. I understand she wasn't at the Florette house when you picked KJ up the other night. Is that true?"

"No, she wasn't there. I called Jojean and complained. I pay Nora to watch my son. She should be there with him."

"Is that something that happened a lot? Nora just dumping KJ at the house and not staying there with him?"

"It happened a few times. She's not a very responsible girl."

"But you kept her for your babysitter anyway?"

"It's not easy to find a babysitter. I don't know anybody here, and I can't afford to pay much, and the Florettes live right on my way home."

"What did Jojean say when you called her to complain?"

"She said what was the big deal, anyway? There are always people at her house. Her sisters or her cousins or nieces or I don't know who all. And there are often younger children there for KJ to play with. It's kind of a crazy place, to be honest. But it was the best I could do. Do you have children, Detective?"

"I have a son," Annie answered, as if they hadn't already had this conversation the day before. "He's five."

"Are you married?"

"I am."

"I wanted KJ to have a father," Genevieve confessed. "But there aren't many men interested in having another man's child."

"I'm sure it's tough to be a single mom," Annie said. "You work and you come home and work some more. Not much time for yourself."

Genevieve laughed without humor. Tears rose in her eyes.

"Lonely, I expect," Annie murmured.

She sniffed and nodded, visibly fighting the need to cry.

"Genevieve," Nick said, "you told us last night that KJ was agitated when you picked him up, that he wouldn't settle down. Do you know what that was about?"

"No. He gets overstimulated. He gets angry," she said, as if her son were still alive. "He gets afraid of all the emotions. There's no consoling him. He just kept running and running and chanting the same thing over and over."

"Chanting what?"

" 'I won't tell, I won't tell, I won't tell.' "

A chill washed over Annie, but Genevieve seemed unfazed.

"The other kids get him wound up, and he just goes on and on," she said. "I know I need to have him tested, to take him to a doctor, but I just can't afford it. Everything costs money, and I just don't have it."

"Who was at the Florette house that night?" Annie asked.

"An old man—I think he's Jojean's grandfather or Duane's grandfather. I'm not sure. He's senile. He just sits in the recliner and watches TV. And the pregnant sister—Darla—and her three-year-old. And Dean. Dean was there," she said with a note of frustration. "I don't like that boy. He's rough, and he uses bad language. KJ always comes home upset if Dean was there."

"Did Dean ever hurt him?" Annie asked, her heart beating a little too hard at the thought. Dean was a bully. He had beat up Cameron Spicer, tried to molest Lola Troiano . . .

Genevieve shook her head, but her expression was unconvincing. "Not that I know of, but I don't know if KJ would have told me. Not if he was afraid."

"I won't tell. I won't tell. I won't tell . . ."

The words pulsed in Annie's head.

"All this fuss for Dead Nora."

It was entirely possible Dean Florette could have done something to his sister, she knew. He was an angry boy with impulse-control issues. He had a track record of being aggressive and sexually inappropriate with girls. He was learning about relationships from an angry mother and an absent father and a stash of porn magazines.

It was entirely possible that he could have hurt Nora and sworn KJ Gauthier to secrecy. But if Dean had done something to Nora, then where was she? Was this going to be one of those terrible tragic stories where the dead girl was found stuffed under a bed or under the house? If that was the case, they should have found her the night before, when they had searched the house. If she was anywhere on the property, the search dogs would already have found her today.

Nick had moved on to his questions, Annie realized, as she brought herself back into the moment.

"I don't want to talk about that," Genevieve was saying.

"I'm sure you don't," Nick said quietly. "But I have to ask the question nevertheless. You went to jail for killing a baby when you were fourteen. I can't pretend that didn't happen."

"I didn't kill her!" she insisted, growing more agitated. "I didn't kill her. She just died. It wasn't my fault!"

"The court found otherwise. You went to jail."

"Everyone was against me!" she cried, sounding fourteen all over again, Annie thought. Life wasn't fair. Everyone was against her.

"Even your own mother?" Nick asked.

"Her most of all! She hated me for getting pregnant and having the baby and keeping it."

"That had to be a lot of pressure for a young girl." He kept his voice low and calm and even, never accusatory, never adversarial. "You were barely more than a child yourself. Suddenly you had a baby to care for, and everybody mad at you, everybody against you. Babies cry, they're demanding, you can't get any sleep. That had to be overwhelming."

Genevieve was crying now. Annie wanted to leave the room. There was no one better at this than her husband. He could find those hairline cracks in a subject's psyche and exert just enough pressure. It wasn't a skill Annie particularly wanted to have. As necessary as it was, she didn't always have the stomach for it.

"How many babies had you ever held?" Nick asked softly. "How could you know what to do? Nobody wanted to help you. And that baby didn't know not to cry. That's all a baby knows to do—cry or not cry. She's hungry, she cries. She's wet, she cries. Her belly hurts, she cries. She can't sleep, she cries. She wants to be held, she cries. It's always something. Every minute of every day . . ."

Genevieve was reliving every one of those moments, Annie could see, remembering the stress, the frustration, the terrifying uncertainty of being a first-time parent. And Genevieve had been just a girl herself. Just two years older than Lola Troiano.

"You lost your patience," Nick pressed on. "You couldn't take it. You didn't mean to hurt her. You just wanted it to stop."

"I didn't kill my baby!" she insisted.

"The evidence suggested otherwise. The coroner ruled her death a homicide."

"I didn't kill her!" she said, sobbing. "She just died! I didn't know what to do. I was so scared! I just buried her. I didn't know what else to do!"

"It's all right, Genevieve," Nick murmured. "You didn't know what else to do. You were tired, frustrated, at the end of your rope. You just lashed out. You had that thought creep into your mind—how much easier life would be without that crying child . . ."

Genevieve's eyes widened in realization and horror. "Oh, my God! You think I killed KJ! You think I did that to him—stabbed him over and over—"

"I didn't say that, Genevieve," he said quietly.

"I couldn't do that!" she cried. "How could you think I could do that?"

"No one would blame you for getting frustrated, Genevieve. He was a handful. You were all alone. He was all wound up, running around, saying that thing over and over until you wanted to scream, you wanted to shake him—"

"Stop it!" she shouted, striking out at him with her good hand, balled into a fist. "Stop it! Stop it! Stop it!"

"Nick . . . ," Annie said, giving him a warning look. *"C'est assez."*

"C'est tout," he murmured, and heaved a sigh.

Genevieve pressed her hand across her mouth and squeezed her eyes shut, trying to contain her emotions. Annie rested a hand on her shoulder in a small gesture of comfort.

"I'm sorry, Genevieve," Nick said. "I don't do this to upset you. My only job here is to find the truth. That means I can't be on one side or the other.

"You've had a hard life, *c'est vrai*. That makes for hard questions. All you can do is answer them truthfully.

"The truth will out," he said. "It always does. We have to choose for ourselves which side of that we're gonna be on, yeah?"

She swiped at her tears and worked to calm herself. Annie handed her a tissue.

"No one wants this to be harder for you than it has to be," Annie assured her. "But your little boy is dead, Genevieve. People are going to have questions. People are going to make judgments. The press is already asking about the baby that died. You need to be prepared for that. For every person donating to your GoFundMe site, there will be someone else who wants to condemn you."

"We'll try to protect you from as much of that as possible," Nick said. "We'll station a deputy outside the women's shelter."

"Who will know I'm there?" she asked.

"Us, and the people at the shelter," Nick said. "We won't release that information to the press, but that doesn't mean they won't get it. I don't know how they found out about your juvenile record, but they did. It's hard to keep a secret in a small town.

"We'll ask you not to talk to the media about the case because the investigation is ongoing," he said. "But that won't stop people from trying to talk to you. It won't stop people from accusing you. You need to know that's coming."

"I can't believe any of this is happening," she murmured, looking toward the window.

From the bed it was impossible to see the reporters gathered below. She had looked down at them before and felt important, felt like a star. Annie wondered what she was feeling now.

"I always wanted to be famous . . ."

"You're gonna trust me, right?" Nick asked. "Last night you said you want me to be your hero in this. Then you need to trust me to do the right thing, to ask the right questions—even if they hurt. It can be a rough road to justice, but the truth will get you to the other side, guaranteed."

She didn't look so sure of that, Annie thought. She looked like she would just as soon quit as keep going. Annie couldn't blame her.

"Just a couple more questions and then we'll let you rest," Nick said. "You have that DUI on your record from Houma, about eight years ago. Did you have drugs in the car that night? A little weed? Some pills, maybe?"

"No," she said. "I told you that was a mistake. I didn't have anything like that."

"So there's no chance you might have given evidence against a dealer or something like that in exchange for having charges dropped?"

"No," she said, but she didn't meet his eyes.

"Did you know any people like that back then?" he asked. "Anyone who might have been nursing a grudge against you all this time?"

"No. Why would anyone bother? I'm nobody."

"And KJ's father . . . ?"

"KJ doesn't have a father," she said quietly, looking away, back out the window at the stunning blue sky. "He never did."

"So, EITHER SHE doesn't know who the father was," Nick said, "or she's afraid of him."

"Either way," Annie murmured. She felt so depleted by the experience of watching Nick's interrogation of Genevieve, she almost didn't want to know more. "Could be KJ was the product of a rape—which she doesn't want to talk about. Or he was the product of an affair—which she also doesn't want to talk about."

They sat in the conference room again, Nick attacking the sandwich she had picked up for him at Po' Richard's. He ate like it was his mission in life, like he hadn't just run a broken woman through an emotional wringer. She snuck a french fry and nibbled on the crispy end, but it was cold and disappointing, like life at the moment. She made a face and put it back in the carton.

"Either way," she said again. "Do you really think someone came up to Bayou Breaux to murder their seven-year-old illegitimate child? Did they just suddenly remember—oh, hey, I still have that kid I don't want?"

"Maybe he's already here," Nick suggested. "Maybe that's why she came here. Maybe she was more desperate now than she has been before and decided to press for money."

Annie sighed, impatient with the subject. She could have been herself a product of rape or of an affair gone wrong. She had no idea who her father was or the circumstances of her conception. Whomever he was, he had never tracked her down and killed her. But then, maybe he was the reason Marie Broussard had come to Bayou Breaux and the reason she had taken her secrets with her to the grave.

Unconsciously, she crossed her arms and hugged herself.

"So she came here to blackmail the father of her son, but she lives in a shit hole and is trying to have an affair with her married boss. And the baby daddy decides he's done with it, so he kills the boy but leaves Genevieve alive."

She shook her head, giving her husband a wry look. "Tante Fanchon crochets doilies with fewer holes than that theory. You're just giving me a homicidal sperm donor theory to cheer me up or to provide a glaringly ludicrous contrast to the theory that Genevieve killed the boy herself. You certainly made a painfully good case for that in there."

Nick sat back and wiped his mouth with a napkin, his eyes never leaving hers. "Are you upset with me?"

Annie heaved a sigh that left her feeling hollow. "No. Not really. That was hard to watch, that's all."

"It was necessary," he said. "Genevieve is not our victim, 'Toinette. The boy is. We need to get to the bottom of her truth to give him justice, yeah?"

"Yes, I know. You're just unnervingly good at it. It was hard not to put myself in her place."

"You don't belong in her place."

"Does she?"

"I don't know," he admitted. "We'll find out."

Feeling the need to either move or crumple, Annie pushed herself to her feet. "Okay. In light of what Genevieve had to say about him, I'm going to go track down Dean Florette, because the prospect of a fourteen-year-old psychopath killing and disposing of his sister is so much more appealing to me. All I can hear in my head now is that little boy chanting 'I won't tell.'"

"What's your next move?" she asked as Nick's phone began to vibrate on the table.

He looked at the screen and frowned as he got to his feet. "Me, I'm gonna go get fired, apparently."

"Great."

"Don't worry, *mon coeur*," he murmured, slipping his arms around her and drawing her head to his chest. She pressed her ear against him and listened to his heart beat. "It won't stop me doing my job."

FORTY

Cameron paced, afraid to be still. His mind was racing. His heart was racing. His sense of self felt connected to the rest of him by the thinnest of invisible threads, sitting perched high in the eye socket of the body. And the body just kept moving, one foot in front of the other, one foot in front of the other, one foot in front of the other . . .

He was alone, and he was afraid to be alone. He was afraid Kelvin might come back and kill him or that he would kill himself.

How stupid was that? He wanted to die, but he was afraid to be killed. That just showed what a loser he was. On top of everything else, he was a coward.

He walked around and around in the family room with the TV on to try to distract from the voice in his head that wouldn't shut up. His mother didn't let him watch TV in the daytime, but what difference did it make now? She was sending him away. Why should he care what she allowed or didn't allow? She was taking the side of the man who had hurt them both over the side of the son she was supposed to love more than anything in the world. She had said she would fix everything, but what she meant was that she would fix it so that Kelvin would still marry her.

The local news was showing the story about the search for Nora

Florette: the mighty Sheriff Dutrow standing on the Florettes' front porch, ranting and raving, red-faced and angry, going on about the importance of protecting the children of Partout Parish, going on about what a family man he was. *"I cannot abide the thought of harm coming to a child under my watch."* Unless he was the one inflicting the harm, Cameron thought.

Kelvin Dutrow was nothing but a phony and a hypocrite, and Cameron felt nothing but shame that a part of him still cared what Kelvin thought of him. He felt shame for being inadequate in the eyes of this man, and he felt disgust for feeling that shame.

He had wanted to measure up. He had wanted the sheriff to like him and to want to be a father to him. But Kelvin Dutrow didn't want to be his father. He wanted to ship Cameron off to military school and be rid of him. Cameron knew he would never measure up. He was weak and timid and there was something wrong in his head that he even for a second thought he might be able to overcome those things.

There was something wrong in his head, period.

One foot in front of the other, one foot in front of the other, one foot in front of the other . . .

If Kelvin wanted a son at all, he wanted a son who was a champion athlete, big, strong, and handsome; a boy all the guys liked and all the cute girls wanted to date. He wanted a son who would hunt and fish with him and not throw up at the sight of guts or cruelty. The only thing Cameron had managed to do to please Kelvin in all these months was to figure out how to row the small boat Kelvin had bought for him.

It was the one thing Cameron had enjoyed doing since coming to Bayou Breaux—taking the little boat out on the bayou and rowing away from everyone and everything. If he could have rowed the boat into another dimension, he would have. But he could only row the boat out into the swamp to be eaten by alligators, and he was too big a coward to do that.

One foot in front of the other, one foot in front of the other, one foot in front of the other . . .

He watched the television from the corner of his eye. The sound seemed suddenly far too loud—the horrible mechanical insect buzz of the search drones hovering in the sky, the baying of the bloodhounds standing on the porch. Along the bottom of the screen, a headline in big bold type announced that volunteer searchers were gathering in the park between the two schools.

Kelvin finished his show with his famous line: "We've got crime to fight!" Then the picture changed to the park, where people had already begun to gather to find Nora Florette.

Annoying Nora. Not even her own family liked her. All her mother ever did was yell at her. Her slutty sister accused her of stealing her makeup and clothes. Dean tricked her into shoplifting for him and spied on her in the bathroom. She was clingy and stupid and weird. She still played with dolls, but all she talked about was how she wanted a boyfriend. She talked about sex like she knew what it was.

Just thinking about her made Cameron uncomfortable. He didn't like her. She was always hovering around him, touching him, like a hairy, ugly fly that wouldn't leave him alone. She managed to make him feel disgusted and weirdly excited at the same time. The feeling scared him. He had run away from her once, and Dean had started calling him Spice Girl and the Houma Homo.

He wished he'd never met the Florettes. He still shuddered to remember how angry his mother had been the day she had come home and caught Nora in the house. He had told Nora over and over he wasn't allowed to have anyone over if his mom wasn't home, but she wouldn't listen. She hadn't believed him—or hadn't cared—probably because there were no rules at all in the Florette house. The kids came and went and did whatever they wanted. Their mom yelled at them, but she yelled so much it didn't mean anything to them anymore.

Cameron had never seen his mother so angry as that day. She had screamed at Nora. She had screamed at him. She had gone to the Florette house and made a big scene and threatened to press charges. Cameron had thought he would die of embarrassment. His mother had ranted at him for days. How could he be so irresponsible? How could he be so inconsiderate? He was living under Kelvin's roof, and there were rules, and rules had to be obeyed. Never upset Kelvin. Never embarrass Kelvin. Never make Kelvin angry.

Stupid Nora. Now half the town was looking for her. Cameron wondered what would happen if *he* went missing. Would anybody even
bother to try to find him? Would Kelvin rant and rave on their front
porch and bring in search dogs and drones? Would his mother go on
television and beg for his return?

They would probably be relieved to have him gone.

Cameron's gone missing. Oh, well . . .

*One foot in front of the other, one foot in front of the other, one foot in
front of the other . . . Might as well go walk into the pool. No one will miss
you. No one will care . . .*

Now the walls seemed to close in on him, and the darkness of the
house and the darkness of his thoughts closed in and tried to suffocate
him. Fear closed around his throat like a hand.

I don't want to be here . . .

He needed to leave. He couldn't be alone. He needed to see other
people—if only from a distance. Just seeing them might somehow keep
him tethered to reality.

The heat and sun attacked him as he stepped out the front door.
Instantly, he felt his pores open and release the sweat from his body. His
nostrils filled with the sour smell of it. Cameron imagined it was toxic
steam. Maybe it was the crazy escaping.

All his senses seemed turned up to maximum sensitivity. He squinted
hard against the brightness of the light and the hyperintensity of the
colors all around him. The sky was too blue. The trees were too green.
The sound of the drones seemed right inside his head. He could hear the
scrape of his shoes against the pavement.

*One foot in front of the other, one foot in front of the other, one foot in
front of the other . . .*

He walked out of Blue Cypress and over to the block where the Florettes lived, careful to keep his head down, staying on the other side of
the street. The crowd on the lawn had dwindled to just a few people
standing, talking with a uniformed deputy. Kelvin was gone. The dogs
were gone. The drones were gone from sight, but he could still hear them.

Turning left at the corner, he headed toward the park. When he reached
the edge of the park, he fell in step with a wide line of people marching

slowly and methodically toward the schools, scanning the ground in front of them as they went. People called Nora's name as if she might actually answer, while the drones buzzed overhead, and someone in the distance shouted over a bullhorn, the sound tinny and distorted.

No one paid any attention to Cameron as he walked along with the group, his head down. He wasn't looking for Nora. He didn't care about Nora. He only wanted to be among people, not that anyone seemed to take any notice of him. He wondered if he was really there or if he was imagining the whole thing. With his sense of self clinging hard to its eye-socket perch, everything seemed surreal and nightmarish. Maybe he was dreaming. Maybe he was dead.

One foot in front of the other, one foot in front of the other, one foot in front of the other . . .

Maybe he was a ghost or an invisible zombie.

The searchers were men and women, older people and kids Cameron recognized from school. They worked their way slowly up the park. Gradually, the schools came into view. The person with the bullhorn was standing near the gazebo next to a woman with a clipboard—the teacher who had brought Detective Broussard to them the day before. Mrs. Blynn, Lola had called her. She looked right at him and then turned away, as if she hadn't seen him at all.

The person with the bullhorn was speaking again. To Cameron it just sounded like *Wah-wah-wah-wah-wah.* Then the crowd began to disperse, people going off to the cars in the parking lots, or walking back toward the schools.

Cameron hung back by the edge of the woods, watching them go, watching the park empty until no one remained and he was all alone. He had no idea how much time passed. He was aware of the silence, of his own breathing, of the heart beating in the chest of the body he occupied. For a long while, he had no thoughts at all. He just stood there until finally his body turned and started back in the direction of home, his gaze on his sneakers.

One foot in front of the other, one foot in front of the other, one foot in front of the other . . .

"Hey, Spice Girl!"

The voice ran through him like a knife. Cameron looked up, his stomach twisting at the sight of Dean Florette standing on the path, his hands on his hips, a nasty, belligerent look on his busted-up face.

"Hey, Houma Homo, what'd you do to my sister? Did you kill her and steal her dress?" he asked, laughing.

"I didn't do anything to your stupid sister," Cameron shot back. "What'd *you* do to her? Kill her and eat her?"

"Well, you didn't eat her, that's for sure, Princess," Dean sneered, snickering as he stepped closer and closer.

"You're disgusting," Cameron said, moving to his left, looking for an escape route, knowing it wouldn't matter if he made a run for it. Dean would be on him in a heartbeat, pounding the crap out of him.

"Ooooh, are you offended?" Dean taunted, making a pouting face. "Poor Spicey!"

Cameron tried to step past him. Dean blocked him.

"Where you going, Fag Boy?"

"Just leave me alone."

"Or what?" Dean challenged, giving him a shove.

Cameron stumbled but caught himself. He kept trying to walk forward. *One foot in front of the other, one foot in front of the other, one foot in front of the other . . .*

There was no one else around. All the searchers had left for some other location to look for Nora. On the downward slope of the park, the schools and their parking lots and playgrounds were out of sight.

"Why are you walking funny, Fag Boy? Did you take it up the ass last night?"

"Just leave me alone!"

Cameron tried to shove him back, but Dean just stepped out of the way, making him look like a fool. Anger and frustration swirled inside him. Everything about his life sucked. And now he was going to get his ass kicked once again by Dean Florette.

"Are you gonna cry, Spice Girl?"

"Shut up!"

"Did I hurt your little feelings?" Dean mocked him and laughed.

"Just fuck off!" Cameron shouted, his voice breaking badly, and as Dean laughed and laughed, to Cameron's horror, he started to cry.

"Crybaby! Cry!"

It was too much. Too humiliating. He couldn't take it anymore.

As Dean stood there laughing, Cameron pulled his arm back and fired a punch, hitting Dean Florette square in the nose.

Stunned, Dean staggered backward a few steps, clutching his face with both hands. As he pulled his hands away and saw the blood, his eyes went black with rage.

"I'm gonna fucking kill you!"

As Dean hit him running, driving the breath from his lungs, Cameron half hoped that was true.

FORTY-ONE

S
he made eleven calls to Jeff Avery's cell phone on the night of the murder," Dixon said, following Nick down the hall to his office.

Dutrow had called his cell three times, leaving curt messages for him to come into his office ASAP, each message sounding slightly angrier than the one before. Fuck him, Nick had thought as he drove past the main building, going instead to the Pizza Hut to check in with Dixon, hoping against hope that she had somehow managed to get her virtual hands on what he wanted.

"And one call to his home phone," she added.

"To his home phone?" Nick asked, sitting down behind his desk.

Dixon handed him the printed call log. The calls to Avery's cell phone had varied in length from a minute or two to twelve minutes. It wasn't hard to imagine the content if Avery had told him the truth. If he had indeed told Genevieve they couldn't be together, that there was no future for them, then these would be the calls from her to beg, to bargain, to try to hang on to whatever slim chance there might have been of having a relationship with him.

The final call, the one to the Avery home, had lasted nearly six minutes. A drunken, high Genevieve calling Janine Avery to confess all? Or calling just as a threat, to show Jeff what she might do if he didn't treat her right. Or she had called with the intention of confessing and then chickened out?

Probably one of the latter two, Nick thought. He couldn't imagine Janine Avery being able to stomach knowingly going to visit her husband's mistress in the hospital.

He glanced at the calls listed for the several nights preceding the murder. Calls to Avery's cell phone each night.

Had the incessant calls been enough to anger Jeff Avery to the point of violence? He didn't strike Nick as having the nerve to kill anyone, but if he was afraid of losing his family . . . ?

Or had the evening of drinking, drugs, rejection, and her son's temper tantrums driven Genevieve past the point of despair?

"Where's Stokes?" he asked.

"Him and Quinlan went down to Dulac and Houma to interview her former employers."

His phone buzzed again, and he checked the screen, hoping against hope it would be Gus. It was not. Dutrow again. Time was ticking.

"And . . . ," Dixon said, holding out another printed page.

Nick glanced up at her, seeing the excitement in her eyes despite her best efforts to look calm.

"You got it."

"I got it."

The arrest report for Gauthier, Genevieve, from Houma PD.

Nick looked it over, shaking his head at the name of the reporting officer: Keith Kemp.

"You can have a seat, Detective," the secretary instructed in a chilly tone. "Sheriff Dutrow is tied up on a *very* important phone call."

Nick leveled a look at her. "I'll stand, thank you, Ms. Comb."

Valerie Comb, Dutrow's secretary, was a holdover from Gus Noblier's reign. She had transferred her loyalty wholeheartedly to the new boss and had hung his framed, autographed campaign poster on the wall behind her desk in Dutrow's outer office. The poster was a full-length shot of Dutrow in his tactical costume, jamming a forefinger at the face of all prospective voters, growling out his favorite tagline, *We've got crime to fight!*

Attractive, blond by design, a few years ahead of Annie in school, Valerie Comb had never gotten over the fact that being head cheerleader did not translate into adult success. She wore her vague air of resentment like a signature perfume every day of her life.

"I don't know how long he'll be," she chattered, straightening stacks of fliers and handouts on the counter, trying to look essential and efficient. "He's had a very hectic morning, what with this missing girl and all. And that murder the other night. But I suppose you know all about that."

Nick said nothing.

"And now come to find out that woman murdered a baby years ago!" Valerie said with shock and outrage. "I imagine she's your number one suspect."

"I can't comment on an ongoing investigation."

Her mouth fell too naturally into a pout. She was a notorious gossip and had reportedly slept her way through the department, from Patrol to Maintenance, not that it mattered to Nick in any way other than as a point of reference.

"Well, it's a shame if that's the case," she said. "Some women just shouldn't be allowed to have children."

"It's a tragedy," Nick said, looking at the door to Dutrow's inner sanctum.

He doubted the story of the very important phone call. It was too easy to picture Dutrow in his office rehearsing what he would say and do, where he would stand, how he would present himself. The star of his own internal movie.

As Nick paced past the ostentatious suggestion box Dutrow had installed beside the office door, the fleeting thought *Don't be such a self-absorbed dick* flashed through his mind.

His phone vibrated on his belt. He checked the screen. Gus.

Valerie was droning on. ". . . and to think she applied for a job here!"

"She what?" he asked, turning his full attention back to her.

"She filled out an application several months ago. I remember thinking she seemed a bit desperate."

"Why do you say that?"

"Oh, you know. A young, single mother . . ."

Which was exactly what Valerie had been when she had first started working for the SO—a divorced mother of three.

"No," Nick said flatly, "I don't know. What does that mean?"

"Well, with all the male deputies and detectives here . . ." She gave a weak laugh and rolled her eyes. "Some girls come looking for more than a job. That's all I'm saying."

Nick stared at her in disapproving silence long enough that she felt the need to move away.

"Did she have an interview?" he asked at last.

"I wouldn't know. I never saw her again."

"What became of her application?"

"I imagine it's on file in the personnel office. We weren't hiring at the time."

Dutrow's voice sounded over the intercom on the secretary's desk. "Ms. Comb, please send Detective Fourcade in."

Showtime.

Dutrow was standing behind his desk when Nick walked in, his hands resting above the tactical belt hung with gear he would never have to use. It was all for show, window dressing on a mannequin, a costume to impress people whose definition of a sheriff was formed from bullshit movies and YouTube videos.

He didn't tell Nick to sit down, having already learned that would be Nick's first subtle act of defiance. But conceding that point automatically still gave Nick the first tiny advantage.

"Detective Fourcade—"

"Were you able to get that original arrest report on Genevieve Gauthier from her DUI in Houma?"

Dutrow's brows knitted. "I haven't had the time or the interest—"

"You're not interested in evidence?" Nick asked. "What a curious position for you to take."

"This isn't why I called you in here," Dutrow said. "Don't try to run me off into the weeds over some minor and undoubtedly irrelevant detail—"

"There is no such thing as an irrelevant detail in a homicide investi-gation," Nick said. "You should know that, but I guess maybe you never worked a murder in your capacity as Special Community Relations Officer."

He pronounced the job title with the barest hint of disdain. The color had already begun to creep up Dutrow's throat.

"Though I'm sure teaching some kind of half-assed karate to the house-wives of Houma had its own rewards."

"The fucking balls on you!" Dutrow barked, not just angry, but of-fended enough to curse. A loss of control. Good.

"So you didn't even bother to request that report?" Nick pressed on.

"How could it possibly be relevant?"

"It could be relevant if it turned out the arresting officer was Keith Kemp."

Dutrow seemed to freeze briefly, as if he'd received the news via an electrical shock.

"You're gonna tell me you didn't know that?" Nick asked.

"Why would I know that?" Dutrow scoffed. "It was years ago!"

"Mm-hmm. Yeah, well, y'all seemed pretty tight back then. You must have been. You must still be. You brought him up here with you."

"This is ridiculous! And not why I brought you in here—"

"Oh, I'm sure not," Nick said, chuckling low in his throat.

Dutrow's scowl deepened. "You think this is funny?"

"Not in the literal sense, *mais non*."

"Just where do you think you're driving this train of thought? Are you going to tell me you think Kemp is a suspect in this murder now? When the mother is clearly—"

"I'm not at a point to draw conclusions," Nick said, deliberately talking over him, eroding any illusion of respect for the man's thoughts or words. "But I don't want him working this case. I sure as hell don't want him handling evidence."

"Because he made a traffic stop on a DUI years ago?"

"No," Nick said. "Though that is an amazing coincidence, wouldn't you agree? What are the odds a man would arrest a woman in one town and, years later, find himself collecting evidence from a murder scene at her home in another town, miles away? Me, I think that is such a coincidence that it can't be a coincidence at all."

"I don't know what you're getting at here, Fourcade."

"Why did Keith Kemp cease to be a police officer?"

"Because he chose to."

"Really? Just like that? He built a career, worked toward a pension, then just up and said fuck it? You expect me to believe that?"

"I don't care what you believe, Fourcade," Dutrow said curtly. "You don't work here anymore. After your performance last night on the news, your manhandling of Bobby Theriot, your belligerent attitude toward myself and others—"

Nick started to laugh, a deep, heartfelt belly laugh. He dropped himself down into the chair that sat opposite the sheriff's desk, leaned back, and crossed his ankles, as relaxed as if he was in his own home.

Dutrow watched him, his expression uncertain. "What the—"

"You gonna fire me now, Sheriff?" Nick asked with a smile. "Really?"

"Despite your high opinion of yourself, we will get along just fine without you," Dutrow said. "You're an arrogant, disrespectful ass, and I won't have it. I know Gus let you run your own show, but I am not Gus Noblier."

"No, you are certainly not."

"I will personally take over the investigation—"

"Will you?" Nick asked. "Well, that should be interesting, all things considered. Especially with the connection to your good friend Keith Kemp."

"There is no connection to Kemp."

"That's how you're gonna spin it? I wouldn't recommend that. I won't hesitate to contradict you."

"Your opinion is of no interest."

"Not to you," Nick said. "But you're gonna cut me loose so that I'm free to go wherever I want, and speak to whomever I choose, and say whatever I choose to say." He shook his head. "I don't think that would be good for your image. The press, they would want to speak to me. And as much as I despise them most of the time, they have their uses."

Dutrow stared at him, stunned at the idea. "Are you threatening to slander me?"

"*Mais non*. Not at all! A slander is an untruth," he pointed out happily then sobered in the blink of an eye. "I have plenty of true, unflattering things to say about you, starting with your *penchant* for threatening women."

It might have been a step too far, too soon, Nick reflected as he watched rage fill Kelvin Dutrow like a flash fire.

"How dare you—"

"How dare *you*, sir?" Nick challenged, on his feet in an instant, so quickly and with such aggressive intent that Dutrow stepped backward with fear in his eyes.

"Don't you *ever* threaten my wife again," Nick warned. "Or any woman, for that matter. I won't care that you have a badge on your chest or ten thousand fucking YouTube followers."

"Don't you threaten me—" Dutrow started.

"Oh, that's not a threat," Nick promised. "I guarantee I will ruin you every way there is. You threaten my family and I will scorch the ground you walk on and sweep the ash with your face."

"I should have you arrested right this minute," Dutrow snarled.

"Oh, you do that," Nick said. "Bring it on. I'll have the slimiest, sleaziest, most media-hungry defense attorney in south Louisiana on this so fast it'll take your breath away."

"You son of a bitch!" Dutrow spat the words.

"Interesting how you haven't denied the charge."

"I have never abused a woman in my life."

Nick arched a brow. "You need to practice that in front of a mirror a few times before you take it to the big screen."

"You severely overestimate your powers of persuasion, Detective," Dutrow said. His hands were trembling ever so slightly at his sides. "Your reputation is already as black as your heart. Who would believe anything you have to say?"

Nick lifted a shoulder in a lazy shrug. "People may doubt me, that's true, but they all will come 'round to listen, just the same."

He smiled again, holding the other man's gaze. "Me, I'm good TV. Maybe you oughta fire me on the air!" he suggested, feigning excitement. "Imagine the ratings!"

"You crazy bastard," Dutrow muttered.

"So they say."

For a moment, Nick just watched him try to process the situation. Dutrow hadn't gotten where he was being a fool or a hothead. He would consider his options like a chess move.

"Fire me or don't. It makes no matter to me," Nick said quietly, backing toward the door. "Me, I work for that dead boy, not for you. And I will keep working until I find him justice, no matter what that takes or what that means.

"Good day to you, Sheriff Dutrow," he said, giving the slightest of bows. "You have a pleasant afternoon."

He closed the door behind him as he left and walked calmly through the outer office, Valerie Comb watching him with the wide eyes of an eavesdropper who had overheard more than she had bargained for. He looked at her and raised a forefinger to his lips in silent warning, just to fuck with her.

As he left the main building for the Pizza Hut, he pulled his phone from his belt and touched Call Back.

FORTY-TWO

Dean Florette was nowhere to be found. Annie had gone back to the Florette house to find no sign of him amid the chaos of family and friends and search volunteers. No one knew where he was, and no one seemed to care. In her absence, Nora had become the much-loved golden child. Dean had been dismissed and forgotten. The irony was lost on them.

With Jojean's permission, Annie had gone through Dean's room, a pigsty of dirty clothes and unmade bed and stinking, filthy sneakers. She found his stash of stolen pornography, some of it quite raunchy and disturbing, depicting bondage and sadism. It turned her stomach to think of a boy as young as Dean steeping his brain in this shit, forming his opinions of women and sex based on the fantasies of adult men—and sick ones at that.

She found underwear he had no doubt stolen from his sisters and a half-full box of condoms he had probably stolen from the Quik Pik. The question put to the remaining Florette women—does Dean have a girlfriend?—was met with laughter and disgust. What girl would go out with Dean?

Why, then, would he have a box of condoms?

He probably used them for water balloons—or maybe to jerk off, though Nicole confessed she'd caught him doing that with a pair of her panties.

Where could he be?

He'd probably gone off with one of the search parties. If not because he cared to find his sister, because he thought the search was exciting, with the drones and the dogs and the people shouting and beating the bushes.

That seemed as good a theory as any, Annie thought as she drove toward the school. She didn't think he'd run off. He hadn't seemed at all bothered to see her at the house that morning. He didn't act like he had something to hide. But then, maybe that was because, judging by the amount of stolen stuff in his bedroom, he was just that used to the feeling. If psychopathy was already baked into his brain, then he was already unburdened by the concept of guilt.

"All this fuss for Dead Nora," he'd said, looking up at the drones in the sky above his house. His lack of emotion had given her a chill.

She thought of what Genevieve had said about KJ running around the house that night, chanting the same thing over and over—*"I won't tell. I won't tell. I won't tell."*

Won't tell what? What had he seen? What had he heard? Had it had everything to do with his death or nothing at all? Genevieve had said she didn't like Dean being around her son. He got him wound up. *"KJ always comes home upset if Dean was there."*

She spotted Jaime Blynn sitting on the steps of the gazebo as she pulled around the circular drive.

"Are you playing hooky?" Annie called as she walked toward her friend.

"Just sitting here melting," Jaime said. Her eyes went suddenly wide. "Oh, my stars! What happened to your face?"

"I asked someone the wrong question and they took exception. It looks worse than it is. Aren't you supposed to be inside shaping the lives of America's youth? I thought I would have to somehow drag you out of the building."

"We combined our classes today so half the teachers could join the search parties. I just stayed out here after the search moved on so I could be morose in private." She glanced at her watch and sighed. "School day's almost over now, anyway. And I've got a meeting to organize a vigil for KJ in an hour.

"I guess it'll be a vigil for Nora, too, now," she said sadly. "I haven't heard any good news; have you?"

"No, I'm sad to say," Annie said on a sigh as she took a seat on the step below her friend. "Unfortunately, good news is seldom my business."

"I don't know how you stand it, Annie. I'm sick one minute and crying the next. If I manage for a second to stop thinking about somebody killing that poor little boy, my head is filled with what could be happening to Nora Florette at the hands of some maniac. The world is an evil place."

"True dat," Annie said. "It's also a place where people give money to GoFundMe campaigns for someone they've never met or barely know and take time off work to beat the bushes in search of a child not their own. You have to hang on to that."

"I suppose so," Jaime conceded. She looked out across the expanse of the park. "You should have seen this place a couple of hours ago. Hundreds of people came out. Young, old, kids from the junior high school on their study hall breaks. A lot of them moved on to other search locations after they were done here."

"Did you happen to see Dean Florette, by any chance?"

"No." She gave Annie a look. "Please don't tell me he's missing, too."

"I saw him this morning at the house, but he's gone now. I need to ask him some questions about that day."

"Maybe he's at one of the other searches," Jaime suggested. "I did see that other boy—that redheaded boy who was out here yesterday with Lola and Dean."

"Cameron Spicer?"

"Is that his name? Spicer? Oh!" she exclaimed as realization dawned. "Is his mother Sharon Spicer?"

"Do you know her?"

"No, not really, but she introduced herself to everyone at the last PTA meeting. She's engaged to the sheriff. She made sure everyone knew that." Her mouth curved into a brief, small frown. "That sounded unkind. She volunteered straightaway for two committees. It's women like her that keep these organizations running like Swiss trains."

Women like her. The always-put-together, terribly efficient, frighteningly organized women who ran Bayou Breaux society, from bake sales to Mardi Gras charity balls. No one ever imagined their lives might not be perfect.

"I want to walk the route those kids took home that day," Annie said, getting to her feet again. "Do you have time to walk with me?"

"Sure."

They fell in step, headed across the grass for the paved path.

"Is it true Genevieve murdered a baby when she was younger?" Jaime asked.

"I'd like to know who leaked that bit of information," Annie muttered. "She claims the baby just died. The coroner says that the baby was suffocated. She did time for it in Ware up in Coushatta."

"Oh, my . . . It's not the first time I've heard a story like that, working with CASA. A teenage mom with no support gets overwhelmed by her situation . . . So sad. And here she is, years later—"

"—a young mother with no support," Annie said, "overwhelmed by her situation . . ."

Jaime gave her a long, serious look. "You think she killed him?"

"It's not my job to draw conclusions. I just collect the facts."

"Genevieve told me that KJ was wound up that night," she said. "She said he kept repeating *I won't tell, I won't tell* over and over. Do you have any idea what that might be about? Did anything happen in school that day?"

"No. It was a normal school day. He was fine."

"You know the Florettes. Do you think Dean could have done something to Nora?" Annie asked, watching her friend from the corner of her eye.

She would want to say no, Annie knew, because Jaime wanted to think the best of all children. But she hesitated to answer, and worry creased her forehead.

"I can't say no," she admitted grimly. "Do you think he might have hurt Nora, and KJ saw him?"

"I have to consider the possibility."

"But you can't think Dean killed him!"

Annie said nothing for a moment, just letting the possibilities hang in the air. Finally, she said, "You've worked in the juvenile court system how long?"

"Long enough to know better," Jaime admitted. "This story isn't going to end well, is it?"

"No matter what, the best we can hope for is justice."

They walked in silence for a moment. Annie scanned the path and the woods on either side, imagining the kids walking home that day, as they did every day. Nothing would have seemed remarkable. No one ever got up in the morning thinking their life would change dramatically before the day was out—especially not children. They lived in the moment, never thinking the moment could end abruptly and permanently.

Jaime had stopped on the path. Annie looked back to find her staring off to the right, into the woods, frowning.

"What is it?" Annie asked, thinking it couldn't have been anything. By Jaime's own accounting, hundreds of people had walked every inch of this park just a few hours prior.

"I'm not sure," Jaime said, heading cautiously toward the trees. "I thought I saw something."

Annie followed, a sick sense of anticipation building in her chest. Could this be the one spot the searchers had missed? Had someone looked right in the split second they needed to look left? Was it possible Nora Florette had been lying here the whole time, within a few feet of the many people who walked on this path every day?

Enough of the afternoon was gone that the light under the thick canopy of the trees was like twilight, dim and diffuse, like the light in a dream. Jaime picked her way through the fallen leaves, going toward something Annie had yet to see.

And then she stopped, and her scream split the thick, still air like a knife.

"CAMERON?" SHARON CALLED as she entered the house from the garage.

She stopped in her immaculate laundry room to unload the detergent from her grocery bag, puzzling again over how quickly they had gone through the last bottle. She was going to have to talk to her son about doing his own laundry. As busy as she was with all the committee work she had taken on, she was grateful Cameron was taking responsibility for his own things, but it seemed he had to be washing one item at a time instead of waiting until he had a proper load to run the machine.

Children. They didn't realize the value of anything because they hadn't had to earn the money to pay for it. She would have to make sure he understood not to be wasteful before he went to spend time with her parents. She couldn't have him be a burden on them.

Her father would be reluctant to say yes to this idea anyway. He was a stern man who believed a person should stand on his or her own two feet and that once you made your bed, you had to lie in it.

Sharon was dreading making the phone call. All day she had gone around and around in her head as to what she was going to say. How could she spin it in a positive light? She would have to somewhat explain the situation to her mother. She would tell her Cameron was having trouble adjusting to the new school. She would say that, what with making the wedding plans and all, and getting established in the community, she was overburdened. And with all of Kelvin's responsibilities with these recent crimes, now was not the time for him to take on the added responsibility of establishing himself as a father to a teenage boy.

She had just outright lied to the junior high principal, telling him she had a serious female health issue to deal with in the coming months, and it would be best for Cameron to go spend that time with his grandparents. She would tell the principal at Cameron's old school in Houma the same thing.

"Cameron?" she called again as she went into the kitchen and placed the grocery bag on the counter.

It was unwieldy, trying to unload and put away groceries using only one arm, and her other hand hurt from striking Detective Broussard. Now, hours after the fact, the memory of that seemed unreal, like something from a bad dream. But the redness and swelling on her right hand gave lie to the theory of a dream. And every time she admitted that, waves of shame and fear rolled through her.

To have someone think that Kelvin had abused her brought a crushing sense of embarrassment. Wondering what the detective would do with that suspicion made her sick with anxiety. And what would Kelvin do if he found out about Detective Broussard's visit that morning?

"Cameron?" she called again, her anxiety rising.

Cameron could have been helping her. Instead, he was in the family room watching television. She could hear the TV mumbling away. Irritated, she wiped her hands on a dish towel and started toward the front of the house. He wasn't supposed to be watching television this time of day. She had expected him to stay in his room, reading, if he wasn't going to go to school.

Ready to snap at him, she poked her head into the family room, expecting to see him on the sofa, but he wasn't there. So irresponsible, leaving the television on! She really was going to have to sit him down and talk to him about courtesy and respect.

She turned around and marched down the hall toward his bedroom, glancing out the side door as she went to make sure he wasn't out by the pool.

"Cameron Spicer, you answer me this minute!" she demanded, banging on his door.

He didn't answer.

"I'm coming in!" she shouted, her temper ready to boil over.

She opened the door and burst into the room, drawing breath to light into him.

The room was empty. The bed was neatly made.

He had written on the mirror above his dresser in marker: I DON'T WANT TO BE HERE!!!

ANNIE SAW THE shoe first. The sole of a sneaker sticking out from under a pile of brush.

Jaime had stopped dead in her tracks. She turned and looked at Annie, her face a pale mask of horror.

Yanking her phone off her belt as she went, Annie ran. She fumbled to punch 911 with one hand even as she tried to clear the brush and leaves and limbs away with her other hand.

"Partout Parish Emergency Services—"

"This is Detective Broussard with the Sheriff's Office. I need an ambulance ASAP to Lafayette Park. I have an individual down and unresponsive, located in the woods about halfway down the main walking path. Tell them to hurry!"

She didn't wait for a response, shoving the phone back onto her belt so she could use both hands to uncover the victim. Heart racing, she tried to sort the information she was taking in through her eyes at the same time another part of her brain was asking questions. Was it Nora? How long had she been here? Could she still be alive?

"Oh, my God!" Jaime cried, rushing up. "Is it Nora?"

"It's a boy," Annie said.

A boy's shoes, sweatpants smeared with dirt, hands battered from a fight.

As she uncovered the face, Jaime screamed again and ran backward, doubled over as if in pain.

The image hit Annie like a hammer to the head, stunning her. Her knees went weak and her head swam.

There was no face. There was blood and tissue, shards of bone and lumps of brain matter. And resting in the center of the mass was a jagged rock the size of a brick.

Annie sank to the ground on her knees and sat back on her heels, drenched in sweat yet cold and trembling. Thinking, as a siren wailed in the distance, that there was no need. There was no hurry. Someone's child would not be going home tonight, and she didn't even know whose.

I DON'T WANT TO BE HERE!!!

Sharon stared at the writing, trying to muster some anger toward Cameron for writing on the mirror. That emotion would have felt better than the feeling that was stirring inside her. She recognized it as fear and tried to talk herself out of it, scolding herself for being ridiculous.

Of course Cameron was here. She simply hadn't found him yet. He was probably on the patio and she just hadn't seen him. But her heart was beating a little faster as she left his bedroom and let herself out the patio door.

The air was still and thick. The sky was a strange color to the south, like a yellow-tinged bruise stacked with mountainous clouds. There had been talk all day of a storm coming. She rushed to dismiss the oddly fanciful notion that she could feel the storm building in her chest. It wasn't like her to be so dramatic.

"Cameron!" she called, looking left and right.

No answer. There seemed to be no sound at all. No distant sounds of traffic or of the neighbors' children. No birdsong or rustling of the marsh grass that grew along the bank down by the boat dock.

"Cameron!"

The silence pressed in on her eardrums like cotton wool until she could hear her own pulse—*whoosh, whoosh, whoosh, whoosh* . . .

Maybe he had gone to a friend's house—

He didn't have any friends she could name.

She should call him—

Kelvin had taken his phone.

Fighting the growing sense of panic that swelled in the base of her throat, she went back inside and went to the family room to turn off the television. She had to think of what to do. She needed a plan. She would feel calmer if she had a plan.

Maybe he had walked to the Quik Pik.

Maybe he had gone to the public library since Kelvin had taken his iPad and he had no other way to get on the Internet. He wasn't allowed to use her laptop, and he didn't know any of the passwords even if he tried to use it behind her back.

As she walked into the family room, a sliver of light caught her attention from the corner of her eye, from the foyer. Someone had left the front door ajar.

"Oh, for heaven's sake, Cameron!" she said out loud as she went to pull it shut. "How many times do I have to tell you to be sure to close the door?"

As she came back, she stopped short halfway across the family room and stared at the lovely flat-screen television that hung on the wall.

A local station was showing breaking news from a scene in Bayou Breaux. The Florette girl, Sharon thought. They must have found the

Florette girl—exactly the way she had expected they would. Dead in the woods.

She spotted Detective Broussard with several other people on the far side of a ribbon of yellow crime scene tape.

And then her eyes focused on the Breaking News headline at the bottom of the screen—*Body of Boy Found in Lafayette Park*—and the bottom dropped out of her world.

FORTY-THREE

The scene was barely contained chaos. Nick blasted the horn, trying to scatter the people on foot as he drove across the park. He needed to get as near as possible to the perimeter of the crime scene. Dirty looks were shot in his direction, expressions changing instantly at the red-and-blue strobe light running on the dash of the Jeep.

The call-out for the ambulance had been picked up by the local news outlets on their scanners, and the reporters, already in town for the Nora Florette search, had instantly bolted for Lafayette Park—some of them no doubt getting there ahead of the deputies who had been dispatched. Camera trucks had parked helter-skelter in the open areas, satellite dishes raised to search the sky for a good signal.

Volunteers from the Florette search were rushing across the grass to join the small crowd already gathered at the edge of the woods. A lone deputy stood with his arms raised, trying to hold the mob at bay.

Nick blasted the horn again, narrowly missing a videographer who didn't want to get out of his way. He slammed on the brakes as he rolled up on the deputy—a fresh-faced kid who looked overwhelmed by the crowd descending on him.

The shouting began before he could even open the door of the vehicle.

"Detective Fourcade! Detective Fourcade!"

"Has the body been identified?"

"Is there a serial killer?"

"Is there a cause of death?"

Nick ignored them, his focus on the scene before him. Someone had managed to get a line of crime scene tape up between a couple of trees to hold off the onlookers. Some distance beyond it, he could see Annie standing with her arms wrapped around herself as if she was freezing. A few feet away, Jaime Blynn sat on a stump, sobbing.

He ducked under the tape, and as he neared the area, his attention went first to the body on the ground. Even in the fading light he could tell the death had been horrific, brutal. Violent well beyond what had been necessary to cause death, this had been a killer in a frenzy, filled with rage and unleashing every ounce of it on the victim. It was the same thought he had had standing over the body of KJ Gauthier.

He took in the sneakers, the dirty sweatpants. A boy, he thought, though in this light it wasn't obvious.

"Mon Dieu," he muttered on a long, sad sigh.

"Are you here in your official capacity, or just for moral support?" Annie asked, her voice shaky and thin.

"That depends on who you ask," he said, turning toward her. She was as pale as milk and trembling visibly. "Are you all right?"

She shook her head, tears welling. "No. No, I'm not."

"Come here," he murmured, reaching for her.

"Nick, there are people—"

"Fuck 'em," he said, drawing her close.

"I'm gonna lose it," she warned, hanging on to him as if she might otherwise be sucked up into the universe.

"No, you're not," Nick told her. "Not here, not now. You're gonna take a couple deep breaths and pull it together, 'cause that dead boy needs you, yeah?"

She took a step back, gripping his forearms hard as she sucked in a lungful of air and visibly worked to compose herself.

"Do you know who this is?" Nick asked.

"How can I say? I can't even tell what color the hair is!" she snapped.

"There were hundreds of people here for the search earlier. It could be one of them. I came here looking for Dean Florette. I didn't find him. Jaime says she saw Cameron Spicer earlier. I don't know where he is now. And I sure as hell don't understand why anyone would do this! Why would anyone do this?"

"I don't know. We'll figure it out."

"I don't know if I want to find out what's in the head of a person who could do that."

There would be a reason, Nick knew. When they finally caught the person responsible, there would be a reason and a logic system that had arrived at that terrible choice, and it would make perfect, terrible sense. But in this moment, it made no sense to anyone. Least of all, he imagined, to the second-grade teacher sitting on a stump a few feet away.

"Do you want to take Jaime home, or do you want to stay?"

Annie took another deep breath and blew it out, putting her game face back on. "I'm staying."

"Good."

He gave her shoulder a squeeze and then turned to the teacher and knelt in front of her.

"Jaime, I'm gonna have a deputy take you home, all right?"

"Thank you," she managed, sniffling.

"Do you think is Reg home yet?"

"I don't know. I hope so."

"I'll have the deputy stay with you until he gets there," Nick said, patting her hand. "I'm sorry you had to see that, Jaime."

"I don't understand people anymore," she said, tears welling anew. "What kind of monster does that?"

"Leave it to us to figure that out," Nick said, offering her a hand and drawing her to her feet as he rose. "You go home and hug your children."

As several more deputies arrived, he tagged one to see Jaime Blynn home. Annie tasked the others with finishing securing the perimeter and keeping the reporters at bay.

The media hounds were baying for information. The illumination provided by their light stands was harsh and glaring. He had to squint hard, looking at them while it was growing darker by the minute under the cover of the trees. He contemplated commandeering their lights for his own purposes around the crime scene.

As he thought it, a siren *whoop-whoop*ed and the crime scene van pulled into view, followed by Dutrow's Suburban.

Dutrow was mobbed as he tried to leave his vehicle. He stood on the running board, holding onto the door like a shield as he called for deputies to clear his way through the crowd as the reporters shouted questions at him.

No one bothered Kemp. He cut straight for the crime scene, leaving his underlings to pull equipment off the van. Nick marched toward the barrier to head him off.

"What are you doing here, Fourcade?" Kemp asked, making a face as if he'd just bitten into something sour. "Shouldn't you be home filling out your paperwork for unemployment benefits?"

"We need lights," Nick said. "How many have you got in that toy truck?"

"I don't take orders from you."

"Fine. I'll get them myself. Stay away from my crime scene." He turned to the two nearest deputies and called out, "Wilson! Rodrigue! I need standing lights back here! And hurry up! There's rain coming! Let's get a pop-up tent back here, too. Check the crime scene van."

"Stay the hell out of my van!" Kemp barked.

Nick sidestepped him and kept walking. Thunder had begun to rumble in the distance. If the wind came up, they stood the chance of losing trace evidence that might have been left on or around the body. If it started to rain, they were in for a miserable evening.

From the corner of his eye he could see they had caught Dutrow's attention, and the sheriff was coming toward them now, his face set in an iron scowl.

Reporters called out to him.

"Sheriff! Sheriff!"

"Is the body Nora Florette?"

"Is it the missing girl?"

"Is Fourcade still on the case?"

Here we go, Nick thought, stopping a dozen feet short of the barrier tape as Dutrow ducked under it.

"Fourcade, what are you doing here?" he demanded, his voice tight and low, his back to the crowd.

"My job," Nick answered calmly, refusing to back up as the sheriff advanced.

Kemp jumped in from the side, furious. "You told me he was gone!"

"Keep your voice down!" Dutrow warned.

"Here's your audience, Sheriff," Nick said, gesturing toward the crowd like a game show host. "You can fire me right here in front of them, and I will walk straight to Kimberly Karstares and tell her the reason you fired me is that I can connect Keith Kemp, your number one crime scene investigator, to Genevieve Gauthier in Houma when you were both in uniforms."

"You son of a bitch!" Kemp wheeled on him. "I told you I don't know that woman!"

"I don't believe you."

"You're calling me a liar?"

Nick shrugged. "You are what you are. It makes no matter. Lie all you want. Me, I have the truth in my pocket."

As Kemp went to lunge at him, Dutrow put himself between them, grabbing hold of Keith Kemp with both hands, pushing him a step backward. Behind them, the television cameras and still cameras were jockeying for position, and the reporters were shouting questions like a pack of barking dogs.

"Go back to the van!" Dutrow ordered, his face inches from Kemp's.

Kemp's eyes bugged out. "You're gonna let him get away with this? What the fuck—?"

"Let it go!" Dutrow growled, driving him backward.

Kemp leaned around him, jabbing a finger at Nick like a spear. "Fuck you, Fourcade! You don't threaten me and get away with it!"

Nick followed them step by step, ever just barely out of reach of Keith Kemp. "If the truth is a threat to you, Keith, you're in the wrong line of work. But then I don't suppose either of you want the general public knowing that the reason Mr. Kemp here no longer carries a badge is that he was trading criminal charges for sex back then."

"That's a damn lie, you coonass son of a bitch!" Kemp shouted, trying to jump around Dutrow to get at Nick.

Nick arched a brow. "Really? Chief Irvin is a liar? I'm sure he'll be disappointed to hear that you said so, Keith."

Kemp tried one last time to lunge around Dutrow. The sheriff, a bigger, stronger man, wrapped his arms around Kemp and shoved him backward like a tackling dummy, toward the barrier tape and the mob beyond. "Get in the goddamn van and keep your mouth shut!"

As Dutrow let go, Kemp stumbled and fell under the tape. He came back up to his feet on the other side, livid and red-faced, shouting without a care for the reporters recording the spectacle.

"Fuck this shit!" he shouted, backing toward the van. "You're gonna pay, Fourcade!"

As he reached the vehicle, he turned around and walked right past it, and kept on walking.

Nick watched him dispassionately, thinking about the amount of rage contained in Keith Kemp, wondering just how far that rage might push him. The police chief in Houma had confessed to Gus Noblier that there had been some rumors at the time. An accusation had been made. Kemp had resigned not long after he had written up Genevieve Gauthier for a DUI, and possession charges against her had mysteriously disappeared.

"That was a mistake," Genevieve had told Nick. Nine months later she had given birth to a baby boy.

"Your career is over, Fourcade," Dutrow said. He stood so close Nick could smell his mouthwash. He could see where he had nicked his chin shaving and tried to hide the cut with makeup.

"I think not," Nick said quietly. "There's no way you didn't know about Kemp, yet you brought him here, just the same. Now a woman he had a history with is attacked, her little boy is killed, and you send him to the crime scene to collect the evidence? That is not gonna look good on your résumé, Kelvin.

"Now, if you'll excuse me," he said, taking a step back. "I have a homicide to deal with."

* * *

Sharon's heart was racing as she drove up over the curb and into Lafayette Park, her car bucking like a horse. There were vehicles everywhere, parked haphazardly and abandoned. She could see the harsh glow
of artificial lights off to one side of the walking path fifty yards ahead.
She could see the gathered crowd of people swarming like insects around
the light.

A deputy appeared in front of her, waving his arms, yelling at her to
stop.

She hit the brakes, slammed the car into Park, and fell out of the
vehicle onto her hands and knees on the grass. Her injured arm buckled
beneath her, the pain shooting through her like white-hot electricity.

"Ma'am! We don't need any more people down there," the deputy
said, coming toward her. "We're trying to contain the scene."

Sobbing, her left arm held tight against her body, Sharon scrambled
to her feet. The deputy was still talking. She couldn't hear him over the
pulse roaring in her ears, and she didn't care. He reached for her as she
tried to hurry past him, grabbing her by the shoulder. She cried out and
wrenched herself from his grasp, trying to run, stumbling, and somehow getting her feet back under her.

"Cameron! Cameron!" she screamed, running toward the crowd.

She couldn't find her son.

A body had been found in the park he walked through every day.

Panic rose with bile in her throat.

I DON'T WANT TO BE HERE.

What if he had killed himself? What if that was what he had
meant—that he didn't want to be *here*, in this life?

She thought of him standing in the rain at the edge of the swimming
pool in the middle of the night.

What if he had meant to step into the pool and drown?

She thought of him standing in the kitchen this morning, sobbing.

She had promised to make everything all right.

There was a dead body in the park.

He had left the front door open . . .

"Cameron! Cameron!"

People on the fringe of the crowd were turning to look at her as if she were a crazy person. She didn't care.

Kelvin's vehicle was parked just behind the mob. If she could get to him, she could get an answer. He would be in charge. He would know what to do.

"Cameron! Cameron!"

She pushed her way through the crowd, not caring about manners, not worrying what anyone would think. She felt just this side of wild, acting on instinct. As she wedged her way through the people, she caught a glimpse of Kelvin on the other side of the crime scene tape, the picture of authority as he gave orders to one of his people.

"Kelvin!" she called, pushing her way to the front of the crowd.

He looked right at her, his expression a mix of shock and annoyance.

"Kelvin!" she sobbed. "Kelvin, help! I can't find Cameron! I can't find him!"

He came toward her, scowling, ignoring the garbled cacophony of questions being shouted by the reporters.

"What are you doing here?" he asked, taking hold of her upper arm and drawing her with him, under the crime scene tape, away from the mob. Beyond him she could see deputies and other people milling around an area set off by several bright, freestanding lights.

"I can't find Cameron!" she cried, stumbling as she tried to keep up with his long strides. "I'm afraid! I saw the news on TV—about a body in the park. Is it him? Is he dead?" she asked as the hysteria rose within. "Oh, my God, is it him?"

Kelvin leaned in close, his grip tightening on her arm. "Stop it!" he snapped, close to her ear. "Get hold of yourself, for God's sake!"

"Tell me!" she demanded, the fear reaching around her throat like a hand, choking her. Pressure built in her head until she thought it would explode.

Kelvin looked down at her with disdain and disgust, this man who was supposed to love her and care about her.

"Tell me!" she shouted.

"I don't know!"

"You don't care!" she said. "You wanted him gone anyway!"

She looked toward the deputies and saw Detective Broussard. They were gathered around the body.

Sharon thought she might vomit at the idea that this could be her son on the ground, dead. She should never have left Cameron alone. She should never have told him she was sending him away. What kind of mother sent her child away because of a man?

"I have to see him," she said, trying to pull free.

"Sharon, no!" Kelvin said, holding on to her.

Detective Broussard was coming toward them, looking concerned.

"I have to see him!" Sharon said again, trying to pull back out of his grip.

"No!" Kelvin grabbed her by both shoulders so hard she thought her bones might snap. "I can't let you!"

"Let me go!" She looked to Detective Broussard. "Is it Cameron? I have to see him!"

"We don't know who it is," she said.

"It's not Cameron?"

The look on her face made a chill go through Sharon—carefully arranged neutrality meant not to give away bad news. But she could see in Broussard's eyes the truth was something terrible, something hideous.

"We can't tell who it is," she said carefully.

"I know my own child!" Sharon shouted. "Let me see him!"

"Sharon, no!" Kelvin snapped. "Stop this right now!"

She turned back on him, her face twisting at the bitterness of the truth. "This is your fault! If it's Cameron, this is your fault! You never wanted him!"

Furious, he turned so his back was to the crowd and she was hidden from their view. They couldn't see the vicious look on his face or see the hysterical woman who was embarrassing him.

"Let go of her!" Detective Broussard ordered as she tried to wedge herself between them. "I'll take care of her."

As Kelvin let go, Sharon fell into the detective, who embraced her and walked her away from Kelvin's anger and away from the bright lights and the onlookers.

She felt limp, spent, her body just a sack of bones and tears.

"Here, sit," the detective told her, helping her ease down onto a tree stump.

"Sharon, why do you think this might be Cameron?" the detective asked her, kneeling down in front of her.

Sharon looked at her, at her swollen lip, remembering their encounter that morning like a strange bad dream. If she said nothing about it, maybe it wouldn't be true.

"Have you checked with Cameron's friends to make sure he isn't with any of them?"

"He doesn't have any friends," she murmured.

She should have tried to help him with that, she thought. She should have enrolled him in some activities where he might have better fit in instead of giving in to Kelvin's insistence that he play football. None of this would be happening if she had done that.

In an instant, every mistake she had ever made ran through her mind like a movie on fast-forward. She hadn't done enough to protect Cameron. Even in her effort to save him from a father who didn't love him, she had saved herself first. And in her effort to get him a better man for a role model, she had thought first of herself and what she thought she wanted, and what she wanted people who didn't matter to think of her. Now she had lost everything, and Cameron had lost everything.

"Please let me see him," she begged, hanging onto the detective's arm.

"I'm sorry. I can't," Detective Broussard said. "I can't tell you it's Cameron, and I can't tell you it's not, and I can't let you look, Sharon. I'm really sorry."

"What color is his hair? I would know by his hair."

"It's . . . It's too dark to tell."

"You're lying," Sharon said. She could feel it, just like she could feel the dread certainty that her son was gone. "Did he kill himself? Is that why you're not telling me?"

"Why would you ask that?"

"Because he didn't want to be here," she murmured as she started to cry. "He didn't want to be here, and now he's gone."

FORTY-FOUR

He watched from a distance, up in the branches of an oak tree, hidden from view and sheltered from the weather as the rain began to fall in big, fat drops. He watched the people below with a sense of unreality, like he was watching a movie from across the street.

At first there had been just the body, hidden from view. Then the body and the two women. Then the body and the two women and a sheriff's deputy. Then the others began to arrive in cars and on foot, all in a hurry. The crowd swelled, people put up lights around the body, and then a white pop-up tent over the body. Then the rain had begun to fall, and the crowd got smaller, and the cars left. A hearse carted the body away.

And then there was no one, and no lights, and he was alone, floating in space, feeling numb and empty. He didn't think about how good it had felt to pound that rock over and over and over. He didn't think about stupid Nora or Vanessa Theriot, or anything else he had done. None of that seemed any more real than photographs in a magazine or pages in a storybook. It was all just a bad dream.

The storm was coming harder as he dropped out of the tree. Thunder rumbled, lightning flashed, the wind came up. He walked out of the woods and stood on the path and let the rain flow over him and wash away the blood.

After a while, drenched to the bone, he started walking.

FORTY-FIVE

Genevieve stood at the back of the TV room, clinging to the doorframe, watching the news coverage. A body had been found in the park near the schools. She wondered if it was Nora. She wondered how long the body had been there. Days had gone by since anyone had seen her, not that anyone in the Florette household would have noticed or cared.

She couldn't even imagine Jojean crying about it.

Had she cried for KJ today? She couldn't remember. She was so tired. She felt so stressed, like she was being crushed by the weight of it all.

Two other residents of the women's shelter sat right up by the television, glued to the scene. One turned to the other and said, "I'd lose my mind if someone murdered my child."

They both cut surreptitious glances at Genevieve.

She backed out of the room and wandered down the hall.

The shelter was a big Victorian house on a corner lot in an old neighborhood a block from the bayou. Conveniently located for suicide, Genevieve thought. Evangeline House, it was called. No relation to Evangeline Oaks Center for Assisted Living—just one of many businesses in Acadiana to take its name from the tragic story of star-crossed lovers. Everything from dry cleaners to bakeries to mortuaries bore the name. First penned as an epic poem by Longfellow, the story had been absorbed into Cajun culture and retold in various forms, all of them ending in madness, death, or suicide. The name seemed especially ironic for this house, considering the residence was for women whose husbands and lovers beat them.

A tall, redheaded female sheriff's detective had brought her to the house late in the day. A staff member had seen her to a bedroom, promising to introduce her to the other women at dinner. Genevieve had stayed in her room, pretending to sleep. She didn't want to meet anyone. She didn't want to see the judgment in their eyes. Now that the story was out, people would judge her for the death of her baby all those years ago. They would look at her with suspicion and wonder if she had killed KJ, too.

Thunder rumbled, subtly rattling the windows as she went into the front room of the house, an old-fashioned parlor with heavy, formal antique furniture and heavy, elaborate draperies framing the bay window. A single lamp burned in the otherwise dark room. She settled into a rocking chair in the window alcove and pulled her cell phone out of the pocket of the sweatpants that had been provided for her. She went to her contacts and punched Jeff's number.

The call went straight to voicemail. She tried the office number, negotiating the automated system to Jeff's extension, which also went to his voicemail. Either he didn't want to talk to her, or he was spending the evening at home with his wife and family. She didn't know which answer was worse.

She felt so empty, so alone. She didn't want to be here. She didn't want to be at this house. She didn't want to be in this town. She thought about taking her GoFundMe money and just leaving. She could go start over someplace new, someplace where nobody knew her as anything other than a young, single woman with her whole life ahead of her.

If her whole life was ahead of her, why did she feel like she was at the end?

If I die young . . . The song drifted through her head like a warm, seductive night breeze.

* * *

"Genevieve?"

She jumped at the sound of his voice, coming back into the present from some deep thought, her good eye going wide at the sight of him. She flinched as lightning flashed brightly in the big bay window.

"I'm sorry to startle you," Nick said quietly as he walked into the room. "I have a few more questions for you."

"I'm tired," she said, her voice barely more than a whisper. "I really don't want to talk anymore today."

"It won't take long, but it's important that you answer me," he said, drawing a chair directly in front of hers. He sat and leaned forward, his forearms on his thighs, his knees just a few inches from hers.

Trapped, she sat back and watched him, frowning.

"Who died in the park?" she asked. "Was it Nora?"

"We don't know yet."

He had left Annie in charge of the corpse, as much as he would rather not have, for her sake. As her husband, he would have spared her. As her superior, he had to make the smartest choice. She was working the disappearance of the Florette girl. She already knew the girl's friends and their families. If the deceased was from among that group, she had already established relationships that would be useful in the investigation.

"I wish I'd never come here," Genevieve said. "There's evil in this place."

"Evil doesn't live in a place," Nick corrected her. "Evil resides in the souls of men—and women. It is a uniquely human attribute. But I'm guessing you might already know that from hard experience.

"Why did you come here, Genevieve?" he asked.

"I told you. I needed a job."

"You had a job. Why did you leave it?"

She looked away from him. "It wasn't working out. I needed to move on."

Stokes had reported to him that the dentist Genevieve had worked for in Dulac had all the makings of another Jeff Avery—a reasonably attractive, pleasant man with a good job and a comfortable lifestyle . . . and a wife and a couple of kids . . . He had given Genevieve a glowing review and claimed he didn't really know why she had left.

"Why you didn't get a job in Houma, then?" Nick asked. "It's a bigger town, more opportunities."

"I came to take a job to be near Aunt Clarice."

"She's not your aunt, though, is she, *cher*?"

She meant to look surprised at his question, but he could sense the panic. "Why would you say that? Of course she's my aunt!"

"Because the office at Evangeline Oaks had only the names of a niece and nephew of Mrs. Marcel's late husband listed as next of kin. There was no mention of you."

"Well, she's not a blood relative," she said, scrambling for an explanation. "But she knew my mother, and I always called her Aunt Clarice. And I just thought it would be nice to be near her—"

"No," Nick insisted gently. "You didn't come here to get a job emptying bedpans so you could be close to your aunt Clarice. You applied for a job at the Sheriff's Office last spring, before you ever went near Evangeline Oaks."

"What of it? That would have been a good job, too. That's just not the job I ended up with," she said. "Being an aide was only temporary, anyway. Mr. Avery is going to move me into the office, so it all works out."

Of course, it wouldn't work out. Jeff Avery would have to let her go, both as an employee and as a lover. He would choose his family, beg his wife's forgiveness, and hope to God his bosses never caught wind of the amateur porn video that would live forever on the Internet. He would save his own hide, and Genevieve would be left to fend for herself. Nick chose not to say so. He chose not to tell her about the cameras Roy Carville and Roddie Perez had hidden in her home—for now. That bad news would serve no purpose tonight.

"Genevieve, I'm not judging you for any of that," he said. "You've had a hard life, and you're just trying to do the best you can, however you can, however misguided your choices may be. Me, I'm just trying to get to the truth."

"You think I killed my son," she said, tears rising in her eyes.

"I never said that, but I have to wonder, and I have to ask. That's my job. I know from experience the truth is not always pretty. It's often not what we want it to be at all."

"No," she murmured, glancing away, blinking as the lightning flashed again. "It isn't."

He let the silence hang for a moment as she lost herself in thought. Looking back on her own truth, he imagined, and not liking what she saw. Mistake after mistake. Wrong choice after wrong choice.

She knew what she wanted—a home, a family, a man to love her and value her. It just seemed she could never get there. She was always on the wrong side of the glass, looking in. It remained to be seen if she had done something terrible to her son to ease a burden from her life. Plenty of people would judge her harshly for the choices she had made. But Nick didn't see malice in her. He saw a yawning chasm of need. Ultimately, she only wanted what every living soul wanted—to be loved.

"Genevieve, does the name Keith Kemp mean anything to you?" he asked, dragging her back from her thoughts.

"No."

"Eight years ago, when you were stopped for driving under the influence, Keith Kemp was the officer who wrote you up. You don't remember that?"

"No," she insisted. "But I was drunk at the time, wasn't I?"

"Were you? Were you that drunk? The arrest report put you at barely over the legal limit. Tipsy, I would say. You were a long way from blacking out."

"It was a long time ago. I just don't remember, that's all."

"You were what? Nineteen? You'd been out of jail a few months? A year, at most. You'd been drinking. You weren't supposed to be drinking, were you?" he said. "That's a parole violation. And you were under-age to boot. You must have been scared, getting pulled over like that—in the dead of night, I'm guessing, yeah?"

She refused to look at him, pretending instead to look out the window.

"Is there a point to this?" she asked. "I'm so tired."

"Genevieve, the man who arrested you that night was forced to resign from that department not long after. There were allegations made against him that he was trading criminal charges for sex. He would, for instance, pull over a young woman who may have had too much to drink, and in exchange for sex, he would maybe look the other way or conveniently forget he might have seen some drugs in the car and settle on a lesser charge."

The idea sickened him. A man in a position of power taking advantage of someone vulnerable disgusted him. The idea went against every reason he had gone into law enforcement in the first place. But that was the yin and yang of the job. It attracted people for all the right reasons, and all the wrong reasons, depending on the individual.

It disgusted him even further that Kemp had paid no price other than giving up his badge. No charges had been filed against him. He had been allowed to resign, and his chief had hired him back to work as a crime scene investigator.

"Is that what happened to you, Genevieve?" he asked. "Is that why that possession charge disappeared? Did you feel you had to make a deal with the devil that night?"

She said nothing. If she could have turned her back to him, she would have. Instead, she continued to stare out the window at the darkness. A single tear trickled down from the corner of her eye.

"Genevieve," he said softly, "if that happened to you, that's not okay. What he did was a crime. It was wrong in every possible way, and he should have gone to prison for it. He still could. I would be happy to see to it. All you have to do is tell me the truth."

"That's not what happened," she whispered. Another tear fell. She reached up to wipe it away with a trembling hand.

"Tell me, then."

"I can't," she said, her voice barely audible. She turned her face as far from him as she could.

Nick leaned forward and took her hand, small and frail and as cold as ice. "Genevieve, look at me. Look at me," he commanded gently. "Please."

She looked at him from the corner of her eye like a skittish wild deer, ready to bolt. She looked down at his hand enfolding hers. She didn't pull away.

"You said last night I need to be your hero," Nick reminded her. "I'll be your hero, Genevieve, but you have to trust me, and you have to tell me the truth."

* * *

GENEVIEVE LOOKED DOWN at the detective's hand covering hers. He was strong and handsome, but he frightened her with his directness and with the intensity of his dark stare. She felt like he could see straight through her, straight through any lie she might tell. He made her feel naked and vulnerable. She was alone and afraid. She had no one . . . except this man reaching out to hold her hand, telling her he would believe her truth if only she would tell him. And it wouldn't matter to him if it wasn't a beautiful story. He didn't care that she had made mistakes. He only wanted the truth, whatever that was.

She had spent so many years trying to hide it, ashamed of who she was and what she'd done and what had been done to her. If she told the truth, would it really set her free?

"Tell me, Genevieve," he murmured, squeezing her hand ever so gently. "Tell me your truth."

Fear swelled up in her throat to choke her.

"Trust me," he said. "Take a deep breath and trust me. You've got nothing left to lose."

Nothing left to lose except the fear, and the shame, and the burden . . . unless she couldn't really trust him, in which case, she could lose her life.

The life that had no value. The life she was ready to throw in the bayou and drown . . .

"Tell me," he whispered. "Tell me your truth, Genevieve. For KJ."

She could do this one thing for her son, after all the times she'd let him down.

Squeezing the detective's hand as hard as she could, she took a deep breath, opened her mouth, and told her truth.

FORTY-SIX

Ulysse Wilson had been the funeral director at Evangeline's Rest funeral home for about a hundred years, or so it seemed. He had been Partout Parish coroner for as long as Annie could remember. A small, formal, meticulous man, she had never seen him dressed in anything but a tidy dark suit and a bow tie, ever ready to greet the bereaved.

Maisie Cormier, his assistant for the evening, helped him into his yellow plastic gown, tying the ties in the back with a sense of ceremony. She had come to Bayou Breaux from her native Martinique and was married to a retired marine who worked as a firefighter EMT for the parish. She turned to Annie and offered her a gown.

"Thanks, Maisie. Sorry you had to come out on a night like this."

They had worked in haste at the scene as the storm rolled in, until the pop-up tent had threatened to blow away and the rain had started coming like a hail of bullets. Ulysse had ordered the body loaded into the hearse. Annie hadn't argued. There was no question as to the manner or cause of death. Better to have the body in a controlled environment than to have any trace evidence that might have been on it blow away.

"I'm more sorry for the reason, Annie," Maisie said as Annie tied her ties for her. "It's so sad the cruelty people do to each other."

"Brace yourself for this one," Annie murmured, still shaken herself, recalling her first look at this victim.

The body had already been transferred from the stretcher to the old white porcelain embalming table—left in the body bag due to the severe damage to the head and the fear that what was left of the head might not stay attached while moving it.

The buzzing fluorescent overhead light cast a harsh glow down as Ulysse unzipped the bag and revealed the victim.

Maisie Cormier made a long, low keening sound of pain, as if she'd been gut punched.

"Pauvre bête," she murmured, and she crossed herself and said a prayer in French.

Ulysse waited patiently and crossed himself at the end of the prayer. It was a ritual they had been through together many times. Then they set about their work, Ulysse taking photographs and measurements, Maisie taking notes.

Annie stayed a step back, watching with a sense of unreality, trying to convince her brain this body on the table had once been a person. Witnesses often said when they first spotted a human corpse they thought it had to be a mannequin, that it couldn't be real, even though it was rare to find a mannequin anywhere outside a department store. The mind wanted to reject the idea of death, especially violent death. And the more damaged the body was, the less real it seemed.

As many bodies as Annie had seen over the years, she still didn't want death to be reality—especially when the victim was a young person. It never got easier looking at a young person's body on that slab, knowing everything they could have been would never be and that every life theirs had touched would never be the same.

"Mr. Wilson?" she asked, drawing the coroner's attention. "Could you please run some water through the hair so I can see the color? I have a mother waiting to hear."

She had sent Sharon Spicer home with a deputy and a promise she would call as soon as she knew something. She hoped they had arrived to find Cameron at home and that mother and son were together right now. Which would mean some other mother's son would never see another day. No matter what, Annie would be giving a family devastating news that would change their lives forever.

Maisie set about the task, softly singing a hymn as she turned on the hose and gently washed the blood and bone fragments and brain matter from what was left of the skull. She did the job with love and care, as if this were her own child she was preparing to send on to eternal rest.

Annie watched the blood and dirt and bits of leaves sluice down the drain channels on the table. She watched Maisie's gloved fingers work through the hair, waiting for the color to brighten, waiting for it to turn the red of rust instead of the red of blood.

According to his mother, Cameron Spicer was suicidal. He was fourteen and sick of a world that bullied him every day. She thought back to the look of misery on Cameron's face as Dean Florette had called him names and laughed at him. She thought back to the night before and the abject terror in the boy's expression as Kelvin Dutrow grilled him like a murder suspect because he'd been in the park after school instead of somewhere else.

"You wanted him gone anyway!"

How many times did a child have to have it made clear to him he wasn't wanted, he was a burden, he was a problem, he was a freak, he was a loser, before he decided he didn't want to be in this life anymore?

But she wasn't looking at a suicide here, Annie reminded herself. This was a murder, an act of rage as savage as any she had ever seen.

Maisie Cormier dried a section of the corpse's hair with a clean white towel.

"Brunette," she said, looking at Annie.

Annie stepped closer to look. She would at least be able to relieve Sharon Spicer's fears for the moment. The body did not belong to her son.

Then whose son was this? And who had killed him? And why?

"Detective Broussard?" Ulysse Wilson asked as he pulled something from the pocket of the boy's sweatpants.

A business card.

Annie's business card.

Her heart sank as she took it from the coroner. It was bent and dirty, had been taken from one pocket and put into another.

"*Now here,*" she had said as she handed him the card. "*You take this card, because one of these days that mouth of yours is gonna get your butt in a world of hurt, and you're gonna need someone on your side . . .*"

"Please excuse me," she murmured. "I have to make a phone call."

She turned and left the room, going out into the hallway of the funeral home with its flocked wallpaper and brocade drapes. She went to the end of the hall and sat down in one of the delicate faux-antique French chairs grouped for mourners in front of the window.

The storm was still flashing and booming outside, the rain pouring down. Tears pressed hard against the backs of Annie's eyes, and her hands trembled as she pulled her phone off her belt and entered Sharon Spicer's number.

"It's not Cameron," she said.

She staved off any questions with a promise to come to the house as soon as possible and assurances that law enforcement were already looking for her son.

She ended the call and sat for a moment, trying to compose herself, trying to gather her thoughts and come up with a plan when all she wanted to do was drive to Remy's and hold her son and read him a story and tell herself the lie that she would never be the mother waiting for a phone call in the middle of the night.

Her phone pinged the arrival of a text message. She looked down at it, expecting it to be from Nick, but instead it was from Jojean Florette. Her stomach turned as she read it: *We can't find Dean.*

FORTY-SEVEN

Kelvin watched the replay of the shit show in the park on the computer in his office, frustrated and angry. He should have been notified immediately when the body was found. He could have coordinated the scene, gotten control of the situation before the media and the crowd had arrived.

It wasn't even their jurisdiction. Lafayette Park was city property. But Broussard had found the body and was already working with a detective from the PD on the disappearance of the Florette girl. The jurisdictional lines were already blurred, and she had proceeded to make a worse mess of the situation, failing to lock down the scene, failing to notify him. Things had already been out of control by the time Kelvin had arrived.

Of course, Broussard wouldn't call him, would she? She had called in her superior—her husband. And of course Fourcade hadn't called him. Kelvin had picked up the call on the scanner.

He watched the video, replaying the confrontation between Kemp and the detective, Kelvin wedged between them. It looked like he had no discipline within his own department, like his own men didn't respect him. All those hours of carefully grooming and presenting his image, gone for nothing as he fought to referee the clash of egos between his underlings.

He wanted to kick Kemp's ass all the way back to Houma. The man had a temper and no self-control. That had always been his problem. He could be useful on a leash. Off it, he was trouble, a train wreck looking for a place to crash.

And now Fourcade knew that.

How he had found out, Kelvin didn't know. He had invoked Chief Irvin's name, but Irvin would never have told Fourcade, a stranger, and a stranger under Kelvin's command at that.

It had all been kept very quiet at the time. One woman had complained to Chief Irvin that Kemp had propositioned her during a traffic stop. She happened to be socially connected to people Irvin didn't want to piss off. He had hauled Kemp in and given him the option of resigning, though to Irvin's mind, what Kemp had done in that particular instance hadn't seemed all that bad. He had no problem reassigning Kemp to the crime scene unit, salvaging a career for the man. Irvin didn't know about the other times, the other women. He didn't care to know. He was a man aging into the twilight of his career. The last thing he wanted was controversy.

Kelvin got up and walked away from the computer, trying to be grateful that at least no microphone had picked up Fourcade's voice as he had spoken. Kemp's shouted vulgar threats had come through loud and clear, but those had been easily explained away. The detective was a controversial figure within the department. The media already had their own ideas about Fourcade being a rogue. Kelvin had readily played on that.

And yet, Fourcade's threat of talking to the media himself was a disturbing dark cloud on the horizon. All it would take was for one reporter to want to dig deeper . . .

He walked to his wall of fame and looked at the photographs and commendations and awards. He had worked his whole life to get where he was. He wasn't going to let anyone ruin it for him. Not Fourcade or Kemp or Sharon, for that matter.

Her behavior at the scene had infuriated him. His private life had spilled out of its box, loud and messy and out of control in full view of the public. Sharon's whole purpose in his life was to further his image, and she had done nothing but embarrass him tonight. He should have rejected her as soon as he had met the boy. Now Cameron was missing, no doubt hiding somewhere, unable to cope with Kelvin's punishment for lying to him.

The anger built inside him like a head of steam. Everything he wanted was within his grasp, and now it was all under threat from people not worthy of shining his shoes.

"Impressed with yourself?" Nick asked.

Standing before his ego wall, Dutrow spun around, startled and angry.

"I don't want you in here, Fourcade. You can leave now, or I can have you removed."

Nick walked into the room, seated himself, and squared an ankle over a knee.

"Me, I'll just sit here while you go try to find two men in this department willing to put their hands on me," he said. "Your friend Keith might volunteer. Other than him . . . Good luck to you."

He was furious, Nick could see by the color in his face and the tension in his square jaw. He paced back and forth in front of his photographs and news clippings and plaques from the Chamber of Commerce and the Rotarians. Dutrow would have said the display was something for visitors to look at, but Nick suspected it was really for himself. This was his reminder of who he was supposed to be, the image he had spent his whole career building. The image Nick had every intention of unraveling with the tug of a single thread.

"I will be rid of you," Dutrow warned.

"You will be," Nick agreed, "but not the way you're thinking. I had a long conversation with Genevieve Gauthier tonight. I asked her about your Mr. Kemp."

"I had nothing to do with Kemp's schemes."

"I wouldn't say that, exactly."

"I don't care what you have to say."

"You made use of his particular . . . talent," he said with distaste. "Which makes you no more innocent than he is."

"I don't know what you're talking about," Dutrow said dismissively. He went behind his desk and set about shutting down his computer.

"One could even say you're worse," Nick ventured, "considering Kemp is an animal of base instinctual needs, an impulsive and reactionary creature. You, on the other hand, are calculating and manipulative. You know right from wrong. You just believe yourself to be above the rules of the common man."

"I tire of your armchair psychoanalysis, Fourcade. Get to the point, if there is one."

"KJ Gauthier was your son."

"The hell he was."

Nick ignored the denial. "You know, I thought on it and thought on it, and I couldn't for the life of me understand why Genevieve would move here if Kemp was the father. What would he have to offer her besides the back of his hand? Of course, I understand you're no slouch in that department yourself."

"I have never struck a woman in my life!" Dutrow barked, leaning over the desk.

"Hang your hat on semantics if you want. Abuse isn't always delivered with a fist. I know what you are."

"You don't know anything about me."

"I know you're a small, entitled, angry man who thinks everyone in your life should bow down so you can step on their backs to elevate yourself," Nick said. "I know you won't hesitate now to throw Kemp under the bus for his misuse of power, but you were no better at all. You took advantage of a vulnerable young woman, and when she turned to you in need, you sicced your dog on her."

"That's a fascinating story, and complete fiction."

"Is it?"

"You'd believe the word of a troubled, mentally unstable drug addict who did time for killing her own baby when she was fourteen over me? You're going to be in a very small minority there, Detective."

A bitter smile turned Nick's lips, and he shook his head in disgust. "I wondered how the press had caught wind of that story—a sealed juvenile record."

"They didn't hear it from me."

"Really? And where did you hear it from, Sheriff? You told me you didn't know Genevieve Gauthier. How could you possibly know her story?"

Dutrow's color darkened as he realized his mistake.

"I heard it on the news," he said, far too late to be believed.

"She's a sad, broken little doll, Genevieve. From way back, I think," Nick said. "I don't know why. It doesn't matter why. All she's ever wanted in her whole life is to feel safe and loved. Unfortunate for her she can't pick the right man to save her life. She always picks someone she can't have. She always picks the man who thinks she's good enough to fuck but not good enough to marry.

"*Pauvre bête.* Poor thing, she thought she hit the jackpot with you— big strong pillar of the community. Single, even, at the time. But you didn't want her any more than you wanted a child with her. She was just an easy bang in a back closet at City Hall."

"This is ridiculous," Dutrow grumbled, slamming a desk drawer and locking it with a key.

"You know what's not ridiculous, Kelvin?" Nick asked. "DNA. DNA is sober as a damn judge."

The sheriff pushed to his feet and shut off his desk lamp. "I'm not staying here and listening to any more of this nonsense. Next you'll be spinning a story of how I tried to kill her."

"*Mais non!*" Nick scoffed. "You wouldn't get your hands dirty and ruin your manicure or mess up the crease in your trousers. You'd hire that out, just like you did before."

"You're out of your mind," Dutrow said, going to the door. "But everyone knew that already. Sad to see such a talented detective deteriorate that way. Hopefully, you have some other marketable skills you might use to support your family, because you will never get another job in law enforcement again."

"Maybe you just hired him to scare her, and things got out of hand," Nick said, slowly rising from his chair.

"That's what you did before," he said, moving slowly and deliberately toward the sheriff as Dutrow opened the door to the outer office. "She wanted more from you than you cared to give. You had Kemp follow her home from a bar. He delivered the message—that her freedom could go away on the say-so of a man with a badge.

"Did he tell you he made her kneel down in the gravel and give him a blow job right there where he pulled her over?" he asked, his temper stirring like white-hot coals inside him as he stalked Kelvin Dutrow into the dimly lit, empty outer office. "Or was that part of his payment? Did you even give a shit?"

"All lies," Dutrow said, angling toward the door to the hall. "None of that ever happened. She's playing you."

"Then you won't mind taking that DNA test, will you?"

Nick stepped to his left, deftly cutting off the sheriff's escape route.

Dutrow stepped back and drew his weapon, leveling the Glock 9mm at Nick's chest.

"Oh, that would be convenient, wouldn't it?" Nick asked. "Shoot me in a dark office. You thought I was an intruder."

"Or I knew that you were crazy," Dutrow said. "I fired you. In a fit of rage, you attacked me, and I defended myself."

"That's a good story," Nick said, moving slowly to the left and slightly forward, one step and then another. "You'd better make sure you shoot me in the head, though, 'cause anywhere else you're just gonna piss me off. And then the only story will be mine.

"Do you think you can do that, Kelvin? Do you think your hand is steady enough?" he asked, his unblinking gaze on Dutrow's eyes, reading the emotions—anger, fear, doubt. He took another step to the left and slightly forward, to the left and slightly forward, turning the sheriff in a small, tight circle.

"Stand still!" Dutrow ordered.

"So you can kill me? I think not. I'm not some target on the shooting range. When's the last time you shot a man, Kelvin? A real man. Not counting some pop-up shooting gallery on a YouTube video."

"You disrespectful piece of shit," Dutrow growled. "You don't have any idea what it takes to be me."

Nick laughed low in his throat. "Oh, it's hard to be you, Kelvin, that's for true. All the time pretending to be someone you're not. And it's about to get harder."

"On the say-so of some trailer-trash dope addict?" Dutrow sneered. "I don't think so."

"Your heart is beating fast now, isn't it, Kelvin?" Nick murmured, his voice low and hypnotic. "You're breathing a little too hard."

"Shut up!"

Nick moved another small step, and another, closer and closer. "Am I making it hard for you, Kelvin? I'm not some paper bad guy hanging on a line. Real targets move and speak and will hurt you if you can't make that first shot."

"I *will* shoot you," Dutrow warned, adjusting his grip on the gun.

"Your palms are sweating, aren't they, Kelvin? You're trying to get your story straight in your head, because once that gun goes off, everything is gonna move real fast, and you can't make a mistake."

"I won't have any trouble at all," Dutrow said, backing himself up against the counter, raising the gun higher, taking aim.

Nick moved as the gun came up, stepping in and to the left, grasping the barrel in his left hand and pushing it to the right as he chopped Dutrow's wrist hard with his right hand. In the blink of an eye, Dutrow was unarmed and the gun was in Nick's hands. Nick stepped back, out of range of contact, popped the magazine, and ejected the cartridge from the chamber.

"You let me know if you want to make a video of that disarming move," he said, dropping the sheriff's weapon into the suggestion box by the office door. "You have a nice rest of your evening, Sheriff."

Dutrow didn't follow him as he left the office. Doubtless he had yet another press conference to prepare for the ten o'clock news. He would compose himself, and no one watching would ever imagine he had nearly shot one of his own detectives in cold blood just moments earlier.

That was one of the most disturbing qualities in men like Kelvin Dutrow—their ability to keep the mask in place, to project the public persona without revealing what lived behind the façade.

That image was what had drawn a young Genevieve to Dutrow in the first place. She had managed to land a respectable—if menial—job at city hall, where she had regular occasion to see Kelvin Dutrow, Special Community Relations Officer.

It had been tempting for her to believe she could have that life—that she could be a respectable girl and marry a dashing pillar of the community. The age difference hadn't bothered her at all. Dutrow's maturity had meant stability and wisdom to her, a girl with no father in her life, a girl who had gotten pregnant and been betrayed by a boy closer to her own age. She had bought the Dutrow image, hook, line, and sinker, only to learn an even crueler lesson in her second try at love.

With two hours to go until change of shift, the building was as quiet as it ever was, the offices of day-shift personnel dark and closed. Nick checked his phone as he negotiated the hallways to the back door.

Annie had texted that she believed the body she'd found in the park to be that of Dean Florette, brother of the missing babysitter. She would speak to the family then go on to see Dutrow's fiancée, whose son had yet to turn up.

He didn't like that last part. The Spicer woman seemed unstable. The domestic situation had been tense the night before—before the woman had punched Annie in the face, before her son had gone missing, before she had shown up at Lafayette Park, hysterical, hurling accusations at Kelvin Dutrow.

Don't go there without me.

Where are you now?

He sent the texts and waited, standing under the overhang outside the back door. The storm had subsided, but the rain continued to fall, a steady shower punctuated by gusts of wind that might have been the leading edge of the bigger storm coming up from the Gulf.

No answer.

He checked the time of her last text to him. It had come while he had been in with Dutrow. Which meant she was probably at the Florette home, delivering the devastating news that their son had been murdered.

What the hell? He didn't believe in anything that smelled like coincidence, but what explanation could there be for this boy to be murdered when his sister was missing? And what connection did the girl's disappearance have to the murder of the child she had looked after? Any? None?

If the death of KJ Gauthier had some connection to Kemp and to Dutrow, if it was about the boy's parentage and Genevieve's reason for coming to Bayou Breaux, how could it be related to the Florette girl? Had she seen something—or more important, some*one*?

"I won't tell! I won't tell! I won't tell!" KJ had chanted over and over the night of his murder. What could a seven-year-old have known that would have been worth killing for?

Annie had suspected the boy, Dean, could have done something to his sister, but now she believed it was Dean Florette lying on a slab at Evangeline's Rest.

He checked the phone again. Still no answer.

He would go to the Florette house and wait for her. They would go to Dutrow's fiancée together.

Decision made, he hustled down the steps and jogged across the parking lot, weaving between vehicles to get to the Jeep, his head ducked down as he ran against the rain, fishing in his pocket for his keys.

He didn't see it coming. He sensed it, throwing up an arm to block the blow before he had any conscious idea of what was happening. A fraction of a second too late.

The ground rushed up at him before he could even realize he was falling, and everything went black.

FORTY-EIGHT

Annie stepped out onto the Florettes' front porch and leaned back against the wall, the ridges of the clapboards pressing into her aching back. Moths flung themselves at the light above. Beyond the porch cover, the rain came down hard enough that the drops bounced high as they hit the pavement under the streetlight.

The sounds of the household drifted out through the screen door— *Family Feud* playing on the television in the living room, a pair of overtired toddlers who should have long since been in bed fighting over a toy, Jojean crying in the dining room, and her relatives trying to console her and talking angrily of injustice and revenge.

She had identified Dean by photos Annie had taken on her phone at the funeral home of a birthmark and a particular curved scar Dean had gotten falling out of his high chair as a baby. The shock had been a terrible thing to watch. Jojean's focus all day had been on her missing daughter. To find out that while she was worried for one child another had been murdered had to have been a nightmare come to life. Then to realize, after the initial shock, that her daughter was still missing . . .

Nora was out there somewhere, Annie thought, staring at the rain. Was she alive? Was she dead? Did she have shelter? Was she exposed to the elements? Was she alone? Was someone torturing her right this very

minute? Had she gone willingly, or had she been taken? What, if anything, did her disappearance have to do with the death of KJ Gauthier—
and now the death of her brother, Dean?

Annie had been halfway to convincing herself that Dean might have
gone further than bullying, that he might have harmed his sister. He
was at an age when boys started having urges they didn't entirely understand or know how to control. He had no adult guidance and an appetite for violence and pornography. She didn't want to think a kid could
be a killer, but she knew plenty of cases that proved otherwise. But with
Dean not just dead, but brutally murdered, she was back to square one.

For a brief moment she tried to entertain the idea that Nora could
be the focus as a suspect rather than as a victim, that she could have
hurt KJ, that she had hated her brother, who tormented her endlessly.
But her brain just couldn't make that plausible. Nora Florette was a silly
tween girl who dotted her *i*'s with little hearts and made friendship
bracelets in her spare time. Annie couldn't reconcile that girl with someone so consumed with rage as to be able to bash Dean's head in with a
rock to the point that he didn't even look real. She had to doubt Nora
would have possessed the physical strength, for starters.

Cameron Spicer might have been physically able. He certainly had
motive to kill Dean. It wasn't hard to imagine months of fear and resentment fermenting inside him and pouring back out like a geyser of
hatred, the kind of rage that wouldn't quit with one or two blows.

Jaime Blynn had seen Cameron in the park during the search for
Nora. No one had seen him since. But could he have gotten the better
of Dean in a fight?

Annie thought back to the day before and the look of misery and
dread on Cameron's face as Dean had called him names and made fun
of him in the park after school. She thought back to the night before,
and the same look on the boy's face as he had waited for whatever punishment Kelvin Dutrow had been about to unload on him. A terrified
child, trapped in a hell of his mother's making.

She couldn't find herself feeling anything but pity for Cameron Spicer.

She pulled her phone off her belt to check her text messages, finding
two from Nick: *Don't go there without me. Where are you now?*

The texts had arrived seven minutes ago, while she had been speaking with the Florettes, in answer to the text she had sent him from the funeral home.

She wrote him back: *Ready to leave the Florettes. Where y'at?*

He had gone from the murder scene in the park to speak again to Genevieve, armed with information regarding Keith Kemp's days as an officer with the Houma PD.

Kemp, the slimy piece of shit. Nick's instinctive dislike of the man had been well founded, as it turned out. Few things disgusted Annie more than a cop abusing his power over vulnerable people. As a law enforcement officer, she was well aware of her position in society and her responsibility to live up to the highest standard that position demanded. But as a woman, she knew what it was to feel helpless against a man with bad intentions. She could too easily imagine the sick fear a young woman like Genevieve would have felt alone on a dark side road with a man like Keith Kemp.

That feeling called Annie's mother to her mind. Marie Broussard had never confessed her story to anyone, as far as Annie knew, but Annie had always suspected her mother had come to Bayou Breaux to hide from a man. To hide from Annie's father, whomever he was. Why had Genevieve come here?

Annie yawned and sighed, feeling exhausted in every way possible. Her body ached, and her brain felt fuzzy from lack of sleep. She wanted to go to Sharon Spicer to assure her they were looking for Cameron, to get any helpful information she could, and then go home and collapse for a few hours. The day had been long and hard, and tomorrow was going to be doubly so. They now had two missing children and two murders to solve. And they would have less manpower if Dutrow had his way and fired Nick . . . not that Nick would listen to him. He had not one shred of respect left for the man.

She might have felt vaguely sorry for Dutrow if she hadn't despised him so. She thought of the expression on his face tonight as he had tried to deal with Sharon, his fiancée, out of her mind with panic for her son. Disgust, annoyance. Sharon had inconvenienced him, embarrassed him in front of his true love—the television cameras. Asshole.

Annie checked the screen of her phone again—no answer—and looked at the time. It was after ten.

She texted Nick again: *R U coming or what?*

She sent it and sent it again, trying to annoy him into looking at his phone. No answer was forthcoming. She stood and stared at her lock-screen picture of Justin for a few minutes, missing him.

Out of patience, she decided to just go. She wouldn't be with Sharon long—less than an hour, she thought. If Dutrow's vehicle was in the drive-way, she would wait in the car for Nick. He couldn't be that far behind.

She texted him again: *Going on to Sharon Spicer. Need this day to be over. 14 Blue Cypress. Come when you can.*

THE INITIAL BLOW knocked him down. Hitting the pavement knocked him out. A fist woke him back up. All in a span of seconds.

Move!

He scrambled to get to his hands and knees, his brain telling him to explode forward and upward, the messages shorting out on the way to his muscles, making his reactions hesitant and his movements slow.

Something as hard as steel hit him a glancing blow across the tops of his shoulders, just missing the back of his head as he lurched forward. The blow dropped him to the wet pavement again, and his breath left him as the toe of a boot caught him in the ribs.

"Coonass motherfucker, take that!"

Kemp.

"Think you're gonna mess with me?"

He was drunk.

"You think you're gonna ruin me? Fuck you!"

He swung a foot back to deliver another kick, and Nick rolled over, swept his arm around, grabbed Kemp's standing ankle, and yanked it out from under him.

Kemp hit the pavement on his ass but rolled away quickly and scrambled back to his feet and came forward, throwing a knee that caught Nick in the jaw as he tried to rise. The taste of blood filled his mouth like warm red wine as he slammed sideways into the door of the Jeep.

He threw up a hand and caught hold of the bracket of the rearview mirror and pulled himself to his feet.

The rain was pouring down, blurring his vision as much as the blows to the head had done. Kemp was backlit by a sodium vapor light twenty yards away, like a silhouette from a black-and-white movie. He saw the man's arm draw back and up, something long and slender in his hand.

A tactical baton.

Move!

Nick rolled to the side, out of the way a split second before the baton struck the Jeep's window and shattered it.

"I will fucking kill you!" Kemp shouted.

As he swung the baton again with murderous intent, Nick stepped toward him instead of away, caught Kemp's arm, turned his body, and twisted his shoulders. The throw was easy, effortless, lacking the violence he wanted to deliver. Kemp flipped over gracelessly, landing hard on his back, the baton bouncing from his hand.

Nick was on him in a heartbeat, straddling Kemp's chest, his thighs tight against his rib cage, weight on his diaphragm, restricting his breathing. Weapon drawn, he pointed the barrel of the gun straight between Keith Kemp's eyes.

"I told you not to fucking touch me, Keith!" he shouted. "I warned you, now look what you're making me do!"

"Don't shoot! Don't shoot!" Kemp screamed, gasping.

"You think you're gonna kill me, you low-life piece of shit?" Nick yelled down at him, adrenaline burning through him like rocket fuel. "I'm not some seven-year-old child you can just stick a knife in! I'm not some young girl you can rape in the back seat of your squad car!"

"I'ma be sick!"

"Good! Lucky me, I've got a front-row seat to watch you aspirate and drown in your own vomit."

Kemp struggled beneath him, trying without success to twist one way and then the other, trying to buck upward as he started to gag. At the last second, Nick eased his weight off just enough for the man to twist over onto his belly, spewing his stomach contents onto the pavement.

Then he rode the asshole flat down to the ground with a knee in the small of his back.

Pressing Kemp's face down into the puddle of vomit with a hand to the back of his head, he leaned close and murmured in his ear, "How do you like it, Keith? How do you like being the victim? Hmm? How does it feel to be the weak one? I can do anything I want to you right here, right now. Ain't nobody here to stop me. I could kill you right here and get rid of your body. Ain't nobody gonna look for you, *fils de putain.* Ain't nobody gonna mourn the passing of the likes of you.

"How does that feel in the bottom of your shriveled little black heart, Keith? Hmm?"

He let the question hang for a moment, let the rain pound down on one side of Kemp's face while the other side was buried in a puddle of bourbon and bile.

"Jesus, Nicky!" Stokes said somewhere behind him. "What are you doing riding that jackass out here in the rain? The least you could do is get a room, man. I can't unsee that shit!"

"Just having a little Come to Jesus meeting with Mr. Kemp here."

Stokes laughed. "Jesus don't want no part of that, son! Put it in a holster, and let's go inside."

Nick holstered his weapon and rose to his feet, one boot firmly planted between Keith Kemp's shoulder blades.

"Cuff him," he said to Stokes.

"Then we're all of us gonna sit down and have a chat with our good friend Keith here. And he's gonna tell us every single thing we want to know. Aren't you, Keith?"

He didn't wait to hear an answer but started toward the Pizza Hut, in search of a dry shirt, checking his phone for a response from Annie as he went: *Going on to Sharon Spicer. Need this day to be over. 14 Blue Cypress. Come when you can.*

FORTY-NINE

Sharon paced in her kitchen, her whole body rigid with dread.

When the deputy had first brought her home, she had walked the house, hurrying from one empty room to the next to the next, hoping against hope that Cameron would be in every room she entered. Maybe he wasn't gone at all. Maybe she had just missed seeing him. Maybe he had come back to the house while she had been out looking for him.

I DON'T WANT TO BE HERE!!!

The reminder printed on his bedroom mirror had brought a fresh surge of terror, so strong she'd had to vomit.

When Detective Broussard had called to tell her the dead boy from the park wasn't Cameron, the sense of relief had been dizzying. She had fallen to the floor sobbing, limp, her heart racing. She didn't know how long she had lain there before the dread had come back.

Her son was missing in a town where two children had died in three days and another had vanished.

How could this be happening to her? Two days ago, her life had been nearly perfect. She had been planning her dream wedding to a wonderful man, establishing her place in her new community, making a lovely home for herself and her son. Then, in the blink of an eye, her perfect

dream had become a nightmare. There would be no wedding. Her fiancé was a monster who would throw her out of her home. Her son was
missing and possibly dead.

I should have done more to protect him.

Trembling uncontrollably, Sharon dragged herself to her feet and
started to pace again, forcing herself to put one foot in front of the other.

She stayed in her beautiful kitchen, her favorite room in the house,
corralled by granite countertops and the glow of under-cabinet lighting.
She walked around and around and around the center island, her arms
banded around herself like the sleeves of a straitjacket.

She felt like she might need one as her world spun out of control, and
her mind along with it.

She needed to think. She needed a plan. She always felt better when
she had a plan.

THERE WAS NO sign of the sheriff's Suburban at 14 Blue Cypress. Annie
breathed a sigh of relief. Hopefully, he was holding court somewhere.
He would have a lot to say to the press after the scene in Lafayette Park.

He had called Annie earlier and left a message requesting information
on the identification of the body. She had texted him back that she believed the body was Dean Florette, but that they would not have a positive
ID until morning. It was late, and the Florettes at least deserved to have
the privacy of their grief for one night. The spotlight would find them all
over again tomorrow, and everyone with a television or radio or newspaper or computer in Partout Parish and well beyond would take in the
news with shock and morbid fascination. The Florettes would be celebri-
ties for their dual tragedies, like a two-headed freak in a circus.

She parked in the driveway and checked her phone, irritated there
was still no message from Nick. Surely, he had long since finished questioning Genevieve. Had he gone back to the office? Was he, at that very
minute, confronting Dutrow with what he knew about Keith Kemp?

It couldn't matter. She was tired, and she wanted this over with. She
dashed through the rain to the door of the house and rang the bell and
waited.

Sharon Spicer opened the door, wide-eyed and pale as a ghost.

"I'm sorry it's so late," Annie said. "May I come in?"

"Do you . . . have . . . news?" she asked, dragging out the question as she tried to brace herself for a bad answer. Her knuckles were white as she clung to the door.

"No," Annie said. "I'm sorry. No news. I need to ask you some questions about Cameron. We need as much information as possible to help us look for him."

She let out a trembling sigh. "Yes, of course. Come in."

"How are you doing, Sharon?" Annie asked as Sharon led the way to the kitchen. Annie imagined that would be the room where she would feel most in control—command central for moms everywhere.

"Is there someone you can call to come be with you tonight?" Annie asked. "You shouldn't be going through this alone."

"No, no. I'm sure Kelvin will be stopping by later," Sharon said, forcing a brittle smile.

"Do you think that's a good idea—for Kelvin to come here tonight?"

"Of course! He'll know what to do. He always does."

Annie held her tongue.

"Would you like a cup of coffee?" Sharon asked, ever the hostess. A well-raised Southern girl, she fell back on good manners and familiar routine.

"Sure. Yes, thank you," Annie said, watching her set about the task, putting a fresh filter into the coffee machine on the counter. She surreptitiously unclipped her phone from her belt, glanced at the screen, and placed it facedown on a place mat as she took a seat at the table.

"I know everyone wants those instant machines now," Sharon chattered. "But I don't believe in that. It's wasteful, and nothing beats a well-brewed cup of fresh coffee! I'm sure you agree. I imagine you drink a lot of coffee. It goes with your job. Kelvin practically has coffee in his veins, he drinks so much!"

"Sharon, can you think of anywhere Cameron might go to hide?" Annie asked. "I know you said he doesn't have many friends, but—"

"*Any* friends," Sharon corrected her. "He doesn't have *any* friends. He goes to school, and he comes home, and no one calls him, and he never asks to have anyone over—not that I could allow that. Not now. Not yet. Kelvin is unused to having children around. I think it's best to ease him into that role. That's only fair."

Fair to whom? Annie wanted to ask, but she didn't.

"Does Cameron have a cell phone?"

"Yes, he does."

"Does he have it with him?"

"No."

"It's here? May I see it?"

"No," Sharon said, bringing a dainty pitcher of cream to the table. "Kelvin has it. He took it away from Cameron last night—his phone and his iPad, as well—in punishment for telling a lie."

Her cheeks flushed with color, and tears rose in her eyes.

"And now he doesn't have his cell phone, and he can't call home. I-if he n-needs m-me, he c-can't call home!"

"Sharon, come sit down," Annie said, going to her, trying to steer her toward the kitchen table.

"But the coffee—"

"It's fine. It can wait. Come sit down."

"It wasn't Cameron's fault," she said. "He got punished, but it was my fault. I told him he could quit football. I just hadn't found a way to tell Kelvin. It was my fault!"

She began to cry as she melted down onto the chair and bent over the table, her face contorted as if she were in pain. Annie rubbed a hand against her back, trying to offer comfort.

"Did Kelvin hurt him, Sharon?" she asked quietly.

Her answer was sobs.

"He tries so hard!" Sharon cried. "He tries so hard to be a good boy! He never wants to make a mistake. He never wants to disappoint me. He tries so hard, and I let that happen to him! What kind of mother am I?"

"Hush now," Annie said, patting her back, her heart breaking for this woman. Everything she said about her child was just as true of her. She tried so hard. She never wanted to make a mistake. She didn't want to disappoint.

"I should have tried harder to protect him!"

"You're a good mother," Annie murmured. "You do the best you can.

"I'd like to have a look around Cameron's room," she said. "Would that be all right? Could you show me his room?"

Sharon dabbed at her tears with a napkin from a clever little decorative holder on the table, trying to pull herself together. "Yes, of course."

The boy's room was down a hall and off the patio, on the opposite end of the house from where the master suite must have been. A little sanctuary to shuttle the awkward child to. Out of Kelvin's way so he didn't have to be reminded he had taken on the burden of his fiancée's offspring from another marriage.

"I apologize if the room has an odor," Sharon said. "Cameron has an irritable bowel. It's been quite bad recently. He's under so much stress, you know, with his studies and all. It's important that he be on the honor roll. He wants to make honors in all his math and science classes. And then the tensions of trying to bond with Kelvin . . . He's even tried to take up fishing. He tries so hard to do everything right."

The room was far too neat and tidy to belong to a teenager, Annie thought, recalling her investigation of Dean Florette's bedroom earlier that day, where she had wished she'd worn a hazmat suit and a gas mask to pick through the rubble. The only thing Cameron's room had in common with Dean's was the swampy smell of sweaty clothes and hormones, though Cameron's room had added layers of fading diarrhea and sickly sweet air freshener.

There were no posters of sports stars or rock bands. Of course, there wouldn't be, lest the posters clashed with the décor. The bed was made. Everything was in place. Only a few toys left over from childhood that had been set at careful intervals on the bookshelves spoke to the fact that the young man living here had been a boy not long ago.

Annie stood in front of the dresser and stared at the message printed on the mirror.

I DON'T WANT TO BE HERE!!!

I don't blame you, Cameron, she thought to herself.

"He keeps his room himself," Sharon said. "I'm so proud of him. You don't see many boys so neat and tidy."

She fussed around the bed, smoothing the coverlet, fluffing the pillows, *tsk*ing to herself as she reached down to pull a dirty sock out from under the bed.

"Boys and their laundry!" she exclaimed, forcing another smile as Annie glanced over.

The expression went from fake smile to puzzlement as she tugged on the sock.

No, Annie thought, not a sock. A strap. A padded strap, like from a backpack.

A strange sense of foreboding washed over her as she dropped to her knees beside the bed. She pulled on the strap as Sharon backed away, dragging a backpack into view inch by inch.

A purple-and-pink backpack.

Nora Florette's backpack.

"What is it?" Sharon asked.

Her voice sounded miles away. Annie's heart was pounding like a war hammer in her chest.

Why would Cameron Spicer have Nora's backpack?

They had walked home together the day she went missing. He had said he didn't know what happened to her. He had said that she was stupid and weird, and he didn't even like her.

But Nora had gotten into trouble for coming to this house once before.

"I won't tell! I won't tell! I won't tell!" KJ Gauthier had chanted those words that evening over and over, driving his mother crazy.

"Whose is that?" Sharon asked, kneeling down to touch the bag. "That's not Cameron's."

Her pulse roaring in her ears, Annie pulled the backpack all the way out, and with it followed the hand of a girl with pink sparkle nail polish.

Sharon's screams split the air and reverberated in the bedroom.

Annie leaned down, raised the plaid bed skirt, and looked under Cameron Spicer's bed and into the glazed brown eyes of Nora Florette.

FIFTY

Go call nine-one-one!" Annie snapped.

Sharon had run backward into the wall, instinctively trying to escape the horror, screaming, "Oh, my God! Oh, my God!"

"*GO!!*" Annie shouted. "*GO NOW!!* We need an ambulance!"

Please let that be true, she thought as Sharon scrambled to get out of the room and ran down the hall.

Frantic, Annie pushed the tangle of friendship bracelets out of the way and tried to feel for a pulse in the girl's wrist. Her own heart was racing wildly. Her fingers were trembling. She couldn't tell if she felt a faint pulse or just wanted it to be so.

She flattened herself on the floor, eye to eye with Nora Florette, and tried to find a pulse in her neck.

Maybe. Weak and thready, but maybe it was there.

The girl looked dead. She had been gone two full days. Had she been under Cameron Spicer's bed the whole time? Could she have survived that?

"Nora! Nora!" she shouted, hoping for some kind of response. A blink, a nod, a spark of life in her eyes. Something. Anything. Please.

If she was alive, she was hanging by a thread. Her body was cool to the touch, but not cold, not stiff, but then, rigor mortis could have come and gone by now.

"You gotta stay with me, Nora!" Annie said. "Help is on the way."

She wanted to pull the girl out from under the bed, but she had no idea what the extent of her injuries might be. She had a head injury, for certain. Blood had run down across her cheek and jaw like a macabre handprint. She might have had a neck injury or a back injury. Moving her might cause more harm than good. Better to let the EMTs move the bed than for her to try to move the girl. They would be here any minute. The fire station wasn't that far away.

"Nora, stay with me!" she said again. "I'll stay right here with you until help arrives. You have to hang on for us!"

She thought she saw an eyelid move a fraction of an inch. It might have been wishful thinking, but she decided to believe it. The Florettes were overdue for a miracle.

Reaching out, she found the girl's other hand and hung on, wondering how the hell this had ever happened.

"How'd it happen, Keith?" Stokes asked. "Did you go there thinking to rape that girl? Did the boy just get in your way?"

"I don't know what you're talking about."

They sat in a small, cramped room in the back of the Pizza Hut that was normally used for storage. Kemp sat behind the beat-up rectangular table, a thin film of vomit clinging to his beard stubble. He had pissed himself at some point during his altercation with Nick. The mix of body fluids and bourbon gave him the pungent scent of a billy goat.

Nick paced back and forth along the opposite wall like a caged tiger, his face twisted in disgust at the smell of Keith Kemp—literally and figuratively. They had yet to Mirandize him. There was nothing official or proper about this interview. But he knew the minute they booked Kemp for assault, the first word out of his mouth would be *lawyer* and they would get nothing from him. Anything they gleaned now would likely not be admissible in court but could serve them as a tool to use for leverage to get them something better later on.

"Or did you go there to kill the boy, and the chance to rape the mother was part of the deal?" Nick asked. "Transactional opportunist and misogynist that he is, I have no doubt Dutrow would be fine with that."

"I never raped that woman," Kemp pointed out.

"So the point was to get rid of the boy."

"And I never touched that boy," he said. Grimacing, he jammed his thumb into his mouth and tested a tooth. "I don't know what you're talking about, Fourcade. I want a lawyer."

Stokes arched a thick brow. "I don't recall asking did you want a lawyer." He glanced back at Nick. "Did you hear me ask him that?"

Nick shook his head. "*Non*. We're just having a conversation here, Keith."

"Arrest me and charge me, or let me go. You can't use anything I tell you here," Kemp said. "Fruit of the poisoned tree, and all that."

"Now he's a stickler for procedure," Nick said to Stokes. "Funny how that abuse-of-power thing just isn't so much fun when the shoe is on the other foot. You liked it fine when you were fucking girls in your squad car in exchange for lesser charges, didn't you, Keith?"

"I never raped anybody," Kemp said. "I negotiated a couple of trades, is all."

"So you lost your badge because one of the women you coerced into having sex with you had buyer's remorse, is that it?"

"Well, who could blame her?" Stokes interjected. "Trading something for nothing is a shit deal."

"They got what they wanted," Kemp sneered.

Stokes laughed. "Yeah, right! The last time you had something a woman wanted, you must have been a shoe salesman!"

"Fuck you, Stokes."

"No thanks, Keith!" Stokes continued laughing. "I can put my own finger up my ass."

"You're a laugh riot, you are," Kemp grumbled.

"Genevieve Gauthier did not want to give you a blow job on the side of the road," Nick said, his dark scowl never leaving Kemp.

"Well, she sure hit her knees quick enough," Kemp taunted him.

Nick lunged toward him. Stokes was out of his chair and blocking his path with a move as smooth as a longtime dance partner.

"She's got you eating out of her hand," Kemp said. "What'd she do for that? Enough to make you look the other way when she killed her own child? That must be some magic pussy she's got. First Dutrow, now you."

Nick went very still. "First Dutrow what?"

Kemp shut his mouth and narrowed his eyes.

A slow, predatory smile turned the corners of Nick's mouth. He nodded to Stokes. "See Mr. Kemp to his accommodations, Chaz. The charge is aggravated assault. Be sure to read him those rights he's so fond of."

Stokes went around behind the table and hauled Kemp to his feet.

"Mind that wet pavement on the walk over, Keith," Nick said, following them down the hall to the back door. "Wouldn't want you to trip and fall with your hands cuffed behind your back that way . . . repeatedly."

He watched them disappear around the corner then pulled his phone off his belt and checked for messages. There was nothing new from Annie. He glanced at the time, frowned, typed:

Hey, 'Toinette. Where y'at?

Sharon reached for the telephone handset on the kitchen counter, stopping just short of touching it. Her heart was beating like a trip hammer. Her pulse was roaring in her ears. She felt like she might explode from the fear and the panic.

There was a body under Cameron's bed.

There was a dead girl under Cameron's bed.

That Florette girl.

What was she doing here?

She wasn't supposed to be in this house.

She had been warned not to come here ever again.

She was a thief and a troublemaker, that girl.

Now Cameron would be in trouble because of her.

What a nightmare. They had moved here to have the perfect life. Now that life was crumbling before her eyes by the minute. She had lost Kelvin, lost her home, lost her future. Now she would lose her son as well. She could have taken him somewhere far away from here and started over. Now he would be taken from her because of Nora Florette. That stupid, useless girl, lying dead under his bed.

And now she was supposed to call the ambulance. She was supposed to call for people to come and try to save Nora Florette when she should have been saving her own child.

I should have done more to protect him, she thought as she backed away from the telephone.

WHERE THE HELL was the ambulance?

Annie held her breath and waited for the sound of sirens. They should have been screaming by now. This house wasn't five minutes from a fire station.

Where the hell was the ambulance?

Where the hell was Sharon?

Had she just panicked and left? Was she in the kitchen making tea?

A few of Nick's favorite French curses rolled through Annie's mind. She didn't want to let go of Nora. She didn't want to leave the girl alone. But she needed an ambulance, and she needed it now.

Annie had left her phone on the kitchen table. Careless. Stupid. She had to put it off to being exhausted, but still . . . Cameron's phone had been taken by Dutrow as punishment for telling a lie, Sharon had said. There was no phone in this room.

Loath to let go of Nora Florette's hand, she forced herself to pull away and get to her feet. She had to get help.

"Sharon?" she called as she hurried down the hallway toward the kitchen. "Sharon, did you call for the ambulance?"

Sharon spun around and looked at her as if she was surprised to see her—or had been caught doing something she shouldn't have been doing. The look registered in the back of Annie's mind, but she dismissed it as unimportant.

"Did you call nine-one-one?" she asked.

"No," Sharon murmured, shaking her head. "I can't."

"What? What do you mean, you can't?" Annie asked, annoyed and impatient. "Sharon, we need an ambulance! Now!"

"No!" she said. "She's dead! That girl is dead! It won't matter now!"

Annie moved toward her aggressively. "Are you out of your mind? That girl could still be alive! Give me the phone."

"No! Please! Don't! Cameron—"

"It's gonna be way worse for Cameron if this girl dies than if she doesn't," Annie said, trying to step around her. "Let me have the phone."

"No!" Sharon shouted.

She hit Annie from the side, knocking her off balance, surprising her and irritating her more than anything. A girl was dying in the room down the hall. There was no time for foolishness.

"I can't let you!" Sharon cried. "He's my son! He's all I have! I have to protect him! Don't you understand?"

No, Annie thought. She understood that a girl had come to this house and that someone had hurt her, that she had been stuffed beneath a bed and left to die, but that she might yet have a chance, if only help could arrive as soon as possible. Those were the things Annie understood in that moment as she turned toward the table to retrieve her cell phone.

In the next moment, she understood something else entirely. In the next moment, she understood that Sharon Spicer was past the end of her rope, that she loved her son more than anything in the world, and that there was nothing she wouldn't do to protect him.

In the next moment, Sharon Spicer hit her hard from behind, with what felt like a hammer to her upper back, knocking her forward. Surprised, she stumbled and fell, crashing into the table. Flinging out a hand, she tried to grab for her phone but knocked it out of reach instead.

"NO! NOOOOOOO!" Sharon screamed behind her, as if she were the one in pain as she struck Annie again and again, hitting her in the back and in the back of the head.

Annie tried to turn but couldn't. Her feet slipped and went out from under her as she scrambled. As she fell, she tried once more to lunge for the phone, knocking it off the table. Her forehead struck the table's edge as she went down, stunning her. She hit the tile floor with jarring force, banging her head again.

Her vision blurred and dimmed and swam. Fighting to remain conscious, she tried to focus on her cell phone and on her need to get her hand on it.

Nine-one-one. Nine-one-one. Punch three numbers. That was all she needed to do.

The phone was on the floor, just a few inches away. In Annie's mind, she was trying her hardest to stretch her fingers out to it, but her body didn't move, and the only help available to her remained just out of reach.

FIFTY-ONE

This is Owen Onofrio, KJUN, all talk, all the time. Our topic tonight: What the heck is going on in Partout Parish? Two murders and two missing children in three days! Let's talk about it, folks!"

Kelvin snapped off the radio in favor of the sound of the windshield wipers, not in the mood for the opinions of people who sat around this time of night calling in to radio shows. Lonely, malcontent, unintelligent gossipmongers, no doubt. House-bound conspiracy nuts. He shuddered to think what they would have to say after the goings-on in the park tonight. Better that he didn't listen. Better that he assumed the worst and took the appropriate measures to regain control of the situation.

He drove toward the house, working to formulate a plan as he went. He needed to right his ship and show his constituents that he was in control and that he could assure their safety. How could they feel safe if the sheriff's own future stepson was missing? How could they have confidence in him if his own fiancée accused him of not caring?

He was furious with Sharon for the way she had conducted herself at the park. She should have come to him directly when she realized Cameron was missing. She should have had sense enough to remain calm at the scene, to stand back and let him handle the situation.

The community looked up to him as a patriarchal figure, a calm, confident, wise leader who would keep them from harm. Now he would have to reestablish that image, thanks to Sharon and her boy.

As much as he wanted to be rid of the pair of them tonight, Kelvin realized now was not the time. He couldn't have these relationships come apart at the seams now. He needed everything to appear normal and healthy. Sharon should continue with her volunteer work. The wedding plans should appear to go forward. They would keep up appearances until such time they could gracefully and quietly stop—or not, he thought.

He needed to cool his temper and consider this with a clear head. He had no desire to start over with the time-consuming hassle of dating—a process that would be especially fraught for him as sheriff. With Sharon, he knew what he was getting. They were already comfortable with their arrangement. If he had to start over, he would have to tread carefully through the minefield of local hopefuls, lest he get snagged by another Genevieve Gauthier. Needy girls, greedy girls, girls willing to get themselves pregnant to snag a meal ticket—they would all come out of the woodwork. He had no interest in sorting through them.

Sharon had been upset this evening, but she would calm herself once Cameron came home. She was probably already regretting her foolish, hysterical behavior in the park.

Kelvin would expect an apology from her, of course, for embarrassing him. And there would have to be some consequences. He would insist that Cameron go away to school. Now was the time to use his leverage for that end. Sharon was a practical woman. She enjoyed the pretty house and the public standing that came with being his fiancée. She would see the need to give in to him on the point of the boy.

It would all work out, Kelvin thought. He was feeling confident.

The situation with Fourcade, on the other hand, was another matter, he thought darkly. He couldn't continue to tolerate a man who had no respect for him. And he certainly couldn't have Fourcade spewing stories to the press about Kemp and things that had gone on in Houma years ago.

Fourcade would have to be dealt with. He had come damned close tonight. No one would have questioned his account of events. Fourcade's reputation preceded him. But he hadn't been able to find the nerve to pull the trigger. He'd never shot a man before. It grated on him to think he had hesitated. All his big talk as a man of action, and he hadn't made good on it.

He drove past the Florette house, making a mental note to call on the mother in the morning as soon as she had ID'd her son's body. With the daughter still missing and the son dead, the media focus would be heavy on the family. He would offer his condolences and assure them justice would be done.

It stood to reason that the two cases were connected. If both could be resolved at once, half of Kelvin's public relations problems would go away. That would leave him with the matter of the Gauthier home invasion and murder, which could be put off to the possible drug connections of a troubled young woman, or on the woman herself.

He was feeling much calmer as he turned onto Blue Cypress. A deputy sat in a cruiser at the curb in front of the house. Not interested in getting soaked making small talk, Kelvin pulled alongside, ran down his window, and dismissed the young man for the evening with a quick sentence.

A black SUV he didn't recognize sat parked in the driveway. Kelvin frowned, easing his Suburban alongside it. Sharon seldom entertained friends during the week. Perhaps this was a woman from one of her committees or someone she had called for moral support after the scene in the park.

He liked that second idea not at all. He would have to have a serious talk with her about discretion. He didn't want her having a confidante. He didn't want to have to worry about her confessing details of their private life to some gossipy woman friend. He was still upset that Annie Broussard had witnessed the tensions of the night before. Clearly, she had voiced her concerns to her husband, and he now felt free to make remarks about the abuse of women. Kelvin would be glad to be rid of the pair of them. The sooner, the better.

Annoyed at having to park farther away from the door than should have been necessary, he got out of his vehicle and made a dash for the front door.

"Sharon?" he called. He shrugged out of his rain slicker and hung it on the coat tree in the foyer.

She didn't answer. He didn't think that much of it. She was probably in the kitchen with the owner of the SUV. He could smell the coffee. They were probably working on the details of some project, the kitchen table strewn with paperwork.

There were no lights on in the living room, which struck him as odd. Sharon liked the house staged—lamps on in the evening, seating areas arranged invitingly with throws and pillows, stacks of books or magazines on the side tables. It didn't matter if no one actually used the room. It was the suggestion that counted. The house was ever-ready for a magazine photo shoot.

"Sharon?"

"Kelvin?" she called from the back of the house.

She sounded hesitant. Understandable, he thought. She was anticipating him being angry, and rightly so.

"Whose car is that in the driveway?" he asked.

She came from the kitchen partway into the dining room, a dish towel in her hands. The dining room was dark as well, leaving Sharon lit from behind and on one side, half of her face light and half dark.

"What car?" she asked, her expression oddly blank.

"The car in the driveway. The black SUV."

"Oh, that deputy brought me home," she said.

"And I sent him on his way," Kelvin said. "I mean the black SUV in the driveway."

"I don't know," she said stupidly, twisting the towel in her hands.

"How can you not know, Sharon?" he asked, irritated. "There's a strange car in the driveway. Who else is in the house? Did someone bring Cameron home?"

"No, he's not home," she said, her voice getting shaky.

Kelvin heaved an impatient sigh. "I expect he's hiding somewhere, sulking."

"He doesn't want to be here," she said.

"Well, that's gonna work out fine for all of us," Kelvin muttered.

"SHARON?"

Dutrow's voice in another room brought Annie out of her trance.

She never would have counted on him to save her, she thought. If he knew she was here, dying on his kitchen floor, would he just leave? Would he save his fiancée over her? He would do whatever was best for himself.

For a moment she lay still, listening to her own breathing, which sounded shallow and labored. She could feel something wet inching down her neck. Blood, she supposed. Whatever Sharon had hit her with had cut her.

"Whose car is that in the driveway?" Dutrow asked.

Annie wanted to muster up the strength to call out, but she couldn't seem to pull it off. Her thought process was scrambled. Her mouth felt dry. Her breath caught in her throat like a crust of bread. The cry for help turned to ash on her tongue.

You've gone and done it this time, girl, she thought, fear stirring in her chest. Her brain was throbbing like it wanted out of her skull. Consciousness kept trying to fade away. She felt like her being might abandon her body at any moment.

"I don't know," Sharon said.

"How can you not know, Sharon?" Dutrow said irritably.

Just inches from her fingertips, Annie's phone began to vibrate with an incoming call. The screen lit up, but she couldn't seem to raise her head to see the name of the caller. *Nick,* she thought—she hoped. He would be wondering where she was, thinking she should have been done here by now. He hadn't wanted her to come to this house by herself. She should have listened to him.

She took as deep a breath as she could and tried one more time to reach those extra few inches. If only she could touch the screen . . .

"OH!" SHARON SAID. "It must belong to that detective! Detective Broussard. She came by to ask about Cameron."

"She's here now?" Kelvin asked, his temper growing shorter. Now he would have to get rid of Annie Broussard before he could have his conversation with Sharon. Broussard, who had already decided he was abusive and had relayed that to her husband. She would try to linger and meddle, as she had the night before.

"No," Sharon said. "She left."

"How did she leave without her car?"

"I don't know. Maybe she got a ride with someone."

"Why would she leave her car?"

"I don't know, Kelvin!" Sharon snapped. "Maybe she's outside, looking for Cameron. My son is missing! Do you understand that? And a boy was murdered tonight!"

"It wasn't Cameron," Kelvin said flatly, already weary of Sharon's emotions. "I'd like a cup of that coffee I smell. We need to talk about what happened in the park tonight, Sharon."

She blocked him as he went to step past her, clutching her dish towel to her like a security blanket.

"Why don't you go sit down in the family room, Kelvin?" she suggested. "I'll bring it to you."

There was something not right about her demeanor. That thought raised a small flag in the back of his mind, but he was too tired and impatient to think about it.

"I'll have it in the kitchen."

"I have such a mess in there!" she said with a strangely hysterical little laugh. "I was just cleaning up."

She was lying. She wasn't good at it. Her eyes went too wide. She forgot to blink. Her mouth moved like a fish's, waiting for words that never materialized in her brain.

"I don't have the patience for this tonight, Sharon," he snapped. "Is there someone in the kitchen? Who's in there with you?"

"No! No one!"

"Don't you lie to me!" he snapped.

She cried out as he grabbed her by the arm and pulled her in close, leaning down over her, enjoying the way it made him feel—the exact opposite of the way he had felt in his office with Fourcade stalking him and taking away his weapon. He didn't have to feel that way now. Now he was the strong one, the intimidating one.

"Do you never learn?!" he snarled in her face. "Don't lie to me!"

"Kelvin, you're hurting me!" she sobbed, shrinking downward.

He yanked her past him into the dining room and let her go. "She's still here, isn't she? Broussard?"

Jesus Christ, he thought, Broussard was in the next room, listening to all of this—

"Kelvin, no!" Sharon cried, hurrying behind him as he headed toward the kitchen. "I have to explain! You won't understand!"

"Understand what?"

"I didn't know what else to do! She was going to call the ambulance. That girl is dead. I can't change that. I'm sure it was an accident. I'm sure he didn't mean to hurt her—"

"What the hell are you talking about?" Kelvin demanded, glancing back at her as he stepped into the kitchen.

"I don't want him to go to prison!" Sharon cried.

"Who?"

"Cameron!"

"You're talking crazy!" he snapped. "What dead girl? What are you talking about?"

"I had to stop her! I didn't know what else to do!"

She was looking past him, into the kitchen, tears welling up and rolling down her face. He followed her gaze and stopped dead in his tracks.

Annie Broussard lay on the kitchen floor, half under the table in a puddle of blood.

"Oh, my God," he murmured. "What have you done?"

"I saved my son!" she cried. And in one quick motion, she dropped the dish towel she had been holding all this time and pushed a knife into his belly.

FIFTY-TWO

Hey, 'Toinette? Where y'at, *bébé*?" Nick asked as he drove out of the SO compound.

She hadn't answered his last text. He hadn't heard from her in more than an hour. He hadn't wanted her to go to that house without him. Now her phone picked up but she said nothing. The silence sent a chill through him.

He pulled the Jeep to the shoulder of the road, pressed the phone directly to his ear, and strained to listen. Was it a bad connection or a bad situation?

Rain pelted him through the broken window. A jacked-up pickup swept past, fat tires hissing on the wet pavement. In the relative silence that followed, he thought he could hear breathing, shallow, quick inhalations.

"I'm listening, baby," he whispered, hoping she could hear him. Hoping no one else would.

In the background, a woman's voice and a man's voice, upset, angry. He could read the tone but not make out what they were saying. The volume rose, slightly louder and louder . . . *"No . . . understand . . . Cameron . . . crazy . . ."*

"What dead girl? What are you talking about?"

Dutrow's voice.

Woman's voice: "I had to stop her! I didn't know what else to do!"

Dutrow: (indistinct mumbling).

Woman's voice: "I saved my son!"

And then Annie's voice—weak and frightened, a single, breathless plea: "Hurry."

Sick with dread, Nick flipped on the dash light and hit the gas.

"YOU BITCH! YOU stabbed me!" Kelvin said stupidly.

Shocked, he watched as Sharon pulled the knife out of his belly and stepped back. He couldn't see any blood against the black of his shirt, and initially, there was no pain. His brain tried to tell him nothing had happened. He was fine. She couldn't have stabbed him. Then, suddenly, came a searing-cold sensation that turned instantly white-hot, taking his breath away. He put a hand to his belly. It came away bright red with his blood.

"Oh, my God!"

Panic bolted through him like a runaway horse. His heart was racing. He was hyperventilating. In the back of his mind, he was thinking he should have had his tactical vest on, but he had removed it for his appearance on the ten o'clock news because it made him look heavy on television. A ridiculous thought. He had no reason to wear ballistic armor to see his fiancée—or so he would have thought.

Sharon gasped, as if in shock, then stepped in close and stabbed him a second time, before he could react at all. The knife came up and into him at a forty-five-degree angle, slightly higher than the first time and just left of center mass.

She ran backward away from him, screaming, looking at the bloody chef's knife as if she'd had no control over it, her eyes wide with surprise.

Shock swept through Kelvin's body in an ice-cold wave, leaving him dizzy and weak. It felt as if every ounce of blood and energy was rushing out of him like water swirling down a drain. The pain now was excruciating, and he had to fight to get a breath.

He was furious and terrified, outraged and shocked that a woman had done this to him. The woman he had chosen to be his perfect partner in the public eye. How could that be? How could he have misjudged her so badly?

"*I saved my son,*" she'd said.

That was his mistake. He never should have let the boy stay.

"You bitch!" He spat the word as he reached for his weapon and staggered sideways as the floor seemed to tilt beneath him. His knees buckled and he sank to the floor, falling against the cupboards.

The thought occurred that he was dying. He dismissed it. This wasn't how he would die—bleeding out on his kitchen floor, stabbed by a woman. He was destined for so much more.

"*I'makillyou,*" he mumbled, the words a single slurred jumble of syllables.

His fingers fumbled as he tried to get his gun free of its holster. His motor skills had begun to fail.

"*I'makillyounow . . .*"

NICK ROLLED IN to the Blue Cypress development with no lights. He pulled up behind Dutrow's Suburban, blocking it in the driveway.

He had deputies coming, running dark and silent, with instructions to sit on the front of the house. Stokes would be right behind them. Nick wouldn't wait for any of them. Procedure be damned. He needed to get to Annie.

She was armed. She carried a Glock 9mm as her sidearm, and wore a little Kurz Backup in an ankle holster. She was quite proficient with both. If she couldn't get to either, something was very wrong. She was being restrained or watched or something worse.

The sound of her breathing on the phone—shallow and quick—suggested she was injured. The possibility made him sick and angry.

If Dutrow had put a hand on her, nothing was going to save him.

Annie believed Dutrow was physically abusive to his fiancée. But it was the thing the woman had said during the phone call that stood out to Nick now: "*I had to stop her! I didn't know what else to do!*"

And what had Dutrow said before that? "*What dead girl? What are you talking about?*"

"*Cameron . . . Dead girl . . . Stop her . . .*"

"I saved my son."

Nick slipped his weapon out of the holster and let himself in the gate to the backyard. Lights were on in what was probably a bedroom or laundry room at the rear corner of the house. The shades were drawn. There were no silhouettes being cast against them. He could hear no voices.

He needed to see what he was dealing with. He couldn't go in blind and get Annie or himself killed for it. Dutrow would be armed, and he would be angry and vengeful, and more than willing to take his rage out on Annie, not just because she was Nick's wife but because she had stepped into the middle of his domestic situation.

He had no way of knowing if the fiancée might be armed as well, but her words on that phone call gave him pause:

"I had to stop her! I didn't know what else to do!"

Not everyone who needed help wanted help. Domestic calls were among the most dangerous calls for law enforcement because of the unpredictable nature of emotional people.

Farther down, along the back of the house, a soft glow came through a bay window that looked out on the patio dining area. There would probably be a table and chairs sitting in the alcove created by the window—potentially good cover for a Peeping Tom. Beyond the table would likely be the kitchen.

Crouching low, Nick moved toward the light.

ANNIE HAD MANAGED to turn onto her side and curl into a fetal position mostly under the table, trying to minimize the trembling, trying to breathe slowly to stave off the nausea from the concussion. Trying to make herself into a smaller target. Dutrow's and Sharon's attentions were on each other, but eventually, attention would be turned to the inconvenient loose end on the floor. Sharon hadn't hesitated to try to beat her head in. She hadn't hesitated to put a knife in Kelvin Dutrow.

Annie considered her options with a foggy, swelling brain. She couldn't get up and run. She would be lucky to make it to her feet at all, let alone get her legs under her enough to stay upright and move forward. She could maybe draw her sidearm, but she didn't think she had the strength to raise and point it, let alone pull the trigger. And which of the triple images she was seeing would be the one to aim for? Shoot the one in the middle and hope for the best?

The strongest temptation she had was to close her eyes and go to sleep, but she knew she needed to stay awake, to stay alive. Nick was on his way, she told herself.

She hoped that was true. She hoped she hadn't imagined his call. Everything seemed unreal now, like she'd fallen into a nightmare—the girl in the bedroom, Sharon attacking her, Dutrow walking in. He made no move to help her. He didn't even say her name. None of it seemed real.

Annie watched the scene between the two of them play out. They looked so surprised, she thought, both of them shocked that Sharon had somehow found the nerve to stab him.

Sharon stared at the knife in her hands, the horror of what she had done slowly dawning on her as her fiancé's blood dripped from the blade onto her spotless kitchen floor.

Dutrow's pallor had gone a sweaty, sickly gray. He was shivering visibly as shock set in. He went to reach for his gun, staggered sideways, and sank down to the floor, leaning against the cupboards. His hand pawed at his weapon with clumsy fingers.

"I'makillyou," he mumbled, fumbling for the gun. "I'makillyounow . . ."

His whole body convulsed and he vomited down the front of his shirt, making no effort to lean out of the way. Slowly, he tried to raise his weapon, but his arm was shaking badly, as if the gun weighed a hundred pounds.

It fell from his hand, clattering to the floor beside him. His empty hand trembled for a moment then fell limp at his side, and he made a terrible, mournful groan as he realized he was dying.

This wasn't how Kelvin Dutrow would have pictured his death, Annie thought. There was no glory in this death. There was nothing distinguished or dignified about it. He wasn't brave or heroic. He hadn't gotten up that morning thinking this would be his last day on earth. He hadn't come to this house tonight thinking he would bleed to death on the kitchen floor, stabbed by a woman he had chosen for her acquiescence. But he died just the same.

Expressionless, Sharon turned and went to the small sink in the kitchen island to wash his blood from her knife.

"It's very important to make sure the blade is clean and dry before putting a knife away," she said, her trembling voice betraying the emotions welling inside. "To avoid rust, of course. And one must always wash a good knife by hand. Never, ever in the dishwasher. That is the secret to maintaining sharp cutlery."

She slipped the knife back into its slot in the block on the island, folded the dish towel, and carefully smoothed the wrinkles from it.

There was something strangely heartbreaking in her actions, Annie thought. Despite the fact that she had just watched Sharon Spicer kill a man, the overwhelming emotion she felt for the woman was pity. Not anger or fear or disgust. Pity. This proper, tidy, fussy woman had spent her whole life building a world that made sense to her, a world with a place for everything, where she made sure everything was in its designated place. That world had spun off its axis and shattered into a million vicious shards she would never be able to put back together. Now, she stood at the island of her lovely kitchen, trying to do something normal and orderly, something that made sense to her, something she was good at, knowing all the while that it didn't matter. Despite her best efforts to hold it together, the life she had built was over.

"I don't understand why this happened!" she cried in anguish and desperation. "I just wanted everything to be perfect!"

FIFTY-THREE

The first thing Nick saw when he peered in the window was the back of Annie's head. She lay on her side on the floor, motionless. His own breath caught in his throat, he stared at her until he could see the slight rise and fall of her side. She was breathing. She was alive.

The second thing he focused on was Dutrow, sitting on the floor, slumped against the kitchen cabinets. He looked dead. His weapon lay on the floor beside him.

Nick grabbed his phone and texted *GO* to Stokes as he ran for the nearest door, thinking the worst—that Dutrow had shot her—that Annie was lying on the floor dead or dying.

The deputies burst in the front door as Nick tried the knob on a side door, finding it unlocked. Leading with his weapon, he ran down a hallway toward the kitchen.

Shouts of "Sheriff's Office! Sheriff's Office!" came from the deputies. They converged on the kitchen, guns drawn. Sharon Spicer cried out in alarm.

"'Toinette! 'Toinette!"

Nick hit the floor on his knees, skidding across the tile to his wife's prone body.

"Baby! Baby, are you awake? Can you hear me?"

His hands were trembling as he touched her pale face, touched her shoulder. He put two fingers to her neck and felt her pulse.

"About time you showed up," she murmured, struggling to smile. She reached out a hand to touch his face and missed by six inches.

"Where are you hurt, baby? Are you shot?"

"No. My head . . . She hit me . . . with something."

"Who? Who hit you?" he asked, gingerly touching the back of her head, his hand coming away sticky with blood. "Oh, Jesus."

"Sharon," she said, squinting against the pain. "She stabbed Dutrow. I think he's dead."

"Holy shit!" Stokes exclaimed as he entered the kitchen and saw Dutrow.

"See if he's alive," Nick ordered over his shoulder. "And take the lady into custody."

"Nick—the back bedroom," Annie said with urgency, gripping his wrist hard. "Nora Florette . . . I thought I felt a pulse."

"What?"

She sounded delusional. Her eyes were glassy, her pupils unequal in size. She had a concussion or worse.

"She's back there," she insisted, tears rising. "Hurry! And you have to find Cameron . . . He hurt that girl . . ." She paused to concentrate on breathing for a moment. "And he shoved her under his bed. She's been there . . . all this time."

"Oh, my God," Nick murmured. He turned to Stokes. "Go! See!"

"I think there's a good chance . . . he killed Dean, too," Annie said.

"No! He's a good boy!" Sharon insisted. "He didn't mean to hurt that girl! I know he didn't! He tries so hard to do everything right. He would never have hurt her on purpose!"

"And did he put her under his bed by accident?" Nick asked, horrified by the thought. The boy was how old? Fourteen? And he'd put a girl under his bed and kept her there for days. Thinking she was dead? Hoping she would die? There wasn't any part of that story that wasn't monstrous.

Two full days had gone by since anyone had seen Nora Florette. If she lived, it would be a miracle.

"Nick?"

"What, baby?" he asked, turning back to Annie, leaning down close. She was breathing too hard, and trembling.

"I'm scared," she confessed, her small hand tightening on his wrist. "S-stay with me?"

As the siren of an ambulance drew near, he raised her hand to his lips and kissed her fingers. "You're not going anywhere without me."

FIFTY-FOUR

The rain stopped around three. Genevieve hadn't slept. She sat by the window in her room at Evangeline House and stared out at the street, feeling restless and exposed, all her nerve endings raw.

She hadn't spoken of Kelvin Dutrow to anyone, ever. What was the point? She had been so young, and so naive, stupid enough to think life might yet be good to her and give her a knight in shining armor. She had found it romantic when he told her their love was their secret, and that they needed to be discreet because of his position.

In truth, she had been *his* secret, and "discreet" had meant he could absolve himself of the sin of her with no one the wiser. And when she had become inconvenient to him, he had turned on her in the worst way.

She should never have gotten pregnant. That had been a foolish choice on her part. She should never have assumed that because he was a responsible man, established in his career, that he would do the "right thing" and marry her.

So many wrong choices. One begat the next. All her life, if there was a choice to be made, she had chosen wrong and blamed someone else.

She never should have come here. After her last affair had crashed and burned, and she had been told to find another job, she had by chance seen on the news that Kelvin Dutrow had become the sheriff in

Partout Parish, and she had convinced herself that, if she could only be near him, let him see her again, remind him . . .

She wasn't even sure anymore what her end goal had been—to rekindle a romance that had never been, or to extract payment in return for her silence? She didn't know which reason was worse. She only knew that the one who had suffered most for that choice had been KJ, the only innocent in the story. None of it had been his fault, but he had paid with his life. And now she would make the only right choice she had ever made and pay with her own.

She took a handful of the pain pills the hospital had given her, slipped out a side door, and as the first faint glow of dawn softened the night sky in the east, she walked slowly down the street to the bayou, singing softly to herself, *"If I die young . . ."*

CAMERON WATCHED FOR hours from his hiding place in the back seat of the neighbor's car. He'd been afraid to go home earlier in the evening. A cruiser from the Sheriff's Office had taken his mother from the park. Had she been arrested? Had they taken her in and interrogated her? What would she have said to them? That there was something wrong with him? That she thought he needed counseling? Or that she planned to send him away?

And when he had finally walked home, a cruiser had been parked in front of the house. Were they waiting for him? He was afraid to go to jail. Junior high was bad enough.

Tired and hungry and scared, he had slipped into the car in his neighbor's driveway to get out of the rain. He'd watched Detective Broussard arrive, and Kelvin sometime after her. They would all be talking about him. Detective Broussard might have guessed about Dean. They might be discussing how, when Dean had been beating on him in the park that afternoon, Cameron had grabbed a rock and smashed him in the face over and over and over and over until he didn't have a face at all. They couldn't know how good that had made him feel, how powerful. Turning the tables on someone who had tormented him every single day. They would think he should be sorry, but he wasn't sorry at all. He was sorry about other things, but he was not sorry he had killed Dean. Dean Florette was a terrible person, and the world was a better place without him. But Kelvin would be happy to put him away for killing Dean, and his mother would be glad to be rid of him.

He wanted to go sleep in his own bed, but more cop cars arrived, and ambulances, and the same hearse that had taken Dean Florette out of the park.

A deputy had led his mother out of the house in handcuffs. Cameron felt as if she had looked right across the street and straight at him, but she hadn't seen him or waved or anything. And then the car had taken her away and it never came back.

All night long the cop cars and crime scene vans had come and gone, people in and out of the house. He had watched and wondered and worried. And then finally they were gone, and Cameron sat and watched the yellow crime scene tape flutter in the wind.

He had never felt so alone. He had never felt so small or so childish. He wanted his mom. He wanted the teddy bear he was supposed to have given up two years ago. He wanted his life to be something different from what it was, but he knew it wasn't going to get better. It was only going to get worse. People would find out about the things he'd done, and everyone would hate him, and no one would ever understand.

Better if he just didn't exist, then no one would have to bother to try.

It wasn't still night and it wasn't quite morning when he slipped out of the car and walked across the street. He didn't see another living thing, not a person or a dog or a bird. He was all alone in the world as he slipped into the house, gathered what he needed, and slipped out again, walking down the driveway toward the dock.

He had never meant to do a bad thing. That was what no one would ever understand, because bad things had happened. That had never been his intent. Unlike Dean Florette, who had gotten up every day plotting to make Cameron's life a misery, Cameron had never meant for anything bad to happen. He had never set out to hurt anyone.

He had gone to Vanessa Theriot because he didn't think she would care. He just wanted to see if what Dean said about him was true. Every day Dean called him a fag, the Houma Homo, and taunted him because he didn't have a girlfriend and he didn't want to grab girls by their body parts, and he didn't want to look at Dean's dirty magazines. Cameron didn't know if it was true. He was afraid to find out, afraid of getting laughed at, afraid someone would tell on him and his mom would be so angry and so disappointed in him, and Kelvin would be disgusted by him and say he wasn't a man.

It didn't seem that bad to go to Vanessa, who would never tell, who probably wouldn't care. He had been to her house with the other kids who went to school with her sister, and she had smiled at him. She wasn't afraid of him. She didn't laugh at him. He hadn't meant her any harm. He was just curious. He even took her a present for letting him touch her, a little trinket box he didn't think his mother would ever miss.

Not in a million years had he ever thought things would turn out the way they had. Dean Florette had done bad things every day of his life on purpose, and no one had ever really cared. Stupid Nora shoplifted all the time and the worst that ever happened was her mother grounding her. Cameron hadn't meant to do anything bad, but bad things had happened anyway. Terrible things.

He walked down to the dock and climbed into the little rowboat Kelvin had given him. If he rowed out a hundred yards, the water was deep enough and too far from shore. He would drown and die because he wasn't any better at swimming than he was at any other sport. And everyone would be happier. He would no longer be an embarrassment to Kelvin. He would no longer be a burden to his mother.

She could have a happy life without him, and he would never have to tell her how Nora Florette had come over with KJ after school that day, even though she knew he wasn't allowed to have anyone over without an adult present. Nora had already gotten in trouble for coming over once before, and she had done it anyway, taunting him and teasing him. She had decided she had a crush on him. She had given him one of her stupid friendship bracelets.

He had told her to leave a hundred times, but she wouldn't. She had followed him out to the pool, pestering him as he skimmed the leaves off the water. That was one of his chores, and he had to get it done before Kelvin came for supper. And stupid Nora had pestered him and pestered him, because she thought it was funny or cute or he didn't know what.

And then she laughed and said, "You have to like me. I know about the trinket box."

Cameron hadn't meant to hurt her. He had just shoved her away. He was angry and scared, and he was going to be in so much trouble. And she fell, and hit her head on the step, and she was dead.

KJ had started crying, and Cameron had yelled at him, "Don't tell! You can't tell! I'll kill you, too!"

And KJ had run off, and Cameron couldn't chase him because his mother was coming home, and she was going to be mad because he wasn't supposed to have friends over after school . . .

He didn't want to get in trouble. He tried so hard to do everything right.

Maybe he could do this one thing right, he thought, as he rowed his little boat, the dock and the house and his world growing smaller and smaller, just as he grew smaller and smaller inside his body, until there was hardly anything left of him that needed to die.

FIFTY-FIVE

awn was a blush-pink promise on the eastern horizon as Nick drove to Blue Cypress. Already the press had choked the street leading into the development, camped out to wait for the story they had picked up in fits and starts on scanners during the night. Their numbers had grown over the past week from local and regional stations and newspapers to include media outlets from New Orleans and Houston, all in Bayou Breaux to cover the "Cajun Country Crime Wave," as coined by the *Times-Picayune*.

He couldn't actually blame them, despite his dislike of having them underfoot. Crime was news. The murders and disappearances of children were news. That kind of crime in particular was an aberration, an attack on the fabric of the local community—and on society writ large. The murder of a high-profile sheriff was news. An investigation, however, could not be "news." Investigations were by nature and necessity secretive. And therein lay the crux of his conflict with the press.

He was not liable to become more popular with them today. He had blocked the entrance to the Blue Cypress neighborhood with a pair of deputies in big SUVs. No one without a badge was getting within a hundred yards of the Spicer/Dutrow crime scene.

Settling in to wait, reporters milled around on the shoulders of the road, drinking coffee, smoking cigarettes, and speculating. Nothing they could come up with in their imaginations would be half as sensational as the truth this time.

Kelvin Dutrow was dead. His fiancée was under arrest. And the girl they had all been looking for was on life support after spending two days stuffed under a bed by a fourteen-year-old boy who was still at large—a boy who may have committed a brutal murder not twenty-four hours earlier.

The deputies pulled back to let Nick pass.

Yellow crime scene tape defined the perimeter of the Dutrow property. The state crime scene van had come and gone. All things considered, it had seemed best and politic to let them handle the investigation of the sheriff's murder. Nick had made the call and then turned the scene over to Stokes to wait for them, while he followed the ambulance to Our Lady.

Ignoring all orders to the contrary, he had stayed with Annie in the ER, leaving her side only during her head CT scan. She had a nasty concussion, but no skull fracture. That her head was harder than the cast-iron skillet Sharon Spicer had struck her with should have come as no surprise. Nick had threatened to never let her out of his sight again, a deal she had readily accepted—for the moment, at least.

He had spent the past two hours lying with her safe in his arms in her hospital bed, comforting himself as much as her.

He turned in at Dutrow's driveway and went past the house back to the oversize garage and the dock where Dutrow's bass boat was moored. He wanted a few moments' peace before the madness of the day began. The best place for him to steal those moments was by the water.

In Dutrow's absence, he would have to deal with the press. The state police investigators wanted a meeting ASAP. He needed to refocus the investigation and the search for Cameron Spicer. He wanted to at least begin the day centered and calm.

As he walked out on the dock, he took in the scene in front of him—the layer of fog skimming over the water and blending into the gray sky, the grasses swaying near the bank, the trees in the distance still shrouded in the last shadows before the light of day. Like a painting darkened by age, the images were as yet indistinct, but he could smell the water and the mud. He breathed deep. *Inhale. Focus. Calm. Release . . .*

A heron lifted off out of the shallows nearby, and Nick called to mind the Wendell Berry poem "The Peace of Wild Things," which spoke of escaping the despair for the ills of the world by seeking out the quiet solace of nature. He wondered if Kelvin Dutrow had ever considered such things while standing on this dock.

The crime scene in the house behind him, where Dutrow had lost his life, housed the chaos of man-made grief—both before and after the murder. The scene in front of him cleansed his soul with its perfect simplicity.

He breathed deep of the moist, earth-scented air and centered himself.

Inhale. Focus. Calm. Release . . .

As the sky brightened and the fog began to dissipate, his focus went to a boat in the distance. A small rowboat or a *bateau*—maybe a hundred yards out, with a single figure seated in it.

This waterway curved around the entire Blue Cypress Point and connected to the north and east to Bayou Breaux proper. Anyone determined to get to this property had only to follow the water. Nick pulled his phone off his belt and made a call as he climbed down into Dutrow's bass boat. He requested a boat from the SO be dispatched ASAP to secure the crime scene from the water side.

He checked the motors then snooped around in the storage compartments until he found a key that started the smaller of the two.

The figure in the *bateau* could be a local fisherman, or it could be an enterprising photographer or reporter looking for a way to get closer to the scene. Whatever the case, Nick wanted them gone. Dutrow would have said he was being paranoid and ridiculous, but Kelvin Dutrow was dead.

What he didn't expect was to find Cameron Spicer, but as he closed in on the smaller boat, and took in the look of the passenger, he believed that was exactly who he had found—a boy in his early teens with a shock of bright red hair.

He didn't look like a killer, that was for sure. He looked young and lost and afraid.

Nick cut the engine and brought the bass boat in gracefully alongside the little *bateau*.

"Bonjour," he said. "It's a fine morning to be out on the water, no?"

The boy just looked at him, wide-eyed. He sat slightly hunched over, his arms close at his sides as if he was cold, like a featherless young bird. At his feet was an odd assortment of belongings—a small bundle of books tied together with string, a baseball autographed with an unreadable scrawl, a framed photograph of the boy and his mother, and a well-loved teddy bear.

"There's weather coming later," Nick said. He fished a cigarette out of his shirt pocket, lit it, and took a long drag, as if he had all the time in the world. As he exhaled, he smiled and made a little gesture with the cigarette. "My wife, she doesn't like me smoking."

"It's bad for you," the boy said.

"*C'est vrai*. That's true," Nick conceded. "But you know, we all do things we shouldn't time to time. Because we're angry or we're scared, or whatever. It's not the end of the world.

"You're Cameron Spicer, yeah?" he asked, looking at the boy from under his brows as he picked a fleck of tobacco off his tongue and flicked it away.

"How do you know me?"

"Whole lotta people out looking for you, son," Nick said. "Me, I'm Nick Fourcade. I'm a detective with the Sheriff's Office."

"You work for Sheriff Dutrow?"

"Well, I did. Something happened last night, and Sheriff Dutrow, he's dead."

The boy's eyes widened in disbelief. "What happened?"

Nick watched him for a moment, contemplating. "I should tell you the truth, yeah? You're old enough to handle that, I think.

"Your *maman*, she wanted to protect you," he said. "She was afraid he would send you to prison, and so she stabbed him, and he died."

Tears sprang up in the boy's eyes—not out of love or remorse for the fate of Kelvin Dutrow, Nick thought, but out of fear for his mother or fear for himself.

"She loves you a lot, your *maman*."

"They took her to jail," Cameron said.

"They did."

"Will she go to prison?"

"She will."

"For how long?"

Nick shrugged. "I don't know. Depends. It helps her cause if she had good reason. Maybe you could help her out with that, yeah?"

The boy stared down at his little pile of odd belongings and said nothing.

"Whatcha got in there, Cameron?"

"Stuff," he mumbled.

Cherished things, Nick thought. Things a boy might take with him if he was running away. But no town kid ran away to the swamp. He wasn't going far in his little *bateau,* at any rate. And there were no clothes, no jacket, no food or drink.

"Why are you out here, Cameron?" he asked. "Do you have a plan?"

Cameron said nothing for a moment. Nick waited, letting the silence build pressure.

"I did a bad thing," the boy said in a small, frightened voice. "I didn't mean to. But I did a bad thing."

"I know."

"I try," he said, his brows drawing together in distress. "I try to follow all the rules, and everything goes wrong anyway."

"I know it can seem that way sometimes—"

"No!" he snapped, his chin quivering as he started to cry. "It's all the time! It's my whole life! I should have never been born!"

He stood up suddenly, the *bateau* swaying beneath his feet. His T-shirt was tie-dyed with blood, probably from the Florette boy. He had clearly been on the wrong end of a fistfight—until he'd gotten his hand on the rock he'd used to obliterate his bully. His lower lip was split. His left eyebrow was busted and swollen, the eye below it nearly shut.

"You know, Cameron, if you hit Dean with that rock while he was doing that to your face—that's self-defense. You have the right to protect yourself. He rode you pretty hard, the way I hear it. Called you names, pushed you around."

"I hit him," the boy said, staring down with a glazed look, as if he were seeing a replay in his mind's eye, horrified by what he'd done.

"I hit him and I hit him and I hit him!" he sobbed.

"These things happen," Nick said calmly. "All that hate, it builds and builds, like an infection in your heart, and then it comes pouring out. You can't stop it."

He glanced again at the belongings in the bottom of the *bateau*. Cherished things . . .

"It's not just Dean," the boy said, shaking with misery at what he'd done.

"Cameron, Nora Florette, she's alive," Nick said. "I know you think you killed her, but she's still alive."

"You're a liar!" the boy cried.

"No," Nick said, slowly getting to his feet. "She's alive. I don't know will she live, but she's in the hospital."

"You don't understand! It's just *everything*!"

"You can explain it to me," Nick said gently. "Me, I'm a good listener. And I've heard stories to make your hair stand on end. There ain't nothing can shock me, *mais non*. You come tell me your story, Cameron. I'll do what I can to help you."

"You can't help me," he said softly.

"Let me try."

"I don't want to be here," the boy whispered to himself.

"Then let's go back," Nick said, reaching a hand out to him. "Come on, son. Get in with me. We'll tow your boat home."

"No. No," CAMERON muttered to himself, shaking his head.

He didn't want to go back.

He didn't want to explain.

He didn't want to go to prison.

He didn't want to be here.

He looked down at all his favorite special things in the bottom of the boat. He had meant to take them with him into the water, but he'd forgotten to bring a bag.

He couldn't even manage to die right.

"Come on, son," the detective said, reaching out to him.

He looked so far away. He sounded like he was down in a barrel. He was looking right at Cameron, but he couldn't see what he really was.

He couldn't see that Cameron was just a tiny being, perched in the eye of a giant, and all he had to do was jump.

SUICIDE, NICK THOUGHT, looking at those cherished belongings. The things a boy might want to take with him . . . to the next life. And in the next instant, Cameron Spicer turned and went over the far side of the *bateau*.

HE FELL SO fast. He went so deep. It was like being swallowed by the abyss. Cameron was terrified and thrilled. He would be free of every useless, stupid thing that he was. He would never make another mistake.

NICK COULDN'T SEE. The water was murky. He kicked and reached and swept a hand from side to side. His lungs were burning. He needed to surface. He didn't want to lose this boy, but he had fallen out of reach.

How true that was in so many ways.

But just as he started to turn and was about to kick for the light above the water, he caught hold of the boy's shirt, and hung on.

FIFTY-SIX

H e keeps saying he never meant to hurt KJ," Annie said, sitting down on the park bench beside her husband. "He says he only went there to scare him."

This was the place they had come to since the start of their relationship when they needed to decompress at the end of the day. The narrow park ran on both sides of the bayou, from one end of town to the other, ending where they sat, fifty yards past the edge of the SO parking lot. It was quiet and lovely, and just far enough away from work that they felt free to be who they were rather than what they did.

A week after the worst of the case, the weather had finally broken. Fall had arrived with a cool breeze and migrating mallards. The trees had changed their colors to bronze and rust, and rattled like bags of bones in the wind.

On the other side of the bayou, Annie's running group went by on the paved path like a flock of brightly colored birds in their fall athletic wear. Still nursing her concussion, she was sidelined. Truth be told, she didn't have the heart for much these days anyway. All she wanted was to hold her family close and feel grateful to have them.

She had just come from visiting Cameron with Jaime Blynn. Jaime, who had taught KJ Gauthier, who had been heartbroken by his death, had volunteered through CASA to help Cameron, who had murdered him. For her there was no conflict in that. Cameron was a broken child in need of help, so she reached out to him. He had no one else.

With Cameron's mother in jail, Sharon's parents had been contacted on Cameron's behalf. Cameron's grandparents, who were church-going, upstanding members of their community, had been reluctant to step up in any real way. Their perfect daughter had failed them. Her son had become something they didn't want to acknowledge or be associated with. Annie supposed she shouldn't have been surprised, but she was disappointed just the same.

"He took a nine-inch boning knife with him," Nick reminded her.

They had found the knife and the steel-mesh glove—which had left the strange, bloody handprint on the wall of KJ Gauthier's bedroom—in Dutrow's workshop, in the big garage where he kept his fishing and hunting gear.

"The only reason he wore that glove that night was so he wouldn't cut himself if the knife slipped. That's premeditation, *bébé*."

"I know. I just . . ." Annie conceded the point and left the rest unsaid. Nick knew she couldn't reconcile the two Camerons in her head— the sad boy she had spent time with over the past week, and the masked killer who had invaded the home of Genevieve Gauthier and her son. It just didn't seem possible the two could be one.

"God help me for speaking ill of the dead," she said, "but I didn't have any problem imagining Dean might have done something to Nora, yet I know for a fact that Cameron did, and I just can't get my head around it."

"He missed Genevieve's jugular by millimeters."

"But he was fighting for his own life at that point," Annie argued. "In his mind, at least. Genevieve came into the room to save her child. They fought. They struggled."

The struggle had initiated in KJ's room and proceeded down the hall into the front room. The friendship bracelet Nora had given Cameron had come apart and fallen off (the tangled mess of colored thread Keith Kemp had wanted to ignore the night of the murder). Genevieve had made it out the front door and had run for Roddie Perez's house.

"He could have chased her down and finished her off," she pointed out, "but he didn't."

"*C'est vrai,*" Nick murmured. "He got scared and he ran away, 'cause he's a little boy."

And then Cameron had gone home and washed himself, disposed of his bloody clothes, and cleaned off his weapon. He had snuck back into his house, crawled into bed over the comatose body of Nora Florette, and gone to sleep. He had gotten up the next day and gone to school like nothing had happened . . . because he was afraid and he hadn't known what else to do.

Despite the things she knew he'd done, Annie didn't want to think of Cameron Spicer as a monster. She couldn't. He had done monstrous things, but when she sat with him and talked with him, he was just a frightened child who wanted his mother.

Her heart broke for him again and again. He had been raised to be perfect, to follow every rule. He had been so afraid to disappoint his mother, so afraid of embarrassing Kelvin Dutrow, that once he had made a mistake, he had committed another and another, each one worse than the one before in the attempt to cover it all up.

He had readily confessed to all of it, going back to the sexual molestation of Vanessa Theriot—which he still didn't grasp as having been anything so terrible. He hadn't set out to hurt her. He had taken her a little gift in exchange for being able to touch her. He had only wanted to see if he would find it exciting, or discover whether maybe Dean Florette was right, maybe he was gay.

He didn't really understand what sexuality meant. He only knew that he had been raised to believe being gay was shameful and wrong. His mother would be so disappointed in him. Kelvin Dutrow would disown him or send him off to military school, or both—or worse.

It had come as a complete shock to Cameron when the Theriot sexual assault made headlines and half the town had been up in arms. He had lived every day with the growing fear that he would be found out. And when Nora had let on that she knew, that fear had boiled over. He had shoved her that day out of fear as much as anger, and KJ had watched it happen. And then Cameron had to fear KJ. What if he told?

"It just breaks my heart, is all," Annie murmured.

Nick slipped his arm around her and pulled her close. She wrapped her arms around him and pressed her head to his chest.

"I know, baby," he whispered, and kissed the top of her head.

Her heart broke for Cameron. Her heart broke for KJ, whose young life had been taken from him before he had any chance at all to live it. Her heart broke for Genevieve, who would have to live with all the mistakes she had made, after being pulled from the bayou when she would have gone from this world forever and ended her pain. Her heart broke for Nora Florette, who had, by some miracle, survived her ordeal, but who would be dealing with the effects of a traumatic brain injury for the rest of her life.

Her heart broke for Jojean Florette, who had buried one child and had a long, difficult road ahead with another. And for the Theriot family, and for Sharon Spicer . . .

There was more than enough tragedy to go around. And they weren't to the end of it yet. Not by any means.

"Smith Pritchett announced today that Cameron will be tried as an adult," she said.

"I heard. As you might imagine, Gus had some choice words."

With Dutrow dead, Gus Noblier had agreed to temporarily step back into the role of sheriff until the situation could be sorted out.

"He's as fond of Pritchett as ever," Nick said. "'Pompous, sanctimonious, grandstanding jackass,' I believe he called him."

"He's too kind," Annie grumbled.

Their preening peacock of a district attorney, Pritchett, was a man who had only become more entrenched and insufferable after every race for higher office he managed to lose.

"I don't have any problem with the boy having to pay for the terrible things he did," Annie said. "But in what universe is it right to equate a boy who sleeps with a teddy bear with hard-core felons? I can't imagine Cameron toughing it out in a juvenile facility. Can you imagine that child surviving in Angola?"

"No," Nick said on a sigh. "I wonder did I do him any favors pulling him out of the water that day."

He remembered it as if it were a movie: diving into the murky water, searching frantically with his hands, being almost out of air as he grabbed hold of Cameron Spicer's T-shirt. He had nearly pulled the shirt off and lost the boy. At the last possible second, he had caught the boy's hand.

"But that's not my question to ask," he said. "I did what I had to do. We can only do what we think is right and hope the universe sorts itself out."

"That's uncharacteristically passive of you," Annie said, looking up at him.

"Not at all. I dragged him out of the water and breathed life back into him. What more could I have done? We do what we can, 'Toinette. You wanna fight for that boy, you fight like a tigress. I expect no less."

He smiled down at her. She was a force to be reckoned with, his wife. She had come into his life and had challenged him to be a better man. God only knew what she could do for Cameron Spicer.

"In the meantime," he said, rising from the bench and drawing her with him. "Let's go home, partner, and love our son, and raise him well. That's what we can do. Raise our family and love each other."

"How'd you get so smart?" Annie asked as they started back toward the parking lot.

"Me," he said with a wink and a smile, "I married well."

EPILOGUE

I t's not fancy," Detective Broussard said, opening the door to the
apartment. "But it's homey, and the AC works."

Genevieve walked in and looked around. To the right was a
small galley kitchen with pale pink walls and a retro fifties-style refrigerator with a huge dancing alligator painted on the door that looked like
the mascot from the elementary school. The clock on the wall was a
plastic black cat with googly eyes and a tail that flicked back and forth
with the passing seconds.

KJ's kitten had somehow managed to find its way onto the counter
and stretched up the wall to bat at the clock's tail.

Straight ahead was the main living space dominated by a glass coffee
table balanced on the back of a five-foot-long taxidermic alligator.

"That's Alphonse," the detective said, gesturing to the coffee table as
she walked through the room. She pulled open French doors that ac-
cessed a little balcony overlooking the bayou. "He used to hang from
the ceiling downstairs back when, until one of his wires broke and he
swung down and knocked a tourist flat. Then I got him."

"You lived here?" Genevieve asked, surprised.

"I grew up here."

They were at the Corners, a boat landing/convenience store/café fifteen minutes outside of town. Genevieve had brought Clarice out here a few times to have the gumbo for lunch and to talk French with the owners, an older Cajun couple.

"Sos and Fanchon, they raised me," Broussard said.

"Excuse me, Miss Gauthier? Where would you like your suitcases?"

Genevieve turned toward the deputy coming through the door, speechless for more reasons than one. He looked at her expectantly, like an eager young spaniel with a sweet face and big brown eyes, ready for her instruction.

Broussard pointed the way. "The bedroom is down that hall."

"That's a little awkward," Genevieve remarked as the deputy disappeared.

"Why? Because he fished you out the bayou?"

"Yeah. Not my finest moment," she confessed.

Annie Broussard shook her head, dismissing the notion. "He's a deputy. That's part of the job."

"I'm just embarrassed, I guess."

The detective gave her a long look. "Don't be. You didn't get to that place on a whim. You earned it the hard way."

The deputy—they called him Young Prejean—had followed her at a distance as she walked away from Evangeline House that night, waiting to see where she might go. She'd gone to the park along the bayou, just a block away, and as the painkillers she'd taken had begun to numb her, she had walked right over the bank, into the water.

She didn't remember much from that night, but she remembered Young Prejean carrying her out of the water and bending over her on the bank. She had wished at the time that he would've let her go. Now here she was, back to square one, relying on the kindness of strangers.

She was being offered this apartment to stay in and a job downstairs to tide her over until she could decide what she really wanted to do. She had the money from the GoFundMe account to help pay her medical bills. One of the local churches had picked up the expense of KJ's funeral.

"Don't think you don't deserve it."

"What?" she asked, coming back into real time.

"This chance," Broussard said, leaning back against the balcony railing. "Don't think you don't deserve it, Genevieve. That's not for you to decide. It's what you do with it that counts."

"I've made so many mistakes," Genevieve murmured. She smoothed her hands along the top of the railing and looked out at the water and the wilderness beyond. "One after the next. How many is too many?"

The detective said nothing as Young Prejean cut back through the apartment to go for another box of Genevieve's meager belongings. When he was out the door, Annie said, "My mother came here when she was pregnant with me. She didn't have anything or anyone. Sos and Fanchon took her in. They gave her a family—they gave *me* a family. I don't know if my mom deserved that chance. But I'm awfully grateful she got it."

"Where is she now?"

A sad smile turned the corners of her mouth. "She's dead. She killed herself when I was nine. She didn't have a Young Prejean there that day to save her.

"That was one mistake too many for her. But you already made that one and survived," she said. "You're getting another chance, Genevieve. Make it count—for KJ. Make it count for everyone willing to believe in you— whether you deserve it or not. Now is when you find out if they're right."

Genevieve took a deep breath and sighed at the weight of that. She hoped she would do a better job shouldering the burden this time. The difference this time would be that she wasn't alone. That, she hoped, would make all the difference.

"No drugs, no drinking," the detective said as she went back into the apartment. "And if you bring grief to these old people, I will drown you myself," she promised, then offered a gentle smile. "But I don't think that's gonna happen. We wouldn't be here if I did. I'm giving you the chance my mother didn't give herself."

"Thank you, Detective Broussard," Genevieve said, scooping up KJ's kitten and holding him close against her chest, immediately comforted by his instant purr.

"And you'd better start calling me Annie," she said as they walked to the door. "You're practically family now."

For the first time in a very long time, Genevieve managed a smile. "I like the sound of that."

"And you'd better get a name for this little fur ball. Your roommate should have a name, don't you think?"

"Yes," Genevieve said, holding up the kitten she had given to her son for a birthday he would never have. Now all she had was the kitten, and the opportunity to try again, an incredible gift, as much as it frightened her. "I think I'll name him Chance."

"I think that's perfect," Annie said. "Go settle in. Come downstairs when you feel like it. I'll introduce you."

Genevieve watched her descend the stairs and then went to unpack to start her new life.

ACKNOWLEDGMENTS

As always, there are people to thank for their patience, for their generosity, and for their support. First, a huge thank-you to Candra Seley, who several years ago now generously donated to the Challenge of the Americas fund-raiser for breast cancer research. Hers was the winning bid for a role in this story, a prize she gifted to her daughter-in-law, Jaime Blynn. Sorry it took so long! Thanks, also, to fellow author Pamela Samuels Young and to Craig and Judith Johnson (yes, *that* Craig Johnson, Longmire fans), for their generous contributions to the Writers' Police Academy for cameo roles in this book. Craig and Judith's adorable granddaughter, Lola Troiano, took their spot.

Thanks also to Karen Ross for her expertise. And to Tina Butler, who brought in the big guns to keep me going at the end when only my spirit was willing and my back was giving me the finger. We both know you cheat, and I am so grateful.

Glossary of Cajun French

allons	let's go
arrête	stop
bateau/bateaux (plural)	a flat-bottomed boat
bébé	This means "baby" in traditional French, but the Cajun version is pronounced "beb" and is used like "babe," as a term of endearment.
bon	good
c'est assez	that's enough
c'est fou	that's crazy
c'est sa couillon	that's a fool
c'est tout	that's all
c'est vrai	that's true
cher	A term of endearment similar to "dear" or "sweetheart." It is pronounced "sha."
chérie	cherished, beloved
coonass	a mostly derogatory slang term for Cajun (depends on who's saying it and why)
couillon	A stupid person, a fool. It's pronounced "coo-yon."

de rien	you're welcome
fils de pute	son of a bitch
gris-gris	A curse, a spell. It's actually a Haitian word.
Ici on parle français.	Here we speak French.
je t'aime	I love you
loup-garou	from Cajun folklore, a swamp-dwelling werewolf
mais	but; often used for emphasis with *yes* or *no*
mais non	but no
ma jolie fille	my pretty girl
maman	mother
merci beaucoup	thank you very much
merci Dieu	thank God
merde	shit
mon ami	my friend
mon coeur	my heart
mon Dieu	my God
oui	yes
pauvre bête	The traditional French translation would be an insult—"poor stupid." The Cajun usage is an expression of pity, the equivalent of "poor thing."
petit homme de mystère	little man of mystery
putain	This literally means "whore" but is used as "fuck."
putain de merde	fuck this shit
s'il vous plaît	please
tante	aunt
T- or 'tite	Preceding a name it's short for petite or *'tite*, and denotes a nickname.
très bien	very good

Continue reading for an excerpt
from Tami Hoag's

BAD LIAR.

Coming soon from Dutton.

ONE

Moonlight on black water, shining like dark glass in the night. Tree branches reflected on the surface, silhouettes on shadow, silent sentinels of the swamp, draped in moss that swayed in the whispered breeze.

A shallow boat glided over the surface, the engine barely running, its low, throaty purr swallowed up by the wilderness with only nature there to hear. A hand trailed in the water over the side, fingers curled as if in invitation for unseen others to follow as the boat slipped deeper into the night.

FINGERS CLUTCHING THE steering wheel, the mother sat in her car, staring at the house. A narrow, rickety little shotgun shack that had somehow stood there well over a hundred years. A sagging roof to match the sagging, postage-stamp front porch. Narrow clapboard siding with paint peeling from the trim in thin, dingy blue shards. Looking like a sad cartoon, the front windows were not quite square in the wall. No light shone through the dirty glass.

How had it come to this?

Her son's life had begun in comfort and security. A big house in a good neighborhood. A respected family. A bright future. Little by little that foundation had eroded, corrupted by things she knew now were beyond his control—mostly—though she had judged him and blamed him. Fought him instead of fighting for him, which would be a stain on her soul for the rest of her life, no matter if he forgave her or not—which he had, or so he said. Sometimes she thought he only said it because he was too weary of the battle to say anything else.

Heart beating quickly, she got out and looked all around, still clinging to the car door, just in case. This wasn't a good place to be. On the ragged outskirts of town, this was a neighborhood that quickly gave way to dirty blue-collar businesses—a welding shop, a scrap yard, a rusty corrugated metal warehouse that housed Mardi Gras parade floats. The old abandoned sugarcane processing plant was just down the road.

A row of small houses like this one squatted like toadstools, side-by-side on weed-choked lots, forgotten by everyone who didn't have to live this way. Those were the people who lived here—people not wanted anywhere else, people without the means to live anywhere else, the marginalized, the outliers, the forgotten. Her son.

There was no one around that she could see, although she was sure she felt the crawl of eyes on her. Just her imagination, she tried to tell herself. A train whistle wailed in the distance, a mournful sound echoed by an owl in a nearby tree. The sound of the owl unnerved her and stirred a long-dormant memory of an old superstition that she would have said she didn't believe in. A folktale about owls being harbingers of death. Despite herself, her stomach clenched and a chill ran down her back as she hurried to the front door.

She knocked and waited. And waited . . . And waited . . .

The mother's trembling fingers tightened on the doorknob.

The owl called a second time.

THE WIFE REACHED out with trembling fingers and pinched out the flame of a candle. *Happy birthday to me*—a thought steeped in sarcasm and sorrow. She was angry and sad and alone. Nothing new there.

This wasn't what her life was supposed to be. This hadn't been part of the deal. Not at all. She had fallen in love with the man of her dreams—handsome, smart, full of fun and promise. They had planned and plotted a life in a better place with a brighter future. They had had so much to look forward to, so many promises their dreams had held out for them like shiny brass rings on the beautiful carousel of youthful romance.

But here she sat, alone in her kitchen, drinking warm chardonnay in the glow of the under-cabinet lighting, in a backwater town in South Louisiana. A place she didn't belong. A fact she was reminded of daily by people she didn't like and who didn't like her. People who had pulled her husband back here on the leash of obligation and loyalty, dragging her along, an unwanted accessory. She often wondered if he thought of her the same way and resented her for it. Was she the constant reminder of what he could have had, could have been if he hadn't come back here and settled for so much less?

Of course he resented her.

No more than she resented him.

This was what her life had become, and she was sick of it, choking on it.

She didn't want to live like this anymore.

She wouldn't.

She wiped away the tears that clung to her eyelashes and reached across the kitchen island for her cell phone.

Happy birthday to me . . .

A PREDATOR ATTACKED. Prey screamed. The swamp was alive at night, a tableau for the drama of life and death, survival and loss. The circle of life turned continuously, naturally, without sympathy or sentiment. One life fed another, which fed another, which fed another. The choreography of nature was graceful, brutal, and honest, a dance carried out in moonlight and shadow.

The engine died. A spotlight swept low across the water.

Eyes glowed back.

The apex predator had arrived.

THE LOVERS' HANDS pressed palm-to-palm, fingers intertwined as they slow-danced barefoot on the cool, damp grass. Black water and the gilded moon painted the backdrop, the bayou shining like polished obsidian in the moonlight.

The warm, smoky voice of a favorite singer set the mood with soulful lyrics—an intimate, heartfelt confession, a pledge of love and wonder. *"You're as smooth as Tennessee whiskey . . ."*

Their hips swayed together, touching, pressing into each other. His breath stirred loose tendrils of her hair. His lips brushed across her skin, traced the shell of her ear. She smiled. He sighed.

Whispered words. Breath caught and held. His mouth found hers. Her tongue touched his. Desire rose like a flame, burning, licking, igniting a deeper need, driving them indoors to the privacy of the bedroom.

The curtains billowed in the night breeze. Clothing fell, sheets whispered. His hand swept down the curve of her side. Her fingers dug into his shoulders. They moved together, slowly and gently, then with strength and passion. The pleasure built to a crescendo and took them both over the edge on a wave of bliss.

The lovers fell asleep one tucked into the other, wrapped up in each other in every way, his hand holding hers pressed against her heart.

THE ALLIGATORS CAME like Pavlov's dogs. The boat had been here before. They thrashed and snapped and devoured what was thrown to them, churning up the water, stirring up the smell of mud and blood and decay.

The pieces were small, bite-sized, alligator fun-sized, meant to be eaten in the moment rather than dragged away and tucked under a log to rot and tenderize. A heart, a liver, a foot, a hand—the hand that had trailed in the water all the way out here like bait.

And then it was done, the evidence gone. The spotlight went out.

The boat started back the way it had come, leaving nature to itself, as if nothing had happened. Leaving nothing but moonlight on black water.

TWO

"Ain't no reason on God's green earth anyone should ever find a murdered body in South Louisiana," Chaz Stokes proclaimed.

He lit a cigarette and took a deep pull on it as he leaned back against the side of a black Dodge Charger and surveyed the area through the dark lenses of his aviator sunglasses. A light-skinned Black man, he was tall and lean, built like an athlete and dressed like a jazz musician in loose-fitting gray slacks and a black-and-white straight-bottomed Cuban-style shirt.

"Umpteen gazillion acres of swampland, marshland, woodland, rivers, bayous, and backwaters, and this genius dumps a body at the end of a road," he said, exhaling twin streams of smoke through his slim nose. "That's just pure damn laziness. Could'a fed that body to the gators with none the wiser."

"If they were geniuses, we'd be hard-pressed for work, *mon ami*," Nick Fourcade said. He slid his backpack off his shoulder and set it on the trunk of Stokes's car.

"Still . . ." Stokes said, making a dismissive gesture with his cigarette. He frowned within the frame of his neatly trimmed mustache and goatee. "This ain't even sportin'."

"Unless you pull a suspect out your ass, that remains to be seen."

They stood near the dead end of a gravel-and-crushed-shell road a mile or so outside the drive-through town of Luck, where the wild began to swallow up what passed for civilization hereabouts on the western edge of the Atchafalaya Basin. The road petered out a dozen or so yards from a shallow slough choked with hackberry and willow trees. It was the sort of place where the occasional drug deal was made and where lovers came to escape scrutiny for a steamy tussle in a backseat or in the bed of a pickup truck. Kids came out here to drink and smoke dope, as was evidenced by the number of crushed beer cans and scattered crumpled Sonic and Popeyes takeout bags.

The tall grass at the end of the road had been crushed down more than once as vehicles had turned around to head back in the direction of town after business had been taken care of. Recent rains had left the ground soft, and a set of muddy ruts indicated someone had nearly gotten themselves stuck venturing too far off the gravel. Just beyond the tracks, a pair of impressively large, bare male feet protruded from the weeds.

The morning was young and clear, with sheer scraps of clouds as thin as gauze contrasting the electric blue fall sky. Too pretty a morning for a murder, Nick thought, watching a squadron of ducks flying toward the Basin, though he knew all too well nature made no concessions for human tragedy. The world turned, the seasons passed. Death was just part of the deal. The man lying dead at the edge of the slough made no more matter to the natural world than a rabbit snatched up by an owl in the moonlight. The sun would still come up the next day and the day after that.

The world of mankind was another matter altogether.

Dressed for a court appearance in a shirt and tie, he had been on his way to the sheriff's office to start the workday early when the call had come. As detective sergeant for the Partout Parish sheriff's office, he ran the department of six detectives, covering 816 square, mostly rural miles, investigating everything from burglary to homicide. He had hoped to get some paperwork done before heading to the courthouse.

He checked his watch and frowned.

"So what's the story here?"

"It's a dump job," Stokes said. "Looks like the victim ran into the wrong end of a shotgun—elsewhere. Looks to me like the killer maybe backed in, thinking to dump the body in the water, sank down to his rims, said fuck it, and chucked the body into the weeds. Like I said, pure damn laziness."

"Any chance we might get a cast of a tire track?"

"Maybe. It's pretty squishy over there right now, but there's one or two might set up enough to be worth a try if we wait a bit for the sun to do its thing."

"You have a plaster kit?"

"I've got one in my trunk. You got any?"

"I think I might have two. Who called this in?"

"Swamper," Stokes said, nodding in the general direction of the blue-and-white sheriff's office cruiser parked a short distance ahead of his car. A bald, stocky deputy sat back against the hood of the cruiser, chatting animatedly with a small, wiry man in overalls and green waders, the pair of them smiling and laughing like old friends catching up at a Sunday picnic.

"Did he see anything?"

"No."

Nick looked over at the bare feet of the victim, the only part of the body visible from the road. The weeds and brush would have hidden the body from view from the water as well. He hitched his backpack over one shoulder and headed toward the cruiser.

"*Bonjour*, Sergeant Rodrigue. *Ça viens?*"

He had grown up in a household where Cajun French was the default language of his parents, people proud to keep that language alive. As was the case with many people in these parts, even his English was seasoned liberally with French.

"Detective Fourcade!" Rodrigue boomed, his usual broad grin lighting his face beneath a bushy black mustache of epic proportions. "*Bonjour! Ça va*. I'm good, me. What a fine day we have in God's country, no?"

"*Mais oui*. That it is."

"Fourcade?" the swamper asked, squinting hard beneath the bill of a worn, dirty green Bass Pro cap. "You related to the Fourcades down Abbeville? Coy and them?"

"No, sir."

"Fourcade—dat's not a Cajun name, but you a Cajun. I can tell," he declared.

"Through and through," Nick conceded. "And you are . . . ?"

"This here's my wife's third or fourth cousin or something like that," Rodrigue said with a chuckle. "Alphonse Arceneaux. My wife, Mavis, she's an Arceneaux on her mama's side. Alphonse, he found the body, him, and he called me."

"Why you didn't call 9-1-1?" Stokes asked, joining them.

Arceneaux looked at him like he was a fool, lines of disapproval creasing his narrow, weathered face. He might have been seventy or forty-five. It was difficult to say. His skin had been turned to tooled leather by years working outdoors in the harsh Louisiana weather.

"That's for 'mergencies!" he declared. "This ain't no 'mergency. That dude, he's *dead* dead, him. He as dead as dead gets. What's the hurry?"

"We'd like to catch the bad guy."

"Bah!" Arceneaux scoffed. "I told you, there wasn't no bad guy. There wasn't nobody but me, and I gotta stay here for y'all. I might as well call a friend, no?"

"You didn't see anyone?" Nick asked. "No car or truck?"

"*Mais* no, no nothing."

"How'd you come to find the body? You got a boat out there?"

"*Oui*, my bateau."

"And what brings you out this way?"

"Running my trap lines. Me, I lease this land. I come this way first thing in the morning and get my nutria before they get stole. This here land's too close to town. Lazy-ass town boys come out here and steal my nutria. Y'all need to do something 'bout that!" Arceneaux said, as if the raids on his trap lines should take priority over a murder.

"We do dead people, not dead rodents," Stokes grumbled.

"Stealing is stealing," Arceneaux said. "Six bucks a tail this year. That's my livelihood they messing with!"

"I don't disagree," Nick said. "But you have to take that up with the Wildlife agents. That's their jurisdiction."

"Me, I'm gonna catch them rascals red-handed this year," Arceneaux promised, clearly relishing the idea. "Give them raggedy-ass thieves some Cajun justice!"

"Dude, don't promise violence on your fellow man in front of cops," Stokes cautioned.

Nick had already lost interest in the conversation. "Show me your boat."

Arceneaux led the way. "You don't wanna see that body first?"

"He's not going anywhere, is he?"

Even as he said it, a trio of stray dogs emerged from a copse of trees, noses scenting the air as they trotted toward the corpse.

"Goddamn it," Stokes muttered, moving off, pulling his sidearm. "I'll stay with the body. Git, you mangy mutts!" he shouted at the dogs. "Go on, git!"

He pointed his weapon off to the side and discharged a round, sending the dogs scurrying back toward the trees.

Nick followed Arceneaux and Rodrigue, pushing through the weeds and the tall grass that had faded from green to blond with the approach of winter.

There was no bank to speak of, just softer and softer ground that gave way to water. They broke through the vegetation where Alphonse Arceneaux's snub-nosed bateau floated, a shallow, flat-bottomed aluminum boat as weathered as its owner's face. A pile of dead nutria lay in the nose of the boat—ugly, orange-toothed swamp rats bigger than cats. They were the scourge of the wetlands, non-native invaders devoted to tearing up the root systems of the marsh grasses, creating erosion in the delicate ecosystem that seemed threatened at every turn these days.

A rifle lay propped near the morning's harvest.

"What you hunting with?" Nick asked.

".22 when I need it. Me, I'd rather use ol' Black Betty and save the ammunition," Arceneaux said, re-enacting clubbing something. "I run a hundred-fifty traps, me. Not going 'round filling the swamp with shot when there's no need."

"You got a shotgun on board?"

Arceneaux laughed and tipped his cap back on his head. "What kind of damn *couillon* hunts nutria with a shotgun?! Dat's a good one! Talk about!"

Rodrigue laughed along as Arceneaux pantomimed shooting and exploding a nutria to kingdom come.

"Why'd you put in right here?" Nick asked, turning to look back toward the location of the body.

As expected, the corpse wasn't visible from this spot, nor was the road. Nothing but a waving sea of grass, and the occasional glimpse of Stokes's dark head a dozen yards away.

"I had me a bad oyster last night," Arceneaux confessed, "and I got me a touch of the *fwa* this morning. Got out the boat to relieve myself and that's how I come to find a dead dude. How 'bout that?"

Rodrigue shook his head. "We got us a case of the diarrhea to thank for the discovery of a murder victim! I been doing this a long time, and that's a first for me!"

"Did you recognize this dead man?" Nick asked.

"*Mais* no," Arceneaux said, shaking his head. "That dude, his own *maman* ain't gonna recognize him. You'll see. It's bad. *Pauvre bête*," he murmured. "May God rest his soul."

He crossed himself, picked up the small crucifix he wore on a chain around his neck and pressed a kiss to it with chapped lips.

"Closed casket bad," Rodrigue said. "Somebody was mad mad at that guy. Maybe a drug thing or some kind of feud. Something personal."

"You don't know him either?" Nick asked the deputy as they made their way back through the grass toward the body. "He ain't your fourth cousin twice removed?"

"I wouldn't know him if he was my own brother," Rodrigue said. "We gotta hope he's still got his wallet in his pants or fingerprints on file. Only God gonna know him now."

Ran into the wrong end of a shotgun, Stokes had said. There was no pretty version of that.

"Did you touch the body?"

"No, sir."

"Did Stokes?"

Rodrigue laughed. "He's just here for show, ain't he?"

"I heard that!" Stokes shouted. "You know I leave the bodies for you, Nicky. You get so testy otherwise."

The decedent had landed on his back with his arms outflung in a pose reminiscent of da Vinci's *Vitruvian Man*. He was a large Caucasian male, over six feet, Nick reckoned, if he'd still had his head. Reasonably fit, broad-shouldered, narrow-hipped. The left hand and wrist were blown to shreds. A defensive wound. The hand had probably been held up in a vain attempt to shield the face from the shotgun blast. Dressed in jeans and nothing else, the corpse was splattered with mud.

Two-thirds of the face and head were completely destroyed, a bloody, unrecognizable mess of shattered bone and pulverized tissue. The remaining portion of the right side of the face was speckled with the tiny red stippling caused by the impact of the fine plastic filler used in buckshot loads. Judging by the damage, the shooter had probably been standing eight to ten feet away from the victim. *Personal*, Rodrigue had said. Indeed.

The man's right eye stared up at him, brown and cloudy, hopeless, lifeless. Flies had begun to swarm on the wounds to feed and lay eggs, but the maggots had yet to hatch out. He couldn't have been lying there more than two or three hours, Nick reckoned.

It didn't look real, what was left of this person. Absent the life force, and so badly damaged, a body ceased to seem human. The reality was so shocking, so hideous, the observer's mind automatically wanted to discount what it saw.

Nick pulled on a pair of purple latex gloves from his backpack and squatted down beside the corpse in the damp grass. The body was cold to the touch, but not stiff. The slight greenish discoloration of the skin on the abdomen and the beginning of bloat told him the man had been dead for a while. A day or two, perhaps. Decomposition was underway. Rigor mortis had come and gone.

Buzzards had begun to circle overhead. Thank goodness for Mr. Arceneaux's bad stomach. If he hadn't come along when he did, the corpse would have become a feast. Mother Nature recycling her own.

Nick glanced up at Arceneaux, who was staring off into the distance, pointedly not looking at the body. The reality was beginning to set in.

"*Merci*, Mr. Arceneaux. We'll need to have you come in to the sheriff's office and make a formal statement. Later today, if possible. Finish running your trap lines, then come in and see Detective Stokes here."

Stokes stepped forward and handed the man his business card, instructing him to call first.

Rodrigue walked Arceneaux back to his boat. When they were out of sight, Stokes said to Nick, "I'm gonna tell you what right now. I know exactly what happened to our dead friend here."

"I'm glad to hear it," Nick said, walking carefully around the body, snapping photos with the digital camera from his backpack. "Do you have evidence to back up this theory?"

"This guy here got caught doing some other dude's lady. I'll bet you a hundred bucks."

Nick looked at the body and its state of semi-dress—no shoes, no socks, jeans half-undone. That was probably a sucker bet, but preconceived ideas were dangerous things in a homicide investigation.

"You know what they say about an assumption," Nick said. "It'll make me kick your ass."

"That ain't what they say."

"It's what I'm telling you."

"Whatever. You mark my words," Stokes promised. "This here is all about a chick. If I'm lying, I'm dying."

"Let this be a cautionary tale then," Nick remarked.

"I don't know what you mean by that."

"Really, Romeo? You standing here in the same clothes you wore to work yesterday. And how is it you came to arrive at this scene before me when you live a good twenty minutes in the other direction?"

Stokes frowned. "I was visiting a friend in the area," he said stiffly.

"Mmm-hmm. At the crack of dawn. Mrs. Who-was-it-this-time?"

"That is not your business, my friend."

"It'd be good if I had a starting place for the investigation when you go missing thanks to a jealous husband," Nick said, squatting down beside the body again to search through the man's pockets for any indication of identity.

"And might I say for nine hundreth time, this judgey side of you is not appealing, Nicky," Stokes complained. "Oh, wait. There *is* no other side of you."

"Good thing you don't want to date me, then, yeah?" Nick said dryly. "And I'm married and everything. Just your type."

Stokes, ever the lady's man, had, in the last year or so, shifted his love life strategy to affairs with married women, on the theory that they were only starved for great sex and weren't out to snag him for a husband—as were most of the single women in his dating pool—or so he claimed. Though any woman who thought Chaz Stokes was husband material needed her head examined as far as Nick was concerned. The apple of his own eye, Stokes was as faithless as a feral tomcat.

"Ha ha," Stokes said, irritated. "All this sassy-ass humor. You're a regular comedian today. You must have gotten laid last night."

Ignoring the remark, Nick carefully pulled out the contents of the dead man's right front pocket. Nine cents, a gum wrapper wadded around a hard knot of chewed gum, and a felted piece of lint that had been jammed down in the pocket corner for a very long time. He slipped the items into a plastic bag and handed it to Stokes, then slid his hand under the man's hip and felt for the shape and bulk of a wallet.

No such luck. Not that he was surprised. A man dressing that hastily, not even managing shoes or socks—his wallet was likely sitting on a dresser or nightstand somewhere. But he worked his fingertips into the hip pocket anyway, and was rewarded with a folded page of paper he pulled gingerly out of the pocket and into the light of day.

Careful not to tear the damp paper, he unfolded it. It was a generic handwritten receipt, a standard form available at any office supply store, the kind that came with carbon copies in pink and yellow. A receipt in the amount of $875, dated three days past, written in some kind of scrawling shorthand Nick didn't immediately understand. The name and address lines for the recipient were blank, but a business name and address were crookedly stamped in red on top: Mercier Salvage, 673 Canal Road, Luck, LA.

"Got a name?" Stokes asked, peering down over his shoulder.

"No. But a motive, maybe."

Nick had certainly known people to be murdered for less. A man walking around with a big wad of cash, flashing it in the wrong bar . . .

Mouton's roadhouse wasn't far down the bayou from here. The kind of place where brass knuckles were a common fashion accessory, and every man—and most of the women—carried a gun or a knife. People looking for trouble looked at Mouton's. Poachers, thieves, drug dealers all made themselves at home there.

"Could be he picked up a hooker, got wasted by her pimp," Stokes speculated.

"Could be."

"I'm telling you, my friend, this'll end with a woman."

Nick arched a dark brow at his partner. "You know the only difference between you and this guy?" he asked, nodding to the faceless corpse.

"Fashion sense?" Stokes quipped.

"Timing."

TAMI HOAG

"Tami Hoag is simply one of the best."

—*New York Times* bestselling
author Lisa Unger

For a complete list of titles, please
visit prh.com/tamihoag